The Cornish Inheritance

The Cornish Ladies
Book Three

Fil Reid

ARE YOU SIGNED UP FOR DRAGONBLADE'S BLOG?

You'll get the latest news and information on exclusive giveaways, exclusive excerpts, coming releases, sales, free books, cover reveals and more.

Check out our complete list of authors, too!

No spam, no junk. That's a promise!

Sign Up Here

www.dragonbladepublishing.com

Dearest Reader;

Thank you for your support of a small press. At Dragonblade Publishing, we strive to bring you the highest quality Historical Romance from some of the best authors in the business. Without your support, there is no 'us', so we sincerely hope you adore these stories and find some new favorite authors along the way.

Happy Reading!

CEO, Dragonblade Publishing

Chapter One

MAJOR NATHANIEL TRELOAR, late of the 18th King's Irish Regiment of Light Dragoons, known nowadays as the 18th Hussars, stepped out of the coach that had brought him up to London from Canterbury and stared around himself at Fetter Lane. He'd been away for over a year and a half, seen a war fought and won, and, somehow, he'd expected London to have something to show for it. But there was nothing. All seemed just as he'd left it in January 1813, when his regiment had taken ship for Lisbon and rejoined the Peninsular War.

His fellow passengers, a bluff gentleman with thick gray hair and whiskers and his stout wife, descended from the coach as well, although unlike Nat, they seemed to know where they were going.

The guard threw down the luggage from the top of the coach with scant respect for whether it might contain anything breakable. Nat picked up his own valise before any of the loitering riffraff could attempt to grab it, and turned toward the hostelry the coach had delivered him to. Large lettering across the smart brick façade above the windows declared it to be the White Horse Tavern and Family Hotel, an establishment recommended by his friend Captain Ned Cavendish. It possessed an added advantage to Ned's recommendation in that it was only a short walk from the Saracen's Head in Snow Hill, from which

Nat had to catch the coach to the West Country first thing in the morning.

Slinging the heavy bag over his shoulder, he pushed open the door and entered the hostelry. He found himself in a long room with a counter running all the way down one side. At this time of day, a few men of somewhat dubious appearance were already sitting around playing cards, tankards of ale gripped in their hands. They looked him up and down, no doubt assessing whether he could be gulled into playing a losing hand with them, and stayed put.

Nat approached the aproned man who seemed to be serving.

This worthy, a long, skinny drink of water with heavily hooded eyes and a burgeoning bald spot, wiped his hands on his wrap-around apron and tugged the scant remains of his forelock in respect. He probably recognized in Nat the gait and bearing of a soldier, despite his civilian dress of blue frock coat and breeches. The long scar on the right side of Nat's face must have reinforced his guess, and might also have had something to do with the card sharps' reluctance to engage him. Nat still hadn't become accustomed to the way people stared at his disfigurement. This man, though, made a creditable effort not to. "Good evening to you, fine sir. And what can I do for you?"

Already the blaring of a horn and the clatter of a second coach arriving at the inn sounded outside on the cobbles. Nat, cocking an ear for the noise of fresh passengers in search of overnight accommodation, was seized by the urgency of the situation. "I should like to procure a room for the night, my good man. The best you have at your disposal."

The barkeeper tugged his forelock again. "If you'd like to foller me, sir, I'll take you up right now. The boss keeps only the best for officers like yourself. Overlooks the street, so you'll not be bothered by the comings and goings of the stableyard too much." His eyes slid sideways toward the scar before he dragged them back again. "This way."

The room, which was of more generous proportions than

Nat had expected, did indeed look out over the street, from which the second coach had now vanished, presumably into the stableyard for the horses to be unhitched. "I'll take it," Nat said. "And a roast chicken for my dinner, along with a flagon of good claret and a bottle of brandy, here in my room."

When the barkeeper had departed, Nat checked the bed. He'd had more than his fill of bad beds in Spain and Southern France, and there could be a lot of things amiss with a bed in a public inn, even in England. The feather mattress didn't feel too lumpy, the sheets seemed clean and well aired, and he couldn't spy any bedbugs or other small visitors. He took off his coat and flung it over the bed's foot, then lay down, still in his dusty boots, and put his hands behind his head. As he stood a little over six feet tall, his feet touched the solid oak foot, and he was reminded of the story of Procrustes and how he would either stretch longer, or cut bits off his visitors in order to make them fit in his bed, until Theseus came along and sorted him out.

Well, what a turn up for the books this was. Only a few short weeks ago he'd been with the army in the South of France, at Bordeaux to be precise, and now look where he found himself. No longer a soldier at all. He glanced down at his long body, virtually untouched by war if he hid the missing fingers on his right hand. His civilian clothes made quite a change from the brocade festooned uniform he'd been wearing as a Hussar, but he liked it. He'd had his fill of fighting, an unsurprising feeling considering how much of the Peninsular War he'd seen and taken part in. Too much. He touched his fingers to his cheek, feeling the raised and thickened flesh. A man could have more than enough of violence.

His grandfather, Sir Hugh Treloar, had bought him a commission as soon as he left Harrow, and a few years later, in July of 1808, he'd been sent as a captain with his regiment to Portugal at the start of the Peninsular campaign.

After Julia.

He'd enjoyed it at first, if that was how he could have described it. Perhaps at best it had been a much-needed distraction from his sorrows. Soldiering had always been something he'd felt he was born for, and he'd sunk into this particular posting like a welcome comforting blanket. For the last six years, he'd allowed soldiering to blot out all else.

Not now though. Not after… No, he wouldn't think about it. If he did, he'd never muster an appetite for his dinner, which must surely be coming up soon. But what to think of instead? He ran his fingers through his unruly hair, a little too long at the moment and much in need of a trim. Rather than let the regimental barber in the Canterbury barracks hack away at it, he'd decided to wait until his return. He'd never been a stickler for following fashion. What soldier ever was? Any of those who did so were rarely good soldiers.

Home. That was it. He'd think of home. Only it hadn't been home now for eleven long years. In all that time he'd only been back to Cornwall once, and that just a flying visit for the funeral of his Aunt Endelyn's husband, John Polmear. Even before he'd taken up his commission, he'd been away at school for six years and glad to be so. Yet, in his heart, it remained his home, as much as any soldier, with his nomadic existence, could call anywhere home.

If he'd been inclined to self-analysis, he'd perhaps have reasoned that he needed its gentle balm, in contrast to the frantic furor of the recent war. As it was, his mind wandered unbidden down winding, flower-strewn lanes to leafy green Cornwall, such a contrast to the stony aridity of Northern Spain and Southern France. How hard it was to conjure up an image of Roskilly House as he remembered it. All he could make out in his mind's eye was a vague shape, devoid even of windows, the gardens remaining invisible. Had he been gone so long it had all but faded from his memory?

His sister Hetty must be all grown up by now. Sixteen? Seventeen? Ready to make her debut in society, such as it was that far down England's long westward stretching toe. Ready, perhaps, to attend local balls and soirées. Having left so young, he'd never tasted the joys of these parties and balls, save the few he remembered peering over the banisters to watch as a small boy at Roskilly, before his father died.

Would it have changed?

So much had happened in his absence. Uncle Robert's wife, a sad shadow of a woman with a mouth downturned by constant disappointment, had finally produced an heir and promptly died, to be shortly followed by Uncle Robert himself, hot on the heels of Nat's own father. Another door in his mind closed: he wouldn't think about how that had happened. He'd think of Uncle Robert instead. Was his orphaned child still living? He had a vague feeling that three years ago when he'd come down for the funeral, his mother had described the boy as sickly. Although, when he'd glimpsed the child playing in the gardens with his little dog, he'd seemed robust enough, despite his slender frame. An imp with the same sea blue, Treloar eyes he and Hetty possessed. His grandfather's eyes.

He doubted if he would see his female cousins, the offspring of his two paternal aunts. The oldest, Eliza, had married an architect and moved to Bath before he'd left Harrow, but she had a brother only a year or two older than Nat, who might be good to look up. Instead of a native returning home, he couldn't shake off the feeling of being a foreigner heading to a land no longer his.

But yes, it might be good to see his cousins if they were around, and young Hetty. He'd like the opportunity to get to know his little sister better. She'd been only six or so when he'd taken up his commission.

But above all, how good it would be to rest his war-torn soul a little and allow the quiet that was Cornwall to cast its spell over him. His eyelids drooped. It had been a long journey.

A knock on the door disturbed him.

He sat up and removed his booted feet from the bedcovers in haste. "Come in."

A maid had brought his dinner.

THE FOLLOWING MORNING, on a day that even that early seemed set to prove a warm one for once, Nat paid his dues to the inn's chamberlain after an early breakfast, shouldered his valise again, and, turning down bogus offers to find him transport, or carry his bag for him, set off along the narrow, crowded London streets to find the Saracen's Head at Snow Hill. It lay barely a few hundred yards from the White Horse, but the route was not a straight one, the streets being as tortuous as a labyrinth and packed with dangers. However, he found it easily, with its two distinctive Saracen busts outside the entrance, and, with his ticket to Penzance purchased from the busy ticketing office, he handed up his valise to the guard, and climbed aboard the stagecoach. He'd chosen this slower mode of transport above traveling by mail coach, which stopped for no man and was anything but restful for its passengers.

After a quick survey of his fellow travelers—a man of business in a somber black suit, a matron in a generously decorated floral bonnet, and a man whose rough hands betrayed him as some kind of gentleman farmer, perhaps, Nat closed his eyes and prepared to ignore their unavoidable stares for his disfigurement and at least feign sleep. He was growing used to the reactions his scarred face provoked, ranging from open horror to pity, and hadn't yet made up his mind which was worse. Best, on the whole, to avoid seeing the looks of strangers.

"Room for two more," called the guard and the door was flung open again. Drat it. The coach was meant for six, but four would have made the journey far more comfortable. Nat leaned into his corner, prepared to stand his ground against all comers for this coveted position, watching from behind half-closed eyes.

To his surprise, the newcomers were a pair of young officers, smart in their brightly colored uniforms and a little the worse for what must have been a long night of drinking and probably gambling as well. He recognized one of them as young Captain Lockhart, whom he'd met on board ship on the journey from Bordeaux.

"Treloar!" Lockhart, who'd acclimatized to Nat's facial disfigurement on the long voyage, exclaimed, as he settled himself into the seat between the man of business and the farmer. "Didn't think to see you here! Where are you bound for?"

The man of business gave him a cold glare.

"Cornwall," Nat muttered, his heart sinking. The last thing he wanted to have to do was to engage in conversation with anyone. That was the worst thing about public transport—being cooped up for hours on end with people you wouldn't normally give the time of day to but who thought you were their new best friend.

The other officer, a baby-faced young man, squeezed his sturdy body between Nat and the bonneted lady, disentangling himself from a sword that seemed intent on tripping him up. "You fellows know each other?" His gaze had fixed on the scar. Being on Nat's right, he could hardly have avoided it.

"Major Treloar of the 18th Hussars," Lockhart said. "Fought at Vitoria and Toulouse."

Nat nodded. "We met on the ship back from France."

Lockhart set his hands on his knees. "I see you're out of uniform. Bought yourself out, have you?"

Nat shifted, irritated by their bonhomie. He gave a curt nod. "Relinquished my commission."

"Oh," Lockhart said, waving a hand at his companion. "I did wonder about doing that m'self, only I don't know what I'd do instead. And you never know with Old Boney. I hear he's been dispatched off to Elba, but allowed to govern it like his own little empire. Not far enough if you ask me. I'd have clapped him in irons if it had been up to me. He'll be back, I'm certain, but we'll be ready for him. Just a bit of furlough for us two at the moment."

He leaned forward and slapped his young friend's knee. "Allow me to introduce my friend and traveling companion,

Lieutenant Talbot. We've been up here in Town a week or so now, since our regiment returned, but we've run a bit low on the readies, so I had the idea to pop off down to Whitchurch where my pater lives. Attending all the celebration balls and soirées can be a terrible drain on one's resources, especially if one has a liking for the card tables. Although all those lovely girls can be quite distracting. We both lost rather too heavily last night in the taproom."

Nat suppressed a smile. No doubt the card sharps had seen these two coming.

"Excuse me, sir," the farmer ventured, his accent broad and rural, saving Nat from having to answer. "Am I to understand that you three gentlemen are all of you freshly returned from the continent? From thrashing Bonaparte?"

"We are indeed," Lockhart said, beaming proudly. "Although we were down in Spain and the South of France, alongside the Spaniards and the Portuguese, and Boney made his surrender in the North. We didn't receive the news down there for several days, but when we did, Soult agreed to an armistice pretty damn sharp."

Talbot nodded. "He'd already abandoned Toulouse and nearly two thousand of his wounded to Wellington. We just marched in and took it over." He stretched out his legs as the coach rumbled out of the inn yard. "We made a fine job of it. And that was that. War over. Boney in chains."

"For now," Lockhart added. "And not actually in chains, remember."

"I hope for good," put in the man of business, a long-faced fellow with heavy bags under his bloodshot eyes. "It's high time we had peaceful dealings across the channel. This has been very bad for commerce."

"Commerce?" Lockhart cried. "Why, it's been bad for everything. But particularly bad if you were a French aristo, I should say!"

"Very true," the matron in the bonnet put in. "I should not

like to be a French lady, even now. In fact, I should not at all like to be French. So frightening. Although I did hear they're planning on restoring their monarchy."

"Louis XVIII," the man of business said. "Brother of the one whose head they chopped off with the guillotine. Dreadful business. Dreadful. Let's hope he's a step up on his brother and wants to improve relations with us British. It'll be good for trade."

"Is that all you can think of?" Lockhart asked, his voice rising. "Venal trade?"

The farmer blustered. "For the likes of us, sir, that's mighty important, even if it's not for gentlemen like you who can go home to your fathers and ask for more money whenever you need it. Most of us have to earn our own livelihood."

Things were hotting up. "Are you saying we soldiers have not been earning our own livelihoods?" Lockhart almost shouted. "Fighting on the Peninsula and in France and Belgium? Prepared to give our lives for our country?"

Time to intervene. Nat held his hands up. "Enough. I may have resigned my commission, but I'm still a major, and as such I outrank both of you two young hotheads. We've a long journey ahead of us, although I don't know how far the rest of you are going." He nodded to the three civilians. "But I'm with this coach nearly all the way to Penzance, and I don't fancy sitting here listening to arguments from dawn till dusk. Let us agree to differ and pass the journey in peace. I've had more than enough of fighting on the continent and don't intend to witness it now I'm back in England."

Lockhart's eyes blazed, but he bowed his head. "Yes, Major."

Young Talbot nodded. "I apologize to the company."

Nat shot Lockhart a hard look. "And you?"

"I apologize as well."

"Thank you."

Nat sat back in his seat, with a sigh, and resumed his attempts to fall asleep.

Chapter Two

A s the coach bumped over the uneven, pot-holed road surface, shaking the passengers from side to side like peas on a drum, twenty-seven-year-old Miss Caroline Fairfield attempted to reread her letter. She'd received it a week ago, and, on an impulse, decided to take up the offer it held. What else could she have done? The prospect of going with her mother to stay with her late father's much older sister, Gertrude, having been the only alternative, it had been an easy choice to make. At the time. Now, being bounced around on Cornwall's less than well-maintained roads, she had an unnerving sensation that she was entering the fabled back end of beyond.

She smoothed the letter out across her lap, and reread her friend Ysella's crabby, untidy, and poorly spelled missive.

My deere frend Caroline,

I was sore upset to heer of your Familys Misfortune. I had it in a Letter from deere Morvoren who was most sad and unhappy for you and your Mama. I had no idea your Papa was in such strates. I am sure my Brother would have helped him had he but Nown. Morvoren told me in her Letter that you are in search of a ~~posishun~~ post as Governess in a welltodo family. I am happy to tell you that I know of just the One for you.

The Treloars of Roskilly House. Mine owners and landed Gentry if not of the True Nobility. Of good stock my Mama would say. Sir Hugh is very old and keeps to his bed and as both the Sons are dead a manager has charge of his affairs which are the estate and mines and other sundries. Mrs. Treloar is the widow of one of the Sons and she seems a stern sort and somewhat imposing. I was a little afrayed of her myself. She has a Daughter just out of the Schoolroom who needs a Companion of good upbringing. I beleeve they wish for someone who can teach her french and musick altho why they want this for her I have no idea as I hated all manner of lerning when I was young.

Mrs. Treloar also cares for Sir Hugh's grandson who is only child to the dead older Brother. I beleeve he is heir to old Sir Hugh just a little Boy I have heard but a sickly one Mrs. Treloar said to me when I met her at the Assembly Rooms in Truro. I have not seen the Child nor Nowe of his age or the Nature of his Sicknesses. They need a Governess for this Child and when I told Mrs. Treloar of you and your booklerning and your ~~sichua~~ hardships she was pleased to ignore that you have no previus ~~exsper~~ skill yet at teaching a child. I sang your prases and told them you can teach musick and french for the girl and spelling and reading for the boy and whatever else it is boys do want to learn and are ~~exsepshu~~ very good at reckoning.

Mrs. Treloar is pleased to take you on if you can come down strate away and start as soon as possibel as there old Governess has upped and left all of a sudden.

Your ever loving Ysella (Beauchamp)
Carlyon Court
Cornwall

Caroline refolded the letter and stowed it in her reticule. Well, Ysella's spelling had not improved one iota for having been married for two years to a grammar-school-educated and intelligent young man.

Sam Beauchamp, Ysella's husband and the father of her baby daughter, Merrin, had once been land agent to Ysella's brother Kit, Viscount Ormonde of Ormonde Abbey in Wiltshire. On their marriage, Ysella and Sam had gone to live and manage Kit's smaller Cornish estate and had been there ever since. Caroline, who'd been close to Ysella's older sisters before becoming friends with Ysella, had not seen her in all that time. At least this employment by one of Ysella's neighbors might mean she'd get to meet up with her friend occasionally.

She leaned back against the coach's faded upholstered head-rest and closed her eyes. The rocking of this rather ramshackle vehicle might have had a lesser mortal ready to cast up her accounts, but Caroline was made of sterner stuff. The sort of stuff that could not abide being beholden to someone like Aunt Gertrude and would rather make her own way in the world. She only wished she could have brought Mama with her, and saved her from the ignominy of having to beg the help of that intimidating woman. Ysella's own mother, Elestren, Dowager Lady Ormonde, had begged Mama to come and live with her, but Mama's pride had made her turn down the offer. Caroline could understand why. At least Aunt Gertrude was a blood relation.

Poor, foolish Papa had been nothing like Aunt Gertrude, thank goodness, although if he had been, he might not have been such a bad manager. She and Mama might not now be cast penniless into the world thanks to his having not only invested what little fortune he possessed in that fake silver mine in Argentina, but also having gambled away his remaining assets, including their former home—Cadley Grange.

She sighed. Poor man, he'd taken the coward's way out and ended his embarrassment with one of his remaining pistols, unable to look either Mama or his only daughter in the face. Anger at his selfishness in leaving them to cope alone had finally subsided into a profound sadness at his weak character, and she no longer burned with fury when she thought of him. Even so, it pained her to picture their lost home and Mama's stricken face as she left it. She pushed these thoughts out of her mind as the coach began to slow down. Was this her stop?

The coach halted. From outside came a distinct thud as the

guard jumped down from his position on the back. The door opened and he poked his head inside. "Miss Fairfield? This be the stop for Roskilly House. I'll get your bags down for you."

He disappeared from view, and, with a quick goodbye for her remaining fellow passenger, a fat, somberly dressed matron who, despite her austere appearance, had proved quite the chatterbox, Caroline set a hand on the edge of the door and a neat, booted foot on the step. Pausing for a moment, she took in the view. The coach had halted on a narrow lane for which the description of "road" would have been far too generous. High, grassy banks topped by hawthorn hedges edged both sides, with one or two stray sheep grazing them and paying no attention to the coach. Straight in front of her, a side lane opened off, a prospect even more rutted and overgrown than the road they were on. No signpost of any kind indicated this was where she should dismount, and no house was in sight. Not even a distant chimney.

The guard dumped her two valises on the grassy verge, only just avoiding putting them in sheep droppings, and Caroline stepped down onto the road.

"Are you certain this is the right place?" she asked, aware that if it were not, and the coach departed, she might be stuck in the middle of nowhere.

The guard nodded. "That's right. Down there a bit." He pointed at the side lane.

"How far?"

"Mebbe a mile." He grinned. "'Tis the only house, so you can't miss it."

"Get a move on," called the driver from his perch high above the road. "I got times to meet, so you got no time to stand there passin' the time o' day with our passengers."

The guard gave a shrug. "Not that far for a strong young leddy like you."

Caroline bristled. Yes, she was tall and robust in appearance, but the implication that because of this she should be expected to cart two heavy valises down a mile long, muddy lane irritated her. Had she been small and dainty, like Ysella, no doubt the guard would not have made that remark. Not that Ysella's appearance didn't hide a tough inner core, because it did. But that was beside the point.

The guard tipped his hat at her and swung himself back up onto the rear of the coach. The driver clicked his tongue at his horses, and they sprang forward into a shambling trot. The coach rattled away down the road and vanished around the next bend.

In the comparative silence that ensued, Caroline stood for a few moments considering her situation. The thought that the Treloar family might not be expecting her rose foremost in her mind, followed closely by the fear that she might not be up to the job, as she'd never done anything like this before. What if the child was of a difficult temperament, or backward? Ysella had said he was sickly. That could mean anything.

She sighed. All she had to go on was what Ysella had written in that letter, and knowing Ysella, it might not be a correct interpretation of what her new acquaintance, Mrs. Treloar, had said to her at some provincial Assembly Rooms. Because surely if Ysella *had* got it right, there'd have been someone here to meet her and help transport herself and her bags to Roskilly House. If, indeed, she was even in the right place.

She peered down the lane. It ran slightly downhill, something she had to admit was better than if it had gone uphill, between high banks and hedges, with here and there, odd, stunted, wind-shaped trees overhanging the way. Nothing about it indicated it was much used by anything other than cattle or sheep. Well, if she was going to get to Roskilly House before it got dark, then she'd have to do it herself on her own two feet. She bent and picked up her valises and immediately regretted bringing so many of her belongings with her. However, the sooner she started, the better.

She set off down the lane.

Although the day was fine, with only a scattering of clouds in the sky, it soon became clear that there must have been a lot of rain in the past few days. The ruts had here and there been filled in with rocks, which made uncomfortable walking, even in her smart boots, but, in between, the ground lay muddy and uneven. Ysella had once told her it rained a lot in Cornwall, and it looked like that must be true. The two valises grew heavier with every step she took, and she couldn't even swap them from hand to hand as both seemed equally heavy. What had she packed in there? Bricks?

Soon she found herself passing through a patch of stunted woodland, the straggly trees bending over the track and stretching out long, spiky arms toward her. Where on earth was this going to take her? Ysella had said this family was gentry, and the name of their house implied she'd had it correct. But was *this* their main entrance?

She struggled on, the summer sun beating down on her in a most discomforting manner. Sweat sprang out on her back, her face began to glow with heat, and some of the branches had snatched at her hair and pulled tendrils loose. Her boots were now mired in mud and the hem of the plain blue gown she'd chosen for a good first impression was liberally spattered. Conscious she no longer looked at her best, she ploughed on. After all, she could hardly turn back now, could she?

After what seemed like a lot more than one mile, she finally turned yet another corner in the track and spotted what had to be her goal. A large, square mansion stood before her, only she seemed to have come upon it from behind, where the oldest part of the house, that would be hidden by a more modern façade at the front, gave away its ancient origins.

She set down her valises in relief and surveyed the building.

The first thing that met her eyes was the stable courtyard, close beside the tidy barns and outbuildings of what had to be the home farm. The coach driver must have dropped her at the back entrance—the servants' entrance perhaps. Did she *look* like a servant? Maybe she did in her rather austere spencer and gown, and with her hair sensibly restrained in a neat bun under a plain and practical bonnet. Not that her hair was neat any longer, of course.

But she was *not* a servant. She was a governess now, and she was *not* going to enter by the back door.

Picking up her valises again, she followed a neat graveled path around to the front of the house, where a sweeping driveway bisected wide green lawns. She'd been right. The front of the house shouted new addition loud and clear. Whoever owned this house had spent a great deal of money on bringing it up to date, and relatively recently by the style of it. An impressive, pillared portico, such as was all the rage in houses nowadays, sheltered a double front door, and, on the far side of the carriage turning circle, an iron grilled gateway marked an entrance into a stone-walled garden.

Caroline set her valises down again and attempted to tidy her hair, tucking the loose tendrils behind her ears. If only she had a mirror. And if only she wasn't now sweating like a navvy. So much for the adage "horses sweat, gentlemen perspire, and ladies glow"—she felt as though she were doing all three at once.

Just then, the gate from the walled garden swung open on creaky hinges, and a small boy in a blue skeleton suit cannoned out of it, short legs going at full pelt, his long golden curls whipping out behind him. An equally small dog, a russet spaniel, ran barking at his heels as though the two of them were racing.

The child skidded to a halt on the gravel ten feet from Caroline, and the dog sat on its haunches, gazing up at its master out of adoring brown eyes.

The dog's master stared at Caroline for a few long seconds before his freckled face broke into a grin. "Hello."

Caroline, who liked children, smiled back. "Hello to you, young sir."

The boy tilted his head to one side as though assessing her appearance. "Why're you so muddy?"

Caroline glanced down at her clothing. She had to admit it was in a state. "I've just walked down that lane over there from where the Penzance coach dropped me off. I think he made a mistake in leaving me there."

"Are you the new parlor maid?"

She shook her head. "No. Were you expecting one?"

He shrugged. "I think so. You don't sound much like a parlor maid, though."

"That's because I'm not one."

"Good. I *like* the way you sound. They don't like me talking to the parlor maids in case I learn to speak like them, but I do talk to them when no one's looking." He frowned. "What are you doing here, then?"

Caroline pressed her lips together. "I did think I was coming to be the governess to a boy who lives here, but I'm not sure his aunt is expecting me. My friend, Mrs. Beauchamp, who lives at Carlyon Court, recommended me to Mrs. Treloar, and sent me a letter telling me to come down here as soon as possible. So here I am, and I very much fear that no one knows I'm coming."

The boy pulled a face. "I think you must be *my* new governess then."

"I was rapidly coming to that conclusion myself."

He frowned. "I'd decided not to like my new governess after Aunt Ruth got rid of Miss Hawkins. I *liked* Miss Hawkins. A lot." His voice took on a note of complaint. "I didn't want her to go. She took me out walking and showed me all sorts of int'resting things. We found a badger's sett, but Aunt Ruth sent Roscarrow out to kill the badgers." The frown deepened. "Miss Hawkins and me, we were going to go back and hide in a bush and watch them, and now I can't, because they're all dead." He rubbed his small nose with a grubby hand.

Caroline wasn't quite sure how to deal with this. Mrs. Treloar, as her prospective employer, would no doubt want her to back up her actions with the badgers, but Caroline couldn't help but commiserate with the little boy before her. He had such a doleful expression on his young face.

"Oh dear," she said, seeking for noncommittal. "Well, if your aunt takes me on as your governess, I promise we'll look for another badgers' sett. There's one in the woods near where I live—*lived*, and my own dear papa took me down there to watch the creatures from time to time. I loved to see the cubs playing together in the spring. But we had to sit very still and quiet. Is that something you can do?"

The boy's face brightened. "Of course I can. I'd like that." He stepped up to her. "I should introduce myself. Aunt Ruth would be quite vexed if she thought I didn't mind my manners. My name is Yves Treloar." He held out a small hand, the dirty nails bitten to the quick.

Caroline took it and they shook. "And my name is Caroline Fairfield. Pleased to meet you, Master Treloar."

He grinned. "Pleased to meet you, too. I think... But I daresay you'd best go in, now, and meet Aunt Ruth. I'll show you the way if you like."

Caroline followed Yves to the front door, which he shoved wide enough open to allow her to step inside.

The interior of Roskilly House, like its front façade, possessed an air of modernity about it, as though someone had taken time with all the decoration and furniture to buy everything of the most up to date. The front door opened into a wide and somewhat spartan hallway with black and white tiles underfoot, and a marble staircase leading to a galleried upper floor.

A liveried servant, the butler perhaps, appeared as if from nowhere. "Master Yves, you're wanted in the nursery for your tea." He bowed to Caroline, disapproval in his cold stare. "May I be of assistance, Miss?"

Yves stood his ground and looked up at Caroline in expectation.

She drew herself up straighter, wishing she didn't look so much the worse for wear. "My name is Caroline Fairfield. I've come to see Mrs. Treloar." She glanced at Yves. Best to start as she meant to go on with him. "Hadn't you best do as you're told and go to the nursery?"

He gave a resigned shrug, but didn't move.

She tried to ignore the way the butler was eyeing her bedraggled appearance and look as though it didn't matter. He cleared his throat. "Perhaps you'd like to leave your bags here, Miss Fairfield, and follow me this way." He glanced at the boy. "Off you go, young man." But she was surprised to see a fond twinkle in his eye.

Yves, trailing his feet, started up the wide staircase, the spaniel trotting at his heels. On the third step, he turned and grinned at Caroline again. She lifted a hand to him, and followed the butler toward an impressively large door on the right of the hall, the feeling of being a fraud washing over her in ever-increasing waves.

Chapter Three

THE DOOR FROM the hall opened into what proved to be the parlor. High ceilinged, and airy, with two long windows either side of a doorway that must lead out onto a terrace, its modernity bestowed upon it a cold atmosphere that matched the face of the woman seated by the empty fireplace.

Ruth Treloar, for it must have been she, set down the book she'd been reading and rose to her feet. A tall, hard-faced woman with graying brown hair scraped back from her face tightly enough to give her skin a stretched look, she wore a navy-blue dress of rich satin augmented by a demure lace fichu about her throat. She was not an unattractive woman, but her pale gray eyes, shining with the hardness of diamonds, pale lips, and cheeks just touched with rouge gave her the distinct look of a harpy from the Greek mythology Caroline's father had been so fond of reading aloud to her.

She looked Caroline up and down, an expression of polite puzzlement on her face that had Caroline's heart sinking into her muddy boots.

"Miss Caroline Fairfield, Ma'am," the butler said.

She gave him a curt nod. "Thank you, Ennion."

Caroline executed as neat a curtsey as possible, considering her bedraggled appearance. "Good afternoon, Mrs. Treloar."

Mrs. Treloar seemed to have been struck dumb for a moment

by Caroline's appearance, but, within seconds, she gathered herself. "Good afternoon, Miss Fairfield. To what do I owe the pleasure of this visit?" Not a shred of recognition or welcome in her voice, only cold disdain, presumably that Caroline had dared to present herself in such a condition. Well, she should make sure her servants' entrance was in a better state.

However, biting back that riposte, Caroline schooled her face to bland impartiality and smoothed her rumpled skirts. The only thing to do here was to brazen it out. "I believe we have a mutual friend in Mrs. Beauchamp of Carlyon Court."

The frosty expression remained. "A mere acquaintance, not a friend."

Caroline ploughed on. "She wrote to me saying you were much in need of a governess and that I was to come down as soon as possible to fill the post."

Recognition at last dawned in those cold gray eyes. "Oh, of course. I had quite forgotten. Please forgive me, but I had no idea she would write to you and have you come down here so quickly. Most obliging of you." Still no hint of warmth showed in her face, although she now indicated a severe, upright chair. "Perhaps you would care to take a seat?"

"Thank you." Caroline settled herself on the edge of the chair, back straight, in an attempt to look more efficient than she suspected her appearance implied.

Mrs. Treloar folded her hands over the book in her lap and addressed the butler without once glancing his way. "Ennion. Have some tea brought in." He departed on silent feet.

Caroline mirrored her hostess's action of folding her hands, although she had no book herself. "I had wondered if Ysella— Mrs. Beauchamp—was mistaken in your need, or that you might already have engaged a governess. Her letter suggested your need was urgent and that speed was of the essence."

Mrs. Treloar shook her head. "There has been no mistake. We had to let the old governess go very suddenly, and have not yet found a replacement. You have French? And play the pianoforte?"

Caroline nodded. "I have had a very competent education, first at home with a governess, and then later at school in Bath. I play both the pianoforte and the violin, and I speak and read French to a high standard, and, thanks to my father, have some Latin and Greek as well. He believed girls should have as good an education as a boy."

Mrs. Treloar raised a thin eyebrow. "That's as may be. You will not need your Latin and Greek for my daughter, Henrietta. My daughter has left the schoolroom behind her now, but her grandfather and I would like her to continue to speak French and improve on her skills at the pianoforte. As well as teaching my nephew in the mornings, I would like you to be Henrietta's companion and ensure she learns all the attributes a young lady requires."

No question of whether it suited Caroline or not. She had to remember that she was now an employee, and her wishes would no longer be taken into account about anything.

The door opened, and Ennion returned with a tray of tea things which he set on the table beside his mistress.

"You may go, Ennion. I will pour." As discreetly and quietly as before, the butler melted away.

"Now," Mrs. Treloar said. "Do you take milk with your tea?"

"Yes, thank you."

Caroline took the proffered cup and sipped the hot liquid. Good China tea, at any rate.

Mrs. Treloar fixed her with that cold stare over the rim of her own cup. "The boy, my nephew, is nine years old. He has no parents. Both of them died very inconveniently before he was three years old." Spoken as though she thought they'd done it on purpose, out of spite. "My father-in-law, Sir Hugh, stands as legal guardian to the child. However, as Sir Hugh has been bedridden these past two years, in practicality, it is I who act as his guardian in all but legal terms. It falls upon me to decide his education. He is a weakly child, prone to all the childhood illnesses and more, and it is my opinion that he should be educated here, at home, where I can keep my eye upon him. He is to learn mathematics, composition, use of the globe and history, as well as French and a little music. As you have Latin, he can learn that too. An improvement on Miss Hawkins, who was not accomplished in the Classics." She tutted. "Not accomplished in very much, it seems."

Caroline nodded. "I can teach him Greek, too, if you wish."

"That will do splendidly. But I don't want the child continuously cooped up inside the schoolroom. For his constitution, I require him to spend some of each day outside, so his lessons will only be between nine and twelve each morning."

Caroline nodded again. Her own governess had done much the same—teaching her in the mornings and then taking her out for walks in the afternoons. Her nervousness at her first proper job began to dissipate. How hard could teaching one small boy be?

Mrs. Treloar set down her teacup. "Yves takes all his meals in the schoolroom, and I require you to do the same. Your room will be in the nursery wing, close to the schoolroom and the nursery, where Yves sleeps." Mrs. Treloar paused. "Do you have any questions?"

TWENTY MINUTES LATER, after sitting sipping her tea in an excruciating silence, and wondering if she should have thought up a few questions, however inane, to fill the gap, Caroline emerged from the drawing room into the wide, soulless hall and followed a young footman carrying her valises up the marble staircase.

The hallway stretched to double height, and a gallery ran around its upper edge, with corridors leading off in different directions into what must be the wings of the house. The livery-clad footman, a young man whose fresh-faced and spotty complexion indicated he could be no more than eighteen, led her down one of these corridors and through a door into what had to be the nursery wing.

"This is the governess's room, Miss," he said, pushing open the door and stepping back.

So, this was how a governess lived. The bedroom was better than a servant would have been given, but not so fancy as a guest room in the main house. A high bed covered in an eiderdown took up most of the room, along with a tall wardrobe, a wash-stand, a desk by the window, and on the floor a slightly worn rug in muted colors. Not the smart new furniture of the rest of the house, but nevertheless, comfortable looking, and enough to remind Caroline of her lost home. Most likely the contents had been demoted when the rest of the house received its modern makeover.

"This will do nicely," she said, going in.

The footman set her bags on the bed. "Will there be anything else, Miss?"

She was about to say no, and thank him for his help, when a small tornado hurtled through the door and flung itself at the footman, closely followed by a spaniel. "Dickon!" Yves wrapped his arms around the young man's waist and hung on.

The footman's cheeks flared with embarrassment and he quickly peeled the boy off, his eyes going to Caroline. "I'm sorry, Miss, that won't happen again."

Yves frowned up at him. "I thought you'd come to play foot-ball with me along the corridor?"

Poor Dickon's cheeks reddened even further. "I can't do that right now, Master Yves. I'm supposed to be working."

Caroline looked from one to the other of them. The young footman was scarcely more than a boy himself, and Yves had taken on a crestfallen, disappointed expression yet again. "Pray don't let my presence stop you from playing ball with Master Yves, Dickon," she said with as kind a smile as she could muster.

"His aunt has just told me she wants him to have as much exercise as possible for his health, so I think a quick kickabout along the nursery corridor should become a staple of his education. If you have time right now?"

Dickon's face broke into a smile, removing any vestige of snooty footman. "If you're sure that's all right, Miss?"

Yves danced from one foot to the other.

Caroline smiled. "Of course it is. You two go and play, and I'll unpack my bags."

Still blushing, Dickon retreated into the corridor, and Yves scampered off, presumably to find his football, his dog bouncing at his heels. As Caroline opened her valises, the thump of a ball hitting the floor and walls sounded outside in the corridor, followed by a high-pitched bark. The dog must be playing too. She smiled to herself. She could only hope that despite the loud noise, the walls and floors were thick enough for no one to hear this downstairs.

By the time she'd stowed all her belongings away, the sound of football being played had died away, so Dickon must have had to return to his footman duties downstairs. The door opened, and Yves stuck his tousled blonde head around it. His pale cheeks had flushed with the exercise.

"I say, that was very sporting of you to let Dickon play with me. Miss Hawkins used to all the time, but since she's been gone, I've had Bridget looking after me, and *she* told me I wasn't allowed to play football inside." He grinned. "It's more fun than outside. The ball can't get away, and I love the noise it makes when it hits the walls." He swung on the door jamb. "I *love* making lots of noise."

Caroline smiled. "What boy doesn't? I used to play football with one of my friends, when I was a girl. And, if you promise not to tell anyone, I'll tell you a secret."

He stepped into the room, nodding. "I promise. I'm good at keeping secrets. You can tell me anything."

"My mother and father sent me to school in Bath when I was

thirteen, intending me to learn to become a lady, but I secretly took my ball with me and would play football in the gardens with my friends. If we'd been seen, we'd have been in trouble because it wouldn't have been considered at all ladylike."

He giggled. "I should like to play football with other boys, but I'm not allowed to play with the farmworkers' children. I've seen them playing together sometimes, in the farmyard or the fields, and it looks such fun. I have to make do with Dickon." His face brightened. "Although now I have you, too. Miss Hawkins didn't play football herself, but she didn't mind me playing. Maybe you might play with me and Dickon? Sometimes we get his sister Patience to play too. She's a nursery maid. A nice one, not like mean old Bridget."

Caroline beamed. "Of course I'll play football with you. But what about your cousin Henrietta? Doesn't she play with you?"

Yves frowned. "She used to, but Aunt Ruth doesn't like her to do boyish things now she's not in the schoolroom. I *like* Cousin Hetty a lot, but she can be a bit boring. Probably because she's a girl and learning to be a lady and can't do the same things I can. Aunt Ruth doesn't mind *what* I do when I'm outside." He peered up at her. "I was wondering. What do you want me to call you?"

Caroline drew in her bottom lip. "We-ell, I suppose you ought to call me Miss Fairfield, to be polite. But my name is Caroline."

Yves bit his own lip. "That's a nice name. Might I call you Caroline when we're not in lessons? And Miss Fairfield when you're teaching me? To be polite."

Caroline pulled a skeptical face. He seemed a very friendly child, and not too pushy. "Perhaps that would work. We'll see, shall we?"

He grinned. "Then shall I take you to meet my cousin, now? She'll probably be in her room getting changed for dinner. Now she's left the schoolroom, my aunt lets her dine with them. She used to eat with me when Miss Hawkins was teaching her too." He seized Caroline's hand. "She only left the schoolroom when

Aunt Ruth got rid of Miss Hawkins. It's been a bit lonely without her, even though she can be boring. I suppose having a girl around is better than having no one."

After this rather scathing dismissal of female-kind, Caroline let him lead her out of the room, down the corridor to the galleried landing and into another wing of the house. They stopped outside a door halfway along the corridor. Yves tapped on it.

"Come in," called a voice from within.

He pushed open the door and led Caroline inside. "Hetty, I've brought my new governess to meet you."

Miss Henrietta Treloar, luckily for her, had not inherited her looks from her mother. She was neither tall nor severe looking. Instead, a girl as dainty as Caroline's friend Ysella regarded them from the chaise longue in the window where she'd been sitting sketching the view of the distant blue sea. Rich auburn hair cascaded in artful curls onto her shoulders, and the corners of wide blue eyes, very much like Yves's own, crinkled as she smiled at her small cousin. "Yves!"

He ran to her and sat down with a thump on the chaise longue. "Can I see your drawing? This is Caroline Fairfield. Caroline, this is Hetty. I mean Henrietta. Aunt Ruth says she can't be Hetty now she's a young lady and not a schoolgirl."

Hetty rose to her feet, her smile illuminating her lovely face. "Miss Fairfield, how lovely to meet you. You mustn't let Yves take liberties with you. He's such a rascal." She ruffled Yves's already ruffled hair. "My mother already informed me you'd arrived. I'm so glad to have someone to keep me company. Now I'm no longer in the schoolroom I'm finding life here a little tedious, but that might be because Yves and I no longer have Hawkie to amuse us. There's a limit to how many sketches I can do, or how much I can play the pianoforte or read. Even though Mama wants me to do *all* these things."

Caroline took her extended hand. "I shall endeavor to find interesting occupations for all of us, Miss Treloar."

Hetty shook her head, making her curls bob. "Oh no no, don't call me Miss Treloar. It makes me sound like an old maid. Like Aunt Agnes, and she's a hundred if she's a day. I should much prefer it if you were to call me Hetty, although *not* in front of my mother who is such a stickler for social etiquette." She dimpled. "We three will keep our own secrets and be Yves, Caroline, and Hetty in each other's company and Master Yves, Miss Fairfield, and Miss Treloar when Mama is present."

She seemed to have very little in common with her mother, especially not her personality, and must, surely, resemble her late father. Perhaps there might be a portrait of him somewhere Caroline could see.

A maid in a mob cap came in. "Miss Henrietta, your Mama sent me to tell you dinner is about to be served." She bobbed a curtsey at Hetty and then another at Caroline, eyes full of curiosity.

Hetty stood up. "I'm so sorry you have to eat in the schoolroom with Yves. I would have liked your presence at dinner to talk to, but that can't be helped. Mama has decreed and what Mama says, goes, every time. Although I am going to endeavor to change her mind. It's so quiet at dinner with just Mama, Aunt Agnes, and me." She gave a little shiver. "Although sometimes Mr. Trefusis eats with us as well. But I am sure we will see each other tomorrow."

And with that, she departed, leaving Caroline and Yves to return to the schoolroom where the dinner served would most likely not have suited the lady of the house one bit.

Chapter Four

T o Caroline's surprise, a maid brought a tray of tea and toast to her room at seven the next morning. A skinny little girl of no more than thirteen, she tapped on the door and pushed it open to peer around it at Caroline, eyes wide with trepidation. "Miss," she called, without coming in. "I've brung your breakfast."

Caroline sat up in bed. "Goodness. Do come in. Thank you very much."

The girl shuffled inside and closed the door behind her with a nudge of her shoulder.

"D'you want it in bed or on the table, Miss?"

Caroline briefly considered the luxury of taking breakfast in bed every morning, but pushed that thought aside as not befitting someone in her position. "On the table, thank you." She swung her legs out of bed and slid her feet into her slippers.

The girl tiptoed across the room as though walking on coals and set the tray down with a rattle of china on the table by the window. As the room was not cold, Caroline didn't bother with her peignoir but took the single chair in just her long white nightgown. The girl made as if to hurry away.

Caroline held up her hand. "Don't go. Pray stop and tell me your name and position in the house." She poured herself a cup of tea from the pretty china pot. "I need to familiarize myself with who is whom and how the house is run."

The girl turned back, hands clasped in front of her. "I'm Patience, Miss, the nursery maid."

Aha, the younger sister of footballer Dickon. Caroline looked her up and down. "You seem very young, Patience, for such an important role. Have you been here long? And what do your duties as nursery maid entail?"

Patience bit her lip. "I'm near fourteen, Miss, and I been here nigh on a year now. I started off in the kitchens, as scullery maid, but then the old head nursery maid was let go. Mrs. Treloar, she did tell me as I'd need to step up, so as to help Bridget. She's the head nursery maid now Hester's gone." She bunched up the edge of her apron, working it in her fingers. Was she nervous for some reason?

Caroline's eyebrows rose. This was indeed a quick promotion for so young a girl. "And how long have you been working in the nursery?"

"A week, Miss. One of my jobs is to bring the governess breakfast every morning, though today's the first day I done that. Miss Hawkins havin' been gone a week an' all. Before that, Hester, the old nursery maid, she and Bridget took Miss Hawkins's breakfast up, along with Master Yves's. Now Bridget says as I have to do both."

Caroline frowned. So, Miss Hawkins *and* the unknown Hester had both been let go at much the same time. How odd. Probably just an unfortunate coincidence, though.

"And what time does young Master Yves rise? I take it you'll be bringing his breakfast up as well, as your predecessor did?"

Patience's honest face took on a puzzled expression, perhaps at the long word. "I've been takin' it up at half past the hour, on Mrs. Treloar's orders, but most times, Master Yves has already been up and about. He likes to come down to the kitchens and eat breakfast with Cook. Then I have to tidy up his bedroom and yours, and do all the cleaning. In the afternoons, 'tis my job to clean the schoolroom after lessons is over and fetch dinner up for half past twelve. Usually, I bring supper, too, only yesterday were my afternoon off." She gave a nervous smile. "I go home to see my ma and pa on my afternoons off."

"Very commendable." Caroline took a bite of toast. Cold. "I'd be most obliged if you would help me with my stays in a moment, as I'm not used to managing them by myself." She'd been worrying about getting dressed, not having a lady's maid to call on. "I should be much obliged for your help with them every morning, in fact. I can manage to get them off at nights, but tying them tightly enough of a morning is likely to defeat me."

Patience bobbed the trace of a curtsey, her hazel eyes brightening. "Like a real lady's maid, Miss? I will, that."

Caroline finished her cold toast and then, with Patience's far-from-clumsy assistance, divested herself of her nightgown and dressed in the plain, dove-gray gown she and Mama had deemed suitable for a governess to wear. Her blue gown, lying on the end of the bed still, caught her eye, as did her muddy boots. "Could you possibly have this dress cleaned for me, and get the bootboy to clean my boots? I had rather a muddy walk yesterday due to having been dropped off by mistake at the back entrance to the house."

"You walked down the back track?" Patience's eyes widened. "Then 'tis not a wonder your clothes and boots are in such a state. I'll get them back looking smart for you, don't you worry. I'm good at that. Master Yves, he do get his clothes in a right mess most days." She gathered up dress, boots, and empty breakfast tray, and, with Caroline holding open the door for her, departed in the direction of the kitchens. The clock on the mantelpiece said the time was five and twenty minutes past seven, so it might be a good time to see if her new charge was out of bed. Now, which was the door to the nursery?

Through good luck, she chose the right one.

Yves's accommodation's close resemblance to her old nursery at Cadley brought a lump to her throat, but it was unoccupied at present. One of the two small beds was neatly made but the covers on the other had been thrown back as though its occupant had leapt out of it in haste. A large, dappled rocking horse stood to one side, alongside a doll's house that must surely belong to Hetty, not a little boy. Tin soldiers had been arranged in tumbled ranks across the floor, and someone, no doubt Yves, had constructed a fortress for them to attack out of building blocks.

But where *was* Yves? The kitchen, presumably. Well, she needed to explore the rest of the house and meet some of the other servants, so an expedition in search of her small charge seemed an excellent idea.

She took the nursery corridor back to the galleried landing and descended the staircase. She'd not really taken it in on her arrival, and only now did its grandiosity sink in. Nothing like the much smaller, oak stairs at Cadley, nor the old-fashioned tower stairs at Ormonde, it more closely resembled the ostentatiousness of Denby Castle, seat of the Duke of Denby. As with the rest of the house, it possessed an air of being almost brand new, and was no doubt very fashionable. Not that she was in any way an arbiter of fashion in housebuilding.

The wide front hall, big enough to hold a dance in, lay empty, the front doors firmly closed. In which direction might the kitchens lie? Presumably toward the back, where she'd seen the stable courtyard, occupying what she'd taken to be the oldest part of the house. Nothing like the modern and austere front face.

An insignificant, plain dark-oak door to the left of the stairs looked promising, so she opened it and went through. The passageway she found herself in was promising as well, its floor stone flagged instead of tiled, and its plain, whitewashed walls indicating its utilitarian use.

She soon found the kitchens, which opened on her right, the warm aroma of cooking assailing her nostrils and leading her on. Yves was sitting at a long refectory table, tucking in to a plate of bacon and eggs. He glanced up as she came in, his lips yellow with runny egg yolk. "Caroline!"

At the far end of the long kitchen stood a large, black range, at which one of the biggest women Caroline had ever seen was stirring what could well have been a cauldron. A girl no older than Patience busily chopped vegetables at the far end of the table from Yves, and a shaggy-headed boy was polishing boots in a corner with great industry. All three heads turned, at Yves's exclamation, to regard Caroline with curious stares. Even a little, no, a lot, suspicious.

Yves jumped down from the table. "It's all right, Mrs. Teague, Molly, Bert. Caroline's my new governess. *You* know. I told you all about her."

Mrs. Teague, who must have been at least six feet tall and half as wide, wiped her hands on her apron and pushed a wisp of gray hair back under her mob cap. "Didn't expect ter see you down in my kitchen, Miss." A definite air of hostility remained. The trouble with being a governess was that you were neither part of the family nor one of the servants, and not really welcome in either situation.

Caroline tried a smile. "I only came looking for Yves. Patience told me he eats down here with you quite often. And I wanted to learn the layout of the house." Best not to say she wanted to get to know the servants as that could be misconstrued. As a governess she would have to watch what she said and maintain a distance between herself and the staff.

"Well," Mrs. Teague said, looking a fraction mollified. "You've seen the kitchens all right now. And Master Yves has finished his breakfast." She picked up his empty, egg-smeared plate. "Have you had enough to eat, young man?"

Yves wiped his eggy mouth on the sleeve of what must have started the day as his clean, royal blue skeleton suit but now was decorated with a few breakfasty stains. "Could I have a cake, please? I still have a small corner that's not quite full yet."

Mrs. Teague's stern face softened as she went to where a tray of small cakes were cooling on a rack. "Hollow legs is what you've got, my lad. Here we are then."

Yves took one in each hand, then glanced up at Caroline. "Do you want one? I bet you only got tea and toast for breakfast. That's what my aunt orders sent up for me, but I fox her. I come down here, and Mrs. Teague always gives me something *much* better. She says my aunt only tells her what to send upstairs, not what to give me down here. That was Miss Hawkins's idea. She said I needed building up." He grinned. "Go on, take one. We don't get much for dinner in the schoolroom, so if you don't, you'll be hungry later."

"Fresh out o' the oven, Miss Fairfield." Did Mrs. Teague's eyes hold sympathy, now, as well as suspicion?

Caroline took a warm cake, the memory of absconding to the kitchens at Cadley for just such a treat almost bringing a tear to her eye. Did children the world over establish friendships in the kitchens of their parents' houses?

"Thank you, Mrs. Teague. That's very kind of you." Best to keep on her good side by being suitably grateful and polite, especially if Yves was right and the other meals they could expect would be small. Last night's supper, that she'd eaten in the schoolroom with Yves, had not been generous, although until now she'd not thought to wonder about it.

"Shall we go upstairs and get your face cleaned up?" she said to Yves. "And you can show me your schoolbooks."

He wrinkled his small nose. "Do I have to? *I* was thinking we could take a walk down to the beach to do some… nature study. Miss Hawkins and I often did natural philosophy on nice mornings. I'm very good at identifying birds and shells. She had a book about them." He waved a hand at the nearest window, although thanks to the heat in the kitchen it was steamed up. "And today's a day for doing that. No rain at all. I already checked. Not that I mind the rain. Although I suppose you might, being a governess and a female." He managed an embryonic sneer. "Hetty doesn't like the rain." A cheeky grin banished the sneer. "She says it makes her hair go all frizzy… and she's right."

Caroline smiled. "Well, let me see your books first, and then we'll decide what needs to be done. And if we don't get to the beach this morning, I promise we'll go down this afternoon. Perhaps Hetty might like to come too, if we ask her. As it's not raining. I'm supposed to be her companion as well as your governess."

Yves's face, which had fallen, brightened. "She'll come. She loves the beach when the sun's shining, and sometimes in winter too." He gave her a sharp look. "But we'd best not tell Hetty's mama, Aunt Ruth, where we're going. She doesn't like the beach at all and thinks poor Hetty should have to stay indoors or she'll ruin her complexion in the sun. Hetty told me that. She says it's very boring being a girl and having to always wear huge bonnets to keep the sun off. It makes me glad I'm a boy."

Caroline laughed. "Well, she's right to a certain extent about the sun, and about bonnets being annoying. But stop delaying, and let's go upstairs. The sooner you show me your books, the sooner we can be about something more interesting for you."

The schoolroom possessed a blackboard on one wall, in itself quite a modern innovation in teaching methods, a teacher's high desk to one side and across the room four small desks with attached seats. At some point there must have been four children within the nursery wing. At the back of the room stood the table they'd eaten at the night before, and an old globe had pride of place on top of a small bookcase.

With marked reluctance, Yves lifted the lid of one of the desks and removed a small stack of dog-eared exercise books. "I'm not *that* good at keeping them tidy," he said, his tone apologetic. A bit. "Aunt Ruth told Miss Hawkins my writing was *un-de-cifrable.*" He said the long word with immense care. "Miss Hawkins told me that means she couldn't read it. But that's a *good* thing, because then she won't be able to read what I've written."

Caroline took the books from him with a frown. "Why is it a good thing she can't read what you've written? When writing, we want others to be able to read our work, otherwise we might just as well not bother to write at all."

Yves narrowed his eyes at her. "Some of the things I write, I don't want anyone reading." He surveyed her for a moment. "Don't tell her I said that, will you?"

Caroline smiled. "I won't. But I must point out that *I* need to be able to read what you've written, so you'll need to do your best handwriting for me. Let me have a look." She sat down at the desk next to Yves's and spread his exercise books across its surface. Mathematics, Composition, French, History and Geography. Well, the missing Miss Hawkins seemed to have been giving him a good variety of lessons.

"Which is your favorite subject?"

Yves, who'd still been standing beside his desk, plumped himself down on the seat. "Composition. I like writing stories."

Caroline opened that book first. His spidery hand crawled across the first page, much augmented by blots and smudges. The title of the piece had been heavily underlined. *The Secret Cove.* "This sounds exciting. Do you mind if I read it?"

His cheeks went a little pink. "No-o… But it's the first one I ever wrote. Miss Hawkins said I have a good imagination. She said I should write my stories down. I'm better at it now, though, and my spelling's improved. I wrote that one when I was quite a *little* boy."

Not that he was big now. Caroline read the two-page story about two boys finding a hidden cove with a cave used by smugglers and being caught by the chief smuggler and asked to join the gang. Some of his writing was indeed hard to decipher, and his spelling was worse than Ysella's, but he could tell a good, exciting story.

"That's lovely," she said, flicking through the book to see how many more there were. It was nearly full. "I love a good story myself and have been known to write my own, just like you." She glanced across at the small but well-stocked bookcase. "Did Miss Hawkins read aloud to you at all? I find reading helps one with writing one's own stories."

He jumped up, nodding. "I'll show you my favorite." Running to the bookcase he pulled one of the books out and handed it to Caroline.

She turned it over in her hands and opened it on the title page. *The Life and Strange and Surprising Adventures of the Renowned Hero, Robinson Crusoe of York*. "Goodness. I didn't know this was for children."

Yves shrugged. "I used to like baby books like *Cock Robin* when I was just a *little* boy, but Miss Hawkins said as I was such a good reader, we should try this one, and it's *very* exciting, so I love it." He leaned closer. "I'll tell you a secret, if you like."

She looked up at him. "Yes?"

"I can read it myself, of course, but I *love* to be read to at bedtime. I used to have a nurse before Miss Hawkins was my governess, and she read to me every night, but only baby books, like *Cock Robin*. But Miss Hawkins said I could have exciting books and she made the stories..." He hesitated as though searching for the right words. "She made me think I was *in* the story." He grinned. "She does... *did* good voices."

Caroline closed the book. "Well, if you work hard this morning, and then show me the way to the beach this afternoon, I shall read to you at bedtime just as Miss Hawkins did. How does that sound?"

His smile stretched almost from ear to ear. "A bargain. But don't tell Aunt Ruth you're doing that. She thinks big boys don't need reading to." He frowned. "Miss Hawkins and Aunt Ruth shouted at each other about that. I think that might be why Miss Hawkins left..."

Caroline rose from the desk and approached the blackboard. There were certainly a few things about Roskilly House she'd like to find out more about.

Chapter Five

AT THE COACH and Horses on Kennegy Downs, just outside Penzance, Nat descended from the stagecoach and stretched his long limbs. Stiffness ached down his back and into his hips. Was he getting too old for such long journeys by uncomfortable, rattly old stagecoach? He could have bought a horse and ridden down in his own time, but a hankering to see the blue Cornish skies and the wild green ocean of his childhood had spurred him on. Not enough to hazard the mail coach though.

Lockhart and Talbot had left the coach at Whitchurch, thank goodness. Despite his attempts to feign sleep, Lockhart, with his slight claim to knowing Nat, had attempted on several occasions to engage him in a conversation he did *not* want to participate in. Nat and the other passengers took rooms overnight at the White Hart, and, after a substantial breakfast of beef and porter, were on their way again early the next morning.

Nat, his stomach full, had leaned back in his corner, his head resting on the upholstered back of his seat, and managed to snatch a few extra hours sleep. This latter was not helped in any way by the guard blowing his post horn with far too much enthusiasm as they approached each and every tollgate. Nor was the noise created by the changing of their four horses every two hours supportable. His sleep was, perforce, of the interrupted type, and not conducive of good temper.

The farmer parted company with the coach at Salisbury, where their stop was at the Red Lion in Milford Street for the midday meal. A dour looking elderly gentleman, with a strong reek of tobacco about him, took his place.

Nat paid little attention to the towns and villages the road passed through until they reached Bridport and stopped for the second night at the Bull on East Street. The following morning, the driver, who no doubt would find himself dismissed if he were late, was keen for them to be on their way, so breakfast was a rushed affair guaranteed to be detrimental to the digestion. Nat contented himself with a quickly fried steak and a cup of strong black coffee. And then it was on again. It was to be another two full days of traveling before his goal was reached.

But now he was here, and, of course, no one knew he had arrived, so no transport had been sent. As the coach rattled back out onto the road, he shouldered his valise and turned toward the inn. Would old Zack Chenoweth still be there in his accustomed place behind the bar?

Pushing the door open, he ducked his head under its low lintel and entered the gloomy taproom, the smell of old soot, tobacco, and ale strong. Yes, much as he remembered it from his boyhood at Treloar Court. Along one side of the room ran a plank-topped bar with a variety of pewter tankards hanging from hooks on the substantial beam above it. A few snugly private booths lay along a second side, and a motley collection of wooden chairs and tables lay scattered across the slate-slabbed floor. All empty but for two old men playing drafts near the empty hearth, and a large dog sprawled in the patch of sunlight streaming in through the leaded front window.

As Nat entered, the dog, a shaggy beast that might have been a wolfhound, raised its head and eyed him, before deciding he merited no interest and dropping his head to the floor again. Could that be one of old Captain's pups? Captain himself couldn't still be alive, surely? Not after eleven years.

Nat set his valise on one of the tables and approached the bar, aware of the close scrutiny of the two old men. No doubt eyeing up his scar, which was enough to render him unrecognizable to those who'd known him as a boy. He knocked on the wood. "Hello? Landlord? Anyone there?"

Footsteps sounded and a sturdy young man of about his own age emerged from the rear of the inn, wiping his hands on a cloth. "Yes, sir? What can I do for you?"

Nat stared. "Jacka?"

The young man also stared. "Nat?" Then he seemed to recover himself. "I mean, *Mr. Treloar*. Or should I say Cap'n Treloar?"

Nat held out his hand. "Don't Mr. Treloar me, Jacka. Surely I've not been away so long that you've forgotten the pranks we used to get up to together? And it's major now, anyway." Somehow, seeing his boyhood friend again after all these years had loosened his long-tethered tongue. He managed a smile, the skin on the right side of his face tightening and pulling at the scar. "But what's put you behind the bar here?"

The two old men were now openly listening, and even the dog had bestirred himself to lift his head again.

Jacka took Nat's hand, and they shook like the old friends they were. "I've been landlord here since I wed Old Zack's granddaughter, my Delen." He grinned. "Last I heared of you, you was off fightin' them Frenchies. I'd not ha' known you 'til you spoke." Jacka's honest eyes ran over Nat's face, and for once Nat felt none of his usual self-consciousness. He didn't mind Jacka seeing what war had done to him.

Jacka grinned. "Make a good pirate now, you would." As boys, they'd played at being pirates, shipwrecked sailors, and smugglers on the beach and in the woods around Roskilly House.

"It's all over now," Nat said, his hand going to his scar, but not, for once, to hide it. "All done and dusted, with Boney a prisoner on Elba and fat old Louis on the throne." He grinned, conscious of how the scar tissue pulled one side of his mouth down as though he'd suffered an apoplexy. "Though how secure those arrangements are, I've no idea. But I shan't think about that. I've resigned my commission and come home to let Cornwall work its magic on me. Nothing will drag me back into the army."

Jacka grinned wider still and fished a bottle of brandy out from beneath his counter. "You'll take a glass with me? For old times?"

Nat eyed the bottle. "I will indeed, but I won't ask you where it came from."

With an elaborate wink, Jacka filled two glasses with generous measures and they toasted one another before knocking back the fiery liquid. "Ah," Nat sighed. "Nothing like a tot of something that's paid no duty."

Jacka chuckled. "Ask no questions, and I'll tell you no lies." He refilled the glasses.

This time, Nat left his on the bar. "Steady on, or I'll not find my way back to Roskilly, or if I do, my sainted mother will see fit to box my ears for drunkenness."

They exchanged glances, faces for a moment serious, then Nat chuckled. "But I'd like to see her try, now I'm no longer a boy."

Jacka downed his brandy. "Aye, 'tis a man grown I see before me today. A warrior returned, by the look o' you. I won't ask, and you don't have to ever tell me, lessen you want to, that is." He poured himself a third measure. "That's good stuff, if I ses it myself. Nothing like stoppin' work for a quick pick-me-up. You'll be staying at Roskilly, then?"

Nat nodded. "I think I can put up with it. I imagine things will have changed since I was last here, as that was more than three years ago. By luck, my regiment was back in England when my aunt's husband died, or I wouldn't have been able to attend the funeral. But I stayed with her at Bodilly House then, not Roskilly, and only went there to pay my respects to my grandfather who was thought too frail to attend the funeral." He rubbed his nose. "I'd be staying there now, with my aunt, if she hadn't closed it up after my uncle died and gone off to Oxford to stay with my cousin Ewella."

Jacka's brow furrowed. "You'll not have heard about the old man, then?"

A chill hand closed around Nat's heart. "No. What about my grandfather?"

"Over two year ago now, it were. Sir Hugh were struck down with an apoplexy. Rumor had it, he were at death's door, but rumor were wrong, and I hear as he's confined to his bed but determined to cling onto life."

Nat digested this disturbing information. An apoplexy was a serious calamity that should, perhaps, have carried his grandfather off, and yet, the old man still seemed to be alive. Two years was a long time to continue confined to a bed. "Does he have his faculties still?"

Jacka could only shrug. "I can't answer that, I'm sorry to say. My sister, Bessie, you remember her?"

Of course he remembered Bessie. Hard for Nat to suppress the color rising up his face as he nodded, but at least the interior of the inn was dark. What young man doesn't remember his first?

Jacka continued. "Her girl, Patience, works at the Court now, and she ses as how the old master has a special nurse who does everythin' for him. The other servants don't get near him." He slanted a sideways look at Nat. "Organized by Mrs. Treloar."

Nat sighed. "It seems I'm returned in good time. I'd hate to not have seen my grandfather before he goes. And by my reckoning, he must now be approaching his ninetieth year." He grinned. "Although he always seemed old to me even when I was a boy."

Jacka nodded. "To me too." He hesitated, as if reluctant to say something.

"Go on," Nat said. "If you have something you need to tell me, spit it out."

Jacka rubbed his bristly chin. "Things've changed more than you'd think since your grandfather took to his bed. Mrs. Treloar, she hired in a man to do the work old Sir Hugh used to do. To manage the estate and mines, and the shipbuilders at Falmouth. Bessie says her Patience and Dickon don't like the man one bit. He lords it about the place as though it's his, and Mrs. Treloar... well, Bessie says there's rumors about her an' him."

"What rumors?"

"I don't like to say, what with her bein' your mother."

"You know why that doesn't matter to me. What rumors?"

Jacka lowered his voice. "That her and Mr. Trefusis, her agent, are more than just employer and manager."

Nat regarded his friend in silence for a long moment. Over by the window, the dog rolled onto its back, legs in the air, relishing the warmth of the sun. "And do you think them true?"

Jacka shrugged. "Not for me to say. But that Jan Trefusis is a handsome man for his age. He do come in here from time to time and my Delen, she told me women do like his looks. With your own father bein' dead these twelve years, could you blame your ma for lookin' at him wi' lively eyes?"

Nat shrugged and picked up his spurned brandy glass. "Waste not, want not." He downed it in one gulp. "I don't know and I don't care. Enough of this idle talk. It's a tidy way to Treloar from here and, as you can see, I'm togged out like a gentleman." He indicated his only slightly dusty top boots. "You wouldn't want me traipsing through fields dressed like this, would you? Do you perhaps have a horse I could borrow?"

Jacka returned the brandy bottle to its place beneath the counter. "I do that, but it won't be what you're used to as a fine soldier. This way."

Picking up his valise, Nat followed Jacka to the rear of the inn where a door opened into a small stableyard. Hens scratched at a neatly stacked muck heap on top of which sat a cockerel, and a pair of fat geese stood on the other side of a wooden gate, peering between the rails. A scrawny boy of about twelve was busy sweeping the cobbles with a besom. Along one side of the yard ran an open shed, housing a flat farm cart and a shabby pony cart.

On the other ran the stables. Jacka led the way through their wide doorway into a flagstone corridor off which a number of stalls opened. In one of them, a stout bay cob was tethered by a rope and log.

"This is Bosun. He's not tall, but he makes up for his lack of height by his width." He slapped Bosun's large quarters and a cloud of dust rose. "Your long legs shouldn't hang too far down."

Nat had seen and ridden worse. He checked over Bosun's sturdy legs for blemishes with a practiced hand and found none. "He'll do me fine. Does it matter when I bring him back to you?"

Jacka shook his head. "Keep him a week, if you have to. I don't need him at the moment, and if I need to go to Penzance, I'll put the pony between the shafts of the cart and take that."

They shook hands on the deal.

Rather less than half an hour later, Nat emerged from the stableyard astride Bosun, his valise fastened to the back of the saddle with some old rope, and took the lane opposite the inn. Overhead, a clear blue sky smiled down on the weary traveler, and Nat pushed any doubts he had about returning to his boyhood home out of his head. He would just glory in being alive, in the warmth of the sun, in the measured tread of a horse's hooves beneath him, and in the birdsong in every tree and bush.

LATE IN THE afternoon, with lessons, dinner, and piano practice over, and the weather still holding fine, Caroline and Yves, accompanied by an excited Hetty and a bounding, yapping spaniel, set off down the narrow path Yves assured Caroline would lead to the beach.

Hetty, dressed very prettily in a long-sleeved lemon gown, dainty white gloves and a capacious bonnet that would indeed prevent every inch of her skin from catching the sun, skipped along at Caroline's side, while Yves and the dog scurried back and forth in front of them, trying to encourage them to hurry. Caroline, conscious of being required to set a good example, had similarly attired herself to Hetty in long sleeves, gloves, and a bonnet, and was even now regretting this fashion choice.

"I think I shall take my bonnet off and leave it here until we return," Hetty said, her hands going to her bonnet strings. "Mama is so mean to make me dress like this on such a beautiful day. I'm far too hot already."

As Caroline was thinking just the same, she could hardly argue. However, Hetty *was* a redhead. "I think you might need to keep well covered," she ventured. "With your delicate skin."

"Oh, poof," Hetty exclaimed. "Don't tell me you're to be as fussy as Miss Hawkins was, and always make me do as Mama says?"

Caroline, regretting she could now no longer remove her own bonnet, sighed. "It's well known that those with auburn hair need to be more careful in the sun. And besides, if you *were* to catch the sun, and, heaven forbid, develop *freckles*, it would be more than obvious to Mrs. Treloar that I haven't been making you obey her command."

Hetty put a dainty hand up to touch her nose. "I do have one or two freckles already, I suppose, even though I dab them with lemon juice every night before bed. But nevertheless, it's so unfair that Yves gets to run about uncovered like this, when you and I must hide every inch of ourselves under clothing. How is it boys are allowed freckles, but we girls aren't?"

Yves came running back at that moment, before Caroline was forced to find an answer for this question, his blonde curls bouncing. "Hurry up, can't you? Dash and me want to paddle in the sea."

"Dash and *I*," Caroline corrected.

The rugged stone walls to either side of the path had fallen back by now and instead they were walking through the start of the sandhills. From up ahead came a distant roar, and a tantalizing smell Caroline didn't recognize. She'd read about the sea and beaches in books, and glimpsed it from afar on her coach journey down to Cornwall, but this would be the first time she'd seen it up close.

The path underfoot turned from solid to soft sand, the gentle rises bedecked with grass resembling long green needles that blew and rattled in the breeze. A breeze which snatched at Caroline's large bonnet as though it were a sail.

Yves raced on ahead with Dash, disappearing from sight between the hummocks, and Caroline hurried her steps, which was difficult on the soft sand that gave beneath every step. She was supposed to be looking after Yves, and that meant keeping him in view the whole time, surely?

As she emerged from the sandhills, she caught her breath in astonishment. Before her opened a vista such as she'd never imagined could exist. The golden expanse of a huge beach stretched to left and right, edged for most of its extent by the same rolling sandhills as she'd just negotiated. In the far distance, or so it seemed, the sea rolled white-capped waves up the beach, and to right and left, at the opposing ends of this wonder, tall cliffs rose toward twin rocky headlands.

"Good heavens."

Hetty caught up with her. "Yes, it is rather striking, isn't it?"

Caroline nodded. "I've never seen anything like it. It's... so huge."

Yves and Dash were already pelting across the sand toward the sea. A sudden worry overcame Caroline. "We'd best follow him. How safe is the sea?"

Hetty wrinkled her nose. "Like this, I believe it's safe enough. But ask not if the sea is safe, but rather, can we trust Yves not to get completely wet. Come along, we'd better run."

Beyond the hot, dry sand, a wide line of dark seaweed separated it from the wet sand. Once they'd stepped over that, they could run more easily. They caught Yves up on the sea's edge, where he was pulling off his boots and stockings while Dash splashed about in the shallows, biting at bits of bobbing seaweed.

As Yves had sat down in what almost amounted to shallow water, he was already halfway to being wet all over.

Hetty picked up his boots and tucked his stockings inside them.

"Don't go in too far," Caroline cautioned, not liking the size of the waves that kept on coming, one after another, like some relentless threat.

Yves paid little attention, but ran into the sea, squealing with delight and kicking up a spray of water, his little dog joining in the fun.

The next wave ran in across the sand, diminishing as it came, and threatened to soak Caroline's feet. She and Hetty retreated out of its reach.

"I think the tide is starting to come in," Hetty said.

"Is it always like this?"

"The tide's on the turn," Hetty explained. "It's low tide at the moment, but Miss Hawkins told me it ebbs and flows with the moon. It'll reach that line of seaweed we had to step over when it does, but it'll take six hours to do that."

Caroline had read about tides but never seen one, nor had one explained to her. "Are you sure we're safe?"

Hetty nodded. "It comes in very slowly. I like it better when it's in, for the waves are so much bigger. Quite splendid to stand and watch. Like so many white horses galloping up the beach."

Caroline wasn't sure she would agree with Hetty on that, but it might be interesting to come down here and see for herself what it was like when the tide was in.

Yves had ventured out a bit further and was now knee deep, the legs of his skeleton suit soaked to a darker blue. As each wave rolled toward him, he did a little leap over it, and Dash was now swimming. There was no denying that the sea was a thing of excitement for a child. Had she still been a child herself, she might have wanted to emulate Yves.

However, just at that moment, a much bigger wave rolled in, and this time it caught Yves as he jumped, wetting him to the chest and bowling him over. He floundered for a moment, and his head went under as a second wave followed the first.

Hetty gave a little scream, clapping a gloved hand to her mouth.

Caroline couldn't afford to hesitate. Instead, she hitched up her skirts and ran into the waves, the chill of the water, even though it was summer, a shock on her legs. The sand under her feet felt unstable, as though it were being sucked back out to sea, and as another wave rushed in, she lost sight of Yves for one heart stopping moment.

There was the dog, swimming still, but where was its owner?

Yves's blonde head, darkened by the water, bobbed up only a few yards distant. She seized him by the arm and heaved him upright, sheltering him from the next wave with her body. Now she was soaked to well above the waist as well. Snatching him up in her arms and holding him pressed to her chest, she struggled back to dry land with him, much hampered by her soaked gown and the fact that he was wriggling. He was also heavier than he looked.

Hetty, hopping from one foot to the other just out of reach of the waves, was still holding Yves's footwear. "Is he all right? Yves, you know you shouldn't go in that far. You're too small."

Yves struggled with renewed determination in Caroline's arms. "Put me down, please. I'm quite all right."

Caroline set him on the sand, completely soaked, just as she was. Dash bounded out of the water to join them and gave himself a vigorous shake, spraying Hetty, who leapt back with a squawk.

Yves pushed his wet hair out of his eyes, a grin spreading across his face. "That was such fun! Just like Robinson Crusoe. I'm going to pretend I've been washed up on a desert island, like he was. Only the natives have rescued me. That's you two. But you're friendly natives, which is good." He did a little dance of glee, oblivious to his waterlogged state. "Caroline, you can be Miss Tuesday, as today is Tuesday, and Hetty can be Miss

Wednesday. Just like Man Friday." He glanced down at his dog, who gave another shake. "And Dash can be Dog Saturday."

"You're both awfully wet," Hetty said, with a hint of wistfulness. "I'd like to paddle in the sea, but Mama says I'm not allowed to. It's not ladylike." She eyed Caroline up and down. "And now I see why."

Caroline smoothed her wet skirts down. This was awful, and despite the heat of the day, she was now cold, so Yves must be as well. Only her first day and she'd nearly let her small charge be washed out to sea before her eyes. And now she was going to have to go back to Roskilly looking like a drowned rat, and so was he. Although perhaps they both might dry off a bit first.

Dash gave a warning bark. He was staring down the beach at the rapidly approaching figure of a rider. A man astride a sturdy bay cob.

Chapter Six

DISINCLINED TO HURRY to Treloar Court and all that entailed, and happy with the cob's generous gait, Nat decided to take the long route back. Turning west, he trotted down the narrow lanes that divided up the small farms until he reached a path he remembered using as a boy. Over to his right, the distinctive shape of the mine workings of Wheal Jenny, and beyond that, those of Wheal True, rose above the skyline, but he ignored them. Time enough to venture that way and see if any of his boyhood friends were still working there.

The surefooted Bosun picked his way down the narrow track to emerge at the western end of Morgelyn Beach, close by the cliffs that bordered Penmar Head.

How tempting the beach looked. What would the cob's gallop be like if he gave him his head? As a boy, Nat had loved riding headlong across the sand when the tide was out, and today was no different. Only instead of the fiery black pony he'd had as a child, he had Jacka's sturdy cob. To do him justice, the cob's ears pricked and his step lightened as soon as he sniffed the salty tang of the sea and felt the breeze stirring his mane and tail. He probably didn't often get the chance for a gallop.

Throwing caution to the wind, Nat gave the cob his head. He set off at a creditable gallop, thundering along at the sea's edge and kicking up a wall of spray behind him with his large hooves.

Nat crouched forward, lifting his seat out of the saddle to encourage him to go faster, heedless of the bumping of his valise on the cob's back.

Wait a minute. Was that *people* halfway along the beach? On *his* beach. Because even now, after eleven years' absence, he thought of Morgelyn Beach as being only his. Maybe at a pinch, his and Jacka's. The cob drew closer, slowing now, as it wasn't built for continuous speed. Two women, a boy, and a bedraggled small dog. His trajectory was going to take the cob right up to them, standing as they were on the water's edge. He could have steered away, but curiosity prevented him.

He let the cob slow still further, and it fell into a trot, sides heaving and neck lathered in sweat. The dog gave a warning bark, and all three of the human interlopers turned to look his way.

Nat brought the cob to a halt ten yards from the little group, out of habit keeping his face a little turned to the right to hide his scar. Not because he wanted to talk to them, but because two of them were soaking wet and common courtesy insisted that he check they were not in trouble. The little boy, who must have been about eight or nine, wore a soggy blue skeleton suit and no shoes, so he must have perhaps been paddling, or even swimming. Fully dressed. Nat himself had learned to swim off this beach alongside Jacka, usually naked, but he'd never once tried it in all his clothes.

One of the women, nothing more than a slip of a girl, her face concealed by an enormous bonnet, was quite dry. But the other woman's gown was soaked, the thin muslin clinging to her shapely body in a most distracting way and showing him far too much of her figure. Her bonnet had taken on a decidedly bedraggled look, as had her dark hair.

She must have been aware of her own predicament, for her hands shot to hold her skirts away from her legs, but there was little she could do to disguise her state.

Instead, she raised her head and looked him proudly in the

eye, as if daring him to let his gaze drop to ogle her all-too-obvious figure. "Good afternoon, sir," she said, with some asperity.

Nat held her gaze, partly from a sense that if she were brave enough to brazen this out, he ought to be polite in return, and partly because her direct stare held his interest. Who on earth could these three be? And what were they doing in the middle of Morgelyn Beach—swimming fully clothed. "Good afternoon to you," he responded, slackening the cob's reins, but still keeping his face slightly averted. His winded mount was going nowhere.

Good heavens, the chit was looking him up and down as though he were on show at Astley's, and, from the look on her face, finding him wanting. He took a better look at her. A plain but interesting face was partly obscured by the size of her now-floppy bonnet, but he could see she had intelligent brown eyes and chestnut hair, as well as a determined chin.

His conscience pricked him, much as he didn't want it to. "Might I offer you some assistance, Miss...?"

She gave her soggy skirts another shake. Really, why *did* girls wear such barely there gowns and then get in a tizz when men ogled them? Although, not many of them went swimming in the sea in them, which it seemed this girl had done. Young woman. She was too old to be called a girl.

"Fairfield," she said, standing up a little straighter. "My name is Caroline Fairfield."

Nat's mouth fought to suppress an unaccustomed smile at her defensive stance. "Might I venture to inquire of you why you have been so far into the sea as to soak yourself?" He glanced at the waves still rolling in. "I did not know young ladies were so fond of swimming as you appear to be."

She bristled a little. "I can assure you, sir, that it was quite unintentional. I had not the slightest idea of even dipping my toes in the water when we came down here. But Yves," and here she pointed at the little boy, who, having lost interest in Nat's arrival, was busy making channels in the wet sand with the fingers of one hand while he held his dog's collar with the other, "got into difficulties. I had to go in to save him."

"Yves?" Wasn't that the name of his late Uncle Robert's brat? The one his mother had spoken of so scathingly at John Polmear's funeral and implied was virtually an idiot.

The child in question stood up, now liberally covered in wet sand, the dog pressed to his side in protective stance. "That's me."

Yes, now he took a better look at the boy, he recognized him, even though the last time he'd had a fleeting glimpse of him he'd been barely out of petticoats. Hadn't he? Hard to remember as children were not something he'd ever been interested in since he'd left childhood behind himself. Three years ago his grandfather had been the main reason for his visit to Treloar, not the old man's heir. The boy had grown upwards a lot, but not outwards. What was he? Seven? Eight? A slight resemblance clung to the child of his mother, Nat's late Aunt Lowenna, who'd topped her achievement of producing an heir for the substantial Roskilly estate and mines by promptly turning up her toes before the child was even two days old.

Better make himself known, as it appeared they must be from Roskilly House, the only large house around here. He swung his leg over the pommel and dropped onto the sand with a splash. "Then we are related, young Yves. I am your Cousin Nat, back from the war."

"Nat!" the younger girl squealed, pushing back her enormous bonnet to reveal her startling red hair. "Do you not know your own sister?"

CAROLINE STARED AT this stranger who'd just surprised her by identifying himself as a hitherto-unknown member of her employer's family. Hetty's brother, no less. She would have guessed him a soldier by his upright bearing, and it seemed she was right. Of course, there must be a lot of soldiers returning from the continent, with Bonaparte now safely under lock and key. Or not, as her dear Papa had scoffed before his demise. No, she wouldn't think of Papa.

Now the newcomer was standing before them, she appreciated how tall he was, with his long legs encased in buff breeches and his top boots spattered with wet sand, a well-cut navy coat, and a conservatively tied cravat. A quick pang of pity assaulted her as she caught a glimpse of the right side of his face for the first time. He might have been considered handsome, were it not for the jagged scar running from above his eye down to his chin, puckering the skin and distorting that whole side of his face. The left-hand side of his face, by contrast, hinted at those lost good looks, although his blue eyes possessed little to brighten his expression.

Yves remained standing close to Caroline, one hand gripping her wet skirts, the other on Dash's head, regarding the newcomer with suspicion. It seemed as though he wasn't at all familiar with his cousin.

How hard it was not to allow one's eyes to be dragged as though by a magnet to that terrible scar, and how rude it would be to linger on it. He was clever at disguising it though, keeping his head partially turned away as if by habit. If he were a soldier, it must surely be from a war wound, so not to be hidden away, but proudly worn, like a medal for valor. How long might he have been like that?

The young man, for he could not have been more than thirty years of age, made a cursory bow, and, straightening, put up a hand to sweep his overly long hair out of his eyes. The sun caught them, and just for a moment they seemed to sparkle with life before he had them veiled again. What was this cold exterior hiding? And did it have to do with that terrible scar?

"Nathaniel Treloar, at your service, Miss Fairfield."

Caroline, somewhat hampered by her wet skirts and the sand her feet were sinking into, made a wobbly curtsey.

Not so Hetty. "Nat? What's happened to your face? Why, Caroline, this is my brother Nat! I would not have known him with that dreadful scar." She glanced at Caroline, a touch of fear in her eyes, then back to Nat, her tone verging on accusatory. "You didn't have it when last you were home, and it has quite changed your appearance."

Not the most tactful of greetings, but her brother, taking her hands, allowed it to pass with the merest hint of pain in his eyes, before, yet again, he had them veiled. He must be used to reactions like this. "And I would not have recognized you either, now you're grown into such a young lady. You were nothing but a schoolroom chit when last I was home. I barely saw you."

Hetty frowned. "Mama is so very strict about what I'm allowed to do. When I was in the schoolroom, like Yves, I hardly saw anyone but Miss Hawkins or Hester from one week to the next." She inhaled as though about to say more, but Nat's gaze flicked to Caroline, and one eyebrow, more mobile than the other, rose in enquiry.

Hetty remembered her manners. "Oh, Nat. Caro… I mean Miss Fairfield, is Yves's new governess. Mama took it into her head that she didn't like Miss Hawkins any longer and let her go. Just last week. Miss Fairfield, who you must of course call Caroline, as Yves and I do, only arrived in Cornwall yesterday."

Nat's somewhat saturnine eyebrow rose again, the impression enhanced by the immobility of the other side of his face. That whole side seemed devoid of expression. "You are not from Cornwall, Miss Fairfield?"

Caroline shook her head. "Wiltshire, sir. My friend, Mrs. Beauchamp of Carlyon Court, recommended me to your mother."

He nodded. "Do the Carlyons not hold the Court any longer? In my boyhood, I recall being taken there to play with the son—Kit, I think his name was."

"Kit is now Viscount Ormonde and lives at Ormonde Abbey in Wiltshire, not far from where I lived with my…" She hesitated, unwilling to share her family's misfortune with a virtual stranger. "Where I lived before I came down here. I knew Kit well, and it is his youngest sister, my dear friend Ysella Carlyon, who is in residence at the Court with her husband, Mr. Samuel Beauchamp. Mrs. Beauchamp was kind enough to intercede for me with your mother, when I found myself… in need of employment."

How hard it was to hedge around the real reason for her sudden need to earn her own living, but he didn't need to know that. No one needed to know.

"How fortunate my mother is, then, that you are so careful of your charge as to allow him to soak himself to the skin on the very first day of your employment." More than a touch of sarcasm tinged his words, which Caroline couldn't fault, as all of it was true.

She felt herself coloring like a green girl and bit her lip. Now there was no way she could disguise Yves's dunking to his aunt, because her newly returned son was bound to tell her. She'd have to be honest and prepare herself for instant dismissal. Her heart sank. Perhaps she could go to Ysella at Carlyon Court if she were thrown out here, at least for a while. How hard would it be to find another post? She'd have no references and couldn't rely on Ysella to find her yet another post amongst her friends, who would all have heard the story of her dismissal from Roskilly.

"I daresay Mama will not care a jot," Hetty said. "He's always getting himself into scrapes, and Mama takes no notice at all. That was part of the argument between Miss Hawkins and Mama, I think. That Mama allowed Yves too much freedom and Miss Hawkins thought it dangerous."

A wry smile curved the uninjured side of Nat's face, made a little macabre by the scar. "I'm not surprised."

What an odd thing to say about an accident to a child.

Yves, who had been silent throughout this exchange, suddenly stepped forward. "I am very pleased to meet you then, Cousin Nat. I believe we've not met before. Yves Treloar, at your service." And he made a neat little bow, made comical by his wet skeleton suit and sand-covered appearance.

Nat held out his right hand to the boy, as solemn as if he were greeting his own father. "Good afternoon."

Yves took his cousin's hand and let out a squeal, but not of horror, of delight. Nat's right hand possessed only the thumb and first two fingers—the little one and the next were gone, leaving only short stumps. Yves turned it over in his the better to examine it. When he looked up, his small face was wreathed in admiration. "You're a soldier, aren't you? Is that how you lost these fingers and came by that scar on your face? Have you been fighting Boney? Will you tell me all about it? Did you see him?" Eyes brimming with eager devotion gazed up into the saturnine ones of his big cousin, both sets as blue as the sea on a summer's day.

Nat snatched his hand back, his face darkening. "Nothing to tell."

The little boy's face puckered in obvious disappointment, and he glanced first at Hetty and then at Caroline for support.

"We should walk back to the house now, before Yves catches a chill," Caroline said, flustered and unsure how to react to this. Best to move on. And her next step was not going to be a pleasant one. Owning up to what had happened in the sea needed to be done, and, just perhaps, if Hetty were right, Mrs. Treloar would not be too angry about it.

Caroline held out a hand to Yves. "Come, let's get back to the dry sand and put your shoes and stockings on at least. You can't walk home barefoot."

Yves, shooting Nat a sulky glare, took her hand, and Hetty, also with a less-than-happy look for Nat, fell in on Caroline's other side. Dash, who seemed to have accepted Nat, raced on ahead of them, intent on chasing any gulls who had the temerity to land on his beach.

Out of the corner of her eye, Caroline saw Nat catch his cob's reins and take his place behind them. Good. She wouldn't be forced to try and make polite conversation with him. Even Hetty appeared to have given up. He seemed such a bad-tempered, reticent young man, perfectly fitting his dour, scarred countenance. Hopefully he wasn't going to be staying at Roskilly for too long.

Chapter Seven

A T THE HOUSE, Nat abandoned Miss Fairfield to her own devices, not really caring whether she admitted Yves's little adventure to his mother or not. Hadn't he had many of the like when he'd been Yves's age? Wasn't that typical of a small boy? And none of them had come to his mother's attention. However, Miss Fairfield had the distinct look of someone who prided herself on speaking the truth. Not always the best policy with his mother, as he'd learned to his cost over the years.

He led Bosun round to the stable courtyard where he was greeted by a young groom he didn't know, but who resembled Pascoe enough to have been a son of his. The groom held Bosun's head while Nat slid down, and Nat handed him the reins. Damned fellow couldn't tear his eyes away from the scar. Turning his head away, Nat unfastened his valise and left the groom to do the necessary for the cob.

He entered the house by the servants' door, stepping into the cool, flagstone corridor to be greeted by the rich smell of roasting meat and baking. Following his nose, he made for the kitchens, hoping there would have been fewer changes in there than in the stables.

He was right. The huge and easily recognized form of Mrs. Teague was just taking loaves out of the bread oven and sliding them onto the floured tabletop. She turned her head as the door opened, and her wide face puckered for a moment in confusion, before breaking into a smile of recognition. "Master Nat!"

Nat allowed himself a smile in return, or at least, the half of his face that could smiled. The army surgeon who'd sewn him up had said he'd never have much mobility back on the right side of his face and it seemed he was right. He gazed around the kitchen he remembered so well. He had so many good childhood memories of this kitchen, and the kindness of Mrs. Teague to a small, ever-hungry boy. "Mrs. Teague. I'm very glad to see you still ruling here in the kitchen."

She wiped her floury hands on her apron. "And I'm that glad to see you back here, Master Nat. Bin a sad quiet place without you, although little Master Yves is heading toward making up for that, I vow. Chip off the old Treloar block, that boy is. Very much like you was." Her gaze ran over his face and he sensed rather than saw an internal wince as she took in his scar.

But Nat refused to think about it. "That bread smells delicious. Might I trouble you for a slice or two with some good Cornish butter? I've sorely missed your cooking."

Mrs. Teague swelled with pride. "You may indeed, Master Nat. And that happy I am to be able to cook for you again." She shook her head in what might have been mock desperation. "Your mama, bless her, don't eat enough to keep a sparrow alive, and she don't think anyone else needs more'n her. It'll be nice for me to have someone around what appreciates my cooking."

She sliced off two thick and steaming slices of the fresh bread, fetched an earthenware pot of golden butter and applied it in abundance to the bread. Nat didn't wait for a plate, but picked up the first slice and bit into it as soon as it was ready. "Mmmmm. Wonderful. I've been four days on the stagecoach down from London, and the food at some of those coaching inns leaves a lot to be desired. What's more, they hurry the midday meal so you don't even get time to eat what you've paid for. Nothing's so good as Cornish food."

Mrs. Teague watched him demolish the bread and now mostly melted butter with a look of immense satisfaction on her face. "I'm thinking I'll be seeing you down here for your breakfast in the morning, along with Master Yves?"

So the child had found a way to get around his mother's insistence that everyone should eat as meagerly as she. Good for him, but Nat had no desire to keep him company of a morning. He seemed the sort who would require answers to constant questions. "You might," he said, finishing off the last crumb. "But now, somewhat fortified, I fear it's time I faced my mother." He wiped his mouth with his handkerchief. "Will I find her in the parlor, do you think?"

"You will." Mrs. Teague's wide face took on a disapproving frown. "She do meet up with Mr. Trefusis in there every afternoon." She pursed her lips primly, hands on hips.

Nat ignored this heavy hint to ask about Trefusis and be given Mrs. Teague's personal opinion, and nodded. "After that, I shall want to see my grandfather." He paused, frowning. "Can you give me any advice on how he is? All I know is what I had from my old friend Jacka, old Trewin the gardener's son. I called in at the Coach and Horses to borrow his cob. It was good to see him prospering. He seems to fit in well behind the bar."

Mrs. Teague sat down with a thud on one of the kitchen chairs. "Not good, not good. Your granfer's not good." She shook her head in what looked like sorrow. "Not the man he was, that's certain. You know it was an apoplexy? Struck him down in church one Sunday. A few folks round here did say it were the wrath of God, but we at Roskilly don't hold with superstition. And your granfer were always good to me and mine."

Nat wiped his buttery fingers on his handkerchief and stowed it in his pocket. "Go on."

"They carried him back here on the vestry door. Unscrewed the hinges and took it down. Luckily, Doctor Rescorla were at the service, and he were able to follow your granfer back here. He bled him directly, and I did hear that was what saved him."

"And the long-term consequences of this?"

"He can't use his legs no more, so he's been confined to his room these last two years. And your ma, she engaged a special nurse for him. Miss Rodgers, she's called. Used to be at the County Asylum, so she ses. Hoity-toity piece she is too. Not like that new governess Master Yves has just got. Now, she's a nice young lady as knows how to treat us servants. Well brought up, that one, not like that Miss Rodgers who's no better than she should be."

"Has no one thought of providing him with a Bath chair?"

Mrs. Teague frowned. "What's one of them when it's at home?"

"A wheeled seat that would give him mobility."

She shrugged. "I can't speak for Mrs. Treloar, but maybe the old master didn't want that. He's a stubborn man, as my old father used to say. Him that was head gardener here before old Trewin, back when the old master was young hisself." She leaned toward Nat. "And maybe Mrs. Treloar don't want Sir Hugh out of that bedroom. Did you not think of that?"

Nat met her gaze. This was no joke. She meant her words. Might his mother be happier with her father-in-law kept out of the way? Particularly so if Jacka was correct and she was carrying on with her land agent. This Trefusis.

He sighed. He'd think about that later. For now, first things first and he'd have to see his mother. "I'll leave you now, Mrs. Teague. Thank you for all that useful information." He pulled a face. "And the best bread and butter in Cornwall, I feel sufficiently emboldened by it to meet my mother."

HE FOUND HIS mother in the parlor, as he'd guessed, reading a book. No doubt some worthy self-improving tome. She looked up as he came in, and her pale eyes widened in shock. For a moment she stayed seated, then she rose to her feet and came toward him, a smile fixed on her face that did little to enhance her looks and he suspected was not genuine. She'd once been an attractive woman, but the years had not been kind to her and a perpetual frown creased her brow.

"Nathaniel. You've seen fit to come home at last."

And then she saw his face.

Her hands shot up to cover her mouth, but she couldn't disguise the indrawn breath and gasp of horror, nor the hesitation in her stance.

Nat stood still, letting her take in his altered appearance, his right hand curling into a fist to hide his lost fingers.

"What on earth has happened to you?" The words came out almost as a cry of accusation, for she was surely suffering from shock. "Your face? What's happened to your face?"

She staggered sideways and caught hold of the back of the chaise longue, her knuckles whitening as she gripped it, but whether this was from concern for him or just shock at the sight of the scar, Nat couldn't be certain. Most likely the latter.

He took a step toward her, thinking to be of help, but she shied away from him as though his very touch repulsed her. "No. I shall be perfectly restored. Give me a moment. Please." Her breast heaved as though she were fighting to regain her self-control.

Nat bit his lip. Perhaps he should have warned her in advance. It might have been kinder than this. Kinder to him as well as her. He should have known she'd react in this way, that she wouldn't be able to see past the scarring. Perhaps he shouldn't have come home at all.

"I *was* a soldier, Mother." He shifted his weight. "And at least I'm not dead."

She shot him a narrow-eyed gaze, sharp as the sword that had wreaked this damage.

He frowned. "Plenty are dead. The surgeon who stitched me back together told me to count myself as lucky that I wasn't lying in a grave in a foreign field."

At the time, Nat hadn't been so sure about luck being involved, as he lay in the makeshift army hospital in Spain with his whole head bandaged. They'd wanted to send him back to England to recuperate, but he'd insisted on staying. Maybe it had been a death wish. He'd certainly thought for quite some time that he'd have been better off dead and had avoided all mirrors, something that had made shaving difficult.

His mother straightened up with what looked like a huge effort. "I am aware of that, Nathaniel." Her gray eyes had hardened to pebbles. Wet pebbles. "I apologize for my reaction." Her eyes were still fixed on his scar as though she couldn't tear them away. "You must know that it will take me some time to become accustomed to… your altered appearance." She cleared her throat. "What was it? A sword?"

He nodded. "A Frenchman. But he didn't live to tell the tale." No, with his own blood almost blinding him and pain lancing through his head, Nat had run the man through with his cavalry sword, as his own men surged to his rescue, surrounding him and sheltering him from further harm. Brave men, all of them. A better band of men it would have been hard to find in all the British army. But he couldn't think of them. Not now. Not ever.

His mother pressed her lips together. "Is this furlough? How long are you home for?"

She didn't sound pleased. He couldn't blame her. Perhaps she'd thought he'd perish on the battlefields of Europe, and, in doing so, oblige her. Perhaps he did her down by thinking this. Who knew? She was a woman harder to read than any he'd met. But he'd come back, and in place of the handsome boy who'd ridden away eleven years ago, she'd got a crippled stranger.

"I've resigned my commission. I have no plans as yet, but I might stay down here a week or so. I've not yet decided what I'd like to do next."

He couldn't read her face. She was too good at hiding her thoughts, and now she'd recovered her composure, a thick veil had dropped over her face.

"Your grandfather will be pleased to see you."

He nodded. "I thought I might go up and see him next."

"And your great-aunt."

Aunt Agnes. He'd forgotten about her. "She's still alive?" She was older, even, than his grandfather.

His mother nodded. "And looks as though she's set on making her century." Was that a note of bitterness in her voice? She and his grandfather's spinster sister had never got on. It would be very like his mother to resent the old lady's longevity and the continued expense of her upkeep on the housekeeping purse.

"Then I'll also try to greet her." Unlike his mother, he'd always got on well with Aunt Agnes and taken her outspokenness in his stride. She'd been a good ally in his boyhood, delighting in his rebellious pranks, especially if they annoyed his mother, whom she seemed to hate.

A thought occurred to him. "When I was down last, Hetty's governess was a Miss Hawkins, I believe. A fearsome dragon, I rather thought. I gather she has left, and you have a replacement. I met Miss Fairfield with Hetty and Yves down on Morgelyn Beach." He paused, eyeing his mother. Would he get the truth out of her? "I thought Miss Hawkins pleased you. Did she seek other employment?"

His mother's eyes sharpened still further and slid sideways as though she were seeking what to say. "We came to a mutual agreement that she no longer met with our requirements."

He raised his one mobile eyebrow. "Indeed?" Although why he was bothering with this, he couldn't be sure. And the new governess, despite having allowed Yves to almost drown, seemed acceptable, and far younger than Miss Hawkins had been. However, he couldn't shake off the feeling there was something more to this than met the eye.

"Yes," his mother snapped. "Indeed. She left us quite in the lurch, but it seems we have found a far better young woman to take her place. This one at least has some Latin and Greek she can impart to Yves."

Nat fiddled with his watch chain. "And I hear that since Grandfather has been bedridden, you have taken on a manager."

Her eyes narrowed. "I have."

Was she wondering who could have told him that? Let her. "Does he know his job?"

She bowed her head, possibly to hide her eyes from him. "Of course he does."

These were strangely short answers. "Will I meet him?"

Her hands had gone rigid in her lap, gripping the cover of her book, the knuckles whitened. "No doubt."

"I shall look forward to that."

Hmm. As there seemed nothing else to say to his mother, Nat bestowed a small bow on her, and performed an about turn. Nothing much changed there. Still a woman who played her cards close to her chest. Aware of her gimlet gaze boring into his back, he strode out of the room and headed for the stairs.

Sir Hugh Treloar had always occupied the best bedroom in the house, its long windows looking out over the wide front drive and giving an excellent view of the distant sea and the rise that was Penmar Head. His wife, the late Lady Treloar, had died while Nat was at Harrow, some twelve years since, not long after his own father's death, and Nat's memory of her had faded long since. But he held a firm picture in his head of how his grandfather had been three years ago when he'd ridden over from Bodilly after the funeral to see him: still over six feet tall, solidly built but not fat, his white-maned head held upright and proud. A lion of a man.

His heart in his mouth at what the last three years and an apoplexy might have done to his grandfather, Nat took the stairs two at a time, turning right where they divided and marching down the upstairs corridor to the east wing, his booted feet loud on the polished oak floorboards.

He reached the bedroom door and halted, swallowing. With his good left hand, he rapped smartly on the door.

Footsteps sounded, and the door swung open a foot, but no

more. Nat kept his face turned to the right to hide his scar as the stern face of a large middle-aged woman, her hair scraped back and hidden beneath a mob cap, peered out. Thick dark brows met in a frown. "Yes?" Almost a bark. She'd have made a good sergeant major.

"I've come to see my grandfather."

She looked him up and down as though suspecting what he'd said was a lie, and he had some ulterior motive for pounding on the door. "Who shall I say it is?" An accusation, her words implying he must be of no importance and his grandfather would not want to see him.

"Major Nat Treloar," Nat snapped, itching to snatch the door from her hands and fling it open. "His grandson." He had to remember his grandfather was not only very old but probably also very weak. He might even be asleep.

"I'll find out if he'll see you," the woman snapped back, and would have closed the door on him had he not stuck his boot out to prevent her. With a withering glare, she turned away, and her feet tapped back across the room. Straining his ears, Nat made out the sound of muted voices. She returned, tap, tap, tapping as though she had hobnails in the soles of her shoes.

This time she opened the door a bit wider. "Sir Hugh will see you now. But don't tire him."

Nat bristled. Who did this jumped-up creature think she was?

The high, four-poster bed Nat remembered from his boyhood occupied the center of one wall. In it, propped up on numerous pillows sat his grandfather, a shadow of his former self. A plaid shawl had been draped over his bony shoulders on top of his nightshirt, and a nightcap sat on his head, wispy white hair escaping around its edges. His thin face, as wrinkled as a walnut shell, had the washed-out pallor of someone who had not seen the sun in far too long a time.

Nat, ignoring the nurse's startled step backwards as she caught sight of his scar for the first time, stepped up to the bed and made a deep bow. "Good afternoon, Sir."

The old man looked him in the eye. He must be able to see the scar as Nat had for once not half turned away. A long silence ensued. Was he, like everyone else Nat met, pitying him for the loss of half his face?

"So," the old man said, his voice every bit as deep and authoritative as Nat recalled, "you've come home to us at last." He glanced at the hovering nurse. "Don't just stand there, Rodgers. Fetch the boy a seat. Then you can go. We've a lot to talk about."

Chapter Eight

CAROLINE HURRIED YVES up the stairs to the nursery, having insisted that he leave the still wet and sandy Dash in the kitchen with Mrs. Teague. If she were lucky, no one would have seen the bedraggled state they were both in. Hetty accompanied them, her hated bonnet discarded to hang by its strings from one hand. At the nursery door, she put a firm hand on Caroline's arm. "You go and change your clothes, and I'll see to this rascal."

Caroline hesitated. As governess it must surely be her responsibility to sort Yves's wet clothes out before her own, but Hetty gave her a firm shove. "I've done it enough times before. He's always in the wars and getting soaked in the sea or in the stream on the far side of the estate. Go on. I know what I'm doing."

Yves looked up at his cousin with a scowl. "I don't need to be dressed by *anyone*. I'm *nine*, not five."

"Nonsense," Hetty snapped. "If we leave it to you, we'll find you dressed as a pirate."

Yves's lower lip jutted. "I like my pirate costume. Miss Hawkins made it for me."

Caroline suppressed a smile. "Then we shall have a day when we all play at pirates, I promise. Just not today."

His face brightened. "Hetty too?"

Caroline nodded. "But only if you let Hetty find you suitable clothes right now. Go on. Off you go with her."

Leaving Yves in a more biddable frame of mind, Caroline headed for her own bedroom in search of a clean gown. If she had much more of this, she was going to run out of suitable gowns altogether.

What a good thing she'd learnt early on to do her own hair, as hers was a windblown mess, despite her bonnet. She stripped off her wet gown and put on a fresh petticoat, then sat in front of her mirror, teasing her chestnut curls into something a little more respectable for a governess. She must have caught the sun, because her cheeks had a warm glow to them that not even an application of powder would disguise.

A tap on her door disturbed her.

"Who is it?"

"Hetty."

"Come in then, as long as you don't have Yves with you."

Hetty, alone, came in. She too had managed to catch the sun, the bridge of her nose being slightly pink. "You mustn't take on about Yves getting so wet." She sat down on the bed. "He's always up to mischief and my mama doesn't mind at all. You can ignore what my mannerless brother said to you. Mama won't care a jot that Yves nearly drowned himself."

Caroline swiveled round on her seat. "Really? I had the impression Yves was considered a trifle sickly, and that I was to take great care of him. At least that's what my friend Mrs. Beauchamp told me in her letter."

Hetty shrugged, her auburn curls bouncing. "What rubbish. He might be a skinny wretch, but he's as tough as... as my old boots." She kicked her boots in the air in demonstration. "Mama doesn't mind in the least what he gets up to. She keeps saying *'he's not my child.'* When Grandpapa was downstairs, before he had to take to his bed, he ruled Yves with a much sterner hand. But then again, Yves was only six or seven so much more manageable. Grandpapa didn't let him go anywhere on his own. He wasn't allowed to climb trees, go down to the beach, or ride his pony any faster than a trot. Not that Blossom ever wants to go faster than a trot, that is. I used to have to ride her before I had Folly." She shrugged a second time. "But when Mama took over his care, she said he needed to learn to be a real boy, like Nat was, and Yves took to it with gusto." She smiled. "I'm not allowed to tell Grandpapa any of that though."

How puzzling. Mrs. Treloar did not at all look like the sort of person who would allow a boy like Yves to run wild and free. Her whole demeanor of stiff control indicated the exact opposite—that she would have liked Yves to be seen but not heard, kept closeted in the schoolroom and nursery so that his presence might not offend the eyes or ears of the adults of the household.

Hetty kicked her boots against the bed. "Miss Hawkins protested that Yves was being encouraged to do dangerous things. I heard her and Mama arguing about it in the parlor one day. I was outside in the hall and I couldn't help but overhear." Her eyes twinkled. "What with having my ear to the door and both of them shouting so loud."

"An eavesdropper rarely hears any good about himself," Caroline said, conscious of the fact she should be discouraging Hetty from such behavior.

"Oh, I heard nothing about me, either good or bad. But I heard a lot about Miss Hawkins and Yves. Goodness me, I didn't realize Miss Hawkins had it in her to face Mama down like that, but she did, saying she thought Mama *wanted* some accident to befall Yves and that Mama shouldn't be giving him something because it was dangerous. Only Mama got the better of her in the end, because she told her to pack her bags and leave if she didn't like the way Yves was being brought up."

Caroline's ears pricked up. "What? Straight after their argument?"

Hetty nodded. "At the end of it. Mama told Miss Hawkins to leave that very day. Had the pony cart brought round to take her into Penzance. I saw her go." She paused. "Although Mama kept Yves and me in the parlor with her until Miss Hawkins left. She said she didn't want us talking to a madwoman. Yves was furious, and Mama had to station Roscarrow, our gardener, outside the parlor door to stop him going out. I was standing at the window, so I saw her leave. Her face was all blotchy and she kept looking back at the house. I think she'd been crying."

Hetty clearly relished the telling of this tale. Her eyes danced in excitement at the drama she'd witnessed. "And then, the next day, Mama sacked Hester as well, who used to be the head nursery maid, and put Bridget in charge. Bridget used to do Patience's job. Bridget's horrible, and I'm glad I'm not in the nursery anymore."

Good heavens. Was the job of governess here a sort of poisoned chalice? Might Mrs. Treloar decide on a whim that Caroline, too, needed to leave? That was a bit of a worry. Caroline made a mental note never to cross swords with her employer if she could avoid it, no matter what happened.

But this had set her wondering. She changed tack a little. "Am I right in thinking that Yves is the heir to Roskilly?"

Hetty nodded. "His papa was my papa's older brother. But he's dead, of course. Well, they both are. Only our two aunts are left now, and we never really see them. Yves's papa drowned while out in his little boat. He liked to go fishing, you see. I was only ten when he died, so I don't remember it very well, but I think his boat sank and he couldn't swim. Yves was three. He doesn't remember his papa at all. I know because I asked him."

Turning this over in her head, Caroline went to her wardrobe and sorted through her clothes until she found a nice fawn gown with long sleeves and a high neckline. Governess style. She stepped into it and Hetty jumped up to fasten the back for her, as she tucked her customary spare long hairpin into the bodice out of the way.

"My papa was killed even before that. I was only five." Hetty fiddled with the ties, tucking them out of the way. "Nat was with him. He was home from school and he and Papa had gone down the mine at Wheal Jenny. I don't know why. Nat wouldn't talk to me about it afterwards, and of course, Mama never would. There was a roof fall, that I do know, and Papa was killed."

"That's dreadful." How sad for his two children and his widow. No wonder Mrs. Treloar seemed so cold. Caroline made up her mind to make allowances for her.

Hetty gave a shrug, returning to her original story. "It's a shame for Yves, really, because he loved Miss Hawkins, but for me it was good luck. With her gone, Mama said I could abandon the schoolroom and become a young lady." She frowned. "Although she still wants me to practice things like the piano, painting, and speaking French."

Caroline pressed her lips together. Hetty was such an ingenue, surely she could ask her a few rather loaded questions without the girl noticing. "And if anything were to happen to Yves, who would become heir to Roskilly?"

Hetty shrugged. "I daresay Nat would, although I don't know for sure. I doubt my two aunts would come into it, even though they were Papa's older sisters. We females are never considered important enough to inherit anything when there are men about. Especially not a house and businesses."

"But after Nat, would it be you?"

Hetty nodded. "I suppose it might be." A frown drifted across her brow. "I'm rather vexed with Nat. I haven't seen him since Aunt Endelyn's husband died and he came down for the funeral. And even then, I hardly had a chance to talk to him. I was only fourteen, and no doubt he didn't want to be bothered with a schoolgirl. He stayed at Bodilly House with my aunt and only came to Roskilly to see Grandpapa. And before that, I think the last time I saw him was when I was six." She sighed. "Back then, before Papa died, Nat used to play with me all the time. He was such a fun big brother. But from what I've seen of him today, I don't think he'll ever be fun again."

Caroline thought about the disfiguring scar running down Nat's face. "I should imagine war has changed him a lot, Hetty, and you may have to be patient with him. And not just his appearance will have changed. If he's been so severely wounded, then, inside himself, he may be hurting very much. You'll need to try to be patient and understanding even if he seems surly and rude." Advice she would do well to adhere to herself, given how she'd taken such a dislike to Nat on the beach.

NAT, MEANWHILE, HAD left his grandfather sleeping and gone in search of Great-Aunt Agnes. This lady he discovered in the library, a room aptly fitting its title as shelves of books lined every wall.

A large stone fireplace occupied the center of one wall, a fire burning in it despite the clement weather outside. Two wingback chairs had been drawn up close to the heat, and in one sat a tiny, bird-like old lady, reading a book with a large magnifying glass. She looked up as Nat came in, and her lined face lit up with delight. "Hugh! Have you just returned from the hunt? Did the hounds make a kill? I asked Mama if I could accompany you, but she made me stay and read to her." She closed the book and set down the magnifying glass on the table by her side.

Nat went down on one knee beside her chair and took her frail hands in his. She'd been reading the book upside down. "It's Nat, Aunt Agnes. Hugh is my grandfather, your brother."

"Nat?" The old lady stared at him, for a moment bemused. "But my Nat's just a little boy. I see him playing out in the gardens, or sliding down the stairs on a tea tray."

"That'll be Yves, Uncle Robert's boy."

She shook her head, suddenly peevish. "And where is Robert, I want to know? I haven't seen him for days. He can't keep hiding from his auntie or I won't have any treats for him." She reached down to the side of her chair and fished up a large cloth bag. "I keep my treats in here, for the little ones. For my little Nat."

Nat sighed. His great-aunt had been heading toward senility when he'd last seen her after the funeral, but nothing as bad as this. Just a little forgetfulness as far as he could tell at the time. Now, her mind seemed addled and befuddled. *I'm your Nat,* he tried again. "Come home from the wars."

She lifted the magnifying glass, and, holding it up to her right eye, peered through it at him. Her own rheumy eye was hugely enlarged by this procedure as she had the glass the wrong way round. She squinted at his face, moving the glass closer to his scar the better to see it. "What's this? My Nat don't look like this." She lifted a bony hand and reached out to touch his scar.

Nat flinched, the effort of preventing himself from starting back enormous. No one had ever touched his scar save the surgeon who'd stitched it back together. Her cool, dry fingers felt the raised and puckered skin. He grit his teeth. She explored the ridges of scar tissue, that the surgeon had said would eventually lessen, from above his right eye, down his damaged cheek to his chin.

"Why," she said at last, her voice soft as an autumn leaf blowing in the wind, "who did this to you, Nat? My little Nat come back to me."

Nat pressed his lips together. "A Frenchman. I've been away fighting Bonaparte, Aunt Agnes, but now I'm back."

Her faded eyes sharpened, and her hand dropped to seize his in a claw like grasp. "You're back for good?"

He shrugged. "I don't know yet. I've not thought about what to do now I've resigned my commission and said goodbye to the army."

Her grip tightened. "You have to stay." Her voice hissed with urgency. "You have to stay and protect the child."

Nat frowned. "What child?" Surely, she didn't mean Yves?

But her moment of lucidity had gone, if it had ever been that. "You have to protect my Robert. My golden boy. I wonder why I've not seen him for so long. He usually comes to sit with me of an afternoon, and I listen to him read. Such a kind boy." She released his hand, looking down at the book in her lap. "Perhaps he'll read to me from this book today." It was *Johnson's Dictionary.*

On an impulse, Nat leaned forward and kissed the wrinkled old cheek. "Dear Aunt Agnes, it's good to see you again." She smelled of lavender water and old lady.

Chapter Nine

CAROLINE ENCOUNTERED MISS Agnes Treloar the following afternoon. Clouds had rolled in from the sea and a light drizzle prevented her from taking Yves out for a walk, as she'd planned, even though he declared himself unfazed by "a bit of rain." Instead, she headed for the library with him and Hetty in search of the chess set Hetty had informed her resided there, a now clean and dry Dash trotting at their heels.

Having spent the morning in the school room introducing Yves to the vagaries of the Latin language in as an appealing fashion as Caroline could think of, followed by algebra and composition, Caroline had seen neither sight nor sound of any other member of the Roskilly household that day. So she was pleased when she and Yves encountered Hetty on the galleried landing and on her advice headed for the library.

Yves dragged his feet. "But I don't *want* to learn to play chess. I'd rather be outside, playing ball with Dash."

"Nonsense," Caroline retorted. "It's a game of tactics that makes you think carefully about everything you do. Most useful for someone in your position. Or the position you'll one day hold."

Yves stuck out his lower lip in rebellion, but followed her meekly enough into the library.

Twice the size of the one at Cadley Grange, the library at

Roskilly boasted a fine array of books. But as Caroline well knew that books could be bought by the foot merely for their appearance and to indicate the supposed scholarship of their owners, she was unimpressed. As with the up-to-date furnishings in the main house, she had a feeling this library had been equipped for show.

Yves, on stepping into the room, let out a cry of delight, and ran across to where two wingback chairs stood close to a roaring fire. "Aunt Agnes! It's me!" He plumped himself down on the footstool beside her chair, and gazed up at the old lady in evident delight, Dash by his feet. How touching it was to see his love for her.

"That's Aunt Agnes," Hetty said, without bothering to lower her voice. "Mad as a hatter and deaf with it. For some inexplicable reason, my little cousin adores her." She wrinkled her nose. "I'll warn you now. I like her too, but she can be a bit smelly."

Such charming honesty. Caroline followed Yves across the room until she was standing in front of the tiny, almost elfin figure in the wingback chair. Thistledown hair, wrinkled apple of a face, rheumy blue eyes that must once have been like those of Yves, Hetty, and Nat, and hands like a bird's claws. In her old-fashioned, wide-skirted, black-satin gown, she looked as though she'd stepped out of the last century, and quite some time back in it, as well.

Caroline performed an elegant curtsey. "Good afternoon, Miss Treloar."

The old lady squinted up at her. "And who might you be, Missy?" The prerogative of the elderly—to be as blunt as they liked. Caroline's own grandmother, whom she vaguely remembered, had been much the same toward the end.

Yves spoke up before Caroline had the chance to reply. "This is Miss Fairfield, my new governess. Only as we're not in lessons, I'm allowed to call her Caroline." His blue eyes twinkled. "But don't tell Mama that. It's mine and Caroline and Hetty's secret."

Caroline clasped her hands together. "We just came in here to find the chess board and set so I can begin to teach Yves how to play. I do hope we haven't disturbed you. We can take the board up to the nursery if you'd rather be left in peace."

The old lady's face clouded over. "Yves? Who's he?" She patted Yves on his curly head. "This is my little Robert."

Yves didn't appear the least put out at having been mistaken for someone else. He must be used to it.

Hetty leaned over to hiss in Caroline's ear. "Yves's father, remember. Aunt Agnes gets confused and most of the time thinks Yves is his father come back to her. Which, to be honest, is no wonder, as Yves is the image of the painting in the dining room of Uncle Robert as a boy."

"I can read to you if you like, Aunt Agnes," Yves piped up. "I'd rather read to you than learn to play a silly board game."

Hetty laughed. "You are *such* a lazy boy, Yves. Grandpapa taught me how to play chess when I was smaller than you. It's an excellent game."

Yves's head came up, his eyes hopeful. "Grandpapa taught you? Do you mean if I learn to play chess, he might play it with *me?*"

Hetty shrugged. "He might, but he won't like it if you forget the moves and do silly things." She glanced at Caroline. "We used to play for ha'pennies. The day I managed to beat him, he gave me a guinea."

Caroline's turn to laugh. "That seems an inordinate reward for a single win."

Hetty tossed her auburn curls. "Not really. Grandpapa is not the sort to allow anyone to win as of an act of kindness, so when I finally managed to beat him, he reflected that in the reward I won."

Aunt Agnes, ignoring this conversation, patted the small round table by her side. "Draw up a chair, Missy, and the girl can fetch the chess set and lay it out on here. I'd like to watch Robert learn."

"Yves, you deaf old biddy," Hetty hissed, then raised her voice. "Very well, Aunt. I'll fetch the board and pieces."

Caroline, resigning herself to having to stay and provide entertainment for the old lady, pulled the other wingback chair closer to the table, as far away from the heat of the fire as she could get. After all, it was July, even though the house itself didn't reflect that.

Yves set his chin in his hands and also appeared to have resigned himself—in his case to learning to play chess.

NAT WAS NOWHERE to be seen at Roskilly that day because he'd chosen to ride out to inspect the estate and see what condition it was in. He set out on his friend Jacka's cob, which had spent a night of luxury in a spacious loose box with the best oats and hay and was full of the joys of spring, despite it being mid-July.

He didn't hurry, despite the fine mizzle of rain. He had his greatcoat and his wide-brimmed hat, and, besides which, he'd suffered much worse in a Spanish winter under canvas. It was good to be out of the stifling confines of Roskilly House that only served to remind him of how glad he'd been to get away from it at eighteen. Although, once he was out in the fresh but damp air, and had time to consider the matter, he realized it was not Roskilly itself that had brought on this feeling, but rather the people within it. Mainly his mother. And no doubt the estate manager whom he had yet to encounter. Jan Trefusis. The one consolation being that she'd had the sense to hire a Cornishman.

It had been good to see his grandfather again, but at the same time poignant to find the old man so reduced. And Aunt Agnes being so confused had brought a sizeable lump to his throat. In a way, it had been good, because after what had happened in Spain, he'd thought he could never feel emotion again. So the sorrow he'd felt on facing up to his grandfather and aunt's decline had brought home to him that he might not be so numbed to feeling as he'd thought.

But the worst thing had been his mother's reaction to his disfigurement. She was the only one who'd been horrified by his scar. Only *she* had withdrawn from him as though from a monster. Not that she'd ever been the sort to hug and kiss her children. Nat had grown up used to her keeping her distance and hadn't expected any difference in her attitude now he was nearing thirty. But her obvious disgust at his facial injury had bitten to the bone. Perhaps he'd been expecting too much of her, though, and an absence of eleven years had given him a false idea of who she was.

She'd noticed his maimed right hand at dinner last night. He'd not been able to disguise it, although she'd made a creditable effort not to recoil in shock this time. Hetty, sitting beside him at the table, had covered his damaged hand with hers in solidarity, but said nothing.

Now Nat was riding over Penmar Head, having visited a few farms and been offered either tea, ale, or a whisky at each. A wet wind blew in his face, and, down on the beach, rollers charged in from the Atlantic. Quite a different day to yesterday, and definitely not a day for the new governess to be taking his grandfather's heir anywhere near the water's edge.

He'd not seen sight nor sound of either her or Yves that morning, when he'd taken breakfast with Hetty in the morning room. No doubt his mother still stuck to her strict regime of keeping children and governesses out of the main part of the house whenever possible. Young Yves had probably been down in the kitchens being fed by Mrs. Teague if he had any sense. Nat had eaten many a meal with the huge cook as a boy.

He put up a hand to jam his hat down more firmly onto his head as the wind snatched at it. Small fields covered the headland, edged by stone and earth-built banks, which themselves were topped by ragged hawthorn bushes, blowing now in the sea wind. The sheep, shorn of their winter coats, sensibly huddled up against the walls, out of the worst of the weather.

He was just heading down the track that would take him to

Balwest Farm, when he caught sight of a rider heading in his direction. Whoever it was wore a greatcoat similar to his own, but was a sight better mounted on a classy, bright-bay horse. Nat drew rein and waited for the rider to approach.

The newcomer brought his horse in alongside Bosun and tipped his hat to Nat. "Good day to you, Sir. Not a particularly nice afternoon for a ride."

Nat, keeping his face turned to the side out of long habit, nodded. "Have you come far?"

The newcomer, a tall and somewhat sturdy young man of approximately Nat's own age, wiped a hand across his rain-wet face. "A tidy ride. My wife insisted that I should come personally and not trust to a messenger, and she's not to be denied when she gets a bee in her bonnet." He held out his hand to Nat. "Samuel Beauchamp, of Carlyon Court."

Nat took the hand. "Nathaniel Treloar." No need for him to give himself the title of major. That was all behind him now, and he didn't need reminding of it.

Sam Beauchamp's face lit up. "Of Roskilly? That's where I'm bound. What luck to have bumped into you. I'm not entirely sure of the lanes around here, and there seems to be a surfeit of them that all look the same. Perhaps you can send me on in the right direction." He tilted his head to one side. "Unless you're heading back there yourself and could show me the way?"

Why not? The rain was worse than he'd expected, the farms much of a muchness, and the beach would be too windswept for a gallop. And breakfast felt a long time ago. He might as well head back to the Court in this gentleman's company. He turned Bosun around, and the two horses fell in side by side, Nat keeping to Sam's right, although he suspected Sam had already spotted the scar but was politely refraining from appearing to notice it.

Sam was clearly a far more garrulous companion than Nat might have hoped for. "My wife made no mention of you being at Roskilly," he began with. "She told me she met Mrs. Treloar and her daughter, Henrietta, last week at the Truro Assembly

Rooms."

He was clearly fishing. No doubt so he could tell his wife all about Nat later. Probably top of his description would be Nat's scar.

A pregnant pause ensued that Nat felt forced to fill. "Hetty is my sister."

"Ah." Sam nodded. "Although I do believe my wife, Ysella her name is, told me Miss Treloar was a redhead." He raised his eyes to Nat's face, pointedly looking at Nat's own dark hair beneath his hat.

Damn the man. Why did he want to make chitchat like this? Nat would have scowled, only his right eyebrow would not have obliged him. "She takes after my grandmother." No need to vouchsafe further information. That would have to do. He'd become the master of the short answer in the last six years.

Sam smiled. Did he consider Nat a new friend on such short acquaintance? "Ysella told me your sister is an uncommonly pretty girl. In fact, this is partly why she had me ride over here in this atrocious weather."

He must be trying to look apologetic, but it wasn't quite working. Was the man under the thumb of his wife that he leapt to do her every bidding like this? Was Nat now supposed to ask him what his visit portended?

It seemed not, because Sam went on without needing to be asked. "Ysella wanted me to call upon your mother for several reasons. The first being out of a desire to invite her and your sister, who she noted is of an age to enjoy dancing and pleasant company, to attend a ball we're giving at Carlyon. And the second is that she wanted me to ascertain if her friend Caroline Fairfield is employed now by Mrs. Treloar. You see, it was Ysella who recommended her to your mother, so she feels a vested interest in the outcome."

Sam regarded Nat as though this time he was waiting for a reply.

Nat sighed. "I'm sure my sister will be very pleased to attend your ball. And I can tell you right now that a Miss Fairfield is indeed performing the duties of governess to my young cousin. I think I was told her name is Caroline. Would that be your wife's friend?" How did this gentleman's wife come to have a friend who was a governess? Although, Miss Fairfield had about her the air of a well-bred young lady, so perhaps she'd fallen on hard times. Not that he cared. He did *not* want to get into discussing the life story of a member of staff.

Sam's honest face lit up. "The very one. Ysella will be delighted. She has asked me to extend the invitation to Caroline as well as your mother and sister. She longs to see her again." He paused, his smile honest and open. "Although of course, she would like to see your mother and sister almost as much."

Nat frowned, doubting very much that anyone might want to see his mother and not at all sure she would approve of an employee being invited to the same ball she and Hetty were going to.

"And now I've discovered your existence," Sam said, with a bit of a flourish, "I daresay Ysella will never forgive me if I don't persuade you to escort the ladies."

Oh no. Nat did not at all want to have to go to a ball anywhere and be stared at by the local gentry, people he'd known as a child and gone to school with, their wives he might never have met, and definitely not the over-friendly Sam Beauchamp's wife, who was probably just like him.

"Shall we trot on?" he asked. "And get out of this rain?"

Chapter Ten

BACK AT ROSKILLY, Nat and Sam left their two horses in the care of Old Pascoe, the man who'd risen to take over his father's place as head groom in the eleven years Nat had been away and was indeed the father of the young groom Nat had already met, and Nat led Sam indoors. Luncheon must be over by now, so Nat escorted their visitor in the direction of the parlor, where his mother always liked to spend her afternoons. However, this involved passing the library, the door of which stood slightly ajar. The sound of merry laughter emanated from within.

Sam ground to a halt.

"No, you can't do that," came Miss Fairfield's voice raised in what sounded like a mix of mock admonition and laughter. "The only pieces that can move diagonally are the bishops and the queen."

"But why can't my *prawn* move the same?" The high-pitched and indignant tones of young Yves carried to Nat's ears.

"It's a *pawn,* you silly, not a *prawn.*" Hetty's voice, brimming with mirth. "But he's right, Caroline. It would be a much more interesting game if they could all move wherever they wanted." For a moment, Nat's stony heart softened. What would it be like to be so carefree and happy again? To be young and reveling in the joys of life as Hetty and Yves did, and perhaps Miss Fairfield as well.

Miss Fairfield's voice came again. "Well, a pawn *can* move diagonally, but only if it's taking another piece. Like this." More laughter.

"I say," Sam said. "That sounds to me like Caroline. I mean, Miss Fairfield. Do you mind if we stop to see her?"

This must have been a rhetorical question, because without waiting for an answer, Sam pushed the library door open wider and stepped through it. Just as a quavery old voice that had to be Aunt Agnes's rose in a plaintive whine. "Let *me* help little Robert. I know how all the pieces move. I'm not so old and feeble that I've forgotten that."

Grinding his teeth at the delay in delivering their guest and therefore making his escape, Nat followed Sam into the library.

Everyone who'd presumably just been staring at Sam suddenly transferred their gazes to him. Reacting without thinking, he turned his head slightly to the right. Miss Fairfield's sympathetic eyes followed the inadvertent move, and he felt heat flood his cheeks as though he'd been caught out in some furtive crime.

Miss Fairfield recovered first. She rose from the wingback chair she'd been occupying and swept Sam a graceful curtsey. "Mr. Beauchamp, how delightful to see you."

Sam bowed. "Miss Fairfield. And this must be Miss Treloar."

"It is indeed," Caroline replied.

"Two Miss Treloars," Hetty responded, also rising to her feet from a stool she'd pulled up, no doubt so she could benefit the players with her wisdom. She executed an elegant curtsey for Sam. "For this is my Aunt Agnes who is also a Miss Treloar and, by benefit of her age, takes precedence over me."

"Prettily put, for such a chit," Aunt Agnes muttered, her gaze flicking from Nat to Sam and then back again. Her sparse, straggly eyebrows lowered. "Do I not merit an introduction to our visitor, young Nat?"

At least she'd remembered his name this time. "Aunt Agnes, may I present Mr. Samuel Beauchamp of Carlyon Court," Nat said. "A friend of Miss Fairfield's."

Caroline edged her way around the chess board. "And as such we are on first name terms. Sam is my dear friend, Miss Treloar, as is his wife, Ysella Carlyon as was."

The old lady sucked her lips over her sparsely toothed gums. "Well connected for a governess, ain't you?" Her eyes darted over Sam. "I remember going to Carlyon Court as a girl. The old viscount settled it on his younger son and he married a local girl. Wise man that he was." Her eyes took on a vacant expression, as though she were seeing back into the long gone past. "Miss Gabriella Polvean, I think her name was. Lovely woman." Her gaze sharpened. "Be you related to them, then?"

"Better shout," Hetty said. "Or she won't hear you."

Sam stepped closer to Aunt Agnes. "I'm married to that Lady Ormonde's granddaughter, Miss Treloar."

Yves, who had remained seated on his stool opposite Caroline, now rose to his feet, a distinct look of his grandfather about him. He made a little bow, made comical by his skeleton suit. "Welcome to Roskilly, Mr. Beauchamp."

"May I introduce Master Yves Treloar," Caroline said. "My pupil."

Nat began to edge toward the door, but Aunt Agnes wasn't about to lose her audience. "Sit down, sit down, boy," she cackled. "And Yves, ring the bell for Ennion and we'll get tea sent up."

Sam obediently pulled up a seat nearer to the fire, and Nat did the same, with distinct unwillingness, and keeping a little further back. Damn it. He'd never escape now. He was stuck having to take tea with a man who was too chatty for his liking, three women, and a far-too-cheeky child.

"Can you play chess, sir?" Yves asked Sam, as he regained his stool after having rung the bell.

Sam nodded. "Not well. I've not a mind for tactics. But I'm good at draughts."

"What's draughts?"

"We have a draughts set," Hetty piped up. "It's much easier

than chess. You'd like it, Yves. I'll fetch it."

While Yves and Hetty delved into one of the chests under the long library windows, Caroline regained her seat. She was tall for a woman, and perhaps not so plain as Nat had at first thought. An intelligent, thoughtful face, that, when she smiled at Yves, lit up. If you were generous, she could even be taken for pretty when she smiled.

"Nat can play chess," Aunt Agnes said. "Why don't you give him a game, my girl?"

Was she talking to Miss Fairfield? Nat, who had been staring into the fire intent on not having to talk to anyone, glanced sideways at Caroline and found her eyes already on him. "Would you like a game?" she asked, face demure and innocent.

It would be rude to refuse. "I am a little rusty." In truth, he hadn't played the game since he'd been in Spain, with a chess set one of his troopers had carved from bone and walnut. But he'd always been a skillful player, schooled by his grandfather, and that wouldn't have left him.

She smiled, her eyes still firmly fixed on his. "Then we shall play while Sam teaches Yves how to play draughts."

Hetty returned clutching a board and a box of draughts. "We'll need a second table. Mr. Beauchamp? Might you help Yves fetch that one over?"

Nat watched as Sam and Yves set up their table and Hetty showed Yves how to lay the pieces out, a memory of his own father teaching him the game leaping into his head. The little dog, a faithful creature, settled itself at Yves's feet.

"I'll be on your side and help you learn the moves," Hetty said, squeezing herself onto Yves's stool beside him. "You'll like this better than chess because it's easier to learn."

When Nat looked back, Caroline had rearranged the chess pieces ready to play. "White or black?" she asked.

"Black," Nat said, trying to keep the gruffness out of his tone. No doubt a woman would not be much of an opponent. Their minds were not constructed for being tactical. And he had the advantage that there'd not been much else to do in the evenings on campaign, so he'd taken the opportunity to play a lot of chess with his fellow officers.

Aunt Agnes leaned forwards, smacking her withered lips in anticipation.

Ennion unobtrusively brought in a tea tray and set it down, but now the games were in hand, no one paid it any attention. Nat lounged back in his seat, his gaze on Caroline.

As she was playing white, she opened the game by moving her queen's knight forward to in front of his bishop's pawn. Nat retaliated by bringing his king's pawn forward two squares. So far so good. Did she not want to gain the vital central squares? Well, he wasn't here to teach her how to play. Just to beat her.

Her brow furrowed in concentration, Caroline moved her other knight forward to occupy the square in front of her other bishop's pawn, mirroring the first. Interesting move.

Nat frowned as well. What was she playing at? He moved his queen's pawn one square forward to open up his back row a bit.

Aunt Agnes cackled with laughter but apart from that stayed silent. She'd been a chess player in her youth, although not as good as his father, and many were the times she'd beaten Nat as a small boy with this exact chess set. The memory surfaced of how pleased he'd been the first time he beat her.

"You hop over the draughts like this," Hetty said, and the sound of Yves doing just that tapped on the draughts board.

"This is much more fun than chess," he cried.

Caroline moved her king's pawn forward to sit facing Nat's king's pawn.

"I wondered when you'd do that," he remarked.

She raised her head and smiled at him. She really was quite transformed when she did that. "Oh, was it something I was meant to do?"

He shrugged. "Up to you." And he moved his king's bishop's pawn forward two squares to threaten her pawn. His favored opponent had been Captain Carnegie, until... No. He wouldn't think about that.

Caroline drew in her bottom lip under her top teeth as though not sure what to do next. Her hand hovered over the board in apparent indecision, then settled on her king's rook's pawn and moved it forward one square. She sat back, a puzzled frown on her face as though she thought that might have been a mistake.

Nat took her threatened pawn, capturing two of the central squares. She was playing into his hands.

She took his aggressive pawn with her knight. Nat studied the board, thinking about what to do next.

"I won!" cried Yves in delight. "Can we play again?"

"You're a natural," Sam replied, his throaty laugh rumbling round the laden bookshelves.

Nat brought out his queen's knight. She'd probably take his pawn next with her knight, and then he could retaliate and take her knight.

She didn't. Instead, she moved it to the right. So that was her game, was it?

"One more game," Sam said, laughing. "And then I really must go and see Mrs. Treloar and complete the mission my wife gave me."

Nat moved his queen's pawn out two squares to consolidate his possession of the center.

"What mission is that?" Hetty asked.

Quite unexpectedly, Caroline moved her queen out on the diagonal to sit beside her knight and threaten Nat's king. "Check," she said, sounding quite surprised.

"I've come to invite you all to a ball at Carlyon Court," Sam said. The draughts pieces rattled as they were laid out again.

Sam brought his king's knight's pawn out to threaten Caroline's queen. She'd have to get out of that for her next move.

As he'd expected, she moved her queen back two squares along the diagonal to protect her other knight.

"A ball?" Hetty gasped. "All of us? When?"

"I don't want to go to a ball," Yves protested.

Hetty laughed. "I don't think Mr. Beauchamp means you."

Nat brought his king's knight out of the back row.

"A ball?" Caroline said, leaning back for a moment as though their game were nearly over and didn't matter to her. "That will be lovely for you, Hetty." With casual indifference she moved her other knight forward out of Nat's pawn's way and sat it between Nat's queen and the second knight. "Oh, I believe that's check again."

Damn it. So it was. She had no need to sound quite so surprised about it. He needed to concentrate better.

Sam joined in the laughter. "I don't think small boys go to balls."

"Thank goodness," Yves muttered.

"You'll want to one day," Hetty said.

Aunt Agnes let out a rather random cackle of laughter.

To get out of check, Nat brought his king forward one space to threaten the pesky knight. He couldn't take the knight though, as it was protected by Caroline's queen.

"But *I* would like to go," Hetty said. "I've only been to one social event so far, at the Assembly Rooms, and it was such fun, but not the same as a ball at someone's house."

Caroline took one of Nat's two pawns in the center of the board with her knight, which put Nat's king back in check again. Damn it. Was she perhaps better at this than he'd given her credit for? Nat countered by moving his king again, feeling as though he was very much on the back foot here but not sure how he'd got there. Women were not meant to be this good at games of strategy.

"I'm sure your mama will let you go," Caroline said, her head tilted slightly to one side as she studied the board. No doubt in search of another way to check him. And she found one. What was going on here? She moved her second knight onto another of the central squares Nat had thought she'd had no hope of gaining. "Check, I think…"

Nat took her other knight with his king, painfully aware he'd left this important piece exposed and that he couldn't take the other knight with it because of Caroline's queen.

"Do you think Mama will let me have a new gown?" Hetty asked. "No, move that piece, Yves. Haha! Got you, Mr. Beauchamp." *Clink clink* went the draughts piece as Yves hopped over Sam's. Probably Sam was letting him win. Not a good thing for a child. Nat's own experience of playing board games with adults had been being beaten time after time, which had made the joy of finally winning all the sweeter.

"You can but ask her," Caroline said, bringing out her king's bishop to threaten Nat's king. "Check."

Nat took the bishop with some little relish, goaded into recklessness by her play.

"I'm winning again!" Yves crowed. "I like this game."

Caroline slid her queen horizontally to take up position threatening Nat's king once more. Drat it. He couldn't take the queen without being taken himself. The only escape he could see was to move back onto the central squares out of the queen's reach. For now. He had a nasty feeling he wasn't going to win this game.

Caroline chuckled and slid her queen along two squares. "Checkmate, I think."

Yves craned his neck. "Did you beat Cousin Nat, Caroline?"

Hetty got up to come and look. "You did! Well done." She clapped her hands together. "And Yves and I have beaten Mr. Beauchamp, again."

Nat looked up from the board, and found Caroline's eyes resting on him. No trace of triumph resided in them, just calm innocence. "You play a good game," he said. "I've not met an opponent such as you before."

She smiled, her eyes suddenly misting over as though she might be about to shed a tear. "I learned from a master. My father liked a game but could never find anyone to give him a good contest. So, he taught me."

Nat's eyes narrowed. Part of him held back from asking her anything further, as clearly memories of her father pained her. Instinct had him recoiling from prying into her past life and thus becoming more involved in her present, as that was the last thing he wanted to do. But another part of him felt curiosity at what might have brought a girl to be a governess whose father had plainly had enough time to spend turning her into the accomplished chess player she was.

He couldn't resist. "And your father no longer plays?"

She shook her head, the sparkle of a tear in the corner of her eye. "No. He does not." She clamped her lips together. That was all he was getting from her.

Sam Beauchamp stood up. "Perhaps I'd better go and see Mrs. Treloar now, and deliver my invitation." He smiled at Caroline. "Ysella sends her felicitations to you, Caroline, and hopes you will also attend the ball. The invitation is for all of you."

"Oh, that would be wonderful," Hetty exclaimed, reaching to catch Caroline's arm. "How perfect. And you are not old and wrinkled like Miss Hawkins was, even if you are no longer in the first flush of your youth. I would be so happy if you were to accompany Mama and me. So much more fun to have a friend like you to go with. At the Assembly Rooms I had to stay with Mama the whole time and it was awful. She insisted on vetting all the young gentlemen who wanted to dance with me in the most discouraging way."

Nat almost laughed out loud at both Hetty's remark and Sam's suggestion. Mama was not going to think much of the idea of taking her nephew's governess to a ball, that was for certain. Good luck to Sam Beauchamp at succeeding in that.

Chapter Eleven

A S IT TURNED out, Mrs. Treloar must have been forced by politeness into saying Caroline could attend the ball as Hetty's companion. A note was delivered to the schoolroom by young Dickon the footman.

Caroline unfolded it while sitting at the teacher's desk, watched surreptitiously by Yves, who should have been writing out an example of a first conjugation Latin verb in his best handwriting.

She read: *Mr. and Mrs. Beauchamp have particularly asked for your attendance at their ball next week. I have decided you may go as Hetty's companion. But there are conditions to this. Firstly, you will wear a suitably plain gown so that no one there will be mistaken in your duties. Secondly, you will not put yourself forward to dance with any young gentlemen. Thirdly, you will carefully supervise all young gentlemen who approach Hetty for a dance and accompany her at all times. Mrs. Treloar.*

What a draconian list of conditions, but at least the writer of this letter could spell a lot better than Ysella. Caroline reread her instructions. A suitably plain gown. Did her employer mean she wanted her to wear one of her drab everyday dresses? She hadn't been to a ball since last year, but she still had the dress she'd worn to that hanging in her wardrobe right now. It was of the palest mauve, a color that suited her complexion well. Might she get

94

away with that?

Yves coughed.

She returned her attention to her small charge. He'd seemed particularly sleepy this morning, as though not properly awake, and was propping his head up on his hand with his elbow on his desk and his eyes only half open.

She smiled at him. "Have you finished your work?"

He glanced down at his ink blotchy page. "Um, not quite."

She gave him a stern look. "Well, best get on with it then. It's nearly midday and you don't want to be still writing Latin verbs out this afternoon."

He rubbed his eyes. "It's so stuffy in here. I can't seem to think."

True. Maybe she should open the window.

With a sigh, Caroline got up and came to peer over his shoulder. "I see you've done *amo* and *ambulo*." She scanned his writing. "And I'm pleased to say both are correct. At least I think they are, given your quite terrible use of blots. Do you know? I think we'll leave it at that for today. No sense in trying to cram learning into your head when you're this sleepy." She shook her head. "Did you not sleep well last night?"

Yves blew to dry the ink on the last word in his list—*ambulant—they walk, they are walking, they do walk.* "I think I must've slept a bit too well. Usually, I go down for my breakfast with Mrs. Teague, but today I overslept and didn't have time." He rubbed his stomach. "And I'm *starving* right now."

Caroline's thoughts went to the meager platters they'd be getting for their dinner in an hour's time. "Perhaps you'd like to go down to see Mrs. Teague now, in that case, and see what she's been cooking. She'll probably have something nice for you to eat."

He jumped up, suddenly lively. "Thank you, Caroline. I can call you that, now lessons are over. I'll collect Dash from down there too. Shall I bring you something to eat as well?"

Why not? "Thank you, Yves. I've some work to do here

preparing for tomorrow's lessons. But that would be lovely."

Like a gangly puppy, Yves galloped out of the schoolroom on his errand of mercy.

Caroline settled down to sort through the work she was planning for the next morning, not noticing how the time ticked past.

The door opening disturbed her. She looked up, half expecting it to be Yves back with a slab of thick-cut bread slathered with butter, but it wasn't. Instead, Patience the nursery maid came sidling in carrying a mop and bucket.

"Ooh, Miss," she said as she saw Caroline. "I didn't think as you'd still be here. Shall I come back later?"

Caroline closed the book on her desk and shook her head. "Good afternoon, Patience. I've finished what I was doing, so I'll leave you to your chores." She stood up, and the girl set the bucket down. Caroline moved to the door, her hand on the knob, but hesitated, her forehead furrowing in a puzzled frown.

"Patience?"

"Yes'm?"

"Master Yves was very sleepy this morning, as though he'd had difficulty waking up." She sucked her lips in trying to decide how to word this. "He missed going down to breakfast with Mrs. Teague because he wasn't up in time. Was there anything… different… about yesterday evening? You *are* there when he's put to bed, aren't you?"

Patience bit her lip. "I'm there in the nursery, Miss, but 'tisn't me what puts him to bed. 'Tis Bridget. I'm doing the tidying."

Caroline nodded. "And was there anything different last night?"

Patience's smooth brow wrinkled. "I b'lieve Doctor Rescorla had left some powders or such like for Master Yves to take. Like he had before. Might've been a bottle. I didn't see it, so I don't rightly know. Bridget give it to him, I think. He didn't like it, but she made him take it."

Oh. Caroline nodded. "Thank you, Patience." She half

opened the door. "And where is Bridget now?"

"Downstairs in the kitchens eating her dinner."

Caroline took a step, and turned to look back at Patience over her shoulder. "Perhaps don't mention I asked you about this. To Bridget, I mean. She might think I'm being interfering, and I don't want to offend her."

Patience was already dipping her mop into the bucket. "I won't, Miss."

Caroline closed the door behind her and headed for the nursery. Empty, as she'd expected. She went inside and closed the door behind herself, standing with her back pressed up against it. What was she doing? Doctor Rescorla had probably prescribed something perfectly innocent for Yves's health. And yet… a child shouldn't be this sleepy in the morning, not when he normally was so robust and lively. She needed to find out what he was being given for herself.

She scanned the room. Where would Bridget keep any medicines? You were supposed to keep things like that out of the reach of children, so surely whatever it was must be stored up high somewhere?

Nowhere presented itself. This was a room laid out for children to play and sleep in, not for the storing of possibly dangerous medications. Caroline's roving gaze settled on a door in the far corner. Aha.

On hurried feet she crossed the floor and put a hand on the doorknob. This might well be where Bridget slept, so as to be on hand if required overnight, and to keep a watchful eye on her charge. She opened the door.

The bedroom was smaller than her own, with a simple, narrow bed and a shabby armoire with drawers at the bottom and hanging space above. It had to be Bridget's room. Caroline glanced around, searching for where Bridget might have decided to keep Yves's new medication. A washstand stood in one corner, with a china pitcher and bowl on it. Above, set into the angle where the walls met, a corner cupboard had been fixed to the wall on eye level for an adult, but out of Yves's reach. Aha.

With a nasty itching feeling between her shoulder blades, and one ear cocked for the sound of Bridget's heavy returning footsteps, Caroline turned the handle on the cupboard. Locked, damn it. Where would Bridget keep the key? Hopefully not on her person. She scanned the room. If it were anywhere but in her pocket, it would be in here.

She opened the drawers in the armoire to find they contained Bridget's clean linen. Careful not to disturb their neatly folded precision, Caroline searched both drawers to no avail. Nothing.

What about under the bed? She got down on her hands and knees but the only things under there were some bits of fluff and an empty hat box. Did Bridget wear hats that came in smart hat boxes or had someone given her the box? Where else was there? Leaning on the bed, she rose to her feet.

The bed. There was only one thin pillow. Caroline lifted it and was rewarded by the sight of a small brass key lying on the smooth sheet. She pounced. It had to be the one.

With fingers that trembled for more than one reason, Caroline tried the key in the cabinet's lock and turned it. With a click the lock slid back into place and she opened the door. There was only one thing within. A large brown bottle, the level slightly down as though one dose had already been administered. Caroline picked up the bottle and read the embossed name.

Dalby's Carminative.

Whatever was that?

She lifted the bottle down, pulled the cork and gave it a suspicious sniff. A bit minty but it also had traces of a not-so-attractive bitterness. Best to taste it. With considerable reluctance, she dipped her finger in the neck of the bottle, withdrew it and licked the tip. Eww. Not a medicine she'd have liked to have taken as a child. But what was it for? Yves didn't appear to have anything wrong with him, so why did he need medication?

Did she dare to ask Bridget?

The thought of Bridget made her heart thump. She'd better

put it back as she'd found it and make herself scarce before Bridget came back from the kitchen and caught her rifling through her room. She locked the cupboard with a shaking hand and restored the key to under Bridget's pillow, then let herself back into the nursery. Patience must already have cleaned in here, because everything was spick and span: toys tidied away, bed made, no clothes lying discarded on chairs. And the wooden floorboards still possessed a dampness indicative of Patience and her mop and bucket's attentions.

Footsteps sounded in the corridor outside. Determined, heavy footsteps. Before Caroline could move, the door swung open to reveal Bridget, stout and sour faced, on the threshold. A Bridget whose rather piggy eyes widened in surprise at the sight of Caroline in the nursery.

Her overly thick brows met in a frown as she stepped into the room, almost, it might have been construed, with an air of threat about her. "What can I do for you... Miss Fairfield?" A hint of unmistakable disrespect colored her words, as though she saw the nursery as her domain and Caroline as an intruder.

Caroline fixed a smile onto her face. "Nothing, thank you, Bridget. I was just looking to see if Master Yves had left one of his books in here. He didn't have it in the schoolroom this morning."

Bridget's ample and well-muscled form took another step closer to Caroline. "There's none of his books in here, that I'll vouch for." She glanced around. "And if there were, Patience would've found them when she cleaned."

Why on earth was she feeling so unnerved by this woman's proximity? Caroline chided herself for being a coward and forcefully straightened her spine, drawing herself up as tall as she could, a good five inches above the short and squat Bridget. "I am inclined to agree with you, Bridget, but it was worth my while taking a look." She narrowed her eyes. "After all, you never know what I might find."

Bridget bustled across the room toward her own bedroom door, where she paused to hurl a parting shot. "Master Yves were down in the kitchens begging food again. Mrs. Treloar said as how he wasn't allowed to. I daresay she'll have something to say to you for letting him do that."

"He was hungry. He overslept this morning and had no breakfast."

Bridget scowled over her shoulder, defensive. "Then he needs to get up a bit earlier. It's not my fault if he can't get out of bed in the mornings."

Accusing Bridget of administering something to make him sleep at nights lurked on the tip of Caroline's tongue, but she hesitated. Best not to reveal her hand too soon. Best to find out who exactly had decreed Yves should take this medicine which she felt sure accounted for his sleepy demeanor this morning. Surely no doctor had prescribed it, no matter what Patience had said.

Leaving Bridget in the nursery, Caroline returned to the schoolroom to find Patience had delivered her and Yves's meager midday meal and a pot of tea. At least with Yves down in the kitchens being fed, she could eat it all herself. She was almost as starving as he must have been, and she wasn't a growing boy.

However, she had other things on her mind now, nagging her and refusing to go away. She sat down at her desk but didn't touch the food. Who could she ask about the medicine she'd found? Who would know? And who if they knew would dare to divulge to her what they knew? No one here at Roskilly, that was certain, not if they valued their jobs. Perhaps a trip into Penzance was called for. She absentmindedly picked at her food, wondering how Mrs. Teague could have produced this. Surely it was yesterday's leftovers.

Seized with determination, she rang the bell and, after a few minutes, Patience returned. She executed a respectful curtsey.

Caroline smiled at her. "I've finished eating now, thank you. But I also wanted to ask you something, Patience. Tell me, is there a pony cart I might use to make a visit to Penzance? I'd like to visit a haberdasher's or dressmaker's to buy myself some ribbons and suchlike to decorate my gown for the ball I'm to accompany Miss Henrietta to."

Patience gathered up the tray. "There is that, Miss. Shall I get Young Pascoe to harness up the pony for you?"

Caroline set her empty teacup on the tray. "Yes, that would be very kind of you, Patience. I shall be taking Master Yves in with me, I think. It's not raining today and the fresh air will do him good."

Chapter Twelve

"I CAN COME too?" Yves danced from one foot to the other in excitement. "I never get to go anywhere. Not since Grandpapa had to stay in bed. Before he got ill, he once took me into Penzance with him on his horse, but I was such a little boy then, I can't remember it at all. Can we go to the harbor to see if any ships are in? I know there's a harbor because Dickon told me so."

Caroline had descended to the kitchens, where she'd found Young Pascoe just finishing his meal and, having enquired of him the correct road to take to get to Penzance, sent him out to get the pony and trap ready. Yves was eating a fat slab of bread, thickly spread with butter, in addition to the slice of pie Mrs. Teague had already fed him, the crumbs of which he picked up with a licked, and rather inky, fingertip.

"You do get to come," Caroline said, choosing to ignore his now ink-stained tongue. "Because every whip needs a groom, and you are to be my groom today."

"I'd rather be the whip," Yves retorted, with a cheeky grin. "But I suppose being a groom will be quite tolerable. Will it be my job to open gates and things like that?"

Caroline nodded. "You will be in charge of that, if we encounter any."

"And Hetty's not coming?"

Caroline had toyed with the idea of asking Hetty, mainly because she might know the way, but the fact that the pony cart only had two places, and even though Yves was small and skinny it would be a squeeze with three of them, put her off. Added to the fact that if Hetty discovered what she was about, she might relay it to her mother, even if not on purpose. And somehow, Caroline did *not* think she wanted Mrs. Treloar to know anything about the true nature of her journey. Just in case there was something to worry about concerning the bottle of medicine. Although, even if there was nothing nefarious about it, no doubt Mrs. Treloar would be offended that Caroline had thought there could be.

"No, we're taking the pony cart, so there's no room for Hetty. I've suggested she use the time for useful piano practice."

"Good," Yves said with satisfaction. "Just you and me, then. And I don't have to listen to her playing the piano all afternoon." He pulled a disgusted face. "That's such *torture*."

They went out into the stableyard where they found Young Pascoe holding the bridle of a pretty dapple-gray mare no more than thirteen hands high, harnessed to a neatly painted two-wheeled pony cart. Caroline thanked him and climbed into the driving seat, and Yves scrambled up beside her.

"She might be a bit lively, Miss," Young Pascoe said as he stepped back. "Not been out for a while."

Caroline gathered the reins and took hold of the whip, keeping its long, dangling end under control with her fingers. "That's quite all right, Tom. I'm well used to handling lively ponies." Having grown up as friends with the Carlyon girls, whose mother was an accomplished horsewoman, Caroline had benefitted from plenty of experience both on the driver's seat and in the saddle.

She clicked her tongue to the pony and it trotted smartly out onto the drive, small hooves and trap wheels crunching the gravel.

"Do you know what her name is?" Caroline asked, as she headed the pony down the way she should have entered by when she'd arrived.

Yves, leaning back in his seat with his spindly legs stuck forward, nodded. Today he had on breeches, miniature top boots, and a short navy jacket with brass buttons. Quite the little dandy. "Blossom. She's the pony that pulls the garden equipment. You know. She does the lawns. She has to wear special shoes for that so she doesn't make hoofprints on the grass. Aunt Ruth would have a fit if she saw a hoofprint. And she has to wear a sort of napkin to catch her poo." He said this last with an air of bravado, his eyes resting on Caroline in speculation, perhaps waiting for a rebuke.

But Caroline had never been shy of referring to waste material—the Carlyon girls' mother, Lady Ormonde, had taught her well. "What a very good idea," she said. "I wish my mother had thought of that. Our poor gardener's boy had to go round with a shovel and put whatever our garden pony did on the rose beds."

Yves chuckled in delight. "I ride her sometimes. She's very lazy. But Aunt Ruth won't let me have a pony of my own. She says I'm not a good enough rider, but how I'm supposed to improve when all I have to ride is Blossom, I don't know." He sighed. "See down there where the road forks? I think we have to take the left-hand lane."

Just as well. The right-hand alternative appeared to be no better than the rutted back way into Treloar and was blocked by a rickety gate. Blossom seemed to know her way and naturally headed left, although with a distinct lack of speed, despite Young Pascoe's avowal that she was fresh. Caroline clicked her tongue again and tickled her rump with the end of the whip, and she sped up her trot. Within five minutes they reached the top road and turned left again, in the direction of Penzance.

Yves seemed much more wide awake now, chattering away about everything they came across, and pointing out the distinctive shapes of the mine workings in the distance. "That one's Wheal Jenny, and over there's Wheal True. Both of them are ours." So the effects of the carminative must have worn off, at last. However, it still disturbed Caroline that something he'd been dosed with the night before had taken this long to lose its efficacy. No child should be as sleepy as Yves had been that morning. She could only presume the syrup had contained something to put him to sleep, and she didn't like the idea of that at all. What might it be? Only an apothecary would be able to tell her that.

Her thoughts wandered to her previous neighbor, young Lady Ormonde, Ysella's sister-in-law, with whom she had become good friends. Morvoren had been the lady of Ormonde Abbey now for a good three years, and was mother to two children. Little George, the heir, now a robust two-year-old, and his new baby sister, Elestren, named after her grandmother, the dowager.

Morvoren was very much what she liked to call "a hands-on mother," a phrase Caroline had never come across before. She played a large part in her children's upbringing and had insisted that neither of them be dosed with something called Godfrey's Cordial that the children's nurse had produced when George first began to teethe. Her aversion to this bordered on the manic, and all bottles of the cordial had been thrown away, much to the nurse's annoyance.

Curious, Caroline had asked Morvoren why she was so set against her children being helped with their teething and colic.

"Because I don't know what's in it," Morvoren replied, jaw set in that determined fashion she had. "And I don't believe in giving anyone, still less my children, something I know nothing about, just to make them sleep to suit the adult who is in charge of their care. I strongly suspect it contains opium, and that's not at all good for anyone. And besides which, it tastes awful. Have you tried it?"

As far as Caroline could remember, the cordial had tasted similar to the carminative, which was what had roused her suspicions in the first place. That and Yves being so sleepy after his first dose of it. It seemed highly likely it contained the opium Morvoren was so set against. And one thing she'd learned from her friend was to listen to her wisdom, which so far had been right every time.

"Look," Yves cried in excitement. "I can see the sea!"

"You can see the sea every day from your bedroom window," Caroline said with a smile. "What makes this sea any different?"

"That." Yves pointed a finger. "A castle on an island."

Caroline stared. He was quite correct. What looked like a small castle occupied a rocky island at the nearest end of a long beach. Surely it was too small to be of much use?

"I know what it is," Yves announced, with pride. "Miss Hawkins told me all about it, even though she was never allowed to take me into Penzance to see it. It's St Michael's Mount and this must be Mount's Bay. Miss Hawkins was Cornish, like me. She knew lots of stories about Cornwall." He paused. "And I think I remember seeing it with Grandpapa that time he brought me with him when I was just a little boy."

Their road, still nothing more than a track with potholes filled by large beach pebbles, began to go downhill as it followed the coastline toward the distant town of Penzance at the far end of the bay.

"Now Blossom's not so lively, can I drive for a bit?" Yves asked.

Caroline narrowed her eyes. "Have you driven before?"

"Oh, lots of times."

Was that too airy an answer? "Are you telling me a fib?"

Yves had the grace to blush. "Well, I've sat on the driver's seat of the barouche a few times beside Old Pascoe. And watched him." He grinned. "And I've been watching you."

This made Caroline chuckle. "Nice try. Normally, I wouldn't let you. But as there's no one else about for you to crash Blossom into or run over, and it's not hard…" She held out the reins to him. "Here. You hold these and I'll keep hold of the whip. Just keep her going and try not to drive into any of the worst potholes. That'll be the hardest thing to do."

Yves seized the reins with gusto, clicking his tongue at Blossom non-stop. However, she seemed to sense the change of driver, and ignored his efforts to get her to speed up.

When they reached a little river tumbling across the road and making the going even more bumpy, Caroline took back the reins. The road was beginning to get more crowded and Yves was prone to being distracted by all the new sights. There was a lot to see for a little boy: a few market carts, people on foot or leading packhorses, a wagonload of hay being brought in from the fields to store for winter, some small boys kicking a makeshift football about. She smiled at him. "That was well done. You'll make an excellent whip."

Yves's thin cheeks colored at her praise, and he settled back to enjoy the entry to Penzance itself, the picture of nonchalant relaxation.

Caroline, on the other hand, was decidedly on edge. This was a strange town, and however small, it represented a challenge to a woman with a child and a pony cart to take care of. The road they were on now led uphill, merging into what had to be the main street, many of the buildings being small, mostly seedy, shops of some kind. Now she just had to find somewhere to deposit Blossom and the cart before she and Yves began her detective work.

Her luck was in. On a corner, where a small side street turned off right-handed, stood a substantial inn—the Star. She drew Blossom to a halt in the road. Most inns possessed stables where you could leave your horse, so surely this one could be no exception. She was right. After a few moments, a scruffy boy not much older than Yves came slouching out, pushing back an old-fashioned tricorn hat that was too big for him and eyeing them up and down.

Caroline dismounted from the trap. "Jump down, Yves." She fixed the disreputable boy with a hard stare. "Good afternoon. Stabling for an hour or so? With some hay for our pony?"

The boy wiped his sleeve across his nose and took hold of Blossom's reins by the bit. "You pays inside."

Caroline followed the boy's advice, Yves trailing after her, but with his chin on his shoulder gawping back at the boy. No doubt he saw very few other children and it must have been a surprise for him to see one so close to himself in age employed at an inn.

The livery charge having been paid, Caroline took him by the hand, as he was much inclined to dawdle and stare at everything wide eyed, and returned to the street.

What she needed was an apothecary. But where to find one. Penzance did not look large, and its selection of shops matched it in size. A milliner's, a haberdasher's, a well-stocked fishmonger's as you'd expect of a fishing village, a small iron monger's, a butcher's, a shoemaker's, a tobacconist, and a plethora of inns and taverns, or so it seemed. But no sign of an apothecary.

A number of people were promenading in the street, each with a purposeful air, but from their clothing, most of them must be of the working class, and Caroline was not sure they'd be the ones to ask. She was saved the effort by Yves, who suddenly yanked his hand out of hers with a high-pitched squeal, and bolted across the road, narrowly missing being run over by a heavy dray.

Where on earth was he going?

Caroline waited for the dray to pass then crossed the road with more decorum only to find her young charge in the embrace of a stern-faced older lady. This lady, dressed in somber dark brown and with a plain shawl drawn about her shoulders, released Yves and straightened up, a wary look in her brown eyes. Her mousy hair was streaked with gray.

Caroline studied her for a moment. Average height and on the scrawny side, with a fiercely straight back and a look of taking no nonsense about her, she nevertheless possessed the sparkle of real tears in her eyes. And as she straightened, she took Yves's hand in hers. A touch possessive.

Yves was bouncing on his feet with excitement. "Caroline! This is Miss Hawkins. My old governess. Isn't it wonderful that we chanced to see one another?" He hopped up and down, beaming up at the woman. "I didn't think I'd ever see you again, Hawkie. Aunt Ruth told me you'd gone to London on the stagecoach to take up a new position." His mouth down turned. "Why didn't you come to say goodbye to me?"

Miss Hawkins held out her free hand to Caroline. "I take it you must be the new governess?"

Was there a hint of distrust in her tone? Caroline took the offered hand and nodded. "Caroline Fairfield, from Wiltshire." She herself felt a strong wariness for this woman, although quite why, she couldn't be certain. Almost as though trouble hovered around her in an invisible miasma.

However, Miss Hawkins's hand in Caroline's was strong and the grip firm. "Imogen Hawkins."

An awkward silence ensued.

Oh well, she might as well ask Miss Hawkins as anyone else. At least if the woman had been dismissed by Mrs. Treloar, she wasn't likely to report back anything about Caroline's enquiries. Caroline cleared her throat. "I'm looking for an apothecary's. Surely there must be one in a town this size?"

Miss Hawkins's eyes narrowed and she glanced quickly down at Yves who was still staring up at her in childish awe. It was clear how much he cared for her, and from the softening of Miss Hawkins's severe face, it seemed she cared for him as well. And she appeared to have been dismissed for wanting to keep him safer than she felt he was being kept. Which in itself was odd.

"Crago's is just around the corner from the Star. Down New Street." Her eyebrows rose. "Might I enquire what it is you need? I might have something I can give you."

This was so clearly a probe, Caroline had to smile. "Nothing for me, nor Yves. I merely wanted to enquire about something I… came across the other day. I wanted to know what was in it."

Miss Hawkins, still holding Yves by the hand, gestured with her other hand to Caroline in the direction of the Star. "I'll show you where it is." She began to walk, her steps unhurried, as though she wanted to elicit more information from Caroline en route.

Caroline might as well try. "I was wondering," she began, walking side by side with Miss Hawkins and keeping her voice down low lest any passersby should hear, or Yves. However, he was staring in at the shop windows as they passed. "I was wondering if, in your life as a governess, you might have heard of something called Dalby's Carminative?"

Miss Hawkins stopped dead. "Dalby's Carminative?"

Yves was craning his neck to look at a pair of dogs fighting over some scraps.

Caroline nodded quickly. "Yes."

"And where did you 'come across' this the other day?"

Why did Caroline get the impression this astute woman already knew the answer to her question. "In the nursery nurse's bedroom. Bridget's room. Locked in her corner cabinet above her washstand."

Miss Hawkins gave an emphatic nod. "It's as I feared. They're trying it again."

Caroline swallowed. "Trying what?"

Miss Hawkins met her gaze. "Not here. Come back to where I'm staying and I'll tell you there."

$$\cdots\!\circledcirc\!\text{\ding{96}}\!\circledcirc\!\cdots$$

Chapter Thirteen

M ISS HAWKINS'S HOUSE lay down a side street whose distant end gave a narrow view of the blue of the sea. Set back from the lane, it proved to be a substantial house with front and rear walled gardens and enough windows to indicate it possessed three floors. She opened the front door and ushered them into a long, tiled hallway. "Come into the parlor. I have it to myself, so no one will disturb us in there."

Caroline and Yves followed her into a fussily feminine parlor furnished with old-fashioned pieces and a surfeit of china ornaments and faded oil paintings of children, dogs, and horses.

Miss Hawkins turned to Yves. "Could you go down the corridor to the kitchen at the back of the house and give Mrs. Penrose, the cook, a message for me, do you think?"

He nodded with enthusiasm.

"Ask her to bring a tray of tea to the parlor and to give you some of her wonderful fruit cake. You can eat it in there with her so you won't get crumbs on the floor in here."

Yves vacated the parlor with alacrity at the suggestion of fruit cake being on offer.

Miss Hawkins turned back to Caroline. "Mrs. Penrose has grandchildren of her own and is very fond of little boys and knows how to feed them. He'll be quite safe with her. Do sit down, Miss Fairfield."

Safe? Miss Hawkins's choice of words set alarm bells ringing. Caroline sat on one of the stiffly upholstered chairs, folding her hands in her lap.

Miss Hawkins also took a seat, perching on the edge of hers and leaning forwards, her brow furrowed in concern. She licked her thin lips. "I expect you're wondering why I invited you back here."

There didn't seem to be an answer to this, so Caroline remained silent, waiting for her to go on.

"As you've gathered, I was Yves's and Hetty's governess until just over a week ago."

Caroline nodded.

Miss Hawkins waved a hand around the crowded parlor. "This isn't my home. This is my place of employment. I hold the position of companion to an elderly, bedridden lady, Mrs. Bristow."

Again, Caroline just nodded.

"I've been praying that something might bring whoever the Treloars hired as a new governess for the children into Penzance, but I could never have hoped you'd come so soon." She clasped her thin hands, fingers intertwining, and two spots of bright color flared on her cheeks. "This is difficult for me to say. Please hear me out before you dismiss what I have to tell you as mad." She held Caroline's gaze. "When I was dismissed, Mrs. Treloar made certain I could have no contact with the children before I left. She had me pack my bags immediately and Young Pascoe drove me into Penzance in the pony cart. I told him I'd be catching the stagecoach up to London to find employment there. But I didn't. I stayed a night in the Star and heard Mrs. Bristow needed a nurse-companion. I applied, and this is where that led me."

Did this have something to do with the bottle of medicine Caroline had found? A bottle Miss Hawkins seemed as though she might be familiar with. Caroline nodded to Miss Hawkins to keep going.

"I didn't want to be far from Roskilly. I couldn't just abandon

Yves to his fate."

Caroline's eyes widened. The nagging worry she'd been feeling almost since she'd arrived at Roskilly began to coalesce into a real fear. "What fate do you mean?"

Miss Hawkins leaned further forward. "He's in terrible danger, Miss Fairfield. Old Sir Hugh can't leave his bed to keep him safe any longer. He's nearly ninety years old and is tended only by the nurse Mrs. Treloar hired. The nurse who used to work in an asylum and is in her pay. His rooms were where I first found a bottle of laudanum. In Sir Hugh's dressing room, where the nurse sleeps." She glanced over her shoulder as though, even in the safety of the parlor, she imagined someone might be creeping up behind to listen. "My suspicions were aroused because lately every time I took Yves to see his grandfather, whom he loves, the old man was either sleeping, or so sleepy he could hardly speak."

"So who exactly is in danger? Do you mean Sir Hugh or Yves?"

Footsteps sounded in the hallway.

"They both are."

The door opened and Yves came in, telltale crumbs around his mouth, closely followed by a rotund woman in a voluminous apron. She set down the tea tray she was carrying on the low table between the chairs. "Shall I take young Master Yves back with me to see the cat's kittens?" she asked, with no preamble.

Miss Hawkins nodded. "That would be lovely. Thank you, Mrs. Penrose. But mind he doesn't try to take one home with him. They're too young to leave their mother yet."

Yves danced out of the room with the cook, and his voice, raised in question about the kittens, vanished down the hall.

Miss Hawkins poured two dishes of tea and handed one to Caroline.

Caroline took a sip but it was still too hot to drink. "Do you mean someone is trying to poison Sir Hugh with a laudanum overdose? Or just keep him sleepy and biddable? I've not met him as yet."

Miss Hawkins nodded. "Both, in all likelihood. But that's not all." She glanced over her shoulder again. "Mrs. Treloar asked Hester, who was the head nursery nurse, and who was in charge of getting Yves to bed after his supper, to dose him with Dalby's Carminative. The same thing you mentioned. She said it was for his digestion and to help him sleep. Hester came to me because she was worried about giving him anything she didn't think he needed, and because she was my friend. I've been caring for him now since he was five years old, so I know him well. He's always been an energetic child in the daytime, and consequently has slept very well at night, woken early and been alert and lively. But three nights of being dosed with the carminative, and he was waking late and half asleep all morning, learning nothing."

"He was like that this morning."

Miss Hawkins pressed her lips together. "I spoke to Mrs. Treloar about it, and she ordered Hester to go to work in the kitchen after nursery supper. Bridget was to put Yves to bed from then on. And Bridget had no qualms about administering the carminative."

"What's in it?"

"Opium, or you might say laudanum. Not a particularly high dose, I've found out, as it's meant for babies and small children, not big boys of nine. But I don't think she was only giving him the carminative. I think she was adding extra laudanum to the bottle. Laudanum from the supply in Sir Hugh's room."

Cold fear traced a finger down Caroline's spine. Could this all be true? After all, why would Miss Hawkins lie to her? Children were astute judges of character, and Yves appeared very fond of her. He surely wouldn't be fond of a madwoman. Might she be right? "Today is the only day he's been like this."

"Perhaps, with no one to blame—and blame someone is what they intend to do—they decided to wait until a new scapegoat had arrived at Roskilly."

"A scapegoat?"

"Yes."

"You mean *me*?" Caroline's voice rose in alarm. "You mean they're planning to poison Yves and blame it on me?"

"Yes. I'm almost certain they intended to blame me when I was there, but I questioned the medication. I questioned some of the other things they were doing with Yves. The things Mrs. Treloar was allowing him to do. Jan Trefusis, the land agent, lets him do whatever he wants in the farmyard. Riding on loaded wagons, running in and out of the barns where the men are working, climbing unsafe trees. Going off by himself. Half the time I couldn't find him because he'd be down in the home farmyard. Or out on the cliffs, looking for birds' nests. At the suggestion of Trefusis."

What had Hetty said? That he was always getting into scrapes and her mother never cared? Of course. Why would she care if he did dangerous things? She wouldn't if she wanted him dead. And if he didn't die by accident while out playing unchecked, then he could be seen to have died at the hands of his governess, who'd wanted him biddable and quiet... and drugged. The woman employed to take care of him who could be shown to have complained about his boisterousness. "Who is Trefusis? I haven't met him yet? I mean—what sort of a man?"

"A ruthless one. Only he intends to *have* his Ruth." Miss Hawkins's eyes filled with venom. "A man with his eye for the main chance. He's after Mrs. Treloar, you mark my words. And he intends her to inherit everything from old Sir Hugh. I'm certain. I wouldn't trust that man as far as I could throw him. Not one inch."

A desire to see this Jan Trefusis for herself assailed Caroline, to discover what manner of man he was and assess the danger to Yves. Although encouraging a child to be daring and court danger was not the same as trying to poison him with laudanum. "If you don't mind me asking, why did Mrs. Treloar dismiss you?"

Miss Hawkins sighed. "Because I argued with her about Yves's care. Because she realized I had surmised her intentions and had discovered she'd ordered Bridget to dose him with the carminative. Because she could see she wouldn't be able to blame me if something happened to him."

Caroline swallowed. "And now you're saying she's going to blame me?"

Miss Hawkins nodded. "She is."

Caroline set down her tea, untouched. "And why is she doing this?"

"The oldest and most obvious of reasons. To do away with the rightful heir so she can inherit the title and money."

"But her son…"

Miss Hawkins's eyes widened. "Her son?"

An image of that scarred and angry face rose up before Caroline. "Yes. Her son. Major Nathaniel Treloar. He returned to Treloar the day after I arrived. He's back from the war."

"Hetty's brother? I thought he was dead."

Caroline frowned. "Very much not dead. And I presume that if Yves were to die, he would stand to inherit the estate and mines from his grandfather some time in the near future. Not Mrs. Treloar or Hetty."

"He would indeed, which would scupper Trefusis's ambitions. This is interesting news. Tell me. What is he like?"

What was he like? Caroline's brow furrowed. "Damaged. He has a terrible scar down the right side of his face and is missing two fingers from his right hand. But I don't mean he's damaged in that way. I mean it feels as though his very soul is damaged. Almost as though he has no soul. When you see his eyes, they're as blue as Yves's, but blank. Dead. I've met soldiers before. Indeed, I once fancied myself in love with a handsome young lieutenant, but he never came back from the war. But those that do come back, they're changed. I would say Major Treloar has probably been changed a lot by his experiences."

"I never met him in the time I taught the children," Miss Hawkins said. "I believe he took up a commission straight from Harrow. I have no knowledge of him at all, but was under the impression he'd died in Spain a year ago. Although, if he were to be anything like Hetty, he would not be like his mother at all."

"He's not like Hetty. You can be sure of that. But I don't think he's anything like his mother, either, from what little I've seen of both of them. Perhaps he takes after his father, the late Mr. Treloar?"

"He may well do. I have no idea. Mr. Treloar died before my time at Treloar. A nasty business as far as I can gather."

"What happened?"

"The son was home from school and his father took him down Wheal Jenny to see the workings. So I was told. Old Pascoe the coachman is a good source of information. Sir Hugh and Mr. Treloar both believed the boy should learn the business from the ground up. They were in one of the adits when there was a cave in. The miners shore up the roofs with wood but there's a lot of rubble on top. Ten miners were caught in the roof fall. Mr. Treloar was killed and the boy escaped with a broken arm. Old Pascoe told me he was never the same after the accident. Went back to school, then, as soon as he could, persuaded his grandfather to purchase him a commission. Couldn't wait to get away from Roskilly."

Caroline bit her lip. She'd been right in counseling Hetty to sympathy for her brother. Not only had war been unkind to him, but so had his boyhood here in Cornwall. No wonder he was so dour and silent.

She looked back at Miss Hawkins. "Do you think he might be a danger to Yves as well?"

Miss Hawkins pursed her lips. "I don't know. When did he return?"

"Only a few days ago."

"Then he can't be a part of the plot to poison Yves because it was in place before his return."

"No, but he would be the recipient of the good fortune his mother wants."

"That won't please Trefusis. He won't want someone stepping between him and his rich heiress."

Caroline swallowed. "What do you want me to do?"

"Keep Yves safe."

Caroline shivered. "I don't know how I can do that if his aunt and this Trefusis are determined to do away with him." How awful and doom laden those words sounded. She was one person, up against at least two very determined people who wanted to remove the obstacle to their inheritance. Should she really include Nat in that bracket as well? Did he look the sort of man who would see a child killed to smooth his way to money and position? But if Nat inherited from his grandfather, Trefusis would get nothing... What a tangled web was being woven at Roskilly.

But Nat had resigned his commission, and without the inheritance, what would he do? If Yves were gone, he wouldn't need to leave Roskilly ever again. Wouldn't need to hide his scars away whenever he went out in public, as he seemed determined to do. He could just inherit the estate and mines when his grandfather died, and, up until then, he could help manage them. And push Trefusis out of his job. Why wouldn't he want Yves removed?

THE MAN IN question was at that very moment riding over to the Coach and Horses to return the cob Bosun to his friend Jacka. He rode his mother's rather aged bay mare, and led Bosun by his reins, as he jog-trotted up the rutted back track Caroline had so recently struggled down.

With the sky only sparsely decorated with clouds, a warm sun heated his back, and from the trees and bushes to either side came the song of small hedge birds, a sound he'd longed for during all those years of soldiering in arid Spain. Despite the drizzle of yesterday, the track wasn't too bad, and the two horses had no difficulty negotiating the route.

For the first time in many years, the urge to whistle came

over Nat.

He rode around to the rear of the inn, where he came upon Jacka splitting logs with a hefty axe. As soon as he spotted his returning friend, he straightened up, the considerable pile lying to one side of the splitting block indicating his industry.

Nat swung down from the bay and held out Bosun's reins. "I said I'd return him, and here he is. Thank you for the loan. How goes it?" Somehow, he didn't feel the same reticence with Jacka he felt with everyone else he met. Maybe it was their boyhood relationship, or perhaps because he knew that Jacka, as the son of a gardener rather than a scion of any of the local wealthy families, had always accepted him for who he was.

Jacka leaned the axe against the splitting log, and held out a work-roughened hand. "Business is good. Two coaches in today." He nodded to where a phaeton stood in one corner of the yard. "And two young men who decided my ale was of the best and have chosen to stay the night."

Nat shook hands. "I'll not go in then. I've no taste for meeting strangers and letting them stare at me. I can do without their pity… or their revulsion."

Jacka nodded, taking Bosun's reins. "Shall I fetch you out a tankard of porter?"

Nat allowed himself a smile. "That would be welcome. I'll tie Duchess in one of your stalls, if I may?"

The two men led the horses into the long stable block, where two matched chestnuts, who must be the phaeton's team, were pulling hay from their hayracks and swishing their tails at the few flies. Jacka slipped saddle and bridle off Bosun, but Nat only took Duchess's bridle off, making it easier for her to chew the hay in her manger, and loosened her girth a couple of notches.

Jacka departed into the back door of the inn, to return a few minutes later with two tankards of the promised porter. They perched side by side on the edge of the well in the center of the yard, the sun on their backs.

"How'd you find being back home, then?" Jacka asked. He'd

never been one to hedge around a subject.

Nat wiped his mouth on his sleeve. "Odd."

Jacka grinned. "I daresay. Eleven years is a long time."

"Time doesn't stand still, no matter how much you'd like it to."

They both drank some more, Nat watching a pair of buzzards riding high above the inn on a thermal. He envied them their freedom. "I'm back to feeling trapped."

Jacka was silent a few moments. "Like before?"

"Yes."

"Not fallin' over themselves to kill the fatted calf for you, then?"

Nat shook his head. "Hetty was pleased to see me. But my mother… well, she could barely conceal her disgust at this." He touched his fingers to his scar. "It was good to see my grandfather, and Aunt Agnes. Although she thought I was my late Uncle Robert come back. Her mind's going."

"D'you see the little heir?"

"I did. A precocious child. And his new governess." Why he'd mentioned her, he had no idea. The image of her ingenuous smile after she'd beaten him at chess had leapt into his head and the words had followed in its wake.

"I did hear as how they sacked the last one. What's this one like? Starchy old spinster?"

Nat frowned. "Well, you got part of that correct. She's a spinster, but she's not old. Well, she's younger than me, I'd say, so not so young as all that." He shook himself. "I'll concede she must be a clever woman, so that bodes well for the boy."

"I saw 'em drive past in the pony cart, not so long ago," Jacka said. "Headed toward Penzance, they was. First time I've seen the lad. I'd heard he were a sickly brat, but he reminded me of you, he did. And you were never sick a day in your life, I don't think."

Nat's mouth, or rather half of it, curved in a smile. "It's a long time since I had golden curls."

Jacka set down his empty tankard. "Didn't see much of her,

though. Had a bonnet on hiding her face."

Nat shook his head. "There's something about her… I'm not sure what it is, but she intrigues me. A little. She's clearly well educated and intelligent, and yet she's down here in the depths of Cornwall, teaching one small boy." He straightened up. "She's a mystery I don't intend to waste my time in solving, however. And now I'd best be heading home." He shrugged. "Home. It doesn't quite sit right with me as yet to call Roskilly home. Not after all this time. I feel like I've been washed up on a beach at high tide, just a piece of flotsam on the water of life. And I don't fit in."

Jacka clapped him on the back. "Give it time. You'll feel more at home soon. And whenever you need to escape, there's room here for you. We can get drunk together."

Chapter Fourteen

CAROLINE REMEMBERED, JUST in time, to go into the small haberdashery and choose some pretty ribbons to augment the gown she intended to wear to the coming ball. *If* Mrs. Treloar didn't change her mind and still allowed her to go. She also bought some to give to Patience in return for her help with dressing in the mornings. Then she and Yves found New Street and the little apothecary's shop. While Yves gazed around at the jars and bottles in wonder, Caroline bought a large bottle of herb tonic which the apothecary allowed her to sniff first and assured her contained not a drop of opium and was merely intended to improve the health of the person who took it. Perfect.

"What's that for?" Yves asked as they headed back to the Star to retrieve Blossom and the pony cart.

Caroline glanced round at the people on the street, any of whom might be an acquaintance of Mrs. Treloar or the house servants. "I'll explain on our way home. Best not to discuss it here." She stowed the cumbersome bottle in the capacious bag she'd had the foresight to bring.

The boy at the Star harnessed Blossom up for them and received a silver sixpence for his trouble, which went a long way to cheering him up. Probably whatever wages the owner of the Star paid for his services went straight to his father, and he saw none of it. He tipped his jaunty tricorn hat to Caroline as she and Yves climbed back into the little cart, and Yves gave him a cheery wave, one small boy to another.

Once they left the outskirts of Penzance behind and had crossed back over the stony ford, Yves returned to his earlier question, blue eyes brimming with curiosity. "Why didn't you want to tell me about your medicine when we were on the street?" Not a child to miss a trick.

Caroline clicked to Blossom to hurry her trot a little, mindful that time was getting on, and turned to regard her charge. "Because we might have been overheard."

He frowned and fell silent for a moment or two, clearly thinking hard. "Who did you fear might overhear us?"

Pursing her lips, Caroline guided Blossom and the cart around a particularly dangerous looking pothole. "Anyone who might know someone at Roskilly."

Yves shifted in his seat. "Why would that be bad?" But he didn't sound shocked. Had he picked up on the undercurrent there, or had Miss Hawkins's fears transmitted to him at some point?

However, Caroline couldn't risk sharing her thoughts with him. She'd have to be circumspect in her reply. "I don't want anyone to know I've bought this medicine. Although it's not medicine in truth. It's just extracts of harmless plants and some sugar water that might or might not make you a little healthier. Although I doubt it very much. But it won't do you any harm, which is what's most important."

He was not going to let this go. "For me? Why don't you want anyone to know?"

Caroline bit her lip. She'd have to tell him. "You know that medicine Bridget gave you last night?"

"Yes. It was horrible. I didn't like it. She poured it into a glass, and I had to drink it all down, *she* said. Or she was going to hold my nose and make me."

"Well, that was what made you so very sleepy this morning."

"Was it? I had a horrible headache too, but it's gone now.

Bridget gave it to me before, when Miss Hawkins was still my governess. Then she stopped."

"I'm not surprised you had a headache." The road was now running past St Michael's Mount, where a stony causeway was just being revealed by the falling tide. "I don't think you need that medicine, do you?"

He frowned. "Don't I? Bridget said the doctor left it for me because I have nightmares. To help me sleep."

"Nightmares? I didn't know. Do you?"

He shrugged. "Sometimes. Not very often. Hester used to come in and cuddle me when I had one, until I went back to sleep again. Hester was nice. *Much* nicer than Bridget." He paused. "Bridget's horrible."

Caroline forbore nodding, despite agreeing with him on that one. "Well, I don't think you should be taking that nasty medicine. For a start, you weren't awake enough this morning to learn anything in your lessons. So *that's* no good. But Bridget won't stop giving it to you, I'm sure, even if I ask her to. I won't be able to stop her." She patted his arm. "So, I've bought this new medicine to replace it with, and hopefully Bridget won't know I've done it. She'll keep on giving you this new medicine and not know the difference."

A broad smile lit his face. "Yes please. I hope it tastes better than the other one."

Caroline returned his smile. "I think it will, but you'll have to pretend it tastes bad to fool Bridget, and complain about having to take it. Do you think you can do that?"

Yves nodded with enthusiasm.

"And perhaps pretend to be sleepy in the mornings when you see her? So she doesn't get suspicious."

Another delighted nod. "Of course I can do that. It'll be fun." His eyes sparkled with mischief at the idea of gulling Bridget. "She deserves to be tricked."

AT ROSKILLY, SUPPER was just arriving in the schoolroom, on a tray carried by Patience, as they arrived, a bit flushed and breathless from their rush up from the stableyard. But it was only a single boiled egg and bread and butter—enough for just one person.

Patience bobbed a curtsey to Caroline, eyes wide with awe. "If you please, Miss Fairfield, but Mrs. Treloar sent up word that you was to come down to dinner with the family. She says at six o'clock."

"Unlucky you," Yves said, sitting down at the table in front of his supper.

What? Why on earth had Mrs. Treloar suddenly decided on this? All sorts of thoughts jostled through Caroline's head but she couldn't come up with a viable reason. "Goodness. That's short notice. I'll need to change into a gown suitable for dinner. Can you come and help me, Patience?" As the clock in the schoolroom declared the time to be five and twenty minutes to six, she didn't have long to prepare for this new ordeal.

Leaving Yves tucking into his boiled egg, Caroline and Patience retired to Caroline's room.

Caroline threw open her wardrobe. What a good thing she'd packed as many of her gowns as possible, the heavy weight of her valises now fully justified. She plucked out a demure, pale-blue gown with short, puffed sleeves for which she had matching gloves, and a lace fichu to disguise a decolletage that would be unseemly in a governess.

"Oooh, that's very pretty, Miss." Patience's work-reddened hands smoothed the elegant silk of the skirt. "I wish I had a dress like this one."

With Patience's over-enthusiastic assistance, Caroline took off her plain daygown and stepped into the fresh evening one. But her hair needed something done with it, and this was where

Patience's skills came to an end. Her hairdressing talents seemed to be confined to the single plait that hung down her back. Caroline would have to manage by herself.

She made an effort that at best might have been deemed barely satisfactory by her old lady's maid, but at least her hair was now tidy after getting windblown on their journey back from Penzance. She tucked her customary spare hairpin into her bodice, pulled on her long gloves and rose to her feet, smoothing down her skirts much as Patience had done. "Will I do?"

Patience nodded with proprietorial vigor. "You look a right picture, Miss." She leaned in close to sniff the perfume Caroline had dabbed on. "And you smell like a flower garden."

Not quite, but she could produce nothing better in the short time allotted to her.

Patience took a step back the better to admire what she plainly considered her own handiwork. "A lot nicer than Mrs. Treloar ever do look. Even when she's preening herself for that Mr. Trefusis."

Caroline, choosing to pretend she hadn't heard Patience's disrespectful remark, stepped out onto the corridor… and remembered she hadn't swapped the two medicine bottles over. Her heart skipped a beat. She couldn't leave the bottle still holding what might prove to be a fatal dose for a small boy. Bridget might just be sloshing it into a glass, careless of how much she administered. Suddenly, she felt like Daniel going into the lion's den in the Bible, which, despite its danger, had always been one of her favorite stories. Only she was *living* in the lion's den. Now she knew how he'd felt.

"Where is Bridget?"

Patience was tidying up Caroline's discarded gown and ankle boots. "Downstairs a-having her supper."

She had to do it now while she had the opportunity. Her bag was still in the schoolroom. If she went now, Bridget wouldn't know. "You go down and get your own supper, quickly," she said to Patience. "Yves will be fine on his own for a short while. I'll just go in and tell him to play with his soldiers. Off you go." Did she sound as stilted and tense as she felt? Maybe Patience would think it because she was afraid of taking dinner with the family, which she was, in a way.

Patience fetched Yves's supper tray, only the well-scraped-out eggshell remaining, and departed along the corridor.

Caroline bolted first into the schoolroom to retrieve her bag, then hurried into the nursery, where Yves was lying on the floor drawing.

She didn't have time to waste. "Quick. Go to the door and watch through a crack for Bridget coming back while I swap the medicines over."

Yves jumped straight into the swing of this adventure, all unaware that it might be saving his life, and ran to the door. Opening it a crack, he peered outside. "All clear."

Caroline fished the bottle of tonic out of her bag and hurried to Bridget's door.

Yves glanced back at her. "I'll hoot like an owl if I see anyone coming."

Possibly not his best idea. Caroline hastened to the bed and lifted Bridget's pillow.

The key wasn't there.

For a dreadful moment, the world seemed to stand still around Caroline, the air thick and difficult to breathe. Had Bridget realized her room had been searched and hidden the key elsewhere, or worse still, secreted it about her person? She heaved in a steadying breath and tried to gather her thoughts. It *must* still be here somewhere, surely? Bridget hadn't taken it with her before.

As fast as she could, she repeated her earlier search. Nothing. A glance back at the door showed Yves still peering out of it. Any minute now, Bridget would be returning, and, on top of that, if she delayed any longer, she'd be late for dinner with the family and be thought rude and ungrateful.

She scanned the room again, but no inspiration came to her.

Could Bridget have decided to keep the key on her person? On a string around her neck, maybe?

Something small caught her eye, almost underneath the spartan bed. Three strides took her to it, and, bending down, she rose with the key in her hand. It must have fallen out from under the pillow somehow.

She threw a glance at Yves, still standing guard, as she ran to the corner cupboard and with shaking fingers opened it. The bottle stood there, the name *Dalby's* embossed in large letters down the front, with underneath that, in much smaller lettering, *Carminative*. Where to empty it?

The sash window didn't want to open. So much for letting fresh air into the nursery. She heaved at it with all her strength, and at last, just when she was about to give up, it slid up a scant three inches. Enough to slide the offending bottle through and tip the contents onto the flowerbed below.

"Someone's coming," Yves called. "I heard the door from the gallery open."

Her fingers shook so much she nearly couldn't do it. A quick rinse out with some of the contents of her new bottle, a second emptying, and she was filling the bottle as Yves disappeared through the door out onto the corridor.

Stopper back in the old bottle, new bottle into her bag, old bottle back into the cupboard, and key turned in the lock. Close the window. It stuck, but superhuman strength came to her. If her heart beat any more violently, it was going to come bouncing out of her mouth.

She returned the key to the floor by the bed and hurried into the nursery. Outside in the corridor, she heard Yves's voice raised in complaint. "But I'd like to go outside and play for a while with Dash. He gets lonely down in the kitchens at night. I need to give him his supper."

Bridget's strident tones rose above his. "You know you ain't allowed downstairs after you've et your supper, Master Yves. And that dog ain't allowed up here, neither. Not at nights."

What to do with the bag and the empty bottle?

"Miss Hawkins and Hester used to let him sleep on my bed."

"And look where that got them. I need my job, and I'm not lettin' you bring that smelly dog upstairs. That's final."

In his toy chest. She lifted the lid, moved some of his soldiers to one side, and slid the bag and bottle under them.

"Grandfather would let me have him up here." The sound of a stamped foot. "One day this is all going to be mine, Bridget, and *then* you'll be sorry."

"That's what you think," Bridget snapped at him. "Now, get out of my way. I've all the work up here to do because that lazy girl, Patience, is downstairs eating her supper."

Caroline, eyes widening at Bridget's first remark, lowered the lid and drew in another deep breath in an effort to compose herself. She stepped out onto the corridor. "Yves, come back in here to play. I have to go down to dinner now. Bridget will look after you."

Yves, who'd been standing halfway along the corridor facing Bridget down, gave an eloquent shrug of his shoulders and a deep sigh, the little dramatist he was. "All right. But tomorrow can I have Dash in the schoolroom with me?"

Caroline stalked past Bridget, who was giving her a suspicious stare. "We shall see. But right now, no arguing. Off you go with Bridget. Good night."

DOWNSTAIRS IN THE drawing room, Nat's mother was tapping her foot with impatience, something that irritated him no end.

Aunt Agnes, dressed as she might have done as a middle-aged woman forty years ago, perched in a stiffly upholstered chair beside the hearth. With her cheeks alarmingly rouged and permanently surprised eyebrows penciled in, she had an amused twinkle in the eyes she had fixed on her late nephew's wife.

But the person who was most annoying Nat right now stood by the fireplace, one arm resting negligently on the mantelpiece, a confident smile on his face that made him look as though he owned the room. No, as though he *thought* he owned the room. Jan Trefusis, the land agent, who plainly felt as though his position was a sight higher than it actually was.

A heavy-set man of about forty, he had thick dark hair with only a hint of gray and a dark shadow of beard on his square jaw. He filled out every inch of his well-cut tailcoat and breeches in a way that might one day soon lead to fat. And his face matched this, being wide and coarse featured, with fleshy lips and heavy brows. He had a glass of whisky in his hand and had been holding forth, a tad ironically, on the merits of allowing governesses to eat with the family.

Which was one of the reasons Nat was having to fight to suppress a strong inclination to draw his cork. Planting him a facer and then throwing him out, perhaps without bothering to open the window first, seemed more attractive by the second.

Trefusis shut up at last, and Mrs. Treloar bestowed a forbidding glare on Hetty. "I don't know why I allowed you and Nat to persuade me to invite Yves's governess, of all people, to dine with us. She clearly has no manners whatsoever. If dinner is at six, I expect those who are to dine to be here by five minutes before the hour, at least. This is *not* good enough."

Nat, standing by the window, remained silent, despite having earlier joined Hetty in her plan to invite Caroline to join them for dinner. He glanced sideways at the ormolu clock on the mantelpiece whose minute hand was only just past the twelve.

Hetty must have also noticed. "It's only one minute after six, Mama. And she *was* given very little time to dress, having been out all afternoon. Would you have wanted her to present herself all windblown and untidy in a day dress?"

Mrs. Treloar raised a sharp eyebrow, homing in with her usual acuity on the nub of what Hetty had just said. "Out?" Her voice rose. "Where has she been out *to*? And who was looking after the boy while she was out?"

Hetty had the grace to look guilty. Maybe Miss Fairfield had asked her not to say what she'd been up to. "Er, Yves went with her, Mama."

Nat had been used to his mother's rages from boyhood, but he'd forgotten about them, or time had diminished them for him. He was about to be treated to a reminder. "She took the boy out with her? How? Where to? What for?" Mrs. Treloar's voice continued to rise with every utterance. Nat resisted the impulse to cover his ears. Trefusis watched the scene with a curl of satisfaction on his thick lips.

Aunt Agnes chuckled, sounding more than ever like an old witch.

Hetty shrank. "She wanted to go into Penzance to buy ribbons for the dress she's to wear to the ball at Carlyon Court." By contrast, her voice, usually so buoyant, diminished and trailed off at the end of the sentence. She studied her gloved hands as though they were the most interesting thing in the room.

Their mother swelled like a bullfrog about to sing. "And *who* gave her permission to take my nephew into Penzance?"

It was at this moment that Caroline entered the room. Nat made a smart bow to her, noticing that Trefusis did as well, his insolent gaze running over the curves of Caroline's body and renewing Nat's itch to plant him one on the nose. At least she looked a sight less dowdy than when he'd first seen her, dressed now in a presentable plain blue gown with a demure lace fichu concealing her neckline. Nothing remotely special about her, and yet an air of calm competence hung about her that was undeniably attractive. No. Wait. What was he thinking? Had he been away from women so long that he was harboring feelings for the hired help? Nat turned away to stare out of the window in the direction of the out-of-sight sea.

His mother kept going, unabashed by any pretense at manners, nor by the irony of having accused Miss Fairfield of lacking them. "Tell me, Miss Fairfield." Her icy tones sliced through the air. "Who gave you leave to take my nephew into Penzance today?"

This was ridiculous. Why shouldn't the woman take the boy out with her if she wanted to? Neither of them were prisoners here. He'd gone out enough as a boy, not that she'd known about many of his excursions. Well, very few of them, in truth.

"I did," Nat said, without turning around. "I thought the boy should get some fresh air and a trip out would interest him."

A stunned silence met this declaration, apart from another maniacal chuckle from Aunt Agnes. No doubt Miss Fairfield was wondering why he'd lied to his mother. God alone knew what his mother was thinking.

She turned her wrath on him with an ease born of years of getting her own way. "You should have consulted me first, Nathaniel. Supposing there'd been an accident? What then? Supposing there was disease in Penzance and the boy caught it and brought it back here?" That last was most probably more due to the worry that if Yves did bring back sickness he might share it about.

"The boy needs to take a few chances," Nat said, smiling inwardly at his mother's uncharacteristic concern for the child. Anyone would think she didn't want anyone outside of Roskilly to set eyes on him. "If he's to be made a man of, that is. And a trip in a pony cart to Penzance hardly constitutes a danger to man nor beast." He turned around. "Now, shall we go into dinner?"

Chapter Fifteen

THE DINING ROOM at Roskilly was much like the rest of the main house: elegantly furnished in the height of fashion. Or at least Caroline supposed it must be. Nothing like her old home of Cadley Grange, with its oak paneled walls and the well-polished furniture her great grandparents had probably purchased. No. She mustn't think about that. Too painful.

The long table that stood on an enormous Persian rug had been laid for six, but not in any sociable fashion. The places were spaced out along its length with Mrs. Treloar occupying the seat at the head of the table that must have once been Sir Hugh's. She had Trefusis close by on her left, with a long gap to where Nat was to sit halfway down one side, while Hetty, Caroline, and Aunt Agnes had seats to her right. None were close enough for quiet conversation.

Caroline had not been in the dining room before, and she had to admit it pleased the eye, with its pale-green walls and exquisite ornamental plasterwork on the ceiling and the delicate cornice at the top of the walls. Despite daylight still ruling outside, the heavy curtains had already been drawn over the windows and a row of silver candlesticks stood down the center of the table. These had been lit, although no fire burned in the grate despite the unseasonable chill in the room.

She kept her eyes averted from Mr. Trefusis, unnerved by the insolence in his gaze, and not wanting to give him the pleasure of knowing how it affected her. She was better than that, but tonight was not a night for staring down his challenge. Tonight was a night for meek obedience and knowing her own place in the hierarchy of the house. Although it didn't look as though he knew his too well.

When they'd all taken their seats, and the soup had been served, Mrs. Treloar turned to Mr. Trefusis. "Did you manage to extract the rent from the Hammetts at Carnwynnen Farm, as I asked?"

Caroline glanced across the table at Nat but he appeared to be concentrating on his soup. Business seemed an odd thing to discuss at a family dinner. Although it wasn't really one of those, with her and Trefusis present.

Trefusis possessed such dark eyes they might well have been black, enhanced by the overhang of his heavy brow. "I did... *Ma'am*, and with the minimum of threat."

The slight emphasis on the "ma'am" had Caroline wondering if in private he dispensed with it, and wanted to hint at this. Perhaps he wanted them to guess that his relationship with his employer was more than it should have been. The thought sent a shiver of revulsion down her spine. For whose benefit had he done this? Hers or Nat's? Most likely Nat's. After all, now Nat was home, would Trefusis be able to justify his job? Surely, Nat could now do that. Trefusis would be keen to let Nat know he had the upper hand here, and would be hard to dislodge.

"Good." Mrs. Treloar spooned up her soup, her spoon chinking on the china. "We can't have anyone thinking they can plead poverty, as they did with my father-in-law and husband, and get away with not paying their dues."

Nat set down his own spoon, his jaw hardening. "My father would rather have seen the Hammetts' children with food in their bellies than forced them to pay what they can't afford."

His mother fixed him with a cold stare. "And look where that got him."

Nat's cheeks colored, his hand twitched and his lips formed a tight line.

Caroline glanced at Hetty, but she had her head bent over her bowl as though she didn't want any part of this.

Nat's brows lowered, but even so were nowhere near as low as Trefusis's. He glared at his mother. "At least he didn't have the empty bellies of children on his conscience when he died. And he died amongst his own people. The people who mattered to him."

Trefusis laughed, a deep, mocking laugh. "You should remember that it's thanks to me, not your father, that you're able to return here and live in the manner you see yourself as entitled to, make no mistake."

Nat's hand gripped the edge of the table so tightly his knuckles whitened. For a moment, Caroline wondered if he might leap up and strike Trefusis.

Mrs. Treloar bestowed an icy smile on her son. "He is quite right, Nathaniel. When your grandfather was in charge prior to his illness, and you were away playing at soldiers, the estate was sliding downhill fast. But he refused to hire a manager as I suggested. It was only when he had to take to his bed, and I had control of the finances here, that I was able to hire Jan." Something stirred in her cold eyes. "He came to me highly recommended."

Caroline's toes curled inside her slippers. The rumors were true. Mrs. Treloar couldn't hide the way she looked at the man by her side.

Nat appeared to be having a great deal of trouble controlling himself. His face reddened and his dark brows almost met. "I was not playing at soldiers." His words emerged stilted and strained.

Caroline took a wary sip of her soup, wondering if all their meals were like this, although probably not, as Nat had only just returned. The challenging look on Trefusis's face when he looked at Nat betrayed the way he saw him. As an interloper, and someone come back to sponge upon the empire he considered he'd helped to build, or at least, to shore up.

But surely Nat's mother would take his side against Trefusis?

Hetty, on Caroline's left, set her spoon down in her empty bowl, but kept her head down. She must be used to keeping silent.

Aunt Agnes gave a cackle of laughter and dabbed her mouth with the hanging folds of the tablecloth. "You'll be packing your bags before the week's out, Trefusis, mark my words. We don't need you now we've got our Robert back."

"For goodness's sake, Aunt," Mrs. Treloar snapped. "For the hundredth time, this is Nathaniel, not Robert. Are you blind as well as foolish?"

Undaunted, Aunt Agnes jabbed her fork at Trefusis. "And I, for one, won't be sorry to see the back of you. Nor our tenants. You with your money-grubbing ways."

Trefusis snorted with laughter. "If you think I care what you have to say then you're wrong, old woman." He flashed a wide smile at Mrs. Treloar, revealing large, tombstone teeth. "You'll find Mrs. Treloar depends on me."

This verbal barrage was so unlike the cheerful mealtimes at Cadley. Caroline's heart twisted as she thought of her mother, then still further as an image of her jovial father came into her head. Happy to the end, laughing away his fortune, until… She bit her lip, unable to swallow any more soup.

Hetty noticed, of course. "Miss Fairfield, are you quite well?" she whispered, leaning toward her.

Goodness. She'd been late to dinner and had taken Yves out without permission and now she was making a spectacle of herself. She kept her voice low. "Thank you, Henrietta, I am well, just a little overcome."

Mrs. Treloar's gaze rested on her for a moment. "Is it a little rich for you perhaps? After the simpler nursery fare?" She twisted her face into a smile that could only be described as chilling. What Trefusis saw in her was a mystery. "I'm anxious not to supply the nursery with any foods that might be heating to the blood, lest Yves should become insufferable. You have to be very careful what you feed to boys."

Oh, how Caroline wanted to ask why she deemed simple bread and butter, and not much of the latter, was sufficient to nourish a growing child. But if she did, it might come out that Yves regularly ate his breakfast in the kitchen with Mrs. Teague. Most likely Mrs. Treloar didn't know that. Best to play along with her. "An admirable undertaking, Ma'am."

Aunt Agnes gave another random cackle as though she thought this amusing, or was as batty as everyone seemed to think.

Nat's hand had relaxed on the edge of the table. "I am sure Hetty is happy she's out of the schoolroom and no longer has to eat the pap you think suitable for a child."

Hetty's eyes widened, probably at her brother's daring.

Caroline shot him a quick glance. Sitting where he was, with the right side of his face toward his mother, he could be taken for unblemished, his handsome face a little hard, with perhaps a coldness about the mouth. Not, though, the visage of a happy young man.

Mrs. Treloar nodded to the waiting footman, Dickon, in his smartest livery, to clear the soup away. "It is character building to avoid eating to excess while young. Henrietta may thank me later, when she realizes I am to be credited with her retaining her girlish figure into married life."

Caroline took a swift sideways look at Mrs. Treloar's scrawny body. Did she want everyone to resemble her? The look on Hetty's face, as she bowed her head again, spoke volumes. Not a girl who wished to emulate her mother.

For the barest of moments, Trefusis's eyes rested on Hetty. Just in passing, but in that fraction of a second, Caroline saw something she'd seen once or twice before in the faces of young men. Not that he was young any longer. Lust. Good God. It wasn't Mrs. Treloar he was after; it was Hetty. Logical, of course. But it looked as though Mrs. Treloar had no idea.

Dickon cleared away the soup bowls and the fish course was

served.

"Your favorite, Jan," Mrs. Treloar said to Trefusis.

Nat's expression darkened again. Mrs. Treloar couldn't have made how she favored Trefusis plainer if she'd kissed him on the lips in front of them all.

Nat poked at his fish with his fork. "What kind of fish is this supposed to be?" His voice had taken on a surly, discontented tone, more angry schoolboy than potential man of the house.

His mother, arrested with a forkful on her way to her mouth, frowned. "Dover Sole. I had the menu up from Mrs. Teague and that was what it said. It was what I requested."

"Overcooked and cold," Nat said. "I'm going to the Coach and Horses for my dinner."

Mrs. Treloar's expression darkened to match his, but there was no other resemblance. "Nonsense. Remain where you are. There is absolutely nothing wrong with the fish. I won't have it said that a member of this family has to take recourse to a common alehouse for his meals."

Aunt Agnes scooped up some of the fish. "'Tis passing tasty with this sauce."

Nat's jaw clenched more visibly than before. No love lost between the members of this family. Caroline was beginning to wish she'd eaten in the schoolroom with Yves. A lot more peaceful and better company. Hetty didn't count as she'd barely said a word. Nat didn't get up and leave, though.

Caroline took a forkful of the fish. "Very pleasant."

Hetty shot her a smile of thanks. "Tell me, Miss Fairfield," she tried, keeping her voice low as though she didn't want to be overheard, "did you find Penzance pleasing?"

Small talk. Hooray. Caroline could do that. "The drive there was most picturesque, as was the town. I was interested by the castle on the little island. Yves told me it's called St Michael's Mount."

"Belongs to the St Aubyns," Aunt Agnes said, without bothering to swallow her food first. "Distant relations of my mother."

As Caroline hadn't heard of this family, it meant nothing to her, so she ate a little more of her fish, which was neither cold nor overcooked.

"It's possible to cross by the causeway to the island at low tide," Hetty said, with the air of peacemaker about her. "But I've not been. Although I should like to."

Mrs. Treloar glowered at her daughter. "You will not behave like one of the vapid masses by going to stare at our neighbor's home." Her gaze took in Caroline. "And neither will you. I will not have my nephew behaving like the common rabble."

An awkward silence prevailed. Eating in the nursery with Yves grew more attractive by the minute. Hopefully she wouldn't be invited to dine with them again. Eating in the kitchen would be better, too.

Hetty came to the rescue. Perhaps she was used to this role. "Mama, I am so excited." She couldn't hide the strain in her voice. "I met Mr. Beauchamp when he called, and I'm so pleased he's invited us all to a ball at his house—in only two days' time, as well."

Dickon cleared away the empty fish plates. Even Nat had eaten his.

Mrs. Treloar took a sip of her wine before replying. "He had some absurd idea that Miss Fairfield should go. I am *not* accustomed to being told by our neighbors to bring our employees to social events."

Trefusis butted in. "Ma'am, I've met Mr. Beauchamp a few times. An astute businessman, it seems, who's set the Carlyon estate on its feet. It would seem a good idea to humor him as he could be useful."

Mrs. Treloar tutted as the beef was served. "I had to agree that Miss Fairfield may accompany us. As you are to be my escort, Jan, I could hardly cavil at her also being one of our party."

Trefusis's dark eyes flashed momentarily before he had them veiled again. He hadn't liked the suggestion that he was on a par with a common governess. Clearly this man saw himself as on a level footing with his employers. Now, what had given him that impression? Were he and Mrs. Treloar actual lovers? Unlikely as it seemed that Mrs. Treloar would have any lover at all, Caroline had to acknowledge that the rumors might well be true and their odd relationship might be a physical one.

Trefusis glanced at Nat. "I assume you won't be accompanying us… what with your *handicap*."

Caroline caught her breath. Did this man have no manners at all? No common decency about him?

Before Nat could answer, Hetty did it for him, her words tumbling out in her haste. "Of course he will. Mr. Beauchamp expressly asked him to come. And as for Miss Fairfield, she'll be coming because Mrs. Beauchamp is an especial friend of hers."

Trefusis's heavy eyebrows rose as he glanced again at Mrs. Treloar. He must know how she wouldn't like this. A governess was not meant to consort with the local gentry, although it seemed a land agent could.

"That is so," Mrs. Treloar said, her jaw so tense she could scarce open her lips. "Miss Fairfield is to accompany us for that very reason." Her eyes snapped. "I can only credit that Mr. Beauchamp sees this as normal as he was once his brother-in-law's land agent, and perhaps is still, for all we know. A *grammar-school* boy, no doubt."

That same momentary annoyance flashed across Trefusis's swarthy face. Perhaps he too had been a grammar-school boy, or not even reached that high in society in his youth.

Caroline bit her lip. Oh, how she longed to lean over and slap Mrs. Treloar across the face for her casual snobbery and bad manners. But of course, she didn't. That would be to sink even lower than her employer, tempting as the prospect was. The more she saw of this woman, the more she disliked her. Thank goodness Hetty did not resemble her, although sour-faced Nat, despite his damaged good looks, seemed as though he might share her acrid personality. Although, she had to admit he had shown admirable concern for starving children. Something her dear friend Morvoren would have approved of.

She took a nibble of the beef, which was very good. Saying what she thought to Mrs. Treloar was the road to instant dismissal, and she had to metaphorically sit on her hands and control herself. She couldn't leave Yves unprotected, so she would have to endure the dreadful manners of her employer. For his sake.

"Nothing wrong with being a grammar-school boy," Nat said. "My own great-grandfather, Sir Hugh's father, was one himself. And it stood him in good stead. None of us would be sitting here now if it weren't for him. It was he who built up the mining business and provided my grandfather with the means to buy this house."

This killed the conversation stone dead.

The meal continued with only sporadic chatter, which Caroline kept out of, content to merely observe her employer's family. Mrs. Treloar maintained a frosty disapproval of everything that went on, except Trefusis, of course. Poor Hetty struggled to keep up a stream of somewhat inane chatter with her aunt, the strain showing in her eyes. And as for her brother, he just sat and silently ate, the expression in his cool blue eyes faraway, as though his mind were in a distant place, divorced from the goings on in the dining room.

What a relief it was when the meal ended and the ladies could withdraw, leaving Nat and Trefusis to smoke and drink port. If that was what they would do together, which seemed highly unlikely.

Caroline and Hetty followed Mrs. Treloar to the drawing room, Aunt Agnes tottering along behind them on two sticks, still cackling to herself every so often as though at some joke no one else appreciated.

Once settled in their respective seats, Mrs. Treloar wasted no time in turning her icy stare on Caroline. "Tell me, Miss Fairfield, how it is you are acquainted with Mrs. Beauchamp and her *husband.* I am curious to know how a governess should know the daughter of a viscount."

How much had Ysella told Mrs. Treloar when she met her at the Assembly Rooms? The thought of revealing her family's misfortunes to this supercilious woman revolted Caroline. "We were neighbors," she said, glancing at Hetty who appeared to be all ears.

"In Wiltshire, am I to understand?"

"Yes. I was more of an age with her older sisters, but once they were married, Ysella, who is now Mrs. Beauchamp, and I became good friends."

"Despite the difference in your status."

Caroline grit her teeth for a moment. "I have not always been a governess."

"So I gather. Do you still possess parents?"

"A mother only."

This catechism on her life grated.

"What of your father?"

If she weren't careful, she was going to commit the fatal sin of rudeness to an employer and ruin all chance she had of saving Yves. "My father is dead."

Hetty stifled a yawn behind her hand. "Mama, I am so tired I think I might retire to my room. Perhaps, Miss Fairfield, I might trouble you to accompany me? I would be most honored if you would help me choose my gown for the ball." Her limpid blue eyes gazed guilelessly at her mother. "You won't mind if we go, will you Mama? I should so love to have some help deciding. You know how I am—cannot decide a single thing by myself. And you have Aunt Agnes to keep you company down here." She rose to her feet before her mother had chance to answer. "And you, Miss Fairfield, can show me the gown you've chosen to wear."

Thank you, Hetty. Caroline grabbed this lifeline with both hands and also rose to her feet. "If you'll excuse me, Ma'am?"

Mrs. Treloar, her mouth screwed tight as the Cadley kitchen cat's bum, waved a resigned hand at them both. "Off you go then. And mind your own gown reflects your position in life, Miss Fairfield. You are not to be the belle of any ball in Cornwall."

Chapter Sixteen

T HE DAY OF the ball came around much more quickly than Caroline expected. She kept a strict eye on Yves for the whole of this time, and he played his part by pretending to be sleepy in the mornings. Although not so sleepy as to miss out on his breakfast in the kitchen, which Caroline had taken to sharing with him. Anything was better than a couple of slices of dry toast and a cup of weak tea, with the added benefit being she could keep watch over him and what he ate. Not that she thought Mrs. Teague would slip anything into his food, but Bridget certainly might if she happened to be in the kitchen too.

She kept Hetty company every afternoon, and organized her piano practice, a little against Hetty's will, in the music room, before taking both children, for Hetty was still very much a child in her eyes, for a daily walk down to the beach. Although she was careful to prevent the adventurous Yves from getting himself soaking wet again.

On one occasion on their way back up from the beach carrying handfuls of shells Yves and Hetty had collected, they encountered Jan Trefusis in the gardens. He appeared from behind a bush very much as though he'd been lurking there waiting for them. A bush that happened to be out of sight of any of the windows of the house.

"Ah," he said, his Cornish accent more in evidence than it had been at dinner. "Miss Fairfield and Hetty, or should I say Henrietta, now you're a woman grown?"

That the implication of that soubriquet was purely sexual, Caroline had no doubt. The man's dark eyes burned with lust.

Hetty shrank against Caroline, dropping her shells as her small hand seized hold of Caroline's.

Trefusis's black eyes ran over Hetty's girlish curves. "Looking pretty today with your hair all windblown."

Yves stepped out from behind Caroline, a little turkey cock ready to fight. "Miss Treloar, to you," he said, some of the gravitas of his statement lost in his youthful rendition of the putdown. "And I will thank you not to approach my cousin without invitation."

Trefusis took a step closer to them all, looming larger and more threatening. "You'll regret those words, boy. *I'm* the one with the power here. Not you. I can get Ruth to send you off to boarding school hundreds of miles away just like that." He clicked his fingers. "And you wouldn't see Cornwall or Roskilly again until you were eighteen."

Yves stood his ground, a sight braver than his cousin. "No, sir. You will regret *your* words. For when I inherit Roskilly and become Sir Yves, you will be the first to go."

Good heavens. Not a wise move, but it was too late now to stop him. This outburst spoke of a long-matured dislike of the man.

Trefusis, his face suffused with anger, raised his hand.

Caroline rose to her two charges' defense.

"Mr. Trefusis. You cannot raise your hand to your employer's heir, or I will have to tell him, and no doubt Sir Hugh will have you dismissed on the spot." She took a quick breath, amazed at her own daring. "And Yves is quite correct. You should not lurk in the garden waiting to accost Miss Treloar. It is my obligation to protect both my charges, and I will do that to the best of my ability against anyone."

Trefusis glowered at her, but now his hot eyes were running

over her body as well, acquisitive and greedy. She had the unpleasant sensation he knew what she looked like naked.

Grabbing Yves's hand and pulling Hetty with her, Caroline marched past Trefusis toward the house, heart pounding in her chest. She could only hope he wouldn't twist this to his own advantage and report it to Mrs. Treloar, who would not look on it in the same way as Caroline did. Well, she might if she discovered how Trefusis was looking at her own daughter instead of her.

As soon as they were out of earshot of Trefusis, Hetty leaned toward Caroline. "You were so brave. I couldn't have done that." She put a hand on Yves's shoulder. "And so were you." She paused, scowling. "I hate that man. I wish he'd never come to Roskilly."

"It was *your* mama who brought him here," Yves retorted, sounding scornful, perhaps at Hetty's lack of backbone.

"Well," she snapped, "it wasn't me. So don't blame me. He's awful. I hate the way he looks at me." She returned her gaze to Caroline. "I wish he wasn't coming to the ball with us. His presence will spoil it entirely for me."

Caroline remained silent, secretly in total agreement with Hetty.

BETWEEN THEM, HETTY and Caroline, with a little reluctant help from Yves, had selected their ballgowns. "You're going to look like one of Mrs. Teague's iced cakes," Yves told Hetty in disgust, "if you wear all those ribbons and things. 'Specially if you wear that bobbly shawl."

The shawl in question could offer no real warmth, being made of finest gauze, but it did have a lot of extra "bobbly" bits attached, in pink to match Hetty's chosen gown.

Yves had more approval for Caroline's demure choice. "That's better. No fiddly bits. You'll look like a real person in this, and Hetty's going to look like one of her soppy dolls."

Hetty did indeed have a collection of very pretty china dolls, all done up in abundant gay finery as though they, too, were off to a ball. That some of the dolls must have been fifty or so years old didn't help, as their gowns were wider and more elaborate than anything a self-respecting doll would wear nowadays.

"*That* doll," Yves said, pointing an ink-stained finger, "looks like she has a really fat bum."

Caroline wagged a finger at him for this lapse. "That is not a word we like to use. Neither Hetty nor I would say it, so neither should you."

Yves grinned. "Can I say bottom then?"

Hetty giggled.

Caroline shook her head. "A gentleman never comments on that part of a lady's anatomy."

"He can think it though, can't he? And anyway, men have them too. And boys," Yves persisted, patting his own bottom in demonstration of its location.

"If you must. But you should never comment out loud."

On the night of the ball, Yves was confined to the nursery in the charge of Patience, as quite by chance it happened to be the awful Bridget's night off. She had, however, left instructions for Yves to be given his dose of medicine before he went to bed.

Caroline, with Patience's help, got into her pale blue gown and set about doing her own makeup and hair. Not easy when she'd been used to having a lady's maid. For every day, she'd taken to just plaiting her hair and then piling it in a bun toward the back of her head, but a ball required more care and attention, and Patience was no help at all in this department.

Hetty came to the rescue. Since her recent emergence from the schoolroom, she'd been given her own lady's maid, Abigail, a young woman promoted, to her delight, from amongst the housemaids. Caroline was sitting in front of her small mirror trying to arrange her hair for the fifth time when a light knock disturbed her and on calling out "come in," Abigail and Hetty bustled in.

Hetty looked quite charming, as Abigail seemed to have toned down the flounciness Yves had pointed out. However, she still wore the pale pink dress she and Caroline had chosen, although with a different, diaphanous shawl, devoid of Yves's "bobbly bits." Her glorious auburn hair had mostly been piled up on her head, but stray curls, artfully arranged, spilled over the alabaster skin of her slender shoulders.

"Abigail will do your hair for you," she exclaimed with evident satisfaction. "Sit back down, and let her work her magic."

And it was magic. In a very short space of time, Caroline's hair looked nearly as nice as her young charge's. Delighted, Hetty planted a kiss on each of Caroline's cheeks. "You look *so* pretty. No one would know you for a governess and old maid."

Although this was meant to be flattering, Caroline wasn't sure she liked being thought of as an old maid. Not even by guileless Hetty. Although, when she'd been seventeen herself, she'd more than likely thought women ten years older to have been distinctly over the hill and on the shelf. She could hardly blame Hetty for thinking the same.

Yves came bounding out of the nursery in his night shirt with Patience in hot pursuit. "By gosh, Hetty, you look like a lady!"

Hetty beamed, despite the implication that she didn't normally look like a lady. "Aren't you supposed to be in bed?"

Patience caught his hand. "He is that, Miss Hetty. Come on you, or I'll tell Bridget you was naughty."

"Not Bridget," Yves gasped, and stopped pulling away from her. "I only wanted to see Hetty and Caroline in their ball clothes." He looked at Caroline. "You look really pretty, too. Not like a governess at all."

"For an old maid," Caroline said, and grinned at Hetty. "Goodnight, Yves. Do *not* be awake when we return or *I* might tell Bridget, even if Patience doesn't. Off to bed with you, right now."

He scuttled off to bed, Patience in hot pursuit, and Caroline and Hetty headed downstairs, Caroline's heart thudding painfully for a number of reasons. Outside the drawing room door, she reached out and took Hetty's hand. "Courage. He can't do anything to you."

Not needing to be told whom Caroline was referring to, Hetty shot her a grateful smile, her fingers tightening around Caroline's. Then she pushed the door open and they stepped inside.

Mrs. Treloar, wearing a maroon satin gown, was seated on the chaise longue. Trefusis stood beside the fireplace, striking a negligent pose as he seemed wont to do, which meant his face was hidden from his benefactress. Taking advantage of this, he let his eyes run shamelessly over both Hetty's and Caroline's bodies as they came in, and Hetty edged closer to her protectress.

Nat, on the other hand, stood by the window, gazing out of it, as though nothing inside the room was of any interest to him. Both men were dressed very smartly in silk breeches and stockings and immaculately cut tailcoats. But there the similarity ended. Nat was the epitome of understated elegance and refinement, despite, or perhaps because of, his eleven years as a soldier. There was nothing of the dandy about him, and his collar points were low and his cravat unostentatious. He looked what he was, the scion of a family of country gentry and an ex-soldier. Trefusis, however, shouted ostentation from every item of his clothing—from the ridiculously high starched points of his collar, through his fancy waistcoat and patterned breeches to his buckled shoes. This was a farmer's son done up how he fancied a lord should look.

After a long moment, Trefusis bestowed a bow on Caroline and Hetty, that look in his eyes making her glad she'd added a pretty lace fichu to conceal her decolletage, for that was where his eyes were looking. Hetty drew her shawl closer about her shoulders.

Nat turned from the window and made a rather stiff bow, and Hetty returned an exaggerated curtsey. Caroline's was more measured.

"Now we are all here," Mrs. Treloar said, her voice laden with disapproval, no doubt at being forced to go out with a governess in her party, "perhaps we can ask Old Pascoe to bring round the carriage." Her tone said what her words didn't—that Hetty, and more specifically Caroline, had made them all wait.

Only five minutes later, for Old Pascoe must have had the carriage ready and waiting in the stableyard, they stepped out onto the graveled driveway and Young Pascoe, who was to ride as groom on the back, let down the carriage steps. Ennion held out a hand to help Mrs. Treloar and Hetty in, then Caroline, to take the rear-facing sea and after them the two men got in to sit opposite. Young Pascoe folded up the step and closed the door, the carriage creaked as he mounted up behind, and his father clicked to his horses to set the carriage rumbling down the drive.

As Caroline had never been down to Cornwall to visit Ysella at Carlyon, she had no idea how far away it lay, nor how long it would take to get there. However, she soon recognized the road as the bumpy one she and Yves had taken to Penzance. Pulled by four strong bays, the carriage fairly rattled along, but nevertheless it couldn't go flat out, due to the ruts and the odd dangerous hole that could lead to a broken axle.

It must have been two hours—two *silent* hours as no one in the carriage spoke much aside from Mrs. Treloar's detailed and several times repeated instructions for Hetty and Caroline— before they rumbled down a tree-overhung lane and through a pair of wrought-iron gates. It seemed Ysella and Mr. Beauchamp lived in an even more far-flung corner of Cornwall than the Treloars.

Old Pascoe drew the carriage up in front of a house that looked as though it had shrugged itself as close to the ground as it could get against the prevailing sea winds, clinging with the determination of the limpets Yves had shown Caroline on the rocks on the beach. Tall brick chimneys rose from a darkly slated roof which overhung the small upper windows as though much in need of the equivalent of a haircut.

Young Pascoe jumped off the back of the carriage and hurried to let down the step. Evening was drawing in and a cool sea wind blew, making Caroline draw her own shawl closer about her shoulders as she emerged. Other carriages were stationed everywhere, so Ysella and Sam must have invited a lot of people to this ball. How good it would be to see her friend again.

The party went inside, Mrs. Treloar and Trefusis leading the way, her hand tucked into the crook of his arm as though he were her escort for the night and she wanted everyone to know he was her property.

The house was as squat inside as out, being much more like the ancient Cadley Grange than Roskilly. Dark wainscotting everywhere, and old furniture just like that of her parents. Immediately, Caroline felt more at home here than she did at Roskilly.

Ysella and Sam were greeting their guests.

Mrs. Treloar approached them first, with Trefusis, who seemed to be brimming with confidence at his inclusion in the party. Caroline watched the bows and curtseys, noting the discontented expression on Mrs. Treloar's face, and the appreciative one on Trefusis as he took in the young Mrs. Beauchamp.

Ysella had always been a pretty girl, but now, as a woman, she'd blossomed into a beauty. Small and dark, delicate as a fawn, she still possessed that ability to charm, despite her previous experiences.

She spotted Caroline. "Caro! You came! I was not sure you would." She bestowed a radiant smile, and a confiding hand, upon sour Mrs. Treloar. "Thank you so much for bringing my dear friend to see me. You have no idea how much this means."

Mrs. Treloar was forced to return the smile, which must have pained her. "As it is thanks to you we have her as governess for my nephew, and you invited her, how could we not bring her with us?"

Caroline couldn't help but smile. The meaning behind these

words would be wasted, as it would sail straight over Ysella's head.

Ysella seized Caroline's hands. "I have so missed you! And I have so much to tell you." She laid a hand across the hint of a rise in her stomach. "Not least this."

"Another child?" Caroline squeezed her hands. "I'm so happy for you. Your nursery will be quite full!"

Ysella pulled Caroline toward her and kissed her cheeks. "Sam is hoping for a boy this time," she whispered in her ear, then raised her voice again. "And who is this?"

Hetty, a little shy in front of all this friendship, blushed.

"This is Miss Henrietta Treloar, for whom I act as companion. Of course, my other charge is asleep in his nursery tonight, being too young, to his relief, to attend balls." A tiny nudge of worry nagged at her, that she'd abandoned Yves all on his own and unprotected. But at least Bridget wasn't there.

"We will talk later," Ysella said. "I must welcome our other guests, I fear."

Sam shook hands with Nat. "Glad to see you've chosen to accompany your ladies."

And they progressed into what seemed to be the main ballroom, although it wasn't large, and further rooms stretched beyond it. A good few couples were already dancing, and around the perimeter of the room others stood talking, watching the newcomers as they arrived, the ladies fanning themselves in the rather stuffy warmth, the gentlemen, even the old married ones, eyeing up the young women on display.

Caroline glanced at Nat. There was nowhere here he could turn his face to in order to hide his scars. But he seemed oblivious to the attention he was receiving, as though he'd determined to brave it out. Her heart momentarily went out to him, as he headed off toward the card room, before she remembered that it would be he who would benefit if something happened to Yves. She mustn't allow herself to feel any sympathy for him. He was probably as coldhearted as his mother.

A handsome, but quite short, young gentleman approached. His hairstyle, which seemed set to defy gravity, had been teased up into many artful curls to add to his height. It bore some semblance to the Grecian style young men about Town affected nowadays, but something more than goodwill must be maintaining its buoyancy.

He made a smart bow to Mrs. Treloar and then to Hetty and Caroline. "William Pendennis, at your service."

Introductions were made all round, as it seemed the Treloars knew his family well, and he procured himself a dance with Hetty and escorted her onto the dance floor.

Trefusis, ignoring the dancing, headed for the refreshment room with Mrs. Treloar gripping his arm in what looked to be a vice, leaving Caroline to keep a weather eye on Hetty. She stood for a few minutes enjoying the music, one foot tapping along, the colorful whirl of dancers and the heady mingled scents of men and women alike.

"Do tell me how you are getting along in your new position." Ysella's voice cut into her thoughts. "Now your employer has absented herself."

She turned around. Ysella, a possessive hand resting on the imperceptible rise of her stomach, stood beside her. Caroline would never have known her condition if Ysella hadn't revealed it.

"I've abandoned poor Sam to greet our guests. I had to find you as it feels like so long since you and I last saw one another. Tell me everything."

"Well," Caroline said with a smile, "Hetty is a lovely girl who reminds me somewhat of you. A little headstrong, a *lot* vivacious and lively." She paused. "Quite unlike her mother."

"And the child? Is he biddable? When I talked with Mrs. Treloar, she told me he is sickly and a little backward. I felt the implication was that he isn't expected to live." She shivered. "As a mother now, that is a sentiment I would dread, although she didn't at all seem upset by it. Although I suppose he isn't her child."

Caroline shook her head with some asperity. "Not at all sickly. He's as robust as any boy his age. As robust as Kit himself was as a child. I keep hearing it said that he's sickly, and yet there's nothing at all wrong with him. I find it very odd that this is said of him."

Ysella's eyes widened. "I suppose no child is entirely safe, is he? With sickness all around that can strike a little one down so easily. I worry for my daughter all the time."

Caroline shrugged. Best not to confide in Ysella any of her concerns about Yves. Not yet, anyway. After all, she had very little evidence to prove anything and was going on what could be construed as merely an educated guess, or a hunch. "He's a charming, quick-witted boy, who likes all the normal things boys like. And he's good at his studies as well. Not in the least bit backward. A bright child who's a pleasure to teach. I'm enjoying my employment as his governess. So far." Although this wasn't strictly true. But she didn't want Ysella to know, at least, not like this, in public.

"Come," Ysella said. "Shall we get ourselves a glass of lemonade?"

Caroline shook her head. "No. I'm afraid I can't, as it's my job to watch Hetty and make sure she doesn't do anything untoward." She smiled. "You know very well what mistakes young ladies make where dashing young gentlemen are concerned."

Ysella had the grace to blush, as she'd made a mistake like that herself and paid dearly for it.

"Then I shall fetch you a glass myself," she said, and spun away into the throng.

Caroline went back to watching Hetty, who seemed to be having a wonderful time with young William Pendennis. Her enchantingly flushed face was wreathed in smiles every time the dance brought them back together, and young William seemed very taken with her. His shortness didn't seem to have put her off any.

However, over on the other side of the ballroom, Mrs. Treloar and Trefusis had returned from searching out their refreshments and were part of a small group chatting together. And Trefusis had his acquisitive gaze on Hetty as she twirled about the dance floor. Now Caroline had two people to keep safe.

Chapter Seventeen

A S THE DANCE continued, several older gentlemen came over and requested a dance with Caroline, men whom Hetty gleefully pronounced as widowers on the lookout for a strong young woman who could look after their broods of motherless children. No doubt they were after other things as well, but Hetty didn't mention that.

Throughout all this, Caroline kept a careful eye on Hetty, who seemed to be very much enjoying herself. She introduced her two cousins, sons of her father's two sisters, to Caroline, and Abel Nancarrow, the older one, took Caroline for a spin around the dance floor while Hetty danced with Thomas Polmear, the younger one, who was home from Oxford. Or was it Cambridge? Caroline hadn't paid that much attention.

Both young men had a slight look of Nat about them, being tall and dark, but that was as far as any resemblance went. What they both had, but he didn't, was a cheerful disposition. Both were jolly and fun to talk to, and after her dance, Caroline let Abel promenade her around the edge of the ballroom. This was mainly to keep an eye on Hetty, who was doing the same tour with young Thomas, whom Caroline had noticed had rather a wicked glint in his eye. She didn't disclose her reason to Abel, who seemed more than happy to parade with her on his arm, despite the hard stare they received from Mrs. Treloar as they passed her.

Trefusis was no longer in attendance, but she seemed to have buttonholed poor Ysella, who had a hunted expression on her face.

"Shall we take a turn into the card room to see who's hiding in there?" Abel asked. "I've a mind to see if my cousin Nat is lurking amongst the hardened gamblers."

As Mrs. Treloar now had charge of Hetty for a while, Caroline allowed herself to be steered through the door and along a paneled corridor.

Nat was indeed in the card room, seated at a table playing Faro, with Trefusis and three other men, all of them with glasses of whisky to hand. Neither raised their heads at the advent of the newcomers.

Abel stopped by the Faro table, watching for a moment. It was well on, and there weren't many cards left to turn over. Nat had a larger pile of chips in front of him than Trefusis, and the other two punters were betting recklessly, no doubt due to the amount of whisky they'd imbibed.

"Calling the turn," said the man in the banker's seat. Everyone placed their bets. He turned over the cards. The dealer won heavily from Trefusis.

"Play again," Trefusis snapped, reaching for his wallet. "I'll have some more chips."

Nat stood up. "I've had enough. I need something to dilute this whisky." He saw Abel and Caroline and a slight frown wrinkled his brow. "Abel, I didn't know you were here."

Abel grinned at him. "But I knew you'd be *here*. Many's the time you've hammered me at Faro, whether I played punter or banker. You have the devil's own luck, man."

"Not so lucky as all that." Nat's hand went to his face. "But in luck tonight."

A moment's awkward silence followed, as no doubt Abel searched for something to say other than *what the hell happened to you?*

Best to leave them alone together. Caroline extricated her hand from Abel's arm. "I think I should go back and make sure Hetty is all right, if you don't mind. Thank you for the dance, Mr. Nancarrow." She bobbed him an elegant curtsey, sure Nat would be glad of her departure, and returned to the ballroom.

Hetty was with her mother, drinking lemonade and talking to Ysella, who seemed happier to be talking to her than she had been with Mrs. Treloar.

Caroline, the oppressive heat making her a little breathless, went in search of refreshment. And was snared by a redoubtable matron, easily as old as Aunt Agnes, wearing what looked like an old-fashioned powdered wig. This lady, who turned out to be even deafer than Aunt Agnes, kept her occupied for a full half hour, by which time Caroline was even hotter and more breathless than before. Escaping when the lady's equally ancient husband came in search of her at last, she decided to sneak out for some fresh air on the terrace.

Night had long fallen and only a few lanterns illuminated the almost empty outdoor space. A low wall surrounded the paved terrace, with steps leading down into the shadowy gardens, and at the top of the steps a lone figure of a man stood, silhouetted in the moonlight.

Caroline hesitated, a nub of unease rising. What if it was Trefusis? Instinct warned her never to be alone with him.

The man swung round at the sound of Caroline's light footsteps on the flagstones and the nearest lamp illuminated his ravaged face in stark clarity. Nat Treloar.

Caroline halted. "I'm sorry, sir. I thought to have the terrace to myself."

He had a glass in his hand, of something that probably wasn't the lemonade the ladies had been imbibing, despite his earlier avowal to seek it out. "Miss Fairfield. Don't let me put you off." He waved his empty left hand. "There seems plenty of room out here for two. Or I can depart and leave you in sole possession."

Caroline tried a smile. "You have the air of one who would

rather be alone."

He gave a shrug. "You have me right. I've grown tired of being the center of attention for all who long to stare at a monster. And there's only so long I can lurk in the card room without either making myself unpopular by winning or in danger of returning home penniless." He paused, perhaps conscious of what he'd just said, although it seemed unlikely he regretted it. "By that I don't mean you. Just the rest of the rabble who can't wait to whisper behind my back at how I've been transmuted into this." His hand came up and almost, but not quite, touched his cheek.

Caroline nodded. "I noticed. There are many fools about who can't wait to comment on another's misfortune."

Perhaps she'd allowed her own bitterness to shine through too much, for his eyes narrowed and he peered at her more closely. "You speak as though you know this to your cost."

She nodded, the darkness between them loosening her tongue, for now he moved out of the light to stand a little closer to her, just a shadowy shape, featureless and without threat, despite his size. "I do."

He was close enough that she could hear him breathing in the silence on the terrace. The muted music and chatter spilling out through the open doors seemed far away, as the night pressed in about her. They might almost be in another world. A world where terrible things had happened to them both.

"My father…" she began.

He held up his hand. "You have no need to tell me."

"I'd like to."

"Then walk with me to the summerhouse and sit a while where we won't be interrupted."

What would Mrs. Treloar say if she discovered Caroline had gone out by herself in the dark and encountered her son for what would seem like a secret rendezvous? Then walked with him into the gardens, to the shelter of the summerhouse. With any man, that would be bad enough, but with her employer's son? Caroline stiffened her resolve. What did she care? She was beyond the age of giddy silliness and compromise, and if she wanted to talk to someone by herself, even if they were a man, then she would.

They descended the stone steps to the lawn and crossed it to where a small, white-painted summerhouse sat in an arbor of shadowy, overhanging trees. How like Ysella to have had this built. Nat pushed open the flimsy door and they went inside. The thin sliver of the moon showed the octagonal, glass-paned building to have cushioned seats around the edge.

Caroline sat down, careful to choose the darker side of the summerhouse where Nat would feel less exposed. He sat beside her, close enough that had she wanted to, she could have reached out and touched him.

Out here, no sound carried to them from the house, but somewhere in one of the nearby trees an owl called. The night was still and warm, and although this felt far away from the house and other people, Caroline felt no fear at being out here alone with Nat.

"My father," she began again. "My father was a kind and generous man, not given to parsimony, but selfish in his own way. I loved him dearly, as did my mother. But he had one terrible fault that made him worse than selfish, and that was gambling."

"Most men like to gamble. I do myself, as you saw."

She nodded. "I know, and some will come in time to the straits my father found himself in, where they have wagered away their homes and livelihoods and still have gambled on." She swallowed. "My father did that. Like all men in his position, he truly believed his luck would change if he kept on wagering. So that was what he did. And lost everything on the roll of a dice and the turn of a card."

"And left you destitute?"

She nodded again. "My mother and myself." Now came the hard part. "But he is not here to share our ignominy with us. It would have been easier, by far, had he chosen to remain, but he didn't. He took the coward's way and left us to face our fate alone." She paused. "He was selfish to the end and shot himself in his study." Her voice shook as she said aloud the words she'd so often thought inside her head but never spoken, not even to her mother.

Nat stayed silent. The owl called again, the sound lonely and haunting, as though even the night bird were joining in with her mourning.

"You hold it against him?" Nat asked, his voice gentle. Perhaps for him, too, it was easier to talk like this when neither could see the other's face.

"I did," Caroline said. "I did for some time, but now, perhaps, I don't. I see him for what he was—a weak and selfish man who could not say no to his vice. But I loved him and love him still, for he remains my father and I shall have no other. And as for me, now I am learning to pay my own way through employment. My mother, though, is with my father's sister and her family. I could not bring myself to do that. I could not live on another's charity." She shook her head. "I just wish I could provide a home for my mother with me, so she needn't remain my sainted aunt's poor relation and charitable cause."

"It does you credit that you don't hold it against your father."

She chuckled. "Oh, I did at first, believe me. I'm no saint despite possessing a saintly aunt. No daughter could have been more angry with a parent. I thought, perhaps rightly, that he'd not loved my mother and me enough to stay with us. Made worse because when he did it, he chose to do it in a spot where one of us would find him."

"But I suspect he did love you in his own way, and you know it."

"You are right. We were a loving family."

"Unlike mine."

What to say to this? Would it be rude to agree? "Hetty is very loving."

A snort. "Oh, Hetty was always so. You would not think her

my mother's child. But then, my mother had no hand in her upbringing. From birth she was in the hands of nurses and nannies, fortunately for her, women with kinder natures to model herself on. I believe my mother only saw her but once a month or so. She is a woman with no feeling for her children although I'd hoped she might find some for Hetty."

Caroline was not at all sure she should be having this conversation, but at least, as they were alone, she could deny it had ever happened were she questioned about it. Although lying was against her strict principles.

"I'm sure your mother loves you in her own way."

Another snort. "You may choose to think that, but I have evidence to the contrary."

Caroline frowned, secure in the knowledge that he couldn't see her do it. If his mother didn't love him, then why was she trying to kill her nephew? Because the person who would benefit in the end had to be Nat, who stood to inherit all that should one day belong to Yves, but only if Yves were gone. Unless it wasn't his mother at all who was attempting to do away with Yves... But it couldn't be Nat, could it, for he'd been hundreds of miles from home when Miss Hawkins had discovered the plot and been dismissed by Mrs. Treloar. No, it had to be his mother. Or Trefusis—although why he'd kill for another man's benefit was a puzzle. Or was Nat lying?

"I've told you my secret," Caroline said. "Will you tell me yours?"

Silence. His hand went up to his face again before dropping into his lap. "I imagine that to be a fair exchange."

She waited.

"You know, of course, that I was a soldier?"

She nodded.

"My grandfather bought me a commission after I left Harrow. I began as an ensign but soon rose to lieutenant, captain and then to major in the 18th Hussars. We were sent to Europe to fight Boney. Not the whole time I was in, mind. I had time back in

England too. Later on, I saw action in Spain and then in Southern France." He held up his right hand, the lack of fingers evident even in the poor light. "I lost these at Corunna, five years since. That coincided with a period back in England so I was able to convalesce. They offered me the opportunity to relinquish my commission, hampered as I was without these fingers, and being right-handed. I refused."

What had driven him to refuse? Out of instinct, Caroline reached out and took his hand in hers, much as she might have done had he been Yves, the stumps of his missing fingers against her palm. "Were they shot off?"

"They were." He made no attempt to free his hand, his remaining fingers curling around hers as though she'd created a link that drew them together in their common suffering.

"Go on."

He cleared his throat. "We were dispatched back to Portugal some eighteen months ago. We landed in Lisbon and battled our way through Northern Spain—I fought at Morales, Vitoria, Sorauren, then across the Pyrenees and into France. My men fought at Nive and Orthez, then on to Toulouse, and that was my downfall." His fingers tightened on hers. "A Frenchman's saber. We were fighting hand to hand, saber to saber." He stopped and she heard him catch his breath. Was he remembering the blow, the slicing open of his face? The pain, which must have been terrible?

"I stumbled. He was quick. But it was the last thing he did. Even as his saber did its damage, mine was running him through." He fell silent again.

She didn't push him. What must it have been like to have your face ripped open like that from forehead to chin? He was lucky to have kept his eye. And what had happened after he'd killed his man? How long had he waited to see a doctor? It didn't bear thinking of.

"The military doctors in our field hospital tried," he said, almost as though he'd read her mind. "But they had little to work with. I'm lucky not to be worse scarred… or dead from an infection. They did their best." The bitterness was back in his voice.

No wonder his mouth possessed that discontented downward curve. Life had dealt him a terrible blow. Had he ever wished he was dead instead of maimed like this? Better to have lost an arm, perhaps, or even a leg, than to have had his face, that must once have been so handsome, mutilated in this way.

"You're wondering how I can bear to live with it," he said, his voice low.

She shook her head. "Not about how you live with it now. I was wondering how you coped in the weeks after it happened. Here and now, I can see for myself how you cope. You turn your head away to stop people seeing. You stand in corners in the shadows, play cards when you fear you'll frighten the ladies, or they will stare, and lurk outside like tonight, keeping the world at bay." How to tell him he didn't need to? That he should wear his scar with pride as it showed how he'd fought for Britain against that Corsican despot and helped procure the hard-won victory. Words her father would have echoed.

He stayed silent.

She reached out with her other hand and covered his so she was clasping his mutilated hand between her two. "You have no need to hide, Nathaniel. You are a hero, like all the other soldiers back from France."

He snatched his hand from hers as though she'd stung him. "Never call me that. I'm no hero. None of us are." His voice rose. "I've seen atrocities that would make your blood run cold in your veins, atrocities I've taken part in. I've seen women and children dead in the streets, and boy soldiers disemboweled, dying in agony. We are not heroes who have stood for that, so never call us by that name."

Stunned, she searched for something to say. "I'm sorry. I didn't know."

He was in full flow now, as though she'd unplugged a stopper in his brain. "I've seen men with their arms and legs blown off by cannon's grapeshot. I know firsthand what cannonballs can do. They're slow, you know, and they bounce along the ground causing maximum destruction. I've seen men who've spotted a cannonball coming and thought to stop it by sticking out a leg or arm, only to have that limb ripped off and the cannon ball to keep on going, reaping death to everything it touches. I've seen horses with their legs broken screaming in pain. I've seen young soldiers who've run in fear at the sound of battle stood up before a tree and shot. We did that. To our own soldiers. To boys who should have been walking behind ploughs in England's rain-washed fields."

"I didn't know."

"No one does. No one tells. We soldiers keep it to ourselves."

He fell silent. She sat beside him for a while before reaching out a hand again and finding his. "I'm glad you told me."

He didn't pull away this time but instead hung onto her hand as though it were a lifeline. "I had to tell someone or I'd have died inside." He paused. "No. I am already dead inside and could not be made more so. Yet it's in me, screaming to get out. I'm sorry to have burdened you with it."

An overpowering urge to put her arms around him and comfort him as though he were Yves washed over Caroline, but the laws of propriety held her back. What might he think if she tried to do that? What might any man assume, out here in the dark garden? That she was an easy conquest? Not worth the risk, no matter how much she wanted to.

Instead, she patted his hand. "You can tell me anything."

He shook his head. "I think you'd best go back inside now before anyone remarks upon your absence. My mother in particular. She has the eyes of a hawk and its claws as well. I wouldn't wish you to lose your position because of me."

He was right, but somehow, she didn't want to relinquish his hand.

Chapter Eighteen

D ESPITE HIS WORDS, Nat didn't want her to let go of his hand. The feel of her holding his was like a balm on his tortured soul. She'd said he could tell her anything, and he'd himself revealed some of his innermost thoughts with few restrictions. Even now, he wasn't sure why he'd done that. The darkness hiding their faces, the peaceful quiet after the hubbub of the ball, the gentleness in her voice, and the honesty with which she'd confided in him her own dark secret, all had contributed to loosen his tongue.

Outside the confines of the tiny world they'd found themselves in, the owl called again, but from a different tree. Or was it a pair of owls, calling to each other as they hunted? He didn't know enough about birds to be sure.

There was more he wanted to say, but even though she'd said he could, had invited his confidences in fact, these were words he couldn't speak, about secrets he'd kept locked in his heart too long to reveal.

The silence stretched on, not awkward, but companionable and reassuring.

At last, she tightened her fingers around his. "Perhaps, Major, we should return to the ball, as you said, in case anyone remarks upon our absence and jumps to untoward conclusions."

She was right. His mother would be the first to point an accusing finger, and it would not be at him, but at Miss Fairfield, accusing her of being an adventuress. Instinct told him that Caroline's character was of the most upright and noble, and the thought of what his mother might say about her infuriated him. "Please don't call me Major," he said. "I've left all that behind me and want no reminder of it."

"Mr. Treloar, then?"

He shook his head. "That is too formal for two people who are to become more than mere acquaintances. No. Call me Nat, as Hetty does, if it doesn't offend you. I much prefer my friends to use that name."

"And do I count myself as one of them now?"

He nodded. "I would be honored if you did."

He couldn't see her smile, but he sensed it.

"I should like that. And perhaps you might call me Caroline? Although I fear we should not indicate such familiarity in front of your mother."

"Wise words."

She stood up, so he followed suit. Her height, which was above the ordinary for a woman, brought her closer to him than any other woman he'd met, and here, standing in the complicit darkness of the summerhouse, he felt a sudden urge to take her in his arms and kiss her. He'd not felt like that for such a long time. What woman would want to kiss a monster like him? One that couldn't see the blemish. One that when she had seen it had not stared, nor looked away in shock. One who'd confided in him her own secret in exchange for his—or the part of his he'd felt able to share.

But he didn't do any of that.

Instead, he let her release his hand and turn toward the door. He saw her smile in the dim moonlight, her face a pale oval. "I think if we are lucky, no one will see us return."

He followed her back through the garden, the moonlight illuminating their way to the terrace and bestowing on her figure an ethereal hint of fairyland. He caught her up at the top of the steps, made brave by her compassion, his hand on her arm. "Will you do me the honor of dancing with me, Caroline?"

She turned to face him, her eyes dark pools. "Inside?"

He shook his head. "No. Not where we can be seen. I've had my fill of drawing stares, and I'm sure you have too. And my mother would be bound to comment. Out here, where none can see us."

She hesitated, studying his face, and he studied hers. Was he wrong? Had he read her feelings for him incorrectly? The urge to take her by the hand and pull her into his arms almost overwhelmed him. But just because she was polite and kind didn't mean she would want the attentions of a man as scarred as he was. A monster. He drew a steadying breath. No doubt it was the lack of female company that had rendered him so vulnerable to the charms of his cousin's rather blue-stockinged governess. She was like Julia in no discernible way, so how could he be feeling like this? He pushed that intrusive thought out of his head. He mustn't think of Julia.

"What dance do you think we can do, all by ourselves?" Her tone was slightly wry, and she was right, because most dances required, at the very least, several couples to perform them correctly. But he'd thought of that.

"The waltz."

A little gasp escaped her. "I know of it, of course, but have never danced it." She chuckled. "My mother, and I am sure yours as well, would deem it far too scandalous to perform. Where did you learn it?"

"On my travels. It's a dance favored by soldiers." And the women who chased after them, but he wasn't going to say that. "And easy to learn."

Caroline pressed her lips together. "I've seen it danced. You are right. It does not look hard to accustom oneself to. The steps are not so complicated as other more respectable dances."

"So, will you?" He held out his hand, giving her the opportunity to turn away if she so wished.

She didn't. Instead, she set her hand in his and took a step toward him. "I think I should like to learn this dance, although it all depends upon if you are a good teacher. If not, I fear such close proximity might lead to me trampling on your toes. I trust you are suitably forewarned."

He smiled, for once unconscious of the fact that only half his face responded. "Then ignore the music from within the ballroom, and let me guide you. All you need to do is follow my lead."

"Very well."

He took her right hand in his left, and put his own right on her waist. Beneath the thin satin of her gown, he could feel the firmness of her stays, oddly provocative, as though intent on suggesting to him how good it would feel to get her out of them. He pushed that thought away. "Now, put your left hand on my shoulder."

She did as she was told, with less than a foot now separating them.

He smiled down at her. "I shall step forward with my left foot, like this, careful not to take too large a step, and you must step back with your right or it will be me trampling on your toes, and I am a sight heavier than you and have solid shoes on. Then, together, with our other feet, we will step to the side, so, then bring our first foot to join the second. One, two, three. An easy rhythm. Allow me to guide you."

She picked up the dance quickly, her lithe body swaying in his arms as they danced around the terrace together to his muttered count of "one, two three" to start with. How long it was since he'd danced with a proper young lady in his arms. How long since he'd held Julia like this. Of course, Miss Fairfield was not Julia in any way. Too tall, too old, too robust. Julia had been delicate and dainty, like the doves on the rooftops in Lisbon. The doves that had reminded him of her in bittersweet memory.

Caroline danced with an energy the delicate Julia had never possessed, a lack of energy that had been her downfall. Sorrow welled up inside him alongside guilt. If only he hadn't wanted a child… but he had, and she had died. Because of him.

Nat came to a halt. "I cannot dance any longer. I'm sorry. Go back inside and leave me out here with my dark thoughts." He released his hold on Caroline. "I am not fit company this night." Turning away from her, he stumbled down the steps and into the darkness.

"CARO!" YSELLA'S VOICE bit into Caroline's jumbled thoughts. "I wondered where you'd got to. It's growing chill out here. Why don't you come back inside with me before you catch your death?"

Caroline, who'd been staring into the dark garden where Nat had disappeared, heaved a deep breath and pulled herself together before she turned, a smile fixed on her face. "Of course. I only came out here for some fresh air. July can be such a hot month for the vigor of dancing."

Ysella linked her arm through Caroline's. "Did I see someone else out here talking to you?"

Should she tell her friend the truth? Somehow it felt wrong to do so. Whatever it was she'd shared with Nat, it didn't feel like something she should divulge. Ysella, being such a flibbertigibbet, might be inclined to broadcast it—inadvertently of course. Two years of marriage and motherhood had probably done little to curb her friend's natural tendencies, which Caroline knew well of yore.

"Oh, no one important. I was just politely bidding him good-night."

Ysella raised her delicately etched eyebrows and pushed open the doors into the ballroom. A wave of heat, music, and voices, hit them. She laughed. "You were never a good liar, Caro."

"Then do not ask me to tell you something I'd rather keep to myself."

Ysella tugged her round. "Then there *was* someone with you! A gentleman, I'd wager."

Caroline sighed. When was Ysella not ready to lay a wager on something? "Please don't ask. I know you want to. Just believe me that it was nothing improper."

Ysella snorted in a most unladylike fashion. "As if I'd suspect *you* of anything improper. Anyone less likely to venture into impropriety I've yet to meet."

If only Ysella knew the truth about how Caroline was suspecting her employers of murderous intentions. If anything was improper, that was, as she had no proof as yet that it was true, and yet she still adhered to it.

She smiled sweetly at her friend. "Well, there you have your answer. Nothing of great note. Just two people exchanging words."

Ysella narrowed her eyes, as though preparing to do battle.

However, to Caroline's relief, Sam, accompanied by a gentleman in spectacles of perhaps early middle age, approached, wending his way around the edge of the room and avoiding the enthusiastic dancing of the many couples in the relatively small space afforded them.

"Caroline. Where've you been? I have someone who would like to meet you. A fellow scholar. May I present Mr. Richard Penlee. I mentioned I knew you and he was most keen to make your acquaintance." He turned to the gentleman in question. "Allow me to present Miss Caroline Fairfield, the lady of whom I was speaking."

Richard Penlee, a man of Caroline's own height, executed a smart bow. "Enchanted to make your acquaintance, Miss Fairfield. Mr. Beauchamp has been extoling your virtues to me and I'm fascinated to meet a young lady with so deep an understanding of Virgil. Perhaps we could take a walk around the dance floor and discuss some of the finer points of his work?"

Caroline caught Ysella's open-mouthed expression and

flashed her a smile. "Thank you, Mr. Penlee, I should be very pleased to do so."

Mr. Penlee's discourse on Virgil's *Aeneid* occupied Caroline until supper was served and Hetty came to reclaim her so they could go in to eat with her mother. Which came as quite a relief to Caroline. At the table in the dining room, Caroline tried to search for Nat without appearing to do so but didn't see him. Was he still outside in the garden by himself or had he repaired to the card room again? Not all the gentlemen had come in to eat, the hardened players having stayed to continue their games. Gambling was the order of the night for many.

However, he did return for the drive home in the dark, although he sat quietly beside Trefusis, who appeared somewhat the worse for drink, staring out at the dark countryside as it passed the carriage window. Caroline had no further chance to talk to him and would not have, anyway, in front of Mrs. Treloar and Trefusis.

Once back at Roskilly, with the hint of a sunrise already on the horizon, Trefusis departed in the direction of the land agent's house, and Old and Young Pascoe drove the carriage round to the stables.

Once inside, Nat departed into the library without a backward glance for anyone, and Caroline bade Mrs. Treloar and Hetty a polite goodnight, which might better have been a good morning. She stifled a yawn as she walked along the nursery corridor. It was going to be difficult to get up in just a few short hours and teach Yves anything meaningful.

Not wanting to disturb his sleep, she took her shoes off and tiptoed into the nursery itself. Yves lay tucked up snugly in his bed, his golden curls on the pillow giving him the somewhat erroneous look of a cherub. The door into Bridget's room was closed, but whether she was in there or not, Caroline had no idea. She tiptoed to the bed and bent over Yves. Was she really checking he was breathing? Had it gone this far?

His chest rose and fell with reassuring regularity. But how

long would it be before Bridget, or whoever was paying her to do this, as paid she must surely be, chose to up the dose of laudanum, thinking it not efficacious or swift enough, and added more of the drug to Caroline's hither-to innocuous bottle? Caroline bit her bottom lip. She had to do something soon to save Yves from the danger his family represented.

She tiptoed out again, closing the door with a soft click, and returned to her own bedroom. No Patience to help her, but getting out of a gown was easier than getting into it, so she could manage on her own. Before very long she was lying in her own bed, trying to fall asleep.

But she could not.

Thoughts tumbled around in her head, foremost the conundrum that was Nat Treloar. Everything about her situation here at Roskilly suggested that she should not trust him. He appeared to be the only one who stood to gain from Yves's death. He was a ruthless soldier who'd fought in a long war and must be accustomed to killing. He'd said himself he'd committed what he termed atrocities, so would the killing of a child be beyond him? Probably not. He possessed a gigantic chip on his shoulder about his own disfigurement. And he appeared to have a short fuse about anything that he disagreed with or didn't like.

Yet she liked him.

She didn't *want* to like him, but she did, however hard he made it for her. His sister, on the other hand, was easy to like, with her winsome ways and innocence. She was like a younger version of Ysella, of whom Caroline was so fond. Mrs. Treloar, though, was a woman surely no one could ever like, unless of course they were after something, which Trefusis surely was. And yet, even if Trefusis was deluding Mrs. Treloar into thinking his interest was in her when really it was Hetty he was after, what good would that do him with Nat next in line for the inheritance? No, she had to absolve Trefusis of any guilt in this. The only suspects were Mrs. Treloar… and Nat.

Yet even after the ball, Nat remained a mystery. He'd confided in her what had happened to him, which must have been difficult, but instinct told her there was more he hadn't divulged. More secrets held close to his heart. Was one of them a desire to inherit his grandfather's title and possessions? Or was he innocent of all her suspicions and was it only his mother she had to protect Yves from? She rolled over in bed, restless and angry that she couldn't get her thoughts straight. She needed to know what Nat was hiding to exonerate him. Perhaps he would tell her, one day, but she didn't have time to wait. What she needed right now was help to save Yves, and she couldn't go to Nat, because he might not want to give it.

So, who could she approach for help?

She rolled over in bed, racking her brain. Who was there in this house she could trust? Bridget was clearly in the pocket of Mrs. Treloar. Patience was little more than a child. Miss Hawkins was miles away in Penzance and she had no way of contacting her. What of the other servants? Dickon liked Yves and played football with him, so, surely, he must be worth trusting, but he would be ineffectual against his superiors, accustomed as he was to obedience. Mrs. Teague had a fondness for Yves as well. Aunt Agnes was too old and frail and far too confused to lend any help, although she, too, seemed fond of Yves.

She sat bolt upright in bed. Of course. Why hadn't she thought of it before? Yves's grandfather, Sir Hugh Treloar, whom she had yet to meet. He might be bedridden, but he was nominally in charge of Roskilly. Surely he must be fond of his little heir. She could go to him. Tomorrow. She'd find a way to see him and tell him everything. But only if she felt she could trust him.

She lay back down again, calmer now than she'd been for days.

Chapter Nineteen

THE FOLLOWING MORNING, Yves wanted to know all about the ball, delaying the start of their lessons, which was no doubt what he intended. "Patience gave me the medicine, just like Bridget does. She said Bridget *insisted* she had to give it me, or she'd be in deep trouble."

"Did it taste the same as normal? I mean, like my medicine, not Bridget's?" Caroline still nurtured the fear that Bridget or Mrs. Treloar might decide to add more laudanum to the bottle, unbeknownst to her.

He nodded. "Just the same as yours. But I pretended I didn't like it, just like you said. I didn't have to pretend *all* that much because it still doesn't taste nice, only in a diff'rent way. Patience got cross and threatened to tell Bridget how naughty I'd been if I didn't take it." He chuckled. "So, I took it in the end, but only after I'd made a *big* fuss."

They were eating a later than usual breakfast together with Mrs. Teague and Dash, who sat under the table awaiting the scraps from Yves's plate.

Yves passed the dog the rind from his bacon. "Can I bring Dash upstairs to the schoolroom today? He doesn't like being left down here."

Caroline laughed. "You know that's not a good excuse. He loves being down here with Mrs. Teague, getting all the tidbits she gives him." However, she wasn't in the mood for an argument after barely two hours sleep. "But, as a special treat, he can come upstairs with you. So long as he sits quietly by your feet while you do your lessons."

Yves bounced in his seat. "Yes! Thank you, Caroline. I'm sure he'll help me concentrate really well on my Latin verbs. He's a very classical dog, you know."

Caroline snorted. "I'll believe that when I see it."

Dash's presence, of course, did *not* lead to the best of concentration from her pupil, as he would keep bending down to pet Dash. However, Caroline, who'd been brought up around dogs and liked the little spaniel, chose to overlook these lapses. Yves was an intelligent child with an aptitude for study, so what did one day of digression matter?

The clock on the mantelpiece at last struck midday, which marked the end of lessons, and from outside on the corridor came the patter of Patience's footsteps carrying up the dinner tray, the crockery rattling as she hurried. It would probably be something small accompanied by more boiled cabbage, a vegetable Mrs. Treloar seemed convinced promoted childhood growth. However, with a substantial plate of bacon and eggs inside them both, that didn't matter.

Yves began to put his books away in his desk.

Caroline waited until he'd finished, which wasn't long as he was shoving them in pell-mell. She cleared her throat. "Yves?"

He looked up, a little worried frown on his forehead as though he suspected she might be about to delay his rush for food, meager and uninteresting as it was. "Yes, Caroline?" Of course, as the lessons were over now, he could call her by her first name.

"Do you often visit your grandfather?"

He closed his desk with a bang. "Quite often. He likes me to read to him. But I haven't been up to his room since you arrived, and he hasn't sent for me." He paused. "He sleeps an awful lot."

Of course he would. The laudanum to add to Yves's medicine

had come from his room. From his nurse perhaps, as he was being dosed with it as well.

Feeling a little manipulative, Caroline continued. "I would very much like to meet your grandfather, as I've now met everyone in your family but him. Do you think you could take me up and introduce me to him after we've taken our dinner?"

He pulled a face. "I was thinking we could walk down to the stream and sail my boat." He fished a small wooden boat with red sails out of the desk where he must have been hiding it all morning. "It's a smuggler's boat loaded with tea and brandy, you know." He tried a winning smile. As he was a handsome little boy, the effect was comely.

"Perhaps a short visit to your grandfather beforehand?"

He shrugged. "I suppose so. He's prob'ly been missing me. He says I make him laugh. He says he only laughs with me. He's very old, you know. Nearly as old as Aunt Agnes and she must be at least *a hundred.*"

"I don't think many people get to be a hundred, so I doubt if your Aunt Agnes and your grandfather are that old. In fact, I'm sure someone mentioned that your grandfather was nearing ninety."

He shrugged. "Aunt Agnes is a bit… well, she's a bit *odd.*"

"She's just old. Er, is your grandfather at all like that?" She needed him to have his wits about him if he were to render her any help. If he could, that was, from the confines of his bed. How much under Mrs. Treloar's control was he?

Yves screwed up his nose. "And she's a bit smelly. So is Grandpapa. He has a nurse to look after just him, all the time, that Aunt Ruth got for him. Rodgers. But she's horrid, like Bridget, and I think she might be a man in a dress. She doesn't like me coming to see Grandpapa." He paused, head tilted to one side as though listening, and Caroline smothered a chuckle at his thoughts on the unfortunate Rodgers. "D'you think Bridget might be a man, too? She walks like one and she has a bit of a mustache. I don't think Rodgers looks after Grandpapa properly otherwise he wouldn't be smelly. When Roskilly's mine, I'll make sure he's looked after properly."

Caroline, still fighting the impulse to laugh, forbore pointing out that for Roskilly to belong to Yves, his grandfather would have to be dead.

"Come along," she said, rising to her feet. "We'd better go and eat our dinner or it'll be cold and the tea will be stewing, and Patience will be taking it all back downstairs."

After dinner was eaten and not a speck remained nor a drop of water in the teapot, Yves led Caroline, with Dash padding at their heels, out into the main house. All was quiet with no sign of any other member of the family. Presumably they were eating either in the dining room or the parlor, as their midday meal would only be a light luncheon, with their dinner in the evening, when Yves would get another helping of bread and butter for his supper. Or maybe an egg if he were lucky and Mrs. Teague could smuggle one upstairs past Bridget's eagle eye.

Yves took Caroline's hand. "This way. Grandpapa's room is down here."

She let him lead her down another corridor past several closed doors until they reached the end.

Yves halted, leaning close to whisper. "We have to knock, and then that horrid Miss Rodgers will come, clumping in her man's boots."

Caroline obliged.

After a long wait, the door opened to reveal Miss Rodgers. The discontented expression on her bony face implied she'd lost a sovereign and found a farthing. Or that she'd just drunk sour milk. Or that she'd trodden in something unpleasant. Most likely all three. "Yes?" she said, her accusing gaze running over Yves and Caroline.

"We've come to see Grandpapa," Yves said, who was not given to beating about the bush. "Let us in."

By his side, Dash wagged his tail in enthusiastic corroboration.

Miss Rodgers's deep-set and already slitty eyes narrowed still further. "Sir Hugh is resting."

Yves, being shorter than Caroline had a better view into the room. "No, he's not," he said. "I can see him sitting up in bed."

"He's about to be resting," Miss Rodgers almost snarled. Had she been told not to let them in?

"Who's that at the door?" called a querulous voice. "Is that my little Yves?"

"Grandpapa!" Yves dived under Miss Rodgers's hammy arm and raced into the room, closely followed by Dash, barking in excitement. Miss Rodgers made a belated grab for him and missed, but in so doing vacated the door space she'd been blocking. Caroline took advantage by stepping inside and closing the door behind her.

Miss Rodgers gave a growl of fury and interposed herself again between Caroline and the bed, hands on hips and legs akimbo. "Strictly no dogs in here."

The old man sitting propped up in the bed was made of stern stuff though. "Rodgers," he snapped, sounding far less querulous than before. "Let the girl through. I've a mind to see a prettier face than yours. And that wouldn't be difficult. Get out of her way. And if I want the dog in here, I'll have it in here. Off you go and do something else."

Rodgers moved out of the way but not without bestowing a threatening glare on Caroline. She moved over to the side of the room from where she had a good view of the bed and stood, arms now folded, glaring at Caroline and Yves.

Yves jumped up onto the bed with the air of someone very much at home in the sick room, and so did the agile Dash. He sat holding his grandfather's hand in his while the old man petted the little dog with his free hand.

"Fetch up a chair, my dear," the old man said. "Come and sit beside me so I can see you properly. My eyes aren't what they used to be."

Caroline glanced around until her gaze fell on an upright

chair which she carried over to the bed. She sat on it, close, but not too close, as that would have been too forward of her.

"That's better," the old man said, his blue eyes, just like those Nat, Hetty, and Yves shared, twinkling in a roguish manner. "Now I can see you. And what a pretty girl you are."

Well, perhaps he couldn't see her quite that well. Caroline had no pretensions to the kind of prettiness Ysella and Hetty possessed, although Kit had once called her striking.

The old man freed his hand from Yves's grasp and waved it at Rodgers. "What're you waiting for, woman? I told you once already. You can go. My grandson will keep me company and this fine young lady. I'll send Yves to find you before they go."

Rodgers scowled even more, but she left, banging the door behind her as she went.

"That's better," the old man said with a sigh. "Can't stand the woman, but she's good at her job, and strong with it. I can't get about the way I used to, and she's more than capable of picking me up when the occasion arises." He gave a chuckle. "Sadly, I'm not the man I was." He held up a bony wrist. "I seem to have wasted away to nothing." He patted Yves's hand. "Now introduce me to your new friend, child."

Yves obliged. "She's Caroline Fairfield, my governess now, after Aunt Ruth got rid of poor Miss Hawkins."

The old man's eyes sharpened. "Miss Hawkins was a good governess."

Yves nodded. "She was. But Aunt Ruth made her go. And Hester." He grinned at Caroline. "Caroline is really nice, though. It's just that Bridget isn't. She's head nursery maid now Hester's gone and she makes me take horrible *medicine*." He managed a disgusted sneer.

The old man held a trembling hand out to Caroline, his gaze penetrating. "Charmed to make your acquaintance, Miss Fairfield."

"You have to call her Caroline," Yves interjected. "I do when we're not in lessons and so does Hetty. Miss Fairfield is too unfriendly sounding. That was why I used to call Miss Hawkins Hawkie. Much more friendly that Miss Hawkins."

The old man raised his eyebrows. "Might I follow my grandson's lead and use your first name also?"

Caroline nodded. "I should be honored if you would." How was she ever going to get a private word with Sir Hugh with Yves in such close attendance? He and Dash looked very much settled on the bed. The little spaniel had rolled over onto his back to have his stomach rubbed and Yves was lounging back, leaning on his hands, as though nothing would budge him.

"Now, Caroline," Sir Hugh said with a smile that reminded her of the undamaged half of his other grandson's face. "Tell me all about yourself and how a young lady such as you comes to be such a scamp's governess."

This took a while and Caroline didn't divulge all of what she'd told Nat. Not that she wanted to hide it from Sir Hugh, but rather because she didn't want Yves exposed to that sad tale. She managed to intersperse the story with a few choice anecdotes from her life at Cadley that had both members of her audience laughing.

At last, an idea came to her. "Sir Hugh," she began, "would you like a tray of tea brought up? And maybe some cakes?"

He snorted with laughter. "Do I look like I drink milksop tea? A glass of brandy would suit me better, but Rodgers refuses to let me have any."

Brandy. Could she send Yves to find some? Perhaps to ask Dickon to bring it up? If Mrs. Treloar found out, and find out she would as Rodgers was bound to tell her, trouble would ensue. She'd have to be firm. "The best I can offer is coffee, I'm afraid."

He pulled a discontented face, all of a sudden childlike. "If that's all that's on offer, then I suppose I'll take it. Ring for Dickon or Ennion and we'll get them to send a tray up."

"I'll go and get it," Yves said, sliding off the bed. The contented Dash, who was still having his stomach scratched, made no move to follow him.

Caroline couldn't have asked for more. "I'll have coffee as well, and perhaps you could ask Mrs. Teague to send up some cakes. No running. I don't want you falling down the stairs because you're in a needless hurry."

Yves ran to the door.

"Remember. No running."

He shot her a cheeky glance and disappeared through it, leaving it open.

Caroline went and closed it. She'd have to be quick, although more than likely Yves would seize this opportunity to eat something in the kitchen with Mrs. Teague while the coffee was prepared.

She turned back to Sir Hugh, suddenly very afraid. She was about to confide her fears in him, and he might well pass them on to the very people she didn't want to know about them. Especially if he didn't believe her. Did she even believe it herself?

"Sir Hugh, might I speak frankly to you?"

His eyes narrowed, all childishness fled. "You sound very serious, my dear."

"I am. It's a serious matter."

"I see it must be for you to have to wait until the child's not here. Go on. I'm listening."

"I don't really know how to begin, so I'll just come out and say it. I'm afraid Yves is in danger."

He regarded her in silence for a moment, the intelligence in his eyes sharp and clear. "I shall not do you the injustice of asking you from what he is in danger."

What? "You knew?"

He nodded. "I suspected. Miss Hawkins came to me with her worries, but she had no proof of malicious intent. I listened, but it was already too late for her to do anything. She only came to see me once and was gone by the next day. Dismissed for bad conduct, Rodgers told me when I asked. With unmitigated glee, I might add. She seemed positively triumphant about the misfortune of others. I get all my news that way or from the children.

Ruth rarely graces me with her presence. She stays away from the sickroom and has her minion, Rodgers, do her bidding. If that woman chose to smother me in my sleep, there's nothing I could do to stop her."

A new fear surfaced in Caroline's head. "Do you think she might?"

"I wouldn't put anything past her. The woman has the build and strength of an ox."

"I think Bridget is in Mrs. Treloar's pay as well."

"The boy's nursery nurse?"

"The same. A few days ago, I found Yves was falling asleep in his lessons. He'd been given some new 'medicine' the night before by Bridget. When she was eating her lunch in the servants' hall, I sneaked into her room and found where it was hidden. It was something that contains laudanum, but in small quantities. I think they've been adding more laudanum to the bottle, or it wouldn't have had such a strong effect on him."

Sir Hugh bowed his head. "And I've no need to ask where they've been getting the laudanum from." He paused, his eyes clouding. "I take it to manage my pain, and at nights to help me sleep. Rodgers administers it. It's the only way for me to get a night's unbroken sleep, and I can't manage without it." He put a hand up to rub his eyes. "Where is the boy's medicine now?"

"I swapped the contents for some harmless tonic I purchased in Penzance. Where quite by chance Yves and I met Miss Hawkins who has found herself a position as companion to an elderly lady in the town. She confided her own suspicions, but there's little she can do from there. It falls to me to keep Yves safe, and I'm very much worried that I don't know how to do that." Caroline bit her lip. "I swapped the contents of the bottle, as I said, but when that runs out, there'll be another bottle and that one *will* have laudanum in it, maybe even more than before, if they think the first doses weren't working. I was reprimanded for taking Yves to Penzance, so I doubt very much whether I can go again, and I've no way of getting word to Miss Hawkins, or the local constable. I can't go on my own and leave Yves unguarded."

Sir Hugh snorted. "Much good the local constable would do you. He's an oaf."

Caroline leaned forward in her seat. "Which is why I've come to you, two heads being better than one. I know you're handicapped by being confined to bed, but can you see a way out of this for us, without Yves ending up… dead?"

Sir Hugh reached out and caught her hand. "You must play your cards tight to your chest, Caroline, for I'm sure now, with what Miss Hawkins told me and what you've just said, that your suspicions are correct. My younger son's wife has always resented that she didn't marry my boy Robert, or perhaps the resentment was caused because Robert provided us with his own heir before he died. With Lowenna losing so many babies before they reached full term, Ruth must have thought he'd never get a living child."

Footsteps sounded outside the door.

Sir Hugh tightened his grip on her hand. "Return tomorrow at the same time, but come alone, if you can. We need to talk. Insist that Rodgers lets you in. Don't take no for an answer."

The door opened and Yves entered, accompanied by Dickon carrying a tray. On it sat a jug of coffee, two small cups, and a plate of cakes. Telltale crumbs decorated Yves's mouth and the front of his skeleton suit. He'd plainly eaten some of the cakes while he waited for the coffee.

He ran across the room and jumped onto the bed again. "Rock cakes," he announced. "Delicious."

Chapter Twenty

NAT, MEANWHILE, HAD decided to take a ride over to one of the several mines Trefusis was now managing, courtesy of his mother, for his grandfather. As a boy, he'd always had a fascination for what went on in them and had been underground on many occasions with Sir Hugh, who had always been a man who liked to keep his finger on the pulse of his own businesses. "What good is a mine owner who doesn't know what it's like to be a miner?" he'd said to the impressionable boy Nat had once been. "If you want to run any business, then you must start at the bottom and learn how every aspect of it works." So, in his holidays from Harrow, the young Nat Treloar had joined the men who worked for his grandfather in the oppressive, cramped conditions underground and found out for himself what it was like to work the rock face deep under the earth, and often deep under the sea as well.

On his way out of the house, he was sidetracked by his mother, who was in the land agent's office with the door open and must have seen him walking past. "Nathaniel, do you have a minute?"

Nat set his jaw and turned around, the old boyhood habit of obedience strong. "Yes, Mother."

She rose from behind her desk as Nat entered the office. By rights, Trefusis should have had a secretary to help him take care of the books, or taken care of them himself, but even when his uncle Robert, and father, Kenver, had been alive, his mother had taken care of the money side of the family business. And neither Sir Hugh nor Robert and especially not his father had protested. All three of them had been more interested in how their empire ran rather than how much money came in. A pair of halfmoon spectacles Nat had never seen before sat on the end of his mother's long nose, making her look the part of office wallah.

"I've been wanting a few minutes alone with you since you returned," she said, fiddling with the pen in her right hand.

He'd been avoiding her, but it was too late now. She had him snared.

"Sit down, won't you?"

Nat took the leather upholstered seat in front of the desk and his mother sat down again as well.

She put her pen down with a clunk. "Now you are home from the wars, I think it is high time you thought of what you are going to do next." Her eyes narrowed. "And as the last male Treloar you owe it to the family to marry and produce an heir."

Well, that was unexpected. For a moment Nat was speechless. Of all the things he'd been expecting, this wasn't one of them.

Her eyes narrowed. "You owe it to your father and grandfather as the last male Treloar."

He had an answer for that one. "I'm not the last Treloar. There's Yves."

She waved a dismissive hand. "He's just a child and a weakly one at that. We cannot be sure he'll even grow to be a man."

Nat frowned. "That's still no reason to be hurrying me into matrimony. And anyway, what am I to offer a prospective bride? My face? My distinct lack of fortune?" Once upon a time he'd been a catch, with his good looks and his splendid uniform. Julia had thought so, anyway. But things had changed since then, and Julia was no longer here.

His mother's thin lips grew thinner still as her mouth pursed into an expression of distaste, perhaps at the mention of his looks. "You may well inherit the whole estate yet. And if not, your grandfather has bestowed a sizeable inheritance upon you and Hetty. Certainly enough to support a wife." Her expression was in direct contrast to her words. As though the last thing she wanted was him inheriting anything and this suggestion of marriage might be a ruse for something else.

Although, if his mother was as determined as he remembered, then she'd have him married off by Christmas. But Nat was no longer a boy and no longer under her control. "Mother, I appreciate your concern for the Treloar name, but I have no intention of marrying just for the sake of continuing it." He might have done so once, but not now. And not with some simpering girl his mother might choose to shove under his nose. "I shall marry when it suits *me*, not you, and it will be on my own terms." He would have liked to say he'd marry for love, only what woman would ever love him, looking the way he did? Or he could have told her he'd already been married and widowed once, and he'd decided never to marry again and put another woman through the agony of childbirth that had snatched his wife from him. Not after Julia. But he had no intention of sharing Julia with anyone.

His mother's eyes narrowed and her brow darkened. Never one to take well to being crossed, even if she hadn't meant what she'd said, she more than ever had the look of an angry harpy. "You will at least attend further social gatherings down here to consider a suitable young Cornish lady as a bride. And you will accompany Hetty." Aha, so that was it—she wanted him to escort Hetty to where *she* might meet a suitable young man. He might have guessed it would be for Hetty's benefit, or rather, their mother's, not his.

He sighed. Like the proverbial horse to water, she could, if she meant it, lead him to various suitable young ladies, but she couldn't make him love them, nor them love him. No doubt one look at his damaged face would have them running for the hills, anyway. The only woman he'd danced with at the Carlyon ball had been Caroline, outside on the shadowy terrace. Almost, a smile tried to curve his up-till-now downturned mouth.

Hawk-eyed, she pounced. "Do you perhaps have a young lady in mind?"

Exasperation had him on his feet. "No, Mother, I do not. And now, if you don't mind, I shall get on with what I was about to do when you called me in here. Please put all thoughts of marrying me off out of your mind, because I have no intention of complying." He touched his face. "Has it not occurred to you that *this* might put off any prospective bride?"

Was that a look of satisfaction on her face or his imagination?

Without waiting for her reply, he marched out of the room, closing the door behind him with a satisfying bang.

Bloody woman. She'd always been like that, trying to control his life from his childhood. Not that she'd seen him often, because she hadn't. Both he and Hetty had been left in the care of nursemaids and nannies, then a tutor for him followed by boarding school with very few visits to Treloar. No wonder this place didn't feel like home, when it should.

In the long convalescence after his face wound, he'd had time to think about his future, and he'd come to the conclusion that it couldn't hold the possibility of another marriage. Not now. Not with this face. What would Julia have thought if she could see him now? For a moment her face rose in front of his eyes: her alabaster skin and lightly flushed cheeks, her cascading golden curls, her wide blue eyes. An angel in human form, or so he'd once told her. But God loves his angels, and she'd been too good to live. God, that most unfeeling of deities, had snatched her from him, along with his infant son, even before the child drew his first breath. And all he had now were his memories.

He clumped down the corridor toward the stables, hands fisted by his sides and, had he but known it, a scowl on his face fit to frighten the devil himself.

Bam. A small tornado cannoned into him and rebounded,

gasping.

Nat's hands went out to steady the tornado and recognized it as Yves.

Caroline came hurrying around the corner. "Yves! You must look where you're going. I'm so sorry, Nat.

"Are you going to the stables as well?" Yves asked, unabashed.

Nat nodded. "I'm riding over to Wheal Jenny."

Caroline raised her eyebrows in a question.

Nat shrugged. "One of our tin mines. The nearest one. You can see its chimney from the upper windows. I once had friends who worked there, and I wanted to see how it was faring for myself." What he didn't say was that he wanted to see how it was faring under Trefusis's iron hand and unsympathetic management. "An inspection, you might call it, as I haven't seen the place for years."

"You're going to the mine?" Yves asked, impressed. "Can I come too? I've never been, and I've always wanted to see inside one of the mines. Are you going down the shaft?"

"I'm riding over," Nat said. "I'm not sure…"

"Oh, I can ride," Yves declared. "I ride the garden pony, Blossom. I'd like a horse of my own, but Aunt Ruth won't let me…" His voice trailed away in disappointment.

"I'm sure Blossom is perfect for you," Caroline said. "You can't have a horse until you're bigger. I only had a small pony until I was twelve, and that's three years older than you."

"But I'm a boy," Yves tried. "Boys get to ride horses before girls do because they're better riders."

"Nonsense," Nat put in. "When I was your age, all I had was a pony." At least, thanks to his father, it hadn't been the garden pony though, and he'd pretended it was a flashy thoroughbred as he galloped along the beach with Jacka, who'd had to make do with his father's cart pony.

Yves squinted up at him. "You haven't said whether I can come."

Caroline caught his hand. "I'm sure your cousin has business he wants to conduct at the mine, Yves, and won't want us hanging about."

The thought that Caroline might come too caused Nat's heart to give an unaccountable little flip. Now, why would it do that? But without a doubt, the thought of riding out in female company, despite what he'd just said to his mother, pleased him, after so long amongst just soldiers. Just to have a woman to talk to would be good. That was all. Nothing more. "Do you possess a riding habit?"

Caroline nodded. "I don't know why I brought it with me. Not many governesses get to ride, I fear. But something prompted me to do so. It was that or give it away, I suppose, and I hate to part with things I love." Her eyes twinkled at him. She must be relishing the idea of escaping from Roskilly on horseback as much as he was.

"Then Yves and I will go and organize the horses while you change," Nat said. Hopefully she wasn't the sort of woman who took forever with her toilette. She didn't look as though she was, but you never could tell.

She flashed him a smile. "I won't be long."

She wasn't lying, either. Young Pascoe was leading out the mare Nat had asked him to prepare for her just as she emerged from the house. There hadn't been a lot in the way of horseflesh to choose from. There being no man of the house with his grandfather bedridden, most of the livestock seemed to be for driving. Maybe Trefusis, who must have a horse or two of his own, kept his in his own stables.

Two riding horses remained, though. He had his mother's aged bay mare, Duchess, again, and Young Pascoe had put a side-saddle on a smaller chestnut with a pretty, Arab head and a long white blaze. Hetty's horse, Folly. Yves was already astride Blossom and lounging with a negligent hand on her rump, looking at Folly with an acquisitive expression as though he'd have liked to ride her.

Caroline's habit was of a rich burgundy that suited her well, bringing out the hidden red highlights in her dark hair, on top of which perched a fetching hat. He could almost have described her as pretty, which had not occurred to him before. In fact, now he paused to think about it, the description he would use for her was striking, especially dressed up like some Amazon princess. Prettiness could be a fleeting thing, but a woman with Caroline's strong features would always be striking.

She used the stone mounting block and was soon on board Folly, gathering up her reins with an air of experience. Nat, who'd waited, mounted himself, observing the way she sat as though a natural. This was a young woman who'd done a lot of riding, perhaps to hounds. Interesting.

Yves, on the other hand, was more of a novice, or if not a novice then a boy who cared nothing for riding style. He had his feet thrust too far into his stirrups, his legs stuck forward and his reins too long. Blossom had the air about her of a pony who intended to get the better of her young rider.

"Can I go first?" Yves asked, the moment Caroline was on. "I know the way, I think. You can see the mine chimney from the nursery window. Just."

"You'll go where your pony fits in best," Nat said. "Which by the look of her is bringing up the rear. She doesn't strike me as a front-line cavalry horse."

"Neither is Duchess," Yves retorted. "Aunt Ruth likes a plodder. I've heard her say so. That's why she won't sell Duchess to the knacker man and buy a livelier mount."

"Nevertheless," Nat said, hiding the smile that threatened to emerge, "you can ride *behind* Caroline and me. Where a good child should be."

Yves's cheeky grin suggested being a good child was furthest from his ambitions just then, but he brought Blossom in behind Folly and Duchess for the time being.

"And don't poke your feet that far through your stirrups," Caroline scolded. "If you fall off, your foot might get stuck and you could be dragged."

"If I fall off," Yves said with a scowl, "Blossom will stop. She's only walking because I keep kicking her. Why's she so slow when she's ridden?"

Caroline laughed. "If you recall, she wasn't fast when in harness, either. I had to keep tickling her with the whip."

"Can I have a whip, then?"

Nat shook his head. "Learn to use your legs correctly when you ride, and only then can you have a whip. Where you have them at the moment, Blossom doesn't even know they exist."

They took the narrow path toward the beach, which seemed to revive Yves's spirits, much as it would once have done for Nat. And even Blossom seemed to pick up her small hooves and increase her speed. A sea breeze wafted the smell of seaweed and salty air to Nat's nostrils. If he felt at home anywhere at Roskilly, it was here on Morgelyn Beach.

BECAUSE OF THE width of the path, Caroline would have been forced to bump knees with Nat, had she not been riding side-saddle as they negotiated the track. She took a quick, sideways look at him, where he rode on her right, the undamaged side of his face toward her.

His mouth had lost some of the twist she'd taken to be cruelty but now suspected might have been unhappiness, and the wind was blowing his hair back from his forehead, revealing just how young he really was. Hardly any older than she and yet with so much suffering behind him. Was he really a man who would see a child dead to gain an inheritance? His demeanor toward Yves didn't smack of threatening at all, but would it, if he were what she feared? Surely, he would hide it well. Like this.

She smiled at him. "Thank you for letting Yves and me accompany you."

He shrugged. "The boy needs to see the businesses that will one day soon be his."

"He took me to see your grandfather today."

A raised eyebrow.

"He seems, despite being confined to his bed, to be in good health. Just very old."

Nat nodded. "At least he still has his wits, unlike Aunt Agnes. She doesn't know what day it is most of the time. But he's approaching his eighty-eighth birthday in August, which is old by any standard. He can't go on forever."

"When he dies, will you take over Yves's guardianship?"

He shrugged. "I suppose I'll have to. I can't see my grandfather allowing my mother such a responsibility."

Did she detect a hint of dislike for his mother there? Might that be a good thing? Caroline couldn't be sure. All she could think of was that if Nat were to have control over Yves, anything could happen. Oh, how confusing this was. Part of her wanted to like Nat, especially since he'd revealed some of his past to her in what had felt like touching candor, but another more wary part was screaming out that *he* would be the one to benefit from Yves's death, and surely, he must be behind any plot to do away with her small charge, or at least in support of it. However, either way, it would be a good idea to get to know him better and keep him close. What was that old saying? Keep your friends close and your enemies closer. But was he her enemy or her friend?

They emerged from the dunes onto the beach, where the tide was half in, or that could have been half out. She had no way of telling. Yves gave a little squeal of excitement and, his legs hammering Blossom's sides in completely the wrong place, trotted past them toward the sea's edge.

Caroline and Nat trotted after him, the fresh sea breeze tugging loose Caroline's neatly confined hair. What a good thing her hat was secured by several long pins and she had the spare one in the bodice of her habit.

Blossom did *not* want to paddle, much to Yves's chagrin. In fact, she seemed to be harboring a distinct suspicion the tiny waves rolling in toward her were intent on her demise.

"We'll have a canter, along the sand and not in the water," Nat said. "This way."

Folly proved to be a moderately well-schooled horse with an easy stride. They rode in a line, with Nat leading and Yves bringing up the rear, with Caroline keeping a close eye on him. He seemed to manage well though, and Blossom, probably relieved not to have to paddle, trundled along behind Folly with an uncharacteristic show of enthusiasm. Perhaps she was realizing how much nicer it was to be ridden than to have to pull the pony cart or the lawn mower.

At the western end of the beach, Nat led the way through the dunes and onto a narrow path edged by stunted, prickly hedging, uphill toward the heather-covered rise of the headland.

"Penmar Head," he said as Caroline brought Folly in beside Duchess again. "Which is like calling it 'head-mark-head' as 'pen' is Cornish for 'head.' And the 'mar' part of the name refers to King Mark of Cornwall, one of King Arthur's knights. I suppose it might be the head of King Mark's head, if that makes any sense to you."

Ahead of them, the outline of a tall, narrow building appeared, with an even taller chimney beside it. "Wheal Jenny," Nat said, with a hint of pride. "My great-grandfather's first mine."

⸻ ❦ ⸻

Chapter Twenty-One

"WE HAVE A steam engine here to pump water out of the lower adits," Nat said, indicating the smoke emerging from the tall chimney. "The best veins head out under the sea—veins of copper and tin, although we're only working tin here, and have been since before I was born. Not much of a market for copper any longer. Not like there was in my great-grandfather's time. That was how he made his fortune. To start with. Unfortunately, it all comes from North Wales now, where it's less expensive to produce."

Caroline stared out across the foam-flecked sea. "If the veins go out under the sea, does the mine as well? Do the miners have to dig tunnels under the sea to get at the tin?" How awful that sounded. Even in her imagination, the thought of tunnelling under the sea seemed terrifying.

He nodded. "They have to be very careful where they dig and not get too near the sea floor or the sea would come flooding in. There'd be no time to evacuate."

A shiver ran down Caroline's back at the thought. "How far out does the mine go?"

"The adits in Wheal True, our other mine, go out a mile at least. These not so far. But some of the old adits in this one are hundreds of years old."

"Have you been down the mine?" Yves asked, kicking the

reluctant Blossom forward. "I'd like to see what it's like."

Nat nodded. "Many times, as a boy. I worked here some of my summers when I was old enough. But not for more than eleven years now."

"Did you go out under the sea?" Caroline asked, another shiver running down her back at the thought of Nat out there with all that water above his head.

Nat nodded again. "Sometimes, when you're down there, you hear the boulders being rolled about on the seabed above your head by the water, and the roaring of the waves when the sea's rough. A bit unnerving to start with, but you get used to it."

"Weren't you afraid the sea would break through?" Caroline had always suffered from slight claustrophobia and the very thought of being in a tunnel beneath not just miles of rock but the sea as well set her heart pounding.

"You don't think about it," Nat said with a dismissive shrug. "Don't forget. I was a boy then and boys never think of danger."

An image of Ysella's older brother Kit, with whom their respective mothers had once tried to engineer a match for her, hanging upside down from a high branch in a tree on the Ormonde estate flashed into Caroline's head, and she laughed. "Very true. I have yet to meet a boy for whom caution is a natural attribute."

"So can I go down the mine?" Yves asked, as if to prove her words. "As it's going to belong to me one day, surely I should be able to see what it's like down there. I really, really want to go down the mine."

Nat shook his head. "Not now. You're too young. Maybe when you're older."

Yves's lower lip jutted in rebellion, but he had the sense not to argue. Nat had about him the air of a man with whom it wouldn't be a good idea to do that.

Nat turned Duchess toward a long, low building off to one side from the mine workings. "We'll tether our horses here, by the count house, and see if anyone's about." He gave a shrug, taking out his pocket watch to consult the time. "Most of the men should be down the mine, but as it's nearly time for the changeover of shifts, they should be coming up soon."

"Do they work at nights as well?" Caroline asked, eyes widening.

Nat nodded. "It makes no difference if you're down in the dark whether outside is day or night. And it increases production."

"Is that something Trefusis introduced?" Somehow, if it were Trefusis who'd brought in this regime, it would feel better.

But Nat shook his head. "No. It's always been done. Shift work employs more men, and puts food on the table of more families. They're glad to have the work." He pointed a finger. "The bal maidens don't work at night though. Just in daylight hours as they work above ground."

"What's a bal maiden?" Caroline asked as she halted Folly beside a handy hitching ring someone had embedded in the stone wall of the count house. Yves was already slithering off Blossom, his eyes fixed in longing on the mine buildings. "Yves. Do *not* run on ahead. This is a mine and it could be dangerous."

Nat dismounted. "A girl whose job it is to break up the ore the men bring to the surface. It earns them a bit of extra money, which helps their families. They don't earn what a miner earns though." He grabbed Yves by the collar. "What did Miss Fairfield just say to you? Stay here. She's quite right about the danger and you know nothing of how to behave at a mine."

Yves's shoulders sagged, but he didn't run off.

Caroline glanced at the ground. Could she manage to slide down from Folly without hooking her habit up too much? Ysella had the right idea. Men's clothing was much better suited to riding horses than a woman's riding habit. But Caroline had until now felt no inclination to dress as a boy, unlike her friend Ysella.

Nat held out his arms.

A curious unwillingness to allow him to help her down washed over Caroline. Not that she didn't want him to touch her, but more that she didn't want to be beholden to someone whose motives she didn't entirely trust. How difficult her feelings were making this for her.

"Let me help you," he said.

Nothing for it but to allow him to play the gentleman. She unhooked her leg from the saddle's high pommel and slid down into his arms. How strong he was and how firm his hold on her waist. Unnervingly so, and really quite exciting. She reprimanded herself for having these feelings. She did *not* want to provoke thoughts like this about him, or indeed about any young man. The only male she could think of right now was Yves. He was the important one in her life.

For just a moment, Nat stared down into her eyes, his hands still firmly on her waist. Was he not going to let her go? She removed her own hand from his arm, where necessity and balance had forced her to put it, and took a step back, out of his grasp. Why on earth was her heart pounding so hard? Had he been able to feel it under her ribs? Under his hands? This was ridiculous. She'd met many men more handsome and eligible than Nat, including the one she'd fancied herself in love with several years ago, before he'd gone off to fight Boney and never returned, but never had she felt quite as flustered as Nat was making her. Warmth crept up her cheeks and there was nothing she could do about it.

Saved by the bell, or rather by the door of the count house opening with a bang.

A large man, in the sort of shabby, workaday suit that told her he couldn't be a common miner but also wasn't a gentleman, strode out into the bright sunshine, one hand up to shade his eyes. He paused for a moment then started forward, a grin on his broad face. "Why if 'tain't Master Nathaniel. Well, I'm blowed." His gaze flicked over Nat's face but the smile barely lessened. "I'd know 'ee anywhere, even after all these years." He held out a huge, square hand and seized Nat's. "I'm that glad to see you back safe from the wars. That glad."

"Gryff Casworan. I didn't dare to hope you'd still be here." Nat's ravaged face twisted itself into a one-sided smile, the most genuine Caroline had seen so far. He must really like this burly stranger.

Mr. Casworan appeared to notice Yves and Caroline for the first time. "And this'll be the little master, no doubting." He held out his hand to Yves, who after a moment's hesitation put his own small one in it and was rewarded by having it pumped up and down in a hearty handshake. "You don't look too sickly to me, young master."

"I'm not," Yves said. "Why does everyone keep saying I am?" He lifted his right arm, bending it at the elbow and clenching his fist. "Feel my muscles. I'm as strong as a…as strong as a piece of Cornish granite."

Mr. Casworan burst out laughing, but he did feel Yves's muscles. "Aye, lad, you are, that," he said, surreptitiously winking at Nat. "You're stronger than Nat here were at your age, I'll give you that."

A wide grin split Yves's face from ear to ear, tinged with a speck of smug superiority as he glanced at Nat, who seemed to be keeping a straight face with difficulty, his lips twitching. Caroline couldn't help but smile at this exchange. She took a better look at the tactful Mr. Casworan.

Taller than Nat by several inches, and more solidly built, Gryff Casworan had a powerful look about him only a little softened by a budding pot belly, as though lately life had been treating him rather too well.

"May I present Miss Fairfield, Yves's governess," Nat said, and Caroline found herself the recipient of a deep bow from this friendly giant. "And this is my old friend, Gryff Casworan. He and I go back a long way."

"To when you was nothing but a slip of a boy scarce any bigger than this one here," Gryff said, ruffling Yves's already wind-ruffled hair. "And if he isn't as like you as a pair of peas in their pod, I'll eat my hat. And it's a new one, so it'd be hard chewing. I can see you two are close related."

"We're cousins," Yves said. "Our fathers were brothers."

"I know that, young master," Gryff said. "I knowed both your fathers well. Not that your own father wanted to make hisself known down here at the mine. He preferred the family ship builders over to Falmouth. Not like your cousin Nathaniel and his pa." He looked at Nat. "Mr. Treloar I should say now, I suppose. Lessen you want me to call you major?"

"Nat did me well enough when I was a boy working with you, and will do me fine now. I've had enough of army hierarchy to last me a lifetime." Nat gestured at the count house. "But how is it that I find you installed in the count house and not working in an adit?"

Gryff's chest inflated with obvious pride. "Mine Captain now, I am. And that's a funny story." He waved a hand to encompass his body. "Grew too big, is what I did. Look at me. I don't fit down those tunnels no more, not like I did when you and I were lads. And thanks to you teaching me to read and reckon, Mr. Robert put me in the count house. I been here ever since, although that new man of your mother's, Mr. Trefusis, he keeps on coming to look over my shoulder. Seems to think I might be swindling him and your ma." He heaved a sigh. "He don't know nothing about how to manage men and win their hearts, that one. There's no one here at Wheal Jenny as cares for him."

Nat's brow lowered. "I suspected as much. That's one of the reasons I'm here today. I've been out over to some of the farms to visit my grandfather's tenants, and I wasn't impressed with Trefusis's methods of management."

Casworan grimaced. "I doubt there's much you can do about it. He's dug his feet in under that table, all right." He shook his head. "I spend most of my time up here in the count house, but I still gets to go down the mine from time to time. Gotta be seen by the men and gotta see the conditions they're working in, like your granfer used to say. And they've gotta see me and know I'm on their side. Trefusis ain't like your pa was, God rest his soul.

He's never set foot in any of the mines." He shook his head again. "He's a hard master, I have to say. Since old Sir Hugh were forced to give up the governance of the estate and the mines, and your mother brung Trefusis in, he's been squeezing it any which way to get more production out of it for less expenditure. Many's the family that's feeling the pinch now, both miners and tenant farmers."

"That was one of the things I came over here to find out," Nat said. "But I didn't think to find someone I knew straight away who could tell me about it. I'm very glad I came."

Yves, bored by the conversation, was wandering off, so Caroline followed him, leaving Nat to discover more of what Trefusis had been up to. As they approached the mine buildings, a whistle blew, making her jump. Yves glanced over his shoulder. "What was that for?"

She didn't need to answer though. A column of people was coming over the brow of the hill, following a rough track from inland. Their voices, carried by the wind, drifted across the heathery hillside. Good heavens. They were singing a hymn she knew—*Love Divine All Loves Excelling*. Out here in the late afternoon sunshine, with a sea breeze stirring her hair, and a throng of tatty miners with their voices raised in worship on their way to work in the bowels of the earth, the hymn she knew so well took on an almost mystical air.

"Shift changeover," Nat said, coming to stand beside her. "The miners down below will be coming up the shafts and these new ones will be taking over."

"But some of them are children," Yves said, staring at the approaching relief miners. "Like me."

Sure enough, a proportion of the new miners were indeed children, who might well have been scarcely older than Yves. They certainly weren't much bigger. Like their elders, they sang with lusty enthusiasm, swinging small pails that might have contained their sustenance for the night shift.

Of course, Caroline knew about child workers, but living in

Wiltshire had done nothing to prepare her for seeing them. Everything in her heart cried out that it must be wrong to send children down into a place she would never go herself. She couldn't argue with children having to work in daylight, although she wasn't sure what they might be working at, if she were honest, but to send children down into the dark seemed a terrible thing to do.

She glanced at Nat and Gryff, standing side by side watching the changeover. "Does the mine need to employ such young children?"

Nat shrugged. "Their families need the money they can bring in. The girls work as bal maidens, but the boys go down the mines, where they're used to squeeze into small gaps a grown man can't fit into."

Gryff met her gaze. "I first went down there when I was eight years old."

That was younger than Yves. "Couldn't their fathers' wages be increased so the children don't need to work?"

Nat compressed his lips. "You'll have to ask Trefusis that one, as he's in charge now. Or my mother, as it seems she still holds the purse strings. And if you do that, then you're a braver soul than I am. She's never taken kindly to being told what to do."

"How do they get up and down the mine?" Yves asked, stepping nearer. Some of the children, now they were up close, were looking in curiosity at him, in his clean clothes and with his striking blonde hair and wind-flushed cheeks that gave him a healthy, rosy-faced look. A stark contrast to the children's dirty clothes, pale faces, and what seemed like uniformly mud-colored hair.

"Ladders," Gryff said. "From level to level. Down the ladder shaft. They'll have to wait until all the men and boys from the last shift are up, then they'll climb down and start work."

Caroline shivered, the hope that she'd never have to find out what it was like to go down a mine at the forefront of her mind.

A few men appeared from amongst the buildings, dirty and

disheveled and walking with their backs bent and their heads down as though exhausted. Amongst them a smattering of children in a similar state. Was this what working all day in a mine did to you? As a boy, had Nat come up from the depths looking like this? But he'd been going home to a hot bath and a fine dinner, unlike some of these workers who might only be going home to a cold hearth and the barest of meals. The hymn singing of the approaching night shift had ceased, and they were standing back, watching the day shift as they blinked in the unaccustomed sunlight.

"They look terrible," Caroline said.

Nat nodded. "You're right. They do." He turned to look at Casworan accusingly. "Why do they look like this? It may be eleven years since I was here, but what's been happening? I don't remember the men being like this when I last worked with them."

Casworan had the grace to look embarrassed. "There's nothing I can do. Mr. Trefusis has reduced wages to save money and the price of bread has done nothing but rise. These people are sending out their children to earn enough money just to eat. They can't afford to put clothes on their backs or boots on their feet."

Nat shook his head. "Why didn't you tell someone?"

Casworan raised his shoulders and grimaced. "Who? Mrs. Treloar lets Trefusis do as he wishes. Sir Hugh's an invalid whose information is filtered through his nurse so he knows nothing of what Trefusis gets up to. No one's going to let me have an audience with him, and even if I did see him, what can he do from his sickbed? Apart from Trefusis and your mother, who don't care, who else is there to tell? And if I were to go to the other local mine owners do you think they'd take my side against one of their own?"

Of course they wouldn't. The landed gentry stuck together through thick and thin. It had been the same in Wiltshire.

"Those children look hungry," Yves said. "Can't we get them

food? Look how thin and dirty they are." He looked up at Caroline. "I don't think I really do want to go down the mine if that's what it does to you."

Nat banged his fist into the palm of his other hand. "How long has this been going on?"

Casworan sucked in his lips. "Since your grandfather suffered his nasty turn. 'Twas said he were going to die, but he rallied. Only with him confined to his bedroom, there were no one to make sure all was fair. He were a hard taskmaster in his day, that's certain, but he were a fair one. He used to say he'd give a fair day's wage for a fair day's work. And he did. Not like Trefusis."

"I see you apportion no blame to my mother."

Casworan stayed silent, but his expression spoke volumes.

Nat punched his hand again. "A workforce treated like this is not a happy workforce. This is more like slave labor. I saw some of that on my travels. But I'm home now and if I do nothing else, I'll see our workers treated better." His brows lowered. "And Trefusis kicked out of Treloar."

"Good," Yves said. "I don't like him and nor does Hetty."

Children were such good judges of character.

Chapter Twenty-Two

MRS. TRELOAR WAS indisposed that evening, so only Hetty, Nat, and Caroline took dinner in the dining room. Aunt Agnes had decided to go to bed early, and Trefusis didn't deign to show his face in the house that evening. Consequently, dinner was a much jollier affair than it could have been. Nat found Hetty was, somewhat unfortunately, on fine form, possibly due to the absence of Trefusis.

"I so enjoyed the ball," she chattered between mouthfuls. "Did you see how many young men asked me to dance? I'm so glad you came here, Caroline, because if you hadn't, we might not have been invited to Carlyon. And Mrs. Beauchamp is such a charming hostess. She said it was quite all right to call her Ysella, as in truth, she's not many years older than I am. She's so pretty. And did she tell you she's increasing? She said she already has a little girl and is hoping for a boy this time. Though if I was ever to become a mother, it would be girls I'd want. All girls. So much more fun as they can wear pretty dresses, like me."

"Good heavens, Hetty," Nat finally managed to put in. "Do you never shut up? Not even to take a breath?"

Hetty pulled a face. "Well, better than never saying a word, like you. Incidentally, I didn't see you dance with *anyone* at all at the ball." Her brow furrowed. "In fact, I hardly saw you at all. Where did you get to? Surely you danced with *some*body? There were lots of eligible young ladies present." She batted her long eyelashes in what had to be an attempt to look modest. A failure on that. "Though I was told by several gentlemen that none were as pretty as me. However, I'm sure one of them would suit you perfectly."

Caroline's cheeks flushed with color as she regarded her plate.

Luckily for her, Hetty was too taken up with herself to notice.

"Stop right there." Nat cut his sister off as she opened her mouth again, his aim being to draw her attention away from Caroline. "It's bad enough with Mother trying to pair me off with some simpering girl without you trying it as well." Not that he didn't suspect there was something behind what his mother had said to him. Never a good thing to trust a word that came out of that woman's mouth.

Hetty's eyes lit up. "Mama is trying to marry you off? How delightful. That will mean I shall gain a sister." She glanced at Caroline. "I know I have you, now, but if Nat marries, it will most likely be to someone nearer to me in age, which would be tremendous fun." She looked back at Nat. "I think that's a splendid idea. I agree with Mama. Now you're home, you should marry as soon as possible."

Nat sighed. "I have no intention of marrying just to give you a girl nearer your age as a sister-in-law. What a thought—two empty-headed chits in one house. That would be torture."

Hetty giggled. "For you, maybe, but not for me." Then she seemed to notice the insult. "And I'm *not* empty headed. You ask Caroline. She knows how diligent I can be at my piano practice and French conversation."

Nat glanced at Caroline, who seemed now to be having trouble keeping a straight face. Was she laughing at him or Hetty? "Perhaps Caroline might like to tell us her views on marriage?" He'd only said it to distract Hetty, but now the words were out, he wanted to know, although why, he wasn't quite sure.

Caroline laid her knife and fork down on her plate. "My own parents were very happily married for thirty years, until my father… died." She paused and he saw her swallow down whatever discomfort this admission had brought to her. "So, I am an advocate of marriage as a partnership of like-minded people. But not just for the sake of being married."

"I shall marry for love," Hetty declared, taking a sip of wine.

"An admirable sentiment," Caroline said, "but not always a wise one. Love does not last forever, Hetty, but friendship does. My parents were the best of friends, although they also loved one another. Not, my mother once admitted to me, with the flush of ardor they felt on first meeting, but with a deep and lasting affection." Her brow furrowed as no doubt she thought of her parents.

"I do not think *our* parents were the best of friends, nor that they nurtured any sense of affection for one another," Hetty said, her eyes sliding sideways to look at her brother. "I remember them fighting. In fact, that is all I remember of Papa."

Nat considered his words with care. "They were not well matched in temperament, I'll give you that. But neither were Uncle Robert and Aunt Lowenna. Although Uncle Robert's marriage was arranged by grandfather, and our father *chose* to marry Mother, so he must have loved her once. I trust that if you do marry for love, Hetty, it will be to someone I, as your brother, will approve of."

Hetty giggled. "I only get to meet the suitable young men of the district, and them not very often, so it would be very hard for me to meet someone unsuitable, unless, of course, you mean that I might fall in love with Dickon or the gardener's boy."

Poor Dickon, who was standing by the sideboard to serve the food, blushed a hot scarlet at this reference. Hetty was a shameless brat. Nat frowned hard at her.

She sighed, ignoring his expression. "Oh, how I would love to have had my coming out in London. To go to London balls and soirées and Vauxhall Gardens. Then I might have met someone deliciously unsuitable and vexed you properly. That must be magical."

Nat allowed himself a reluctant smile. "You are very unlikely to have that opportunity, I'm afraid, and I fear you wouldn't like it near so much as you think. London is full of false friends and spite, as well as the dangers of fortune hunters and cads, who you would undoubtedly be taken in by, being such an empty-headed chit. You are best off here, choosing a suitable husband from amongst the eligible sons of our neighbors."

Hetty gave a derisive snort, but just then, the dessert was brought in, which distracted her. Ice cream had always been Nat's favorite as a boy, and Mrs. Teague must have made it specially, using the ice stored in the underground icehouse in the gardens. As Nat ate, he made a mental note to go down to the kitchens in the morning to thank Mrs. Teague personally.

He took another look at Caroline, delicately spooning up the ice cream in sharp contrast to the almost greedy way Hetty was eating it. Her soft brown eyes looked troubled. What was it about her? She seemed almost to be holding her breath as though expecting something dreadful to happen; to be waiting for the strike of doom. Outwardly, her demeanor was all friendly kindness, but he had a distinct sense that she was holding something important back from him.

It being not long after midsummer, after the dessert was finished, it was still light outside in the gardens. As they rose from the table to retire to the drawing room, Nat caught Caroline's arm to detain her. "It's such a lovely evening, would you care to take a stroll in the gardens?"

Hetty's brows rose almost into her hairline. He didn't need to guess what *she* was thinking.

With a pretty smile, Caroline consented, and, leaving Hetty to go upstairs and sit with her grandfather, at Nat's suggestion, they walked out into the walled garden at the side of the house.

Here, paths wound between luscious flowerbeds replete with brightly colored flowers Nat had never known the names of. Climbing roses covered the walls, and trees and bushes grew in profusion. This was the garden his grandmother had designed, and where he'd played as a small boy with Jacka, whose father had been the head gardener. Although despite his father's horticultural employ, Jacka had been no wiser about the names of the plants than Nat.

Caroline had tucked her hand into the crook of his offered arm, and now she strolled by his side in the warm twilight, the mingled scent of the many flowers pervading the air.

"So," she said, smiling up at him, "it seems your mother intends you to marry."

He nodded, still unsure if that was truly what his mother wanted; half convinced that something else had lurked behind her words. "A rather foolish idea. I pointed out to her that no girl would want to see this face every day, or words to that effect."

"If you find a girl who loves you, she will not hesitate."

He laughed. "In order to love me, she will have to get past her first sight of my face, and I fear no girl, not even one with the capacity to eventually come to love me, could do that. Save if she were blind."

"Beauty is only skin deep."

He shook his head. "Whoever said that knows nothing of wooing. For physical beauty is the first thing that attracts people to each other. Only then do they discover if the beauty of the body is matched by the beauty of the soul. And by then it's often too late. Whereas for me, my lack of beauty is something all too evident. I am unlikely to find a bride who can overlook my all-too-obvious faults in search of a beauteous soul."

"Then all girls are fools."

Nat stiffened. Did she class herself in this statement or mean something else by it? He wanted to ask her, but diffidence kept him silent. And besides which, if all girls were judged by Hetty, then they were definitely fools.

They walked on a bit further until they came to a particularly fragrant rose bush where Caroline halted. "I know this one. Common Provence. We had these roses in the gardens at Cadley Grange, my old home." She bent to inhale the intense scent. "The smell reminds me of my mother. She always had vases of them about the house all summer long."

Nat's heart did a skip of shock. That her mother should have chosen this particular rose above all others as her favorite was too much of a coincidence. He bent to smell them as well, their fragrance sending images flashing through his head that he wasn't sure he wanted to see. Despite playing in here as a child, he'd never taken a lot of notice of what grew here, except for these roses. It had been more fun to race around the paths with Jacka and the dogs, but every so often, when this bush was in bloom, he'd stopped to drink in their evocative scent.

And remember.

On an impulse, he reached out and plucked one of the best flowers from the bush. With careful fingers he pinched out the few thorns, and held the stem out to Caroline. "Might I put this in your hair?"

Her eyes met his, suddenly serious. "You may."

How long it was since he'd touched a woman's hair. In Spain, of course, he'd had a few dalliances with young women who'd been little more than camp followers. After Julia, that was, but they'd been unsatisfactory, and he'd come away from those liaisons discontented and unfulfilled. He'd had to acknowledge that none of them had been what he was searching for, and give up on them. And of course, since his face... well, that had made any further amors of any sort out of the question.

He settled the rose just above her left ear in her soft brown curls, so silken under his touch. The urge to run his fingers through her hair and luxuriate in the sensation was strong.

She smiled up at him. "Thank you... Nat." She had an uncommonly deep voice for a woman, with a hint of huskiness in it that was most attractive. Odd that he'd not noticed this before. And that he'd also not noticed how clear her skin was, nor the generous curve of her lips...

He stepped back, flustered. He was reacting like a green boy would to the first woman he ever encountered. Not like a man who'd already been married and widowed, and… No, he wouldn't think of that.

"It's odd how certain things remind us of home, isn't it?" he said, the words tumbling out in far too much of a hurry. "When I was in northern Spain, I had occasion to see the ocean and a long sandy beach. It reminded me so much of Morgelyn Beach I was nearly overcome. Silly, but true, and yet now I'm here, it doesn't feel any more like home than Spain did."

Caroline touched her fingers to the rose in her hair as if to make sure it was secure. "I understand, I think. Cadley, my parents' house, will forever be my home, but were I to return to it now, and find others living there, it would no longer give me the same feeling I used to have. The safety it imbued in my soul would be gone." She began walking again and he kept pace with her. After a bit, she turned to look up at him. "Tell me, Nat, do you feel safe here?"

What an odd question. But now she'd asked it, he felt obliged to consider his answer. "I'm not sure. I hadn't thought about it before, but there is, perhaps, a feeling of insecurity here that I hadn't noticed at first. A sense of waiting for something to happen. Something bad." There, he'd said it. Would she agree with him?

Caroline bit her lip. Was there something else she wanted to ask him? He waited.

She gave herself a shake. "I'm sure it's probably just that both you and I are unused to being here, even though this is your childhood home. You must be glad to be back within the bosom of your family, with your mother and sister."

Now it was his turn to hesitate, wondering if he should reveal more to her. She had such an air of quiet reassurance about her, as though he could tell her anything he fancied. Why not? "She's not really my mother, you know."

Her eyes widened. "Hetty didn't say. And you refer to her always as your mother. I had no idea."

"Hetty doesn't know. Almost no one does."

He could see she was twirling all sorts of theories in her head so he'd better come clean and tell the truth. "My father was married before. My mother's name was Margaret. I remember very little of her, as I was barely three years old when she died. Soon after her death, my father married Ruth, who'd been my grandfather's housekeeper, and instructed me to call her mother. I think perhaps they hoped I'd never remember and grow up thinking she was indeed who they said she was. But I have fought to keep my memories, fragmented as they are." He paused, and she gazed up into his eyes, lips slightly parted, as though hanging on his words. It was a long time since a woman had looked at him like that.

He hurried on, again pushing aside that urge to take her in his arms and kiss her. "And by some strange coincidence it is the scent of this very rose..." He indicated the flower in her hair. "That brings back images of my mother the most strongly. Like your mother, she liked to bring flowers into the house, and my clearest memory is of her holding a bowl of roses with the scent all around her like a mist of fragrance. She's standing at the foot of the stairs, and like you, there's a rose in her hair. Sunshine is pouring in through the windows, and I am happy."

Her eyes filled with sympathy. "I had no idea. So, you and Hetty are only half-brother and -sister." Her eyes narrowed. "And that makes all the difference, I fear."

He frowned. "What do you mean?"

She shook her head. "Nothing. I shouldn't have said that." She glanced back at the house. "I think I need to go inside and make sure Yves has gone to bed. He's inclined to misbehave for Bridget, whom he doesn't like."

And she turned on her heel and strode away, head up, determined, a woman on a mission. Nat watched her go, confused. That she'd meant something by that last remark he was certain. And whatever it was, he felt sure he needed to know it.

Chapter Twenty-Three

YVES WAS SLEEPING soundly, his golden curls spread across his pillow, one thumb close to his mouth as though he might have been sucking it, not something Caroline would tell him she'd seen. The tatty stuffed rabbit lying on the bed reminded her of how young he was. She sniffed the air. Had Bridget augmented the fake medicine in the bottle and if so, was it possible to tell by smell? Or was this just a natural, childish, deep sleep? Caroline had no way of knowing. She tucked the blankets in around him more closely and tiptoed out of the room.

She had a lot to think about tonight, despite the tiredness that weighed her down like an oppressive shroud.

Back in her room, she changed into her nightdress and hung her evening gown in her wardrobe. A quick wash followed by a diligent brush of her teeth with her Bott's Toothpowder, and she was in bed, pulling the covers up to her chin. Despite it being July, this house with its high ceilings and drafty corridors was not of the warmest.

But she couldn't sleep. Again.

The moon had risen, a little fatter than it had been on the night of the ball, visible through her window where it was silhouetting the leafy branches of the trees in the garden. She tried shutting it out by closing her eyes, but instead, Nat's scarred face rose before her, half of it managing to smile as he held her close in the waltz.

How good looking he must have been before his wound had damaged not just his features but also his self-confidence and his soul. If you ignored the scarred side of his face, he was still a handsome man, but unlike beauty, his wound was more than superficial. His whole persona seemed to have been deeply affected by what had happened to him. Whose wouldn't be? He'd gone through so much, and it had left an indelible mark on him.

There'd been a moment out there in the gardens with him when she'd thought he might take her in his arms and kiss her. She'd seen it in his eyes. And she'd shocked herself by wanting him to, and by being disappointed when he didn't. What would it have been like to have felt his lips on hers? To have had him press his powerful body against hers... What on earth was she doing? Behaving the way she'd expect of Hetty, that was what. She should know better than to nurture fanciful dreams of handsome suitors at her age. She was indeed an old maid and should remember it.

She rolled over in bed, her back to the window. No doubt Nat would be horrified to learn she was feeling sorry for him. Not the sort of man to wallow in the pity of others, nor in his own pity for himself. More the sort to walk away and never talk to you again if you showed compassion. She would need to tread carefully around him.

Which brought her back to Yves and whether Nat might be complicit in what she saw as an attempt on his young cousin's life. Every part of her wanted to exonerate Nat, to clear him of all suspicion. But the fact remained that he was second in the line of inheritance and would get Roskilly if Yves were somehow removed.

Irritated by her inability to clear her mind of her suspicions, or of Nat, she rolled back over again, glaring at the fat sliver of the moon. What he'd confided in her tonight might well be something that could indeed mark him as innocent in all of this. He was not Ruth Treloar's son. The woman had been an ordinary housekeeper who had taken advantage of her position to inveigle a grieving, recently widowed man to marry her, thereby gaining for herself a social position and the money to sustain it.

Or had she? Just because Caroline didn't like the woman didn't mean she was as black as she fancied painting her. Did it? She might once have been a kind and beautiful woman, to whom Nat's unhappy father had turned for comfort, not the seductress Caroline wanted her to have been. However, that sounded over generous. Surely no one could start out kind and gentle and end up as bitter and twisted as Mrs. Treloar seemed. Hetty said she only remembered her parents fighting. So, they could never have loved one another, could they? Only that wasn't true either. People *did* fight even if they loved one another. Her own mother had often tried to prevent her father's rash ways with money, but failed, and Caroline had overheard some of their heated arguments.

When had Nat's father died? It had to be a long time ago for Hetty's memories to be so vague. Ten years since perhaps? No, it had to be longer, because it had happened before Nat had left to take up his commission and that was eleven years ago. Miss Hawkins had said he'd been a schoolboy. But, to go down the mine with his father, he couldn't have been too young. Over twelve, at least. Maybe she could ask him about it tomorrow. Using care and tact to avoid having him retreat into angry silence.

Another face swam into focus. Trefusis. Old Sir Hugh, whom she must remember to go and see tomorrow, had suffered his apoplexy two years since, and Mrs. Treloar must have promptly brought in Trefusis to take over the running of the estate and mines. Had she had him lurking in the wings, ready for the takeover? Were they lovers then and now, or just partners in crime? Or was she stringing him along? Mrs. Treloar didn't have the look of a woman ruled by her passions, but Caroline had to acknowledge she herself was not a great judge of passions, so, despite her employer's austere exterior, she might be.

It seemed obvious, now, that Trefusis was playing the long

game. If she had him right, he didn't intend to rest content with the middle-aged Mrs. Treloar, who would necessarily lose her inheritance to one of her children as soon as Sir Hugh and Yves were out of the way. He had his roving, insolent eye on Hetty. But, even if Yves were to be disposed of, there would still be Nat, standing squarely now between Trefusis and Roskilly, and all the riches that entailed.

Fear clutched her heart as the import of this washed over her. Yves and Hetty were not the only ones in danger here. Nat was too. Trefusis had probably thought Nat would never come home. So many soldiers died in Europe, it seemed likely Nat would as well. Maybe he'd even thought Nat had already perished. Miss Hawkins had. And now Nat was home, and the campaign to remove Yves had commenced, surely Trefusis, who could be complicit with Mrs. Treloar over the laudanum, would want to remove this unexpected obstacle.

Caroline's skin prickled with cold terror.

Of course. That was it. Trefusis intended to remove both heirs and marry Hetty. Mrs. Treloar would be sidelined, despite thinking herself his chosen one. Fear for Hetty burgeoned. That she was afraid of Trefusis was obvious; repulsed by his occasional look of lust when he thought no one was looking.

That made three people she had to save.

Sleep was not going to come easily tonight.

THE NEXT MORNING, when Caroline went into the nursery to suggest they go down together to the kitchens for breakfast, she found Yves still sound asleep. A gentle shake produced only a muffled groan. Her heart pounding with fear, she shook him again, more forcefully this time, and his eyes creaked open, unfocused and sleepy.

She didn't need telling. Bridget must have added more laudanum to the medicine bottle in the corner cupboard.

"Wake up, Yves," Caroline hissed, glancing across at the closed door to Bridget's room. "Breakfast time."

He rubbed his eyes. "Can't I stay in bed a bit longer? I'm sooo tired."

"No, you can't. Get up." She pulled him into a sitting position. "You need some fresh air to blow away the cobwebs. Come on. I'll find your clothes."

Bridget, or it might have been Patience to whom Bridget seemed to delegate most of the work, had laid out his clothes for the day on the chair by the bed, but it took some bullying to get him into his breeches, stockings, shirt, and jacket.

"Downstairs," Caroline said when he was finally ready. As there was still no sign of Bridget, she gave Yves's hand a tug and he followed her with unaccustomed meekness, and trailing feet, down the corridor, out into the gallery and down the stairs in the direction of the kitchen.

Mrs. Teague was busy at the stove and the little kitchen maid, Molly, was peeling vegetables for dinner, a resigned expression on her face.

Yves slumped onto a chair, folded his arms on the table and put his head down to rest on them. "I'm going back to sleep."

What to do? Bridget must have administered a very large dose last night. Caroline needed something to combat it. No use trying to make him sick as after nine or ten hours it must be securely in his system.

"What's the matter with young Yves?" Mrs. Teague asked, coming over to the table. "He don't usually want to sleep at this time o' the morning."

The urge to take the burly cook into her confidence rose. But Caroline couldn't be sure she wouldn't tell someone else who might report back to Mrs. Treloar. If this happened, Caroline would be dismissed just as Miss Hawkins had been, and Yves would be at the mercy of his aunt and Trefusis again. Probably Mrs. Teague would be dismissed as well. "He's just a bit sleepy after a bad night," Caroline said, instead. "Do you have any coffee prepared?"

"Coffee?"

"For Yves."

Mrs. Teague's face registered her shock. "For a child? I never heard of such a thing. That's a drink for grown men and women, not little lads like him."

Caroline pursed her lips. "Coffee is a stimulant, as you probably know. Yves needs stimulating to help him wake up." Oh, if only this would work.

Mrs. Teague looked unconvinced. "If you're sure?"

"I am. Look at him. He's going back to sleep again in the middle of the morning. He needs to wake up properly."

With a huff of disagreement, Mrs. Teague returned to the stove where she did indeed have a pot of coffee keeping warm. She took down what had to be the smallest cup she could find and filled it only half full. This she returned to Caroline. It did *not* look an appetizing drink for a small boy, and it was too hot for him to swallow. What to do? Inspiration came to her. "Milk. Do you have some creamy milk? That will make it taste better and cool it down. Quickly now."

Yves's eyes had closed and he looked as though he'd fallen asleep again.

Mrs. Teague took a cloth off a jug and topped the coffee up with the milk. Caroline added two large spoonsful of sugar and gave it a stir, then roused Yves who had relapsed into minimal responsiveness. "Here. Drink this."

He obeyed her, if with a wrinkled nose, and swallowed down the coffee.

Caroline held out the empty cup. "I think a second cup. The sugar will do him good as well."

When Yves had drunk three cups of milky coffee and sugar, he finally began to wake up, and Mrs. Teague served both him and Caroline with bacon and eggs. Once he'd eaten that, he seemed almost back to normal.

What a relief.

Then it was back up to the schoolroom to his lessons, despite his wheedling suggestion that as he needed fresh air, they should go to the beach and have a philosophical science lesson instead.

In the front hall, though, distraction awaited them. They encountered Nat, carrying his riding whip and with a determined expression on his face.

Yves ran over to him. "Where are you going?"

Nat favored him with a raised eyebrow. "Does your governess not insist on you learning how to greet someone you haven't seen since yesterday a little less abruptly?"

Yves grinned. "Good morning, Cousin Nat. Where are you going?"

Nat met Caroline's eyes, a distinctly more friendly expression on his face and the left side even suggesting he might be hiding a smile.

Caroline returned a tentative smile of her own, still worrying about how she was going to prevent Bridget from dosing Yves with the medicine again that night. "Good morning, Nat."

Yves danced up and down. "Are you going out riding? Can I come?"

Nat tapped his riding whip against his leg. "I am indeed going riding, but I also happen to be well aware that your mornings are for learning, not gallivanting with me to far-flung mines." Despite the stern words, he had a twinkle in his eyes that was both unusual and most attractive. Could she dare to hope he'd lain awake last night like she had, thinking of her?

"They most certainly are," Caroline said, perhaps with a touch too much asperity. "But perhaps if you are especially good, Yves, we might prevail upon your cousin to let us accompany him this afternoon?"

Yves danced up and down some more. "Oh, please! I love riding even if it has to be on Blossom." A thought seemed to occur to him, bringing a furrow to his smooth forehead. "And if I ride out a lot, and get better at it, perhaps Cousin Nat might persuade Aunt Ruth to let me have a bigger pony?"

Nat snorted. "If she refuses, then I'm sure you and I can ask Grandfather if he will approve it. He is, after all, your guardian and not your Aunt Ruth. So, he should have the final authority on this. And I'll help you choose it. The mount for a prospective baronet needs careful selection."

Good heavens. He must be feeling in a better mood this morning. Caroline couldn't help but smile a little more, mainly because Nat's words seemed to bolster her theory that he could not be involved in the attempts to poison Yves. However, that final thought had the frown returning. "Thank you, Nat. We will hold you to that. But for now, Yves needs to come with me. I wish you a pleasant ride this morning."

"Where're you going?" Yves asked, his chin on his shoulder as she took a firm hold on his hand and pulled him away.

Nat waved a hand in the vague direction of Penmar Head. "To our other mine, Wheal True. I've a mind to see and hear for myself the conditions the miners are living in, so I'll be a while. I might be going down in the cage." He glanced at Caroline. "It's beyond Wheal Jenny and is the larger of our two mines."

"I wish I was going too," Yves managed as Caroline started up the staircase with him. "I want to go down in the cage like Nat. Much more fun than learning Latin verbs." He must have forgotten already the plight of the child miners he'd seen.

A snort of what could have been laughter sounded from the hallway, followed by the clunk of the front door closing. Nat had gone.

Chapter Twenty-Four

YVES DID NOT seem to be in the right frame of mind for learning all morning. Whether it was the lasting effects of the laudanum dose, or the unfortunate encounter with Nat off to do something Yves regarded as a much preferable alternative to Latin verbs, Caroline couldn't work out. But she had the distinct sensation she was trying to knock her head against the proverbial brick wall. All the verbs he'd learned had gone out of his head, and he kept yawning and staring out of the window at the enticing blue sky outside.

Caroline couldn't blame him. What small boy in their right mind would want to be sitting at a desk indoors when they could be out on their own private beach, or riding an admittedly recalcitrant pony across the sand and pretending he was Robinson Crusoe. She quite fancied being out of doors herself, given the beauty of the day, but she didn't intend to let him know. So, while he pored over his Latin grammar book with a discontented frown on his small face, she turned over in her mind what she was going to say to Sir Hugh that afternoon.

That he knew Yves was in danger had been obvious, but now she had to tell him everything she surmised about Trefusis's intentions toward Hetty, and the danger she suspected Nat might be in. Would Sir Hugh believe her? She still wasn't sure she believed it herself. In the cold light of day, or rather in the sunny, warm light of a July day, it seemed increasingly unlikely and more and more like something out of the Gothic novels she and Ysella had liked to read.

The sound of galloping, or at the least cantering, hooves on the gravel in front of the house disturbed her thoughts and Yves's studies. He was out of his seat and climbing onto the bench by the window before she could utter a reprimand, his nose pressed against the glass.

"It's Duchess. By herself. And she's not wearing her saddle."

Caroline, who'd been about to launch into a diatribe about how schoolboys should not leave their seats unless given express permission, threw caution to the wind and leapt up to join him at the window.

"Oh God." Fear closed around her heart. He was right. Duchess, flanks heaving and flecked with foamy sweat, was now standing close to the porticoed front doors, her head down, reins hanging broken, and devoid of her saddle and rider. Even as Caroline watched, young Pascoe came running from the stables, his father, Old Pascoe stumping along behind him.

"Where's Cousin Nat?" Yves's voice rose in panic. "He must have been riding her. There isn't any other horse he could've taken. How's she lost her saddle?"

Yves was right. If Nat had ridden to Wheal True as he'd said, he'd have taken Duchess. Folly, although a livelier, younger ride, would have been too small for his six-foot frame.

Caroline glanced at the schoolroom clock. Ten o'clock. He'd been gone barely an hour.

Young Pascoe grabbed Duchess's reins and Old Pascoe ran his hands down her legs, no doubt to see if she'd done herself any damage. Caroline caught the sound of the front door opening, and in a moment Ennion was there, closely followed by Trefusis and Mrs. Treloar. From above, their faces were invisible, but their voices carried up to the schoolroom window.

"There looks like there's been some kind of an accident," Trefusis, on the top of whose head Caroline was absurdly pleased to see a sizeable bald spot coming, said. "Did Nathaniel ride her out?"

A muffled yes from Old Pascoe, standing, cap in hand.

Mrs. Treloar joined in, her voice strident and accusing. "And where is the saddle? How is it not on the horse? Who is in charge of checking the saddlery?"

Old Pascoe fiddled with his cap, head down, only his gray hair visible from above. "I am, ma'am."

Silence, but Mrs. Treloar must have been glaring at Old Pascoe because he cringed like a beaten dog.

Trefusis put his oar in again. "We'd best organize a search party. I'll get round to the farm and requisition all the men. And I'll send Dickon out on Folly to the other farms on the estate. We'll get a hundred men out looking for him. Don't worry, Ruth, we'll find him."

"Nat!" Hetty burst out of the front door onto the gravel, making Duchess startle. "Is it Nat? What's happened to him? Oh my God." Her voice rose into a wail.

Her mother took her by the shoulders. "Do *not* take the Lord's name in vain, Henrietta. And stop making a show of yourself. Our men will find him, have no fear."

Hetty wasn't to be stopped though, not in the full flow of hysteria. "What if he's fallen over the cliffs? Or on the beach and hit his head on a rock and the tide is coming in? Or down an old mine shaft?"

Mrs. Treloar raised her right hand and a resounding slap echoed. But it worked. Hetty shut up. "Be silent, you stupid girl. He will be perfectly all right and just having to walk home which will take him a lot longer than it has his horse. Go inside and find Miss Fairfield and remain with her. She can look after you."

Yves jumped down from the window. "I'm going looking for Nat, too."

Caroline just managed to grab his arm. "No, you're not. We're to let the farm workers and servants do that. They know the countryside far better than we do. And you heard your cousin—there are old mine shafts out there. We don't want to make things worse by giving them more people to look for. Besides, Hetty's coming to find us. We have to look after her."

Despite her words, if only she hadn't had Yves to look after, Caroline would have been out there herself, searching for Nat. This couldn't be a coincidence, surely. How did a saddle come off a horse if it had been maintained properly? Old Pascoe was going to get the blame for this, without a doubt, and it probably had nothing to do with him. Unless he was in the pay of Trefusis, of course, which seemed unlikely.

Hetty burst through the door, her face waxy pale with a glare of red on one cheek and tears running down her face. "It's Nat!" she wailed. "His horse has come back without him."

"We know that, silly," Yves said, displaying zero compassion. "And now we have to look after you, while everyone else goes out to search for him. Which isn't fair, because I want to look for him as well."

"Something bad's happened," Hetty continued, oblivious to his reply. "I know it has. Bad things happen all the time here. Like when Papa died, and then Uncle Robert. Our family *always* dies in accidents. At least the men in our family do. It's a curse, I know it is."

"Be quiet, Hetty, you're frightening Yves." Caroline kept her voice level and calm.

"I'm not frightened," Yves protested. "I'm cross because I'm stuck in here with *her*."

Caroline shot him a fierce frown. "Yves. You can be quiet, too. Ring the bell for Patience and we'll have some tea brought up to the schoolroom. No running off."

Luckily, a bell rope hung by the schoolroom door for just such an eventuality. Yves gave it a vigorous tug and returned to Hetty and Caroline, a cunning expression on his face. "If we're not doing lessons but looking after Hetty, do I still have to call you Miss Fairfield until twelve o'clock?"

Caroline shook her head in exasperation. "Caroline will be

fine. Come and sit down, Hetty. Here at this desk. Now breathe deeply and try to stop crying."

"What a baby," Yves observed, going back to the window. "Nothing to see. They've all gone."

"You can come and sit down too," Caroline said, taking hold of Hetty's hand. "Your cousin needs us to be brave for her."

"I *am* being brave," Yves said, brow furrowing. "It's *her* that's not."

"I'm a girl," Hetty sniffled. "I'm allowed to not be brave."

"Girls." Yves curled his upper lip in an attempt at scorn that only made him look rather silly.

Hetty gave a watery smile. "One day you'll like girls."

As Yves seemed about to enter into an argument about why he would never like girls, Caroline held her hand up. "No arguing. We have to support one another while the search goes on."

A timid knock came on the door, and Patience pushed it open. "You rang, Miss?"

"We need sweet tea, for shock," Caroline said. "And for you to tell us if the servants are all going on the search party?"

Patience nodded. "There's only me and Mrs. Teague left, and that Rodgers up with Sir Hugh seein' as he can't be left on his own."

Aha. Just what Caroline wanted to hear. This was the perfect opportunity to get rid of that laudanum-loaded medicine for good. Even if it risked the wrath of Mrs. Treloar. She couldn't let Yves take another dose or it might be fatal.

Patience shortly returned with the tea, and Caroline asked her to remain. Then, leaving Hetty and Yves with her, and all three of them drinking the tea, much to Patience's mixture of delight and embarrassment, Caroline went into the nursery.

Bridget, presumably co-opted onto the search, was not there. Thank goodness. It was a work of only a minute to retrieve the key from under her pillow, unlock the cupboard and take out the medicine bottle. She uncorked it, sniffed it, and just for good measure inserted her finger then licked the tip. Yes, the bitter taste of the laudanum had returned. Presumably Mrs. Treloar, or Trefusis, or both of them, but not Nat, had decided the initial dose had not been enough and they should increase it.

She hauled up the sash window and tipped the entire contents of the bottle into the flowerbed. A jug of water stood on Bridget's washstand, which made it an easy job to refill the bottle and return it to the cupboard. At least this gave her a little over twenty-four hours to try and do something. Tonight, Bridget would go to dose Yves and find only water in the bottle. Even if she noticed, which she might not if Caroline was lucky, she wouldn't be able to do anything right then. Although, surely after Yves was in bed she'd be reporting to Mrs. Treloar. And if she did spot the substitution tonight, when everyone was back in the house, she wouldn't know it had been Caroline who'd emptied it. Hopefully. Although she'd most likely suspect it was. But with no proof, what could anyone do?

With determined fingers, Caroline locked the cupboard, returned the key to under the pillow and went back to Hetty and Yves.

AFTER HE'D LEFT Caroline and Yves to continue on their way upstairs to the schoolroom, Nat strode around to the stables in search of a horse. Well, in search of Duchess, as there was nothing else there except for the carriage horses, Hetty's mount, Folly, or Blossom. He encountered Young Pascoe engaged in mucking out the loose boxes. The groom set down his wooden, manure-laden barrow. "Shall I get Duchess ready for you, Mr. Nathaniel?"

Nat shook his head. "No need. I'll see to that myself. You look like you have plenty to do already, and I formed a habit of taking care of my horse for myself while I was in the army."

Young Pascoe picked up the barrow again. "Thank'ee, Sir."

Nat found the saddle he'd used before in the tack room and carried it, with Duchess's bridle hooked on the cantle, down the passage to the loosebox she occupied. Her ears pricked as she saw him set the saddle on the stable door, and she gave a little, welcoming whicker. She might be getting on in years, but she'd been a good horse in her time.

Ten minutes later, he was riding out of the stableyard and onto the track that would lead him in the direction of Wheal Jenny. With Wheal True lying on the far side of the headland, he didn't need to take the main road but could thread his way along the narrow farm tracks that wound between the small, square fields. Bright sunshine beat down on him, tempered by the usual sea breeze that lifted his still-too-long hair off his forehead. What a day to be alive. He could almost feel his heart swelling inside his ribs. Something about Cornwall, that he'd forgotten in his long absence, was sneaking its way back into his very bones.

Duchess seemed full of the joys of life as well, stepping out smartly with her ears pricked at each and every bird, sheep, or cow they came across. Although he liked her well enough, it might be nice to find himself a horse of his own, for in truth she was a lady's mount, not a man's. And at the same time, he'd look for a pony for that imp of a cousin of his. A boy his age deserved a pony with some life in it, not the old plodder that pulled the pony cart and worked in the garden.

He urged Duchess into a trot, the wind lifting her black mane, as they reached the open moorland that rose toward Penmar Head. Maybe he'd let her have a canter. From a boyhood spent exploring the surrounding countryside with Jacka, he knew where all the abandoned mineshafts were, and had no fear of riding into one.

Duchess sprang into a canter with enthusiasm and, out of sheer joy, Nat encouraged her to go faster as the track ran uphill toward the distant mine buildings.

She was in a skittish mood, possibly in season, which always made a mare more of a handful, but he didn't mind, and stood in the stirrups to encourage her to go faster. The path wove between clumps of gorse and the many rocks that peppered the heathery moorland, but she was sure-footed and he had faith in her.

As they breasted a low rise, from out of the heather on his right, a female hen harrier rose, a vole clutched in its talons. The bird's brown wings flapped, Duchess's ears shot forward, and she leapt to the left as though she were a just-broken three-year-old.

Nat would normally have had no problem sitting out a sudden shy like that, but as she leapt, her saddle slid violently to the right. Nat's weight was thrust too far to the right, and he had no chance to readjust it. The saddle kept on going, and he and the saddle spun through the air. The uneven, rocky ground came up to meet him with a bone-jarring smack, as though he'd run into a brick wall. He rolled, blue sky and heather spinning, dimly aware that he was tumbling downhill, for what felt like forever, until he hit something even more solid than the ground and his head snapped back. Bright lights flashed in his vision for a moment before darkness descended. He knew nothing more.

❦

Chapter Twenty-Five

CONSCIOUSNESS RETURNED SLOWLY, accompanied by the raucous sound of gulls calling, their intrusive cries gouging uninvited into Nat's pounding head. The vibrant heat of sunshine on his face followed, with an awareness of brightness lurking beyond the inadequate shelter of his eyelids. Then a disconcerting sense that he was lying with his head lower than his legs on what had to be rocky ground seeped over him. And pain. Not just the throbbing in his head, but a sharp, nagging pain like the worst toothache imaginable, encompassing the entire right side of his body.

Nat groaned.

After he'd groaned a bit more and cursed himself for falling off his horse, he ventured to open his eyes. He was right about the sun. It appeared to be directly overhead and trying to blind him out of a cloudless blue sky that otherwise he would have enjoyed. He tried turning his head to the right but found his cheek up against a sizeable rock, so he closed his eyes, heaved in a breath and held it, and turned his head to the left instead.

When the rocking dizziness had subsided, he forced his eyes open again. Purple heather met his gaze, both close up and far off, stretching uphill to a not-too-distant, blurry horizon.

He lay for a minute or two trying to organize his jumbled thoughts. That he must have fallen off was obvious, but apart from that, he had no idea how that could have happened to a cavalry officer who'd almost lived in the saddle for a good number of years. Nor could he recall why he'd been out on a horse, nor where he was.

Gradually, though, shards of memory fought their way to the surface, and he waited while they slotted back together. He'd been riding over to Wheal True to see what conditions were like there for the miners. On Duchess, who'd been particularly lively that morning and probably in season. Yes, she'd shied at a good few things along the way, but hadn't a large bird of prey startled her? He saw again the dappled browns of the hen harrier's large flapping wings and felt Duchess leap to the left, but what had happened after that remained hidden. Surely, he hadn't fallen off when a horse did a simple sideways shy? What kind of a green-horn rider did that make him?

His brain couldn't seem to work its way around any of that, so he closed his eyes for a minute or two, hoping things would improve. They didn't, much.

Common sense prevailed, though. He needed to make an assessment of what damage had befallen him. His head hurt with a vengeance with every move he made, but what else had he done? The pain down his right side had localized to his upper body, which felt tender from the shoulder down, and he didn't fancy trying to move. However, he couldn't stay here in what appeared to be the bowl of a rocky gully. He had to get up into the open, where perhaps he might spot a cottage somewhere, or even someone on an errand who could help him. Instinct told him he very much needed help.

He tried moving his legs first, one at a time. They seemed inclined to mobility which was a relief. Arms next. His left arm and hand were fine, but not so his right. Any movement of that arm resulted in a wave of pain that threatened nausea. He grit his teeth; he would *not* lie here and puke on himself. He *had* to get up.

Perhaps he could pull himself up into a sitting position against the rock to his right.

It took some time and frequent pauses to grit his teeth and wait for the pain to subside, but he managed it. Panting for breath, he leant against the boulder and surveyed his situation. His right arm hung useless, pain pulsating out from the shoulder, and his ribs hurt as though he might have cracked at least one. But apart from that, and whatever head injury he'd sustained, he seemed to be in one piece.

Overhead, the wheeling gulls kept up their cries, but they were no indicator of how close he was to the cliffs. Did he just have to hope someone would eventually come looking for him? How far did the moorland stretch? Too far. With lots of little gullies like the one he'd so unfortunately fallen into. He peered up at it again. It wasn't steep sided, just dotted with lumps of granite amongst the heather, and if he could get to his feet, he could perhaps use those rocks to lean on as he fought his way back to the higher ground.

In a few minutes. He just needed to close his eyes and rest.

When he opened them again, the sun had shifted in the sky and the rock behind him was throwing a giant shadow across his body. He tried to muster some spit to lubricate his mouth, without success. He'd lain here too long. The day was moving on, and even though it was only just past midsummer, he didn't want to spend the night in the open. For all he knew, he hadn't yet been missed, and no one was out searching for him. He had to do something for himself.

It took far more effort to stand than it had to pull himself into a sitting position, but through sheer determination, he did it. Leaning heavily against the boulder, he surveyed the easiest way out of the gully. Every part of him ached as though he'd been trampled by a herd of wild horses, and his whole being focused on the pain in his right shoulder, which managed to overshadow his aching head with no trouble.

Touching wary fingers to his scalp, he found sticky blood matting his hair and explored no further. If a head wound like that had been going to kill him, then he'd be dead or dying by now, and his shoulder pain told him he was anything but.

Moving slowly, from boulder to boulder, rock to granite rock, he began what had looked at first to be the gentlest of ascents but rapidly turned into major mountaineering. But eventually, he made it to the brow of the gully and stood, swaying slightly, surveying the view. His saddle lay in the heather a few feet away, testament to how he'd managed to fall off. Damn it. He'd saddled Duchess himself. Had he done something stupid? Surely not. He'd been riding since he was younger than Yves. Only a fool would have failed to do a girth up properly, and anyway, a loose girth wouldn't have made the saddle come right off.

He couldn't bend over to pick the saddle up now, not one-handed, so he left it lying in the heather.

To his right, at a distance of perhaps only five hundred yards, rose the buildings of Wheal Jenny, the pump house engine busy working to empty the lower parts of the mine of water. He hadn't even made it past there.

Deciding they were the best place to head for, as it was much further to try to walk back to Roskilly, Nat took a first, shuffling step, anxious not to jar his shoulder too much. He failed on that. Pain lanced through his body leaving him gasping for breath.

It was no use letting it get the better of him. He had to keep moving.

A thousand more steps, almost exactly, as he was counting them to take his mind off the pain, brought him to the walls of the count house. The afternoon's shift change must have already happened, because the sun was now even lower in the sky, and the count house looked quiet and deserted. With his good arm, he banged on the door, then leaned against it, forehead resting on the flaking paintwork.

Nothing. No one was there.

He let his body sag and nearly collapsed to the ground, only willpower holding him up. All the pain he'd been holding at bay on the walk from the gully threatened to overwhelm him and the world spun out of control. Nausea welled.

"Nat!"

A voice he knew broke through the wall of pain.

In a moment strong arms were supporting him and he was being helped inside the count house. "Mind my arm," he managed to mutter. "I think it's broken."

Gryff Casworan, for it was he, helped Nat into the high-backed chair in front of his desk, and Nat leaned back with a deep sigh that transmuted into a groan, partly of relief but mostly from pain. He closed his eyes and tried to relax, but his whole body felt tense, as though he were holding it taut in an effort to lessen the pain.

"What happened to you?" Casworan's deep voice asked. "We heard you was missing, and I spared some men from the mine to join in the search, but Mr. Trefusis wouldn't let them all go. Said as how the mine had to keep working, come what may."

Bloody Trefusis. Probably he'd been rubbing his hands and hoping Nat had met with a fatal accident. Well, he nearly had done.

"Fell off my horse," Nat managed through gritted teeth.

Casworan huffed a sharp breath. "What? *You* fell off a horse? How'd'you do that then? The boy that used to gallop bareback along the beach when we was lads?"

"Saddle slipped. I think the girth must have broken. She was in the mood for shying. A bird startled her, something must have broken, and the saddle came right off with me. I couldn't save myself. I rolled into a bloody gully about five hundred yards from here."

"Thassa long way to've walked in the state you're in. Here, let me get your coat off and take a look at your arm. I'll do your left sleeve first, to make it easier on you."

Nat gritted his teeth yet again as Casworan helped him extricate his left arm from his snug-fitting coat. It made getting his injured right arm out a lot easier, as his friend had said, but nevertheless, it had him swearing, and *not* under his breath. A relief not to have to watch his language.

Casworan chuckled. "Where'd'you learn to swear like that then?"

Nat managed a weak grin. "You'd think my troopers, wouldn't you? But no, I learnt most of that at Harrow."

Casworan's strong hands gently lifted Nat's right arm, feeling along it no doubt in search of broken bones. Nat screwed his eyes shut and stayed silent as fiery pain shot through his shoulder, although his breathing came fast and furious.

"Nothing's broken, I don't think," Casworan said, his hands still on Nat's arm. "My guess is what you've got here is a dislocated shoulder. I've seen a lot of them in this line of work. That's what's paining you so much." He paused. "He needs putting back in, an' that'll take most of the pain away."

Nat opened his eyes. "It will? Can you do it?"

Casworan shifted as though uncomfortable. "Like I said, I've done it a fair few times for miners what've been injured. But to do it for you, for Sir Hugh's grandson…" He shook his head. "I don't know. It do hurt something bad while it's bein' done."

"I don't care. Do it. Who else is going to? Doctor Rescorla is miles away in Penzance and will have to be sent for. I have to get back to Roskilly somehow. I won't do that with my shoulder the way it is. You do it, Gryff."

Casworan released his gentle hold on Nat's arm and went over to a wall cupboard behind the desk. Opening it, he took out a bottle of brandy. "You'll need some of this first, then."

He poured a generous glass and brought it back to Nat, then took a swig himself from out of the bottle. "Gotta boost my confidence for treating the gentry."

Nat knocked back the brandy in one long gulp, feeling it leave a pleasant trail of fire down his throat. He held out the glass. "Another."

When he'd done the same with the second glass, and Casworan had also taken another fortifying slug from the bottle, he nodded to his friend. "Best get it over with. Ignore me if I shout stop. I won't mean it."

Casworan came around to Nat's right side and picked up his arm. "I'm going to just turn him gently so he should slide back into his socket. Try and relax your muscles as that makes it easier to slide him back in. Breathe deeply, look at that clock over there and tell me what time it be. I gotta get back to dinner tonight or my wife's goin' to be right cross with me. She don't like it if the dinner gets spoiled."

Nat looked at the clock, Casworan turned his arm, the bones shifted, pain shot through Nat, and the joint clicked back into place. For a moment all he could do was concentrate on breathing, aware of the pounding of his heart and the throbbing in his head. Then the pain began to subside, down well below the level it had been at before. It still hurt, but the worst of it had gone.

He looked up at Casworan. "You missed your calling. You should've been a surgeon."

Casworan grinned and shook his head. "Not for the likes of us miners' boys. I only got the job here because you taught me to read'n'write'n'reckon."

Nat managed a grin in return. "I'm very glad you have this job, or where would I be now? Leaning against the door while some lazy appointee of Trefusis was at home pleasing his wife by not being late for dinner. You can tell your wife it was my fault, and that I'll be sending over a big joint of beef she can cook for you and your family come Sunday. I owe you and her my heartfelt thanks."

"You don't need to do that, Nat. You don't owe me nothing. Like I said, I wouldn't be here were it not for you. I'd be stuck down that mine with my back all bent and twisted on account of me bein' so gurt big." He chuckled.

Nat leaned back in his chair while Casworan busied himself making a sling out of a scarf he found hanging on the coat stand. "Gotta keep it supported. Once you done this to your shoulder, it can happen again, easy as sneeze." He tied the scarf in a knot at the back of Nat's neck. "Now, we'd best locate that useless search party and let 'em know you're found safe, if not quite sound."

Chapter Twenty-Six

A T MIDDAY, CAROLINE ate a meager dinner with Yves and
Hetty, no doubt each of them, like her, wondering in silence
what might have become of Nat. Only, for obvious reasons, she
probably had darker thoughts about this than her two charges
did. The day was creeping past, and still the search parties had
come back with nothing.

When Patience had cleared away the dinner things from the
schoolroom, Caroline suddenly remembered she'd told Sir Hugh
she'd return to see him that day. The trouble now was that she
was supposed to be taking care of Yves and Hetty, who, if she left
them alone, would probably set out to stage their own rescue
party and get into difficulties themselves. She couldn't abandon
them to Patience, as neither were likely to do as she said, and the
more threatening Bridget, whom they might not have dared to
cross, had been co-opted into the search. There was nothing for
it, they'd have to come with her.

Rodgers had not been included in the search party, and although unwilling to allow three people in at once to visit Sir
Hugh, fell back under their combined onslaught. Sir Hugh
shouting at her to let his grandchildren in or he'd have her fired,
preferably out of an upstairs window, no doubt helped.

"You can go," he snapped at Rodgers. "And take that bowl of
pap you brought up for my lunch with you. I need beef and ale,

and a bottle of port. No. Brandy. You can go and find some for me and bring it back with you later. Be off." He waved his hands at her in dismissal.

Glowering like a storm cloud, Rodgers departed, muttering under her breath about ungratefulness, but no one, especially not her patient, cared. Hetty slammed the door shut behind her.

"Hetty, Yves, Miss Fairfield," the old man said, his face changing instantly from irritated wrath to friendly smiles. "I didn't think you'd come. There seems to be something going on downstairs, but that bloody woman wouldn't tell me about it. She said it might give me palpitations. Well, if anything's enough to give me those, it's not being told. So, you three can tell me or take the consequences." He folded his thin arms, a mulish expression on his heavily lined face.

Oh dear. In all likelihood the truth was indeed enough to give an old man like him palpitations. Caroline wasn't sure she should be disclosing anything to him.

She didn't have long to wrestle with her conscience though. Hetty stepped in. "Nat is missing. He rode out this morning on Mama's horse, Duchess, and she came back without him and without her saddle."

"We saw it from the schoolroom window," Yves put in. "She was all lathered up as though she'd been galloping, and her eyes were rolling." He demonstrated what he thought a horse with rolling eyes might look like, tossing his curly head.

Sir Hugh's anxious gaze met Caroline's. "Is this true?"

Yves and Hetty both opened their mouths, no doubt to object to him suspecting they might be fabricating, but this time Caroline got in first. "I'm afraid it is. Mrs. Treloar and Mr. Trefusis have organized a search party. They've been gone about three hours. We haven't heard any news though. Not yet."

"The horse came back without her saddle?" Sir Hugh grimaced. "Something must have gone amiss with the tack—the girth, most likely. But Old Pascoe is such a stickler for maintenance. I can't believe he'd have let anyone ride out on a saddle that was unsafe."

Hetty gave a sniff.

Oh no, was she going to resort to the vapors again?

Hetty sniffed a second time, more dramatically. "It's like fate. Every man in this family dies in an accident and not in their beds. It's as if there's a curse on this family."

Yves shook his head. "Not Grandpapa. *He's* going to die in his bed because he can't get out of it."

Caroline frowned at him. "Yves. Don't say things like that. It's not polite."

But Sir Hugh greeted it with a loud guffaw. "The boy's right. Although both my sons were carried off in accidents, 'tis true. And my father."

Yves leaned forwards from the position he'd assumed on the end of the bed. "Will you tell me about them? No one ever speaks of them here, and I want to know."

Caroline glanced at the window. She felt impotent and powerless sitting here looking after these three, but they'd surely hear if the search party returned. Where she wanted to be was out there, on the moors, searching for Nat. Her heart, which had not slowed down much since Duchess's return, ached in a way she couldn't quite fathom. And her stomach twisted, threatening to give her a second view of her meager dinner.

What she needed to do was get Hetty and Yves away from Sir Hugh so she could talk to him in private.

But he was already settled in to telling them the stories of how their respective fathers had died. "Your father, Hetty, he went first. 1802 it was. I was quite a young man then, by present standards, and I'd been intending to go down Wheal True and take young Nat with me. But something came up, and my boy, Kenver, went with Nat instead. Nat was about fifteen, I think, no more, but used to going down the mines with me and his father. A good boy, wanting to learn the business from the bottom up."

"How old was Hetty?" Yves asked. "Do you remember your papa, Hetty?"

"Only a little."

"She was a little slip of a thing of five years old, pretty as a picture with her grandmother's red hair. The only one to inherit it out of all my children and grandchildren."

Hetty patted her curls.

Caroline's ears pricked at the sound of voices outside.

Yves bounced off the bed and ran to the window. "Nothing. Just Old Pascoe and Dickon."

Caroline, throwing all thoughts of etiquette aside, joined him at the window. "Perhaps they've found him?" She undid the catch, slid the window up and leaned out. "Pascoe!"

Old Pascoe squinted up at her. "Yes, Miss?"

"Have they found Mr. Nathaniel?"

Yves shouldered his way in beside her. "Is he dead?"

What a question. How typical of a small boy.

Old Pascoe shook his head. "Not found him yet, Miss, but they sent me back to fetch a flat cart from the farm in case when they finds him, he can't walk nor get back on a horse."

Or if he were dead. But at least Pascoe sounded optimistic. Caroline withdrew her head and pulled Yves away from the window as he was leaning too far out. She didn't want him accomplishing what his aunt wanted all by himself.

"Leave the window open," Sir Hugh said. "We can hear better what's going on, and it's nice to get a bit of fresh air. I don't get much of that because Rodgers thinks I'll catch a chill."

They returned to his bed.

Hetty, who hadn't moved and was now chewing her nails, patted her grandfather's hand. "Go on. Tell me what happened to Papa. I've never dared to ask Mama."

The distraction would be good for her.

Sir Hugh covered her hand with his wrinkled, age-spotted one. "Nat and Kenver, your papa, went down the mine in the cage. Wheal True's a deeper mine than Wheal Jenny and the main shaft runs straight, not like the ziggy-zaggy the miners have to do to get down Jenny's ladder shaft."

Yves scrambled back onto the end of the bed. "Maybe I should go and get Dash from the kitchens."

Caroline shook her head. "He's fine down there with Mrs. Teague."

"He could be a search dog and follow Cousin Nat's trail. He's really good at sniffing out rabbits."

"No, he couldn't," Hetty said. "And shut up. I want to hear this story."

Despite herself, Caroline did too.

Sir Hugh sighed. "There was a roof fall when they were down the mine. The miners shore up the roofs with wood, you see, and there's a lot of broken rock down there, lying about loose, that has to be held back out of the way. The miners have to follow the line the ore takes, and that's never straight. They dig out stopes, which are like steps, and pile the rock up behind them as they go. A mine's not a safe place at the best of times." His eyes took on a faraway expression, as if he was remembering what it had been like down Wheal True, and what had happened to his younger son.

"Were they buried under the rocks?" Yves, typically tactless, asked.

Sir Hugh nodded. "Most of the miners in that adit were. By chance and good luck, Nat wasn't. But his father was. And the fall let water into the mine from an abandoned working. They were at such a depth it was below high tide mark. The roof fall coincided with high water and it all came rushing in. The few miners who survived got Nat to the cage just in time, and the winding engine took them up to the surface." He sighed. "Nat wanted to go back down to get his father straightaway, but we couldn't, because of the water. We could only work down there when the tide was out. It took a week to clear the roof fall and fetch out the bodies."

Hetty's expression had not improved. This was not a cheery tale for a day when they were awaiting news of Nat.

"And my father?" Yves, ever the ghoul, asked.

"Your father went out one day in his little sailboat, for some fishing, and never came back. Simple as that. We never found his body, nor the boat."

"What was the weather like on the day it happened?" Caroline asked.

"A fine day with a stiff breeze blowing. Good for sailing. Stayed fine all day. I remember it like it was yesterday. Your guess would be as good as mine as to what caused his little boat to sink, for sink it must have."

"I don't remember him much," Yves said. "I think I was very little when that happened."

"But I was right, wasn't I?" Hetty put in. "Accidents happen to Treloar men. You'll have to watch out, Yves, because after Nat, it'll be you."

Sir Hugh's eyes met Caroline's over their heads. "Wouldn't you children like to play a game?" he asked, sounding hopeful.

Yves bounced off the bed again. "Oh yes. Draughts. Shall we go and fetch it from the library?" He looked a question at Caroline, hopping from one foot to the other in impatience.

Should she let them go? "As long as you promise to come straight back here. I shall be timing you."

"Come on, Hetty," Yves said. "I'm going to beat you at this."

"No running," Caroline called, but it was already too late as they charged out of the door.

She turned back to Sir Hugh. "I think someone has tried to kill Nat."

To do him credit, he didn't look at all surprised. "What makes you think that?"

"The saddle. And I only found out yesterday that he's not Mrs. Treloar's real son. Trefusis is after the inheritance, I'm certain. Mrs. Treloar thinks he's interested in her, but he's not. It's Hetty he's after. And Hetty's terrified of him."

He did look surprised this time. "Good heavens, girl, what are you, some sort of detective? You sound like you've been very busy. How do you know this is all true?"

She glanced toward the door, still slightly ajar. "Firstly, Nat is a cavalryman. He wouldn't just fall off a horse. And Old Pascoe is, as you say, a stickler for maintaining the saddlery." Were that footsteps outside? "I've been at dinner with the family, and Trefusis was there too. When Mrs. Treloar isn't looking, you should see the way he ogles Hetty. She hates it. He even ogled me a bit too. But I'm twenty-seven, and I know the difference between a simple ogle and one that means more. He intends to have Hetty for himself, and I'm sure he must want the estate and mines as well. He's got Mrs. Treloar in his pocket because she fancies herself in love with him and thinks he loves her back. There's no fool like an old fool, as my mother would say." Frequently about her father, but she wasn't going to add that bit.

"Slow down, slow down. You're getting ahead of yourself."

Caroline threw another glance at the door. She could now hear running footsteps and the scampering of paws.

"I think you could be in danger too," she got out, just before Dash ran into the room and launched himself at the bed. No respecter of etiquette, he climbed into Sir Hugh's lap and began licking his face with enthusiasm.

Yves and Hetty ran in.

Yves was clutching the draughts set to his chest. "We saw Old Pascoe take the cart out. Mrs. Teague wouldn't let us go with him."

Thank goodness for Mrs. Teague.

Hetty ran to the window. "There he goes now. I do hope they find Nat and nothing's happened to him."

Caroline suppressed a shiver. The longer the search went on, the more likely it seemed that something had befallen Nat to prevent him coming home on foot in pursuit of his horse.

"Use that table and those stools," Sir Hugh said, waving a hand at the far side of the room. "Set your game up by the window, over there."

They did as they were told, and Caroline moved her own chair closer to the head of Sir Hugh's bed. "What are we going to do?" She kept her voice down but needn't have bothered as Yves and Hetty were now arguing as to who should have which color.

"We don't have any proof," Sir Hugh muttered. "But if Nat's found, he might be able to offer some."

Caroline nodded. "And you shouldn't take any medicines from Rodgers. Whoever is providing the laudanum must be getting it from her, I'm sure. She must know what they're doing. And Nat and Yves aren't the only ones standing in the way of Trefusis. You are too."

He nodded. "I realize that. But I can't do without my laudanum. I have to have it in order to sleep."

Caroline glanced at Hetty and Yves. "Well, don't let her give you too much. Try to take the minimum amount necessary, if you can."

The old man's eyes clouded. "That'll be hard to do."

⸻ ❧ ⸻

Chapter Twenty-Seven

YVES, WHO MUST have had the sharpest ears, heard the wagon returning first. He leapt up from the table, scattering the draughts board and its pieces in all directions, and ran to the window, Hetty on his heels.

"They're back. They're back, and they have the cart with them. I can see Nat sitting on it!" squealed Hetty. "He's not dead."

Caroline rose from her seat by the bed, where she'd been sitting quietly with a book while Sir Hugh dozed, and hurried to join them. Sure enough, the cart was rumbling over the gravel with Nat sitting upright in it, his right arm in a sling. He looked disheveled and pale, but he was alive. And that was what mattered. Whoever had tried to kill him today, if that were what had truly happened, hadn't succeeded. Caroline's heart gave a great leap of relief. Thank God.

"Can we go down to see him?" Yves asked, jumping up and down at the window. "I want to ask him what happened."

Sir Hugh stirred. "What? What's that?"

"Nat has been found," Caroline said. "He's being brought back on the cart, but he doesn't look badly hurt. Thank goodness."

Were those tears glistening in the old man's eyes? Had he, like Hetty, been inclined to think some curse hung over the

Treloar family males? A sobering thought, and one, no doubt, Trefusis might try to use to his advantage.

Hetty ran to her grandfather and caught his hand. "Nat's safe, Grandpapa. He's not lying dead. I'm so happy I could sing."

"Please don't," muttered the old man.

"He's got his arm in a sling," Yves pointed out. "So he's not absolutely all right. I wish *I* had a sling. Can I have one too, so I can look like Nat? Can I, Caroline? Can I?"

Caroline laughed, a little hysterically due to the relief she was feeling. "Next time you play at pirates you can have a sling, but not just now." She bit her lip. "And I think, if we're all very quiet and you two don't get carried away, we could go to the gallery and maybe down to the hall and see how Nat is. But you have to promise to behave. Both of you."

"I promise," Yves said.

"Me too," Hetty added. "Although why you think I need to make the same promise as Yves, I don't know. I'm always very well behaved, aren't I?"

"Come back and tell me how he is," Sir Hugh called. "Leave the dog with me. He can keep me company." He hooked his bony fingers into Dash's collar, but the dog didn't seem inclined to give up his comfortable billet.

Caroline, Hetty, and Yves hurried to the top of the stairs, where they peered over the banisters. The front door stood wide open, and Ennion, in unaccustomed shirt sleeves, was standing in it. A moment later, Nat walked in, accompanied by Dickon and Young Pascoe, hovering to either side of him as though they feared he might buckle at the knees. His hair was in a mess, his buff breeches covered in dirt, and he'd lost his coat. Feeling Yves start forwards, Caroline put a restraining hand on him and Hetty.

EVERY STEP NAT took jarred both his shoulder and his head, but he was determined to show nothing. After all, he'd had much worse than this in battle, hadn't he? And he had rather a large audience.

His stepmother had emerged from the parlor, her face even colder than normal, her eyes like icy pebbles. She didn't look in the least bit pleased to see him. "Nathaniel. I see you are returned to us. What a furor you have caused, upsetting the whole household who had to leave their work and turn out to search for you."

What was this? Was she accusing him of doing this deliberately? Of it being somehow his own fault? It wasn't as if he'd just fallen off like some novice. His saddle had been faulty and come off with him.

His stepmother's hard eyes ran over the sling and his dirty appearance. "I trust you are not badly hurt. Do I need to call Doctor Rescorla out?"

Nat shook his head, wishing immediately that he hadn't but even more determined not to show it. "I've been well looked after by Gryff Casworan." He didn't need to tell her what his friend had done for him. "No need to trouble the doctor. Just a sprained shoulder and a bump on the head." He turned to Young Pascoe and Dickon. "I can see myself upstairs to my room, thank you. I'm not an invalid yet."

They stepped back, diffident and wary probably at his tone of voice, much as they'd been all the way back from Wheal Jenny. Having supported Nat's mended shoulder with his makeshift sling, Casworan had sent a couple of young bal maidens to look for the search parties, and it hadn't been long before Pascoe and the cart arrived. There being no women present to make a big fuss, Nat had allowed them to help him into the cart without further ado, and they'd set off for Roskilly.

Footsteps sounded in the still open front doorway, and Trefusis stepped into the hall, his face as dark as Nat's stepmother's face was cold. Anybody would think they weren't glad to see him back safe and sound. Well, not all that sound, as Casworan had said, but practically so.

"I heard you were found," the land agent said. "You seem to have the luck of the devil."

Did he sound put out? Nat's head ached too much to ponder that for long.

Instead, he nodded. "I've been right through the Peninsular War, so it's going to take a lot more than a simple fall from a horse to kill me off." They must know his saddle had come off as Young Pascoe had told him Duchess's return home without him had sparked the search.

Trefusis managed to get his expression under control and even forced a smile onto his rugged face. "It's a relief to have you back safe at Roskilly, Nathaniel."

Why did he get the feeling Trefusis didn't mean a word he was saying? And he didn't like the man using his first name. He had ideas above his station.

Nat turned away and glanced around himself. There was about the gathering in the hallway a certain tension, as though everyone there wanted to say something of their own, but none dared. Even the servants looked as though they wanted to speak.

Dickon and Young Pascoe stepped back, and Nat took a step toward the stairs, anxious to be away from everyone and lie down somewhere dark and quiet. He needed something for his head and the persistent ache in his shoulder and arm. Perhaps he could ring for something from Mrs. Teague, who kept an arsenal of herbal remedies in the kitchen.

As he reached the bottom step, he turned around to stare straight at his stepmother. "Someone needs to go and fetch my saddle back. I'd like to have a look at that later on and find out exactly what failed. Perhaps Young Pascoe could go. It was at the top of the gully I rolled into, not far from Wheal Jenny's count house. It'll be easy to spot."

What was that lurking behind her eyes? He couldn't read her expression at all. And, if he admitted it, which he didn't want to, his head was swimming too much to cope with working out what the woman was thinking about. Her eyes bored into his for several seconds too long. "Very well. He may go."

Trefusis butted in. "He'll need to deal with the cart and the other horses first. The saddle's not as important as his usual work."

Nat's stepmother's eyes slid sideways to Trefusis, and she gave him a slight nod.

That would have to do. Nat didn't have the strength to argue the point. Young Tom Pascoe could bring it back this evening and he could scrutinize it. Perhaps he'd take a bath while he waited. A long, hot bath. He could ring for one to be brought up. But first the daunting prospect of the stairs.

He started up them, and the group in the hall broke up, although he didn't look back to see. The door into the parlor closed, presumably on his mother and Trefusis, and the servants dispersed. Head down, he trudged up the wide staircase.

He'd reached the half-landing before he spotted he had an audience in the gallery. He stopped, heaved in a deep breath, and continued up the stairs.

Yves met him at the top. "Are you hurt? What did you do to your arm? Caroline's being mean and won't let me have a sling."

"Silence, brat," Nat said. "Your chatter is hurting my head." His hand went automatically to the back of his skull and came away sticky with blood.

Hetty gave a horrified squeal, which made Nat want to cover his ears.

A firm but gentle hand rested on the small of his back. "Come into your room and let me take a look at your head. Someone needs to, and as you've turned down Doctor Rescorla's attentions, it seems it falls to me to be your nurse."

Caroline, of course.

Nat would have argued, but he found he didn't have the energy. "Not her," he said, indicating Hetty. "She's too noisy by half."

Caroline turned to Hetty. "Take Yves and go and reassure

your grandfather that Nat is home safely. I'll deal with his head wound. Off you go."

Hetty and Yves, both rather reluctant, vanished off to Sir Hugh's room to relay the good news. Thank goodness. He did *not* need Hetty squealing and Yves's constant questions. He needed peace and quiet. Although he wasn't quite sure Caroline should be coming into his bedroom with him. He pushed that aside. No one was going to know.

She kept her hand in the small of his back all the way along the gallery and down the corridor to his room, the feel of it reassuring. But as he pushed the door open, she removed it, and turning to the bellpull, jerked it. "We need warm water and cloths. Sit down on that chair and let me have a look at you."

Nat sat down, obedience being the easiest thing. For some reason exhaustion was washing over him, despite having spent what must have been half the day asleep in the gully. Or at worst, unconscious.

Caroline stood behind him, her fingers gently parting the hair on the back of his head. Ouch. He winced. She didn't hesitate though, but kept up her gentle probing. "It's not too bad. A big lump, which has bled quite a lot. I'll try to get the blood out of your hair. Not enough to need stitches, so you were right that you don't need the doctor." She paused. "Unless, of course, you have a concussion."

"Since when have you been a nurse?"

She chuckled. "Since forever. As a child, I was friends with a big family and they were always getting into scrapes they didn't want their parents hearing about. They turned to me every time."

"Good luck for me."

"Do you have a bad headache?"

"Crippling."

"And what have you done to your arm? I'm assuming if it were broken, you'd have agreed to see the doctor."

"Dislocated my shoulder." He felt her startle. "Don't worry, Casworan put it back in for me. But he says I have to be careful because it's easy to do it again."

"I have to admit, I have no knowledge of shoulder dislocations. Bumps and scrapes are my limit."

Dickon arrived, and Caroline sent him to fetch water and cloths and ask Mrs. Teague for both an ointment for Nat's head wound and something to dull the pain. "Brandy," Nat said, but Caroline shook her head.

"That'll only make you worse. Do you want the pain of a hangover as well as the headache you already have? And it's a bad thing to have after a bang on the head. No. Warm water, Dickon, if you please, and a pot of tea."

When Dickon returned with all the required list, Caroline laid them out on Nat's washstand and returned to his head. Her fingers were so gentle, he could have closed his eyes and nodded off to sleep, but for the constant throbbing. He watched her wring out the cloths in the water and begin to dab the back of his head clean. Very soon the water had darkened with blood.

"That's better now," she said. "All clean. But if I were you, tonight I'd sleep on your side, not your back. That bump has got to hurt."

"It does."

"I'll just dab on some of the ointment Mrs. Teague sent up. I don't know what's in it, but it smells nice."

Nat sat mute under her ministrations, enjoying the feel of her cool fingers in his hair and not wanting her to have to stop.

However, all too soon she finished. "Now, let me see your shoulder."

"What? It's fine. No need."

She came round to stand in front of him. "Nonsense. Let me have a look. I'm sure I can fashion you a better sling than this as well. And let's give you the painkiller."

The painkiller had come in a little bottle. She uncapped it and took a sniff, then gave a huff. "I might have guessed. Laudanum. It'll have to do and will help you sleep as well. Just a small dose and I'll take it away with me in case you feel the need to augment."

"I'm not a child who can't be trusted."

"I know you're not. But laudanum can be quite dangerous." She automatically thought of Yves. "Take this." She held out the small cup to him and he swallowed it down.

He gave a snort and a wince. "No chance of me overdosing on that. It tastes foul."

"Probably a good thing, although I do believe some people become addicted to it, so they must be able to get over the taste. At least, so I've been told. A substance to be avoided, in my opinion."

He looked up at her as she busied herself constructing a better sling out of the spare cloths Dickon had brought. How practical she was. And how beautiful. Why had he not noticed this before? She had about her an inner beauty that transcended mere good looks in other women. Her calm demeanor, her wide, dark eyes, the curve of her pale cheek, that delicate nose. How had he ever thought her plain? The urge to take her in his arms returned, despite his pounding head and aching shoulder. Well, take her in one arm at least. He felt his mouth curve into an involuntary smile.

"I didn't know it could work so quickly," she said.

"It isn't. I was smiling for another reason."

She didn't ask him why. Maybe she suspected. Instead, she moved to the window and closed the heavy curtains. "I think you should lie down and get some rest. Hopefully the laudanum will help ease the pain. I have to go and rescue Sir Hugh from Hetty and Yves. They *are* my charges, after all. Not you."

Was there a wistful note in her voice?

He rose from his chair and went over to the bed. "Could you send Dickon up to help me with my boots?"

She turned from the window. "Nonsense. I can do that for you."

Oh, the longing to let her do so. And more. He hadn't felt like this about a woman in… how long? Julia had been gone six years.

Six *long* years. He felt impotent to resist, as, without waiting for an answer, she approached him, a determined look in her eyes.

"Sit down then. I can't pull them off if you're standing up, can I?"

He sat on the edge of the bed, his heart hammering much faster than it should have been. It was only boots, after all. He was getting carried away by an action such as the soldier who served him in the army might have done, or a valet, if he had one. Just boots. He had to get a hold of himself.

She seized one of his boots. They were a snug fit and she had to pull hard, and he had only his good arm to balance himself on the bed. It necessitated bracing his other foot hard on the floor.

The boot slid off into her hands and she laughed. "I used to sometimes pull my father's boots off for him, so he could toast his toes in front of the fire of an evening."

"Thank you."

She set about the other boot which soon joined the first, but didn't leave. Was she intending to tuck him up in bed? She was a governess, not a nursemaid... but... No. This was ridiculous. "And thank you for the second boot. I shall be fine now. You'd best get off to Hetty and Yves. They might themselves need rescuing from my grandfather."

"You're sure you'll be all right? Would you like me to look in on you later?"

Damn it. He was blushing. Thank goodness the closed curtains hid it. "I'll be fine. You don't need to bother yourself."

She shook her head. "It's no bother. I'll bring you a light supper from the kitchens when I come." And with a smile, she was gone.

Nat sat for a while on the edge of the bed, turning his thoughts over and finding they were just as jumbled as when he started. It must be the knock on the head. Or the laudanum dose on top of Casworan's brandy. That was it. He'd best try and sleep it off. He'd be more sensible after a sleep.

CAROLINE FOUND HETTY still with her grandfather, but Yves and Dash had gone. She'd been reading aloud to him but the old man had nodded off, and Hetty had moved over to the window and was sitting reading to herself when Caroline stole in on tiptoe.

"Where's Yves gone?" Caroline whispered, with a glance at the bed, but Sir Hugh didn't stir. His grandchildren must have tired him out. That, and the worry about Nat. Or the laudanum. The worry that she didn't know how it worked bothered Caroline.

Hetty closed her book and rose to her feet, the evening sunlight dancing in her rich auburn hair. "Yves said this book was boring and he wanted to go outside. I couldn't stop him." She didn't sound worried, though. But then, she didn't know about the conspiracy. A conspiracy Caroline felt had grown much more real since Nat's accident.

"Do you know where he went?"

Hetty shrugged. "Where does he always go? The kitchens in search of food. I swear that boy has hollow legs. And he never gets any fatter, which is most unfair."

"Shall we leave Sir Hugh to sleep? Come along. And it's time you did some more piano practice—you've not done any at all today, what with the chaos going on. Now Nat's safe and sound, you can do half an hour before you have to get ready for dinner."

Hetty pulled a face. "If I must."

Leaving the book behind on Sir Hugh's bedside table, they tiptoed out of the room and descended the stairs to the quiet front hall. Hetty headed off to the music room, and Caroline took the corridor to the kitchens at the back of the house. Mrs. Teague was in there with Molly the kitchen maid, but there was no sign of Yves.

"Good afternoon, Mrs. Teague," Caroline said. "Have you seen Master Yves?"

Mrs. Teague wiped her greasy hands on her stained apron. "I have that, Miss. He were down here looking for something to eat. When isn't he, I'd like to say. That boy eats like more'n one horse, I can tell you. I gave him some bread and jam and he spotted Mr. Trefusis passing down the corridor and ran off after him."

Caroline's heart skipped a beat. "When was this?"

"'Bout ten minutes gone."

"Going which way?"

"Out into the stable courtyard."

Caroline hastened back into the corridor and headed for the back door. That Yves was alone with Trefusis chilled her blood, but surely, surely, he wouldn't try anything on the day Nat had almost perished? That would look like too much of a coincidence, even for someone as determined as he appeared to be.

She pushed open the door into the stableyard. Empty. Where could they have gone? No sign of either of the Pascoes either. She'd better look in the stables and tack room.

No one there either, just a row of contented horses munching hay.

For a moment nonplused, Caroline stood biting her lip in the wide, arched doorway into the stable block. Could Trefusis have taken Yves off somewhere?

Laughter sounded from beyond the arched gateway of the yard, and Yves came running in, Dash barking at his heels, all by himself.

Caroline let her breath out with a sigh. "Yves, where've you been? I've been searching for you and thought you'd gone off and got lost like Nat, and I was going to have to get a search party out after you."

Yves skidded to a halt, a decidedly guilty look on his face. "Nowhere." Dash bounced around him in excitement, uttering little yips.

"Mrs. Teague told me you went off with Mr. Trefusis."

Yves regarded his booted feet. "Oh, he's gone now. He had work to do."

Why did his attempt at nonchalance sound so stilted? Caroline narrowed her eyes at him but couldn't think of anything else to ask. "Well, it's nearly time for your supper, and I ought to change for dinner. Although I think I might send my apologies to your aunt and tell her after today I have such a headache, that I'd best eat with you in the schoolroom." Anything was better than another meal with Mrs. Treloar, Trefusis, and no Nat.

Yves brightened. "I'll ask Mrs. Teague if she can send up an egg tea for us. I'd like that, and so would you. Come on, Dash."

Yves extracted the required promise from Mrs. Teague for the egg tea, and she shortly proved as good as her word. A tea of two boiled eggs apiece along with ample bread and butter came upstairs with Patience and was served in the schoolroom with a pot of tea. Quite a banquet by the normal standards of nursery tea. Yves's slightly reluctant demeanor, as though he was hiding something, vanished, and Caroline dismissed her worries. He might have gone running after Trefusis, but the man hadn't dared do anything to him.

After tea, Caroline left Yves playing with his toy soldiers on the floor of the nursery and carried the tea tray down to the kitchen. Dinner upstairs was over, and Mrs. Teague made up another tray, also of boiled eggs, bread and butter and tea, for Caroline to take upstairs for Nat.

At precisely seven o'clock, by the striking of the hall clock, she knocked lightly on Nat's door. No answer. She waited a minute then tapped again. Still no answer. Should she go in? Several not so comforting reasons for his lack of answering flashed through her mind, including the fact that the head wound she'd treated might have been worse than she thought and caused his death, which would undoubtedly lead to her being dismissed on the spot. Or he could be concussed and in a coma. A young man near Cadley had fallen from his horse out hunting and sustained a head wound similar to Nat's which had resulted in a coma that lasted for nearly a week. And then he'd died.

Fighting to control her nerves, she pushed the door open and went in.

Nat was lying on the bed, not in it, long legs outstretched. Was he dead or in a coma? She approached the bed. What a relief. His chest rose and fell as he breathed and he looked peaceful rather than at death's door. Although the thought that someone about to die might look peaceful, too, surfaced.

"Nat?" She couldn't keep the quaver out of her voice.

His lashes fluttered and he opened his eyes.

What a deep blue they were, just like those of Yves and Hetty, as blue as the sea on a summer's day.

He pushed himself up on the bed with a wince as he leaned on his bad shoulder. "Ouch. Caroline. I didn't think you'd come. I'm sorry. I was asleep."

She set the tray down on the ornate table beside the window. "You need to eat something. Mrs. Teague did you a tea such as she just sent up to Yves and me." She wanted to reach out and touch him, but held herself in check. She was the governess, he the son of the house. She must not take liberties.

"That's very kind of you, and her." He swung his legs off the bed and padded in stockinged feet over to the table. "This looks excellent and reminds me of nursery tea when I was a boy."

Caroline couldn't resist a snort. "We don't often get eggs for tea in the nursery. Your stepmother seems to think little boys exist on thin air. Well, on thin bread and a scrape of butter."

He sat down. "She only became like that after my father died. Poor Hetty and Yves. You'll take tea with me?"

Mrs. Teague had sent two cups. Now why had she done that? Caroline sat down at the table, opposite to Nat, and poured the tea. "Sugar? It's good in this sort of situation."

He nodded and winced again. "Three spoonsful."

She smiled. "Very bad for your teeth."

He lopped the pointy end off one of the eggs and runny yolk ran down the side. "Just as I like them. And I don't take three spoonsful normally. I'm just following your advice. We soldiers learn to look after our teeth, thank you."

Caroline smiled. "As do we governesses."

He broke off a piece of bread and dunked it in his egg. "The food of the gods."

She watched him eat, sipping her hot tea. It was the best China tea and very aromatic. He looked much recovered with some color in his cheeks but not too much, and appeared to be using his right arm as much as the left, as though the pain had diminished considerably.

He'd finished the bread and eggs and picked up his cup of tea before she spoke again. "What happened to you?"

His eyes narrowed at her tone. "My girth broke, I assume, or the straps holding it to the saddle. Young Pascoe might be back with it by now. I might go down and look now I'm feeling so much better." He regarded her with a thoughtful expression. "Bad luck, I assume. Duchess shied, the saddle came loose, I couldn't save myself and by bad luck I was by a rocky gully. I rolled into it and spent much of the day lying sleeping in the sun, with a broken head and dislocated shoulder." He wrapped one arm around his chest. "And my ribs feel as though they've been well trampled by a herd of wild horses. I thought at first they might be broken, but they're not. Believe me when I say I know what that feels like."

"They could be cracked."

"I doubt it, as it doesn't hurt too much to breathe. I've had broken ribs before and they were worse. I think in all probability they're just bruised."

She nodded, catching her bottom lip in her teeth. Dared she say anything to Nat? Would he be horrified at what she was suggesting, or would he be up in arms in defense of Yves, his grandfather, and himself?

Nat rose from the table. "I'll put some shoes on and we can go down to the stables and see Young Pascoe and that saddle. Would you like to come?" A hopeful glint showed in his eyes, so winning that Caroline smiled at him.

"I would. Where are your shoes, and I'll fetch them for you."

With his shoes found and his feet slipped into them, they headed down the corridor to the gallery and from there down the stairs and into the passage to the stableyard. Caroline carried the tea tray to return to Mrs. Teague as they passed.

Young Pascoe was in the kitchen eating his supper, but he jumped to his feet when he saw Caroline and Nat.

Nat waved his free arm at him. "It's all right, Tom. Sit down and keep eating. I don't want to disturb you. Miss Fairfield and I are just on our way to the tack room to take a look at that saddle you went to retrieve."

Tom Pascoe looked guilty and didn't sit down. "I'm right sorry, Sir. I went and looked where you said it were, but I couldn't find it not nowhere. I scoured the heather, and I found the gully you was in. There were fresh blood on a boulder from your head, I reckon, but not a sign of no saddle."

Caroline stiffened. Nat had described exactly where to go, and Tom Pascoe had gone. But he'd had to sort out the flat cart first and no doubt do a few other chores in the stables. How long had the delay been? Long enough for anyone else who'd heard the directions in the hall to go and retrieve the sabotaged saddle. And dispose of it so Nat couldn't find out what had gone wrong with it.

"Are you sure?" Nat asked, as though he didn't quite believe Tom.

Young Pascoe nodded. "Proper sure, Sir. I looked around the whole top. I could see where you fell and rolled and hit that rock, right hard. Flattened heather where you'd lain. But no saddle."

"Might someone have taken advantage and stolen it?" Nat muttered.

Unlikely. Caroline caught his arm. "Thank you, Tom. Shall we go and see how Duchess is faring after her flight?"

Nat went back into the corridor with her and from there out into the yard. Duchess's loose box was at the far end of the stable block from the tack room. The warm smell of straw beds and hay in racks tickled Caroline's nostrils, and the sound of contented masticating came from every loose box. Duchess turned her head from her hayrack, but didn't come over.

"She looks better for her adventure than I feel," Nat said, leaning on the stable door.

Caroline leaned beside him. "She was lucky. Her reins broke. They could have caused her to fall. She could have broken a leg."

He nodded.

She licked her lips. "You were lucky, too. You could have been killed."

He nodded again. "I wish I could take a look at that saddle."

Now or never. "Do you think someone doesn't want you to see it?"

She felt his body stiffen beside hers, but he didn't turn his head. "Do you think that?"

"I do."

He stayed silent for a full minute, the sound of Duchess eating loud. "Who do you think would want that?"

She watched his profile. He was on her right, so she couldn't see his scar. "Who heard your directions to go and find the saddle?"

"Everyone in the hall. Dickon, Tom Pascoe, you, Hetty and Yves, my stepmother, Ennion, Trefusis…"

"And who ordered Young Pascoe not to go and find it until he'd finished his day's work?"

"Trefusis."

She let the name hang between them.

"You think Trefusis went out there and took the saddle? So Tom wouldn't find it?"

Caroline nodded. "I do. I think he gave himself enough time to get out there and dispose of it so you couldn't see someone had tampered with the girth, or the girth straps."

Now he did turn his head to look at her, his face close to hers. His voice dropped as though he feared someone might be listening. "You think he interfered with my saddle? Why?"

"Men," Caroline huffed. "You're all blind to what's going on around you. My friend Lord Ormonde is much the same, and dear Sam Beauchamp, as well. Look beyond the end of your nose. Trefusis is after the Treloar fortune."

Nat shook his head. "But how could he hope to get it? After my grandfather dies, it'll go to Yves." He frowned. "Does he think to be guardian to Yves until he reaches his majority?"

Caroline shook her head. "Look a bit further. Who inherits if anything happens to Yves?"

"I do, I suppose."

"Yes. And if anything happens to you?"

"Hetty."

"Precisely."

"But Trefusis is my mother's lover. I had it from Jacka at Kennegy Downs. Everyone knows it. Why would Hetty inheriting Roskilly make a difference to him?"

"Haven't you seen the way he looks at Hetty when your stepmother isn't looking? It's Hetty he's after, not her mother. Think. Why would he go after your stepmother who is older even than he is, when he could have a young and beautiful bride—with a huge inheritance. Your stepmother can't give him children, for a start."

Did he believe her? She held her breath.

"So, you're saying he tried to kill me today?"

She nodded. "I'm almost sure he did. Think about it again.

He won't start with the first in line—your grandfather. He'll go last because he's sure he's going to die soon and he can afford to wait for nature to take its course. All he needs to do is remove you and Yves, then marry Hetty and the inheritance is his to keep. Yves, whom everyone's been told is weakly and not expected to live. You and Yves are in terrible danger."

"And my grandfather."

"Him too, but nowhere near as much as you and Yves. Trefusis tried to kill you today and failed. That saddle's probably down an old disused mineshaft where you'll never find it. And he won't stop at today. He's going to try again. Don't forget what Hetty said—that there's a curse on the male Treloars. If something happens to you, the locals will say it was the curse."

"And Yves?"

"At first I thought it was only your stepmother who wanted him gone so you could inherit, but now I think it's not just her. It has to be Trefusis, although how he would have persuaded Bridget to do it for him, I don't know. Well, I can imagine but that's too horrible to put into words. I think it's probably both of them. Together."

"What're you talking about? Explain yourself."

"Bridget has been dosing Yves with large quantities of laudanum. Miss Hawkins discovered it and was dismissed, as was Hester the old nursery maid. She thinks—Yves and I met her in Penzance—that whoever's behind it—she thinks it's Mrs. Treloar—was trying to make *her* the scapegoat, so they could blame her for doing it to him. I found the bottle in Bridget's room and swapped it for a harmless liquid, but last night it was topped up again and Yves was half asleep this morning. It's a very dangerous thing to give so small a child."

She waited, hardly daring to breathe, gazing up into those troubled blue eyes.

"How long have you known?"

"I didn't know all of it until you told me you were only Mrs. Treloar's stepson. Before that..." She hesitated. "Before that I thought perhaps it was you who wanted Yves out of the way so you could inherit. When you told me she wasn't your mother, I realized she couldn't be doing it for you. And then I worked out it had to be Trefusis with his eye to marrying Hetty and taking the inheritance all for himself."

He nodded. "Quite the detective. I'm impressed." Exactly what his grandfather had said.

"We have to stop them."

He nodded. "There's nothing I can do tonight, but I'll speak to my grandfather in the morning about dismissing Trefusis. That would be a start. He seems the catalyst to all of this. Without him here, my stepmother will have no reason, surely, to ill wish Yves and me."

"You think? She'll still want Hetty to be the only heiress, you mark my words. If she's involved in this, and I'm becoming more and more certain she is, although it might not be her idea and she *may* just be under the influence of Trefusis because she thinks he loves her." She refrained from mentioning how convinced she was of Mrs. Treloar's guilt. Let Nat accustom himself to this first.

"I think after today Yves should be safe tonight," Nat said with a sigh. "And I should be, too." He gave her a wry smile. "But tomorrow, I promise, we'll see the back of Trefusis if I have to kick him down the drive myself."

Caroline chuckled. "I have to say, I'd like to see you do that. If you decide to, promise to warn me in advance so I can come to watch."

He chuckled. "I promise. Now, you'd best get back to your watch on Yves, I should think. Just in case. It doesn't do to become complacent. I shall be quite all right now. Trefusis won't dare do anything to me right here at Roskilly. He'll be planning to wait a while before he strikes again."

Caroline nodded. "I'll go and read Yves a chapter of his favorite story." She laid her hand on Nat's. "Goodnight."

His blue eyes met hers. "Goodnight, Caroline." For a moment she couldn't drag her own away. His were almost hypnotic, or was she just at her most vulnerable right now?

With an immense effort of will, she tore her eyes away and hurried out of the stables. Yves would be very pleased to have her read to him.

Chapter Twenty-Nine

CAROLINE HAD TROUBLE getting to sleep that night, and even more trouble staying asleep, so it was a rather the worse-for-wear start to the morning. Patience, arriving with her breakfast tray, found her still in bed, yawning and heavy eyed.

Caroline sat up. "How is it," she said, "that one spends all the night tossing and turning and unable to sleep, only to fall into the deepest and most refreshing of sleeps just before one has to get up?"

Patience giggled. "I'm sure I don't know, Miss. It don't happen to me. I'm asleep the moment my head touches the pillow, because I has to be up at five every morning."

Suppressing another yawn, Caroline climbed out of bed. "I really need a strong cup of tea. Have you taken Yves his breakfast? Or is he already downstairs in the kitchen?" At least Bridget couldn't have given him a laudanum-laden dose of the carminative last night. If she'd tried, she'd have had a shock when she found it was just water.

"I'll go and take it to him now, Miss. He weren't in the kitchen this morning. At least, I didn't see him there. Shall I come back here after and help you with your stays?"

"That would be lovely. Thank you, Patience."

Patience departed and Caroline poured herself a cup of tea, but this time it was nursery brand and rather weak and tasteless.

She added a spoonful of sugar to give her some much needed energy, and nibbled on the bread and butter. When she was dressed, she could go down to the kitchen and ask Mrs. Teague for a nice doorstep slice of bread with some of her fresh butter, all golden and thick. Mmmmm. How ridiculous it was to have that available in the kitchen but send up these thin slices with barely any butter on them. Not enough for a mouse to survive on. For all she knew, Mrs. Treloar might well have decided starvation was a slow but sure method of disposing of Yves—and his governess at the same time.

Patience was back in ten minutes, by which time Caroline had drained the teapot and changed into her shift and drawers, ready to be laced into her stays.

Patience picked up the stays. "Master Yves weren't in his bedroom, Miss, but I left his tray there, just in case he comes back."

"And still not in the kitchen with Mrs. Teague?"

Patience fastened the stays around Caroline's body and started tightening the laces. "No, Miss. Not a sign of him. And I been in there working with Molly, the kitchen maid, for a bit before I brung up your breakfast. I don't think he's been in there this morning, which is a bit unusual, I has to say."

Caroline twisted her head round to peer over her shoulder at Patience. "That's odd. It's not like him to miss his food. Whether it's from Mrs. Teague or what his aunt perceives as suitable for a nursery meal."

Patience pulled on the stay laces. "Breathe in, Miss."

Caroline obliged. "Did you ask if anyone had seen him this morning?"

"No, Miss. I'm sure he's around somewhere, though. He's a good boy, and he knows he has to do his lessons with you of a morning."

The stays firmly laced, Patience helped Caroline on with her petticoat and gown and fastened the ties down the back. "There. Would you like me to help with your hair?"

Caroline shook her head. "No, thank you. I'll just braid it and make a bun. Could you take my tray down and, if Yves turns out to be in the kitchen, ask him to come up as soon as he can? And if he's not… well, you could ask around the servants to see if anyone's seen him."

"Yes, Miss."

Patience scuttled off carrying the tray and Caroline dealt with her hair. Where could that scamp have got to? Perhaps she ought to go down to the kitchens and question the other servants herself rather than rely on Patience, who clearly wasn't bothered about Yves's absence. After all, she didn't know what Caroline knew.

With hurried steps, as now a nub of unease had formed in her stomach, she made her way down to the kitchen.

Mrs. Teague was busy at the stove, as usual, her face flushed red with the heat.

"No," she said, on being questioned. "I haven't seen the lad. I thought as maybe he was still in bed. Like yesterday. Patience already asked me. Like I said to her, Dash's still here, so he hasn't been in to get the dog yet." Her brows met in a worried frown. "What d'you think he's up to, then? Some mischief, I'll be bound, knowing him."

Caroline shook her head. "I have no idea, but I need to find him." She bit her lip. "It's very important that I find him."

Questioning of the other servants who kept coming in and out of the kitchen provided no clues. No one had seen Yves that morning. Had he even come down here? Thanking them, Caroline went out into the stableyard. It might be a good idea to check if Blossom was there.

The little gray was snug in her small loosebox, munching away on her breakfast hay. But Folly was not. Had Hetty gone out riding? Caroline retraced her steps and ran along the gallery to Hetty's room.

With no preamble, she pushed open the door. Hetty was still in bed, but she sat up when Caroline came in, rubbing her eyes.

"Goodness. What is it? It's too early to be getting up yet."

Caroline improvised. "I thought Yves might be with you."

Hetty yawned. "I should hope not at this time of the morning, but I wouldn't put it past him. He can be quite horrid when he tries."

"He's a boy, that's why." Caroline scanned the room. "Did he happen to indicate where he might be going today? I have an uneasy feeling he might be up to no good as he's missed his breakfast."

Hetty yawned again. "I need to go back to sleep. This is far too early for me."

"Think. Please."

Hetty snuggled down into her bedcovers. "We-ell, when I was in the garden yesterday, I glimpsed him with Mr. Trefusis." She gave a little shiver. "I hid behind a bush when I saw them coming."

Little wonder. She wouldn't want to bump into Trefusis in the gardens if she was alone. And Yves wouldn't count as much of a chaperone.

"And?"

"Once I'd hidden, I couldn't get away, so I had to stay crouched there while they walked past. I couldn't help but overhear. Yves has such a loud voice. He was asking Mr. Trefusis all about the mines. And Mr. Trefusis was telling him how exciting they are and what the tunnels are like."

That didn't surprise Caroline at all. Yves had been curious about the mines when they'd gone to Wheal Jenny, although a little put off by the sight of the miners.

"What did Mr. Trefusis say to him?"

"I couldn't hear everything once they were past my bush, but I heard this bit. He told Yves he'd first been down a mine when he was younger than Yves, and that he'd loved it. He said it was like exploring—a big adventure. He'd gone along the beach here and found the old adit in the cove beneath Penmar Head and got in that way, because his father had refused to let him go in by the ladder shaft."

Caroline had heard of people's blood running cold but had never thought it could be true. Now she discovered it was. Icy fingers ran down her spine. Trefusis had told Yves there was an entrance into the mines from the beach and called going into it an adventure. What self-respecting, red-blooded boy would balk at the challenge? He would see it as exciting and illicit—two things that would make it even more attractive to him.

Without even thanking Hetty, Caroline sped from the room, her feet leading her straight to Nat's bedroom door. She rapped hard on it and, a moment later, he opened it. His hair was tousled and he needed a shave, and his shirt was undone to reveal dark hairs curling on his muscled chest. Dark bruises shadowed his ribs. If she hadn't been in such a panic, she might have admired the vision.

"Caroline." He hastily buttoned his shirt and tucked it into his trousers, then pulled his braces up over his shoulders. "What can I do for you?" He must have been able to see from her face that something was very amiss.

"Can I come in?" She kept her voice down low, glancing up and down the corridor, fearful lest anyone should spot her.

He stood back. "Of course. If you think it appropriate."

"I do." She stepped inside, closed the door behind her and leaned against it. "Yves has gone missing."

He drew his bottom lip under his teeth, his blue eyes troubled. "Missing as 'he's in danger,' or he's just out on some boyish prank?"

"The former."

"How do you know?"

Caroline repeated what Hetty had told her. "And he's taken Folly, whom he's never ridden before. How he got a saddle on her, I have no idea." She was only a large pony really, but nevertheless, reaching her back would have been hard for him. Could someone have helped him? Trefusis, perhaps?

Nat sat down on his chair and started pulling on his boots. "I know the adit Trefusis referred to. I've been in there myself as a boy, and I can tell you, it's not safe. The roof is shored up in places with ancient, rotted wood, and when the tide comes in, it floods the bottom of the mine. Plus, there are shafts cut in the floor from time to time, and they stay full of water."

"Oh my God."

He grabbed his jacket. "Can you give me a hand with this? We have to go after him. I'll tell…" His voice trailed away.

Caroline nodded. "Yes. Who can we tell? No one. If we tell Trefusis he'll insist on looking for him himself, and if he finds him, well, I expect he'll find him already conveniently 'drowned' or 'buried' by a fall. And we'll be none the wiser."

He grimaced. "We don't have time to get other help. We have to go alone. Come on."

As it was still early, Mrs. Treloar wasn't up yet, but Trefusis might well have been in the estate office, so Nat led Caroline out through a side door and they skirted around the stables to the path to the beach. If they were lucky, no one would have seen them leave.

Once out of sight of the house, they ran, and as they burst out of the dunes onto the beach, Nat was relieved to see the tide a good way out, and the wet sand marked by a single telltale set of hoofprints heading toward the cliffs of Penmar Head. If they were lucky, they should have several hours in which to find Yves before the tide cut off Penmar Cove. If he'd been foolhardy enough to go into the adit alone, that was. There remained the chance that he'd either not been able to find it, or had seen it and been frightened off. But there were no returning hoofprints.

At least when Nat had gone exploring the adit as a boy, he'd been with Jacka, and they'd had the sense to take a ball of string with them. Nat had just read about Theseus in the labyrinth of

Knossos, and Ariadne's helpful ruse had been fresh in his mind.

He'd brought several candles and a supply of matches with him this time, trusting his own knowledge of the mine workings. Experience had taught him how dark a mine adit could be. If only his shoulder wasn't aching so much, but at least his headache had gone, although the back of his head remained tender to the touch.

Once down on the hard, wet sand, they could move faster than they had done in the dunes. Caroline jogged along by his side, her face creased with worry, as they followed the clear trail of hoofprints. What was that foolish, but bold, boy thinking of, going off on his own like this? But he had no friends to take with him. Poor little chap lived such an isolated life away from other children. No wonder he craved adventure.

Penmar Head seemed to have retreated into the far distance, but they reached it at last, and headed around the rocky foot of the imposing headland where it stretched out across the sand in long, jagged fingers. On the summit, the shape of Wheal Jenny's engine house and chimney rose up against a cloudless blue sky. If only he'd taken the boy down a few levels the other day, by the ladder shaft, then he might not have been so curious about the inside of a mine. Or he might have made it all worse. After all, mining ran deep in the blood of the Treloars.

Penmar Cove was a small inlet curved into the foot of the headland, with high cliffs rising behind it edged by tumbles of fallen rocks. Now, where was that adit? There was only one, he was sure. Thank goodness. Something moved between the piles of boulders, drawing Nat's attention. For a moment he thought it was Yves, before the chestnut shape of Folly wandered into view, reins trailing on the sand.

He approached her, holding out his hand, and she approached, soft eyes relieved to see him. Her stirrups had been adjusted short enough for Yves, but there was no sign of him. He put her reins back over her head. "If the tide comes in, and she's here in the cove, she'll drown." He led her around the outcropping cliff and rocks into Morgelyn Bay, ran her stirrups up, tucked the buckle end of her reins behind them and gave her a smack on her rump that set her trotting off across the beach. She'd be safe now and probably find her way home.

"I don't see any cave entrances," Caroline said. "Is it even still here?"

Nat nodded. "I very much doubt it'll have been hidden by a rock fall. We don't get many of those here. Wrong kind of rock. This way." He held out his hand and helped her onto the barnacle- and mussel-covered rocks. They scrambled across the banks of slimy weed, feet scraping on the coarse shells. The dips and crevices of all sizes that sheltered rock pools would have transported Nat back to the days of his carefree boyhood, had their mission not been of the most urgent.

"These rocks are covered as the tide comes in," he said. "You can tell by the covering of seaweed and shellfish. And out here, it'll be well before high tide itself. We have to hurry. If we're still in the cove when the sea comes up to these rocks, we'll be stuck." He squinted up at the sheer cliffs. "And these are unclimbable."

Caroline regarded him for a moment out of determined eyes. "Then you are right. We shall have to hurry. Folly's being here only reinforces my conviction that this is where Yves has gone."

Nat turned back to the cliffs, scanning their rocky crevices. He hadn't been here for… what was it? Fourteen or fifteen years. Treading in his youthful footprints, he scrambled over a particularly large boulder, and there it was.

The jagged, dark mouth of a cave, maybe five feet high by three feet wide, opened up before him, the path to it as rough as the rocks he and Caroline had been clambering over. He paused to survey it, a little daunted by the prospect of entering this adit, but not about to admit it to his companion. If she was prepared to go into it in search of Yves, then of course he was too. He tightened his grip on Caroline's hand. "Come on then."

Chapter Thirty

CAROLINE STARED AT the small cave in the cliff face, not even high enough for her to enter without having to almost crouch. This did not look as though it could lead anywhere. Had Yves really gone into this uninviting hole? Why would anyone even want to? Sweat began to prickle out across her skin.

She glanced at Nat, but he was already scrambling over the remnants of what must once have been a path along the cliff edge, but had now been almost all washed into the sea through lack of maintenance and many years of rough weather. Over her shoulder, the waves seemed a lot closer than they had been, but that might have been an optical illusion… or her nerves. Had the tide turned, and was it even now creeping closer by the minute and threatening to shut off the little cove and them with it? She swallowed. She had to think of Yves and not her own safety, hard as that might be.

Nat ducked his head and disappeared into the dark mouth of the cave. In a moment he was outside again, holding up a garment Caroline recognized. Yves's short blue jacket, the brass buttons on it glinting in the sunlight. "He left it lying just inside the entrance," Nat said. "He can't be too far ahead of us. Give me your hand and I'll pull you up."

Using his left hand, he hauled her up to stand in front of the cave entrance on a little platform of flat rock. He seemed to be holding his right arm against his chest as though in pain. A pang of guilt assaulted Caroline that she'd asked him to help her so soon after his injury. "I'm sorry. Your arm must be hurting you. I should have asked Young Pascoe to come with me instead."

He shot her a reproving scowl. "He'd be no good to you at all. Never been down a mine in his life, and I doubt he even knows where this adit is. I've spent enough time in this one in particular to know my way about. We'll find him, don't worry."

His positive air comforted her as much as his physical presence did. A man used to command and to facing danger. However bad they were at noticing things going on under their noses, men could be useful in a crisis.

Nat looked past her at the sea. "Time presses on, and we only have until the tide reaches the furthest rocks. We'd best get in there."

He went first, and, having taken a huge, steadying breath, Caroline ducked her head and followed. Immediately darkness rushed in around her, compressing her body and making it hard to breathe. Her heart began to race and a fresh lot of cold sweat stood out on her skin. Her terror of enclosed spaces filled her head. She couldn't do this. She couldn't.

A flame flickered as Nat struck a match and lit one of the candles, sending the darkness fleeing. The interior of the cave leapt into immediate shadowy reality—a little larger on the inside than the entrance implied, but with walls and ceiling of jagged rock. How narrow it felt, with the walls close enough to touch without stretching out her arms. Underfoot lay soggy sand and lumps of rock, indicating just how far in the sea would come before too long.

Yes. She could do this. For Yves. She took another quivering breath. "Yves!" She shouted, but the rocks seemed to soak up her voice and dwindle it to nothing. Perhaps she was hoping for too much that he might still be near enough to hear her.

"Yves!" Nat joined in, his voice deep and strong, but still swallowed by the walls.

Nothing.

"Take hold of my coat and follow close behind me," Nat said, seemingly oblivious to her terror. "Step carefully. I don't want you stumbling and breaking your ankle." She didn't want that either. The last thing on earth she wanted was to be stuck in here with a broken limb. She swallowed; she was just going to have to be brave… for Yves.

Nat held the candle out in front of him, and Caroline did as she was told and took a tight hold on his coat tails. They progressed at snail's pace into the tunnel. The *adit*. She had to remember it was called an adit. Somehow, remembering the proper name felt like a lifeline that might keep her mind off the reality of her situation.

A glance over her shoulder showed her the tiny dot of daylight that was the entrance disappear around a bend in the tunnel. *Adit*.

She mustn't think of the tons of rock above her head, of the headland, the mine buildings on the top of it, of the sea chasing them up the beach. *Adit*. This was an *adit*. Think of Yves, lost in here somewhere. In this *adit*.

After about fifteen minutes of this slow progress, the flickering candlelight illuminated, badly, a fork in the narrow tunnel. To the right, the adit veered off slightly downhill, into murky brown water that must never drain away when the tide was out. To the left, the adit rose a little and headed very gently uphill, the path altogether drier, but considerably narrower. If that were possible. No wonder they sent skinny young boys down here. She swallowed down her fear yet again, an action made hard by how dry her mouth had become.

"He won't have gone down that tunnel," Nat said, his voice barely above a whisper. "The boy has some sense, I believe."

Not that much or surely he wouldn't have gone down here on his own in the first place.

Nat turned uphill, at over six feet, a tight fit, with his head scraping the tunnel roof and his shoulders the sides. As for

Caroline, her skirts caught at the walls of the tunnel, snagging on the rough surface and her feet scuffed over the wet, rocky floor. Thank goodness she'd worn boots and not light shoes.

The flickering candlelight illuminated the walls, revealing streaks of blue running down them. "Copper leaching out of the rock," Nat said. "See up there?" He pointed where a narrow shaft in the tunnel roof rose above them at an angle. "That's where the old miners followed the vein of copper upwards."

"I thought this was a tin mine."

"It is, but there's copper here as well. Or there was. Not much left now and too expensive to dig out. So we stick to tin."

Water dripped and trickled down the rocks on both sides, pooling on the rough floor, and Caroline was glad again of her boots. How far were they going to have to go? She was a mole, blindly tunneling ever deeper into an earth that terrified her. Progress was by necessity slow, and Yves could be anywhere in here, even now lying injured somewhere they might not find him. She tightened her hold on Nat's coat as they continued.

They hadn't gone a lot further, or so it seemed, when Nat ground to a halt.

Caroline peered around him only to find the tunnel up ahead blocked by a pile of rocks and rubble. "It's blocked," she said, stating the obvious. "Where can he have gone?"

Nat shook his head. "Not fully blocked. Look."

Sure enough, up near the top of the fall of rocks was a hole. Not a very large hole, but one a small boy could have wriggled through if he had a fancy to. However, it didn't look large enough to allow either Nat or Caroline through.

Nat scrambled up and put his candle and face to the hole. "Yves! Are you there? Yves!"

Nothing.

Caroline, abandoned in the dark, her heart beating so fast and hard it might at any moment leap out of her mouth, bit her lip as she strained her ears for a reply. Oh, please let him be there. If only so they could get out of this dreadful tomb-like warren of ever-narrowing passages. Please.

"Yves!" Nat shouted again.

Nothing.

Caroline glanced over her shoulder into impenetrable blackness where anything could be lurking. No. She mustn't go down that road or she'd go mad. "Maybe he didn't come this way?" Her whisper hissed in the quiet of the tunnel.

Nat twisted to look at her, the candlelight throwing his face into stark planes of light and dark, highlighting his scar and bestowing on him a sinister appearance. "He must have. We found his coat, and I doubt he'd have taken that semi-flooded tunnel. He must have squeezed through here. I'm going to try and move a few of these rocks and see if I can make the hole big enough for me to get through. Stand back a bit, because I'll be throwing them down." He grimaced. "In fact, stand well back in case I bring the roof down on us."

Caroline's poor heart performed a fresh leap of terror. She stared at the pile of rocks. "Is that likely?" She couldn't keep the tremble out of her voice. Thank goodness for the darkness that must be hiding the tears in her eyes. She had to be brave.

He shrugged. "Possible. Go back ten paces, but be careful not to fall."

Into the darkness?

She retreated the required ten paces into the darkness with careful slowness. Should she have asked him to give her a candle? If there was another rock fall and he was buried, so would his candle be. Too late now.

She watched the small circle of light as Nat pulled at the rocks. He'd set the candle down and was using both arms for this, which couldn't be good for his shoulder. A few of the smaller rocks tumbled down the pile onto the floor of the tunnel, location unseen. He strained at a larger one for what seemed forever, then that too tumbled down.

She kept her eyes fixed on the roof above his head, waiting for any sign of movement that might indicate another fall.

Nothing.

"I've done it," he called back. "Make your way back to me very slowly. There are rocks where you won't expect them." He held up the candle and she did as he said. When she reached him, he moved the candle to illuminate the not-much-larger hole. "I'll get through there now, and look for him. I'm going to light another candle for you, and send you back to the beach and safety."

She shook her head. "No. I want to come with you."

He sighed. "It's too dangerous for a woman. It's best if you go back."

She shook her head again, surprised at herself. "No. What if he's hurt?"

"What if the tide comes in and cuts you off?"

"It'll do that to you as well. These tunnels will flood and you'll drown."

"That's why I don't want you here."

She bit her lip. "Whether you like it or not, I'm coming too. You can't stop me." Was she mad? Probably.

They were at an impasse. He drew himself up to his full height, glowering at her. "Has anyone ever told you that you are the most frustrating of women?"

She glowered back at him. "Of course. And while we're about it, has no one ever told you how difficult you are? No wonder I suspected you might be behind the attempt on Yves's life."

His eyes caught the candlelight. "You are the most outspoken young woman I've ever met. Only you would have been tenacious enough to bring us searching into a mine like this when it's blatantly obvious you have claustrophobia."

She opened her mouth to make a retort, but he forestalled her, catching hold of her shoulders and pulling her to him. His mouth came down on hers, hard, insistent, and hot with a mixture of what might have been frustration and… passion. His tongue parted her surprised lips, invaded her mouth, and found her tongue. She was too astonished to respond, but the shock rippled through her body, from the top of her head down to her legs, where her knees nearly buckled with a sensation quite new to her.

He released her mouth and retreated half a step, but without releasing his hold on her shoulders. "I'm sorry. It was the only way to shut you up."

For once, Caroline could think of nothing to say for several long moments. When words returned, all she could manage was a rather hoarse, "I'm still coming with you."

He gave a shrug, removed his hands and climbed up to the hole again. "Well, you'd best follow me then." As though he hadn't just kissed her like a lover, he shoved his head and shoulders through the hole, his legs scrabbled for an instant, and he was gone.

She was alone in the pitch blackness with her thoughts. And what thoughts they were. Never had anyone kissed her like that. Not even the dashing young officer she'd fancied herself in love with, who'd gone off to fight in the French wars and never come back. Her lips tingled with the feel of his mouth on hers, her knees still had trouble holding her up, and a curious sensation had inhabited her stomach, reminiscent of how she'd felt as a child when waiting for something exciting to happen, like Christmas or her birthday.

She didn't have long for these thoughts, however. The light appeared in the hole, along with Nat's face. "Hurry up, then." He was back to being all practical.

Hitching up her skirts, she scrambled up the rocks and inserted her head and shoulders into the hole. The tunnel on the far side looked much the same as the first. But what if she got stuck? She probably had wider hips than Nat, being a girl, and he'd looked a tight fit.

She kicked out with her legs, to the sound of fabric ripping, wriggled as fast as she could, mainly out of rising panic, and she was through, an easier fit than Nat had been with his wide shoulders. He helped her to her feet on the other side and, for just a moment, they stood gazing into one another's eyes. If she looked anything like he did, with his dirt smeared face and clothes, then not even her own mother would recognize her in the street.

"Onward," Nat said, and set off along the tunnel. *Adit.*

Caroline, holding tight to his coat tails, struggled along behind him, only now she had something more to think about than how frightened she was. No, terrified. Now she had that kiss to think of. And how much she'd liked it. Had he meant it as more than a means of shutting her up? Had it made him feel the way it had her? Did she want him to do it again? Yes, she did. She wanted to feel that glorious shiver run through her body, so strong it had pushed aside her terror. She hugged the feeling to herself like a comforting blanket as she trudged along the tunnel. *Adit.*

After a bit, a thought broke through her ruminations on that kiss, and she tugged Nat's coat to get him to halt. "Do you have your pocket watch? We need to know how much time we have left before the tide cuts us off." Saying it out loud, although she'd been thinking it for a while, somehow made the reality of what might happen to them much more real. If only she hadn't said it.

He frowned. "I came out in too much of a hurry. I'd say we might have to abandon any idea of going back to the beach and make our way up to the Wheal Jenny workings instead. This adit should connect to them still, if we're lucky, and it hasn't been completely blocked by another fall of rocks. I think we're probably safe here from the sea. We've climbed for long enough that we should be well above high tide level, but we can't go back that way unless we wait for the tide to go back out again, which won't be until late evening."

Small comfort. At least the threat of drowning like rats in a drain had retreated.

Caroline heaved in a lungful of the damp air. "Yves!"

She listened hard. Nothing. Or was that the faintest sound? It could have been dripping water, a falling stone… anything.

"Yves!" Nat called, his voice louder and stronger than hers.

Another faint sound.

Nat's eyes lit up. "Did you hear that?"

"Was it an echo?"

"No. I don't think it was. Come on."

They hurried now, their boots scraping the rocks, their light bouncing around the low roof of the tunnel. Water ran down walls, stained here and there with the blue of more copper. If Yves had been this way, he'd have liked that.

Nat halted, his finger to his lips. They both listened.

Nothing.

"Yves!" Caroline shouted.

"Caroline!" His voice carried faint but clear through the echoing tunnels. "Help!"

"Yves! We're coming. Hang on."

Nat sped up, with Caroline stumbling along behind him in near darkness, expecting at any moment to fall flat on her face but, for once, her terror ignored.

"Caroline!" Yves's voice grew louder, but high with fear.

Nat came to such a sudden halt that Caroline crashed into him. She steadied herself and squeezed past him. The inky surface of water twelve feet across reflected in the candlelight, nearly filling the tunnel floor from wall to wall. A good three feet below them, Yves's small, pale face stared up from water that covered him to his neck, his hands clinging limpet-like to the rocky wall of the water-filled shaft he must have fallen into. He hadn't been able to get out because the water level was too low.

"Caroline," he whimpered, and one hand came away from the rock as he reached toward her.

"Hold on," she cried, throwing herself down onto her front and reaching for his hand. "I'm here."

But she couldn't reach him and his remaining hand was slipping.

Nat dropped with a thud to the wet ground beside her and reached his longer arm for Yves's hand, automatically using the right one. She saw his fingers close around Yves's wrist and he heaved, his face contorted in a grimace of pain. Yves's other hand slipped off its precarious grip on the rock, and, for a moment, all the boy's weight hung from Nat's right hand. Caroline stretched for him, their fingers touching as Nat gave a grunt of pain.

With a concerted heave, Nat pulled Yves partly out of the water and Caroline managed to snare his other hand, gripping him as tightly as she could. Together, they dragged the little boy further out of what had been going to be his watery grave. Nat's other hand closed around Yves's arm and the boy slid up over the side of the shaft to lie beached on the tunnel floor.

Caroline gathered him into her arms, holding his freezing body against her.

He might have been nine years old and a brave adventurer like his hero Robinson Crusoe, but he burst into tears, his whole body shaking violently.

Nat rose to his knees and pulled his coat off. "Get his wet shirt off and wrap him in this. Quick. We have to get him warm."

Caroline did as she was told, pressing Yves against her own warm body, terrified by the iciness of his limbs. It was possible to die of cold, and Yves was frozen.

Nat stood up. "There's nothing for it now. We have to go on and get to Wheal Jenny and the ladders. We can't wait for the tide to go back out or he'll die of cold down here." He stepped closer to Caroline and put his long arms around her and Yves, sandwiching the little boy between them. "This is our only way of getting him warm."

Yves was still crying, but less noisily, his face pressed against Caroline's chest.

Caroline pressed him closer still. "Why ever did you do this, you cuckoo?"

He sniffled, his teeth chattering. "M-Mr. Trefusis said how exciting it would be and that if I wanted an adventure I should sneak off and do it by myself. He said he'd done it when he was a boy, and he was sure Nat would have." He paused. "I wanted to be like Nat."

Nat growled but said nothing. What more proof did they need?

Caroline held Yves closer still, his body trembling against hers, and Nat's strong arms were around them both.

"We have to move," he said, after another minute or two. "Give him to me and I'll carry him."

"What about your shoulder?"

"I'll manage. Look at him. He can't walk."

"It might get his circulation going."

"He's not strong enough."

He was right. Yves didn't look capable of sitting up on his own, never mind walking. She nodded and Nat gathered Yves into his arms, his coat wrapped tightly around him. "We'd better get going. If we're lucky we might come upon the miners after a bit and they can help us."

One behind the other, they edged their way around the flooded shaft to the tunnel on the far side and, with Nat now following Caroline, who had the candle, set off along the narrow tunnel.

Chapter Thirty-One

"WE'RE GOING TO have to climb up this stope," Nat said, adjusting the hold he had on Yves's limp form. "We have to get up toward the worked adits, and this is the only way."

Luckily, the candlelight didn't show much of the steeply uphill climb they were going to have to make, but it did show how narrow it was. Caroline didn't want to know what lay ahead of them. She'd been taking this trek a little bit at a time for some time now. Just another ten steps. Just round that next bend in the tunnel. Just while she declined some Latin nouns and adjectives in her head to keep from thinking about their situation and her own fears. Just another ten steps. A *stope*. Another word to add to her litany. *Stope. Adit. Tomb.* Don't think.

Exhaustion had long since taken its toll. Not that they could have walked that far. Rather, it was the nature of the walking: in the dark, by the light of a single candle, along narrow adits that ran with water so she was near as wet as Yves, now. Having to walk bent over where the roof came down low, and splashing through puddles of water on the uneven floor so that her boots and feet were soaked.

Added to all that, the sensation of being miles under the ground with tons and tons of solid rock above their heads, and the knowledge that no one knew they were there, pressed down on her like a physical weight. She mustn't think about being stuck down here forever. In the dark. Entombed. She mustn't. Of course, the moment she tried not to think those things, they became the only thing she *could* think of.

In obedience to Nat's command, she started up the uneven, rocky slope that would hopefully take them to the next level. Nearer to the worked adits. Nearer to safety. If it was hard for her, it must be even harder for him. Yves wasn't a heavy child for his age, but he was nine and not a baby anymore. And Nat's shoulder should not be taking such a punishment so soon after his injury. She could hear his panting breath from behind as she climbed. But at least he wasn't hampered by wearing a long gown. She was holding it and her petticoats up with one hand, but still her clothing hampered her movement. Once more, the thought that Ysella had it right about wearing boys' clothes rose to the surface. Too late now. Unless, of course, she ripped off her skirts and climbed in just her drawers. What a thought. Only the hope that they were going to get out of there, in the end, and someone would see her in her underwear, prevented her from doing just that.

Before long they had to rest. Climbing the stope was worse than walking along the adits had been. Her own breath was heaving, and the air felt thick and heavy and difficult to force into her lungs. Hadn't she once read somewhere that bad air in mines could kill you? The urge to burst out laughing washed over her and she only just managed to hold herself in check. Because if she started laughing, she'd end up sobbing. And she mustn't do that in front of Yves.

Nat sat down on a large rock and shifted Yves so he was lying in his arms like a baby, his blonde head resting against Nat's shoulder.

Caroline sat down beside them and felt Yves's face and hands. A little warmer than they had been.

He opened his eyes. "Caroline?" How feeble his voice sounded in the darkness.

"I'm here. We'll have you out of this dreadful place soon,

don't you worry."

"Am I going to die?"

She bit her lip and forced a smile. "Of course not. Do you feel a bit warmer now?"

He nodded, but she couldn't be sure he was telling the truth. "I'm so tired. My candle went out. I was in the water in the dark for so long. I didn't think anyone would ever come." His voice faltered. "I-I thought I was going to die and never see Dash again."

How dreadful that must have been, afraid that no one knew he was there, that he'd die alone in the cold dark of the maze of tunnels and never be found. He might only be nine, but those thoughts must have run through his mind as he clung to the rocky wall of his wet tomb. What bravery and determination it must have taken not to give up and let the water take him. He'd never given up hope. She squeezed his hand. Thank God they'd come in time.

"We're all tired," Nat said. "But not long now. We can't be far off the worked levels, and there should be men there who'll be able help get us out."

"Am I having an adventure?" Yves asked.

Caroline nodded, keeping her voice light and cheerful, which was difficult, as what she needed herself right then was reassurance. "You are indeed. And so are we, thanks to you. But I have to say, it's an adventure I could have done without."

Nat laid his free hand on her knee. "But you have turned out to be a fine and brave adventuress."

She chuckled, glad of the warmth seeping through her wet and torn skirt. "If only that were true."

"You are," Yves whispered. "You came to save me."

"Technically, Nat did that. I couldn't reach you."

"He's brave too. Like Mr. Crusoe and Man Friday." He closed his eyes and nestled closer to Nat. In a few moments he was asleep.

What a sweet picture the two of them made. Nat, with his

hair all awry and the little, sleeping boy cradled in his arms. Despite her fears, Caroline found a smile.

Nat glanced at her. "My father died down here."

She would have liked to tell him not to talk about dying while they were still not sure they could get out, but she didn't. "I know. Sir Hugh told me."

Nat sighed, shifting a little on his rocky seat as though uncomfortable. "I was with him."

She nodded. "He told me that, as well."

"I couldn't do anything to save him."

Unable to think of a response, she waited for him to go on.

"He was buried under a roof fall that let the water in from an old, blocked up adit. We were further down than this and the sea came rushing in. All the miners who were trapped on the far side of the fall drowned. I don't know if the fall killed my father or the water. Gryff Casworan was with me. He dragged me out. I wanted to stay and dig my father out, but he made me leave. Forced me to. He saved my life."

"It wasn't your fault."

He shrugged. "I know that now, but then it felt as though I'd abandoned him to die. It took me a long time to get over it. A long time."

If he ever had.

He licked his lips as though unsure whether to go on.

She patted his hand. "You can tell me anything."

His eyes met hers. "Somehow, I *want* to tell you everything. I don't know why. I've never told anyone before. I feel… as though you understand."

"Tell me, then."

"I joined the army and met a girl. In London. A beautiful girl. Her name was Julia. We married young. I was twenty-one and she only nineteen. She…" His voice trailed off and his Adam's apple bobbed. "She was with child. We were so happy. We had a small house in Town, near to her parents."

He fell silent and she squeezed his hand again.

The darkness, suddenly companionable, pressed in close to her. "I wondered."

He nodded. "I thought you did. No one at Roskilly knows about Julia. She died. The baby as well. My son. I never thought I could feel anything again. Not after that. It was my fault. The birth of the baby killed her. I did that to her."

Oh God. No wonder he was so cold and distant. Life had not been kind to him.

"It wasn't your fault."

He shook his head. "It was, and so was what happened in Spain."

Yves stirred in his arms and snuggled closer.

"What happened in Spain?" Surely it must be doing him good to finally speak about his demons?

"I was leading my men through a mountain pass. Just a small group of us on patrol. The road clung to the side of the mountain, and up ahead someone had dug a short tunnel through the rock. We didn't reconnoiter but rode straight into it. The French had set explosives. The roof came down on us. My best friend was killed. The man who used to play chess with me every night. Captain John Carnegie."

"How was that your fault? Surely it was the fault of the French who laid the trap?"

"I was their Major. I led them into it. I should have foreseen the danger."

She shook her head. "Nonsense. It was warfare, plain and simple. You had no way of knowing what would happen. It wasn't your fault."

Yves stirred again. "What wasn't my fault?"

"Nothing," Caroline said. "Nat and I were just talking. That's all."

Nat grunted. "Enough of that. We're not out yet. Up you get, Caroline. We have the steepest bit to do next. Do you think if I put you on my back, young Yves, you could put your arms around my neck and hold on? I could climb better that way."

The little boy's eyes, so like those of his big cousin, filled with doubt. "I don't know. I'm not feeling very strong."

"I've nothing to tie you on with, I'm afraid."

Caroline stood up, shoving aside thoughts of Nat's dead wife and friend. "I have. My skirt. I'll tear it off at knee height. I've still got my petticoat, so I'll be fine. I'd use that, only I think my skirt will be stronger fabric."

Thank goodness Nat didn't argue. How refreshing to meet a man who realized what was necessary. She stood up and managed to rip a strip of fabric about two feet wide from her gown, long enough to tie around Yves and secure him on Nat's back. This took a bit of doing, as they had so little space, but at last Yves was fixed in place, with his small hands locked around Nat's neck.

They set off again, climbing steadily in the narrow space of the stope, a space not meant for more than one small miner at a time. Once again, the thought that it was no wonder the mines employed children rose to the surface. Neither she nor Nat were built for cramming themselves into tight spaces.

"Keep your head down, young Yves," Nat said, right after she heard him bang his own head and swear.

"If I bang mine, can I say that too?" Yves asked, at last sounding a little like his normal self. That short sleep must have done him good.

"No, you cannot," Caroline retorted, glancing back over her shoulder. "If it became a habit, think how shocked your Aunt Ruth would be."

"Pooh to Aunt Ruth," Yves said, with a little more spirit.

They'd climbed for another ten minutes when Caroline stopped, head on one side and ears cocked, listening.

Nat's breathing filled the silence.

She swung round. "Ssh. Try not to pant. I can hear something."

They stood still, waiting for their own heavy breathing to lessen. Silence gradually fell. Was that a tapping up ahead? Faint and faraway? Surely not just the drip of water.

"That sounds like hammering." Yves's voice rose in excitement.

"Keep going," Nat said. "We must be nearly there."

Caroline started climbing again, holding the candle up ahead of her. Another five minutes brought her to a halt again. This time the tapping sounded much closer.

Nat grinned at her out of his filthy face, his teeth flashing white in the candlelight. "We've done it. They must be up ahead. Look, we're out of the stope and into an adit. We're in the current workings and must be near the main shaft, by my reckoning."

Caroline set out again with renewed determination, along a tunnel even narrower than any in the lower levels, where she had to squeeze herself between the crowding walls. Hope that they would soon be out in daylight drove her on. From ahead came the distant, muffled sound of voices rising in song. Was that a hymn, like the one she'd heard the miners singing on their way to work? Did they feel the sound of worship made them safer down here, in these dark, depressing tunnels, so alike to hell itself? Was their religion their crutch?

She trudged around a corner in the tunnel and found it widened out. At the far end, four miners, dirty and scruffy and akin to Satan's own demons, were hammering at the walls, the candles set in small alcoves each throwing a tiny circle of feeble light. And yet it seemed to Caroline as though they'd reached heaven.

All four of them stopped working and swung round to stare. As well they might, for she must be a sight, with her ripped gown, filthy face, and messy hair. As for them, they were more like angels than if they'd been arrayed in heavenly white with wings and haloes. She'd never seen a more welcome sight.

Nat emerged from behind Caroline, Yves peering over his shoulder.

"Mister Nat!" One of the miners started forward. Impossible to guess his age as he was as dirty as Caroline and Nat, but he appeared to be in charge. "What're you doing down here, surr? I didn't see you come down with the shift change."

Nat sat down on a rock, looking relieved to take the weight off his feet. "I didn't, Opie, but I'm very glad to have found you. We came up through the old workings from Penmar Cove searching for Master Yves, who'd gone exploring on his own. We had to find our way up here because the tide was coming in and the cove would have been shut off. I'm just glad there were no significant roof falls to stop us."

Opie looked at Yves. "Why, 'tis the young master hisself. What were'ee doing lost in those old adits?"

"Learning to be a miner," Yves said with some asperity. "But I fell into a shaft full of water and couldn't get out."

Opie's eyes widened. "Right little miner you are then. But I 'spect you all want to get out o' here." His eyes ran over Caroline again. "You an' the young leddy."

Caroline could have cried with relief, but held herself in check. "I want nothing more than to never go down a mine again, Mr. Opie. Once I'm up in the fresh air, I shall be the happiest woman on Earth."

Opie grinned, his teeth showing white in his dirty face. "You'll have to climb a few ladders to git out, I'm afraid. This ain't no place for a leddy." He wiped a dirty hand across his eyes. "But if you've come all the way up from the old workings, I think you can do it." He turned back to Nat. "Here, you give me the lad, and I'll tek him on my back. You look knackered, my luvver."

What an odd expression that was, but how kindly said. How very Cornish.

Yves was transferred to Opie's broad back, and the miner led the way along more narrow passageways, past other groups of miners working away at the lode, until the main shaft was reached. Here, the first of what was to be a series of wooden ladders rose upwards.

Caroline heaved in a resigned breath. At least this was the last stage of their journey and ahead lay the great outdoors. A great outdoors she never wanted to leave behind again.

Chapter Thirty-Two

AFTER THE LONG climb up from the bottom of the shaft via a series of wooden platforms which Opie called sollars, Casworan greeted them at the pithead. Each sollar had offered the opportunity for a breather, with the next ladder stretching twenty feet up to a small hole in the next platform. But by the time they reached the surface, Nat was far more exhausted than he'd have liked to admit, and his right shoulder was throbbing like the worst toothache with every beat of his heart. He could only be glad he hadn't had to carry Yves up.

One of the other miners had gone on ahead, and Casworan had blankets ready, which he quickly wrapped around Caroline, to conceal her shredded gown, and Yves. Nat turned his down as, despite being wet from the running water down below, he was hot and sweating from the climb, and the warm sun would dry him off better than a blanket would.

Opie set Yves down on a low wall, wrapped in his blanket, and the little boy gazed around himself, blinking in the bright sun. Of the three of them, he seemed to have weathered the ordeal the best, despite their worries that he might die from the cold, and to be on his way to recovery from his long immersion. Such is the resilience of children.

The wind caught Nat's hair, and from beyond the headland the thunder of waves crashing on the cliffs rose into an air peppered with wheeling gulls. The tide must be right in. He couldn't deny his relief to have made it out of the mine.

How long had they been underground? Nat squinted at the sun. This had to be mid-afternoon. He looked at Caroline, who was making a forlorn and hopeless effort to tidy her hair. She looked as though she'd been dragged through the dirt by a wild horse, and then thrown in a few bushes, and no doubt he did as well. What a trio. Nothing like the scions of a noble house. More like beggars you'd pass on the road without a second glance, or villains.

She met his gaze, her dark eyes brimming with confidence. What a woman. He'd never met anyone like her before. Someone prepared to enter a maze of underground tunnels she didn't know she could get out of in order to rescue her charge even though she so plainly was terrified. A woman who had trusted him enough to follow him ever deeper into the mine when he'd assured her he'd known the way out. She must have guessed he couldn't be certain a way out still existed after all these years. Yet she'd conquered her fears and followed him in.

The impulse to snatch her into his arms grew to epic proportions. He wanted to press her body, scantily clad as it was, against his, and kiss those lips until they bruised. He'd not felt desire like this for years. Not since Julia. He'd never thought he could find another woman like her, and yet he had, although in truth she was nothing like Julia. He felt himself harden at the thought of kissing her again, and turned away, wishing he'd accepted that blanket from Casworan.

She cleared her throat. "We'd best get Yves home. He needs to be in a warm bed." And the moment was gone.

Casworan loaned them his horse, a sturdy cob as like Jacka's Bosun as to be his brother. There was only an ordinary saddle, of course, but, after considerable argument, he succeeded in persuading Caroline up onto it. She, of course, was of the outspoken opinion that he, as the one injured by yesterday's fall, should take the horse and she could walk. Ignoring his throbbing shoulder, Nat assured her he was fine. A lie, but an expedient one. Then Casworan lifted Yves up in front of her and they set off back to Roskilly.

Yves, who was clearly not as recovered as he would have liked them to think, fell asleep again in Caroline's arms, as Nat led the cob down from the headland and onto the tracks between the small, stone-walled fields, every step jarring his aching shoulder. But it was a satisfying ache, because of how he'd gained it, and he could put up with it.

WITH NAT LEADING the cob, Caroline was able to hold onto the sleeping Yves with both hands. Thanks to the blanket and the warm July sun, he was warming rapidly, which relieved her. But nonetheless, a visit from the doctor would be in order.

She looked down at Nat. Each step he took seemed to be undertaken with care, as though his shoulder pained him. How could she ever have suspected him of evil intent to Yves? He'd leapt into action at her request for help, and risked his life to save his young cousin. And he'd kissed her. Oh, how he'd kissed her. Kissed her in the way all young girls dream of. Throughout most of the time underground she'd refused to think about it, but now, in the clear light of day, she allowed herself to remember his demanding lips on hers and the arousal she'd felt shiver through her body.

She'd been kissed before, by the young lieutenant who'd gone off to war and never come back, but it had been nothing like the passionate kiss Nat had given her. And once, many years ago, her friend Kit had kissed her, in a chaste and innocent way, as they'd both been no more than thirteen and merely curious to find out what a kiss might feel like. It had been somewhat disappointing, and not one whit like Nat's hot and hungry kiss down there in the dark bowels of the Earth.

Did she want Nat to kiss her again? She most certainly did. In fact, she felt her cheeks heating at what she wanted Nat to do, that shiver of arousal cascading through her body once more. If he only knew what improper thoughts she was having about him, he'd be shocked. Or maybe not. Maybe he was having them himself. He was a man, after all, with a man's needs. Clearly women had similar needs because, right now, all she could think about was not just being kissed but being undressed by him and taken to bed. How very risqué and daring of her. She smiled to herself against Yves's tangled curls.

To distract herself from these naughty but pleasurable day-dreams, she looked out to sea. A few fishing boats dotted the expanse of blue, idyllic in the sunshine, but the lack of wind was probably not good for sailing, or fishing. Overhead, the gulls continued to wheel, their raucous cries tearing at the air, and the now familiar smell of the sea wafted to her nostrils. How good it was to be alive and out in the sun again. She was *never* going in a mine again. Never, never, never. She couldn't say that to herself enough times. Never. Never. Never.

They were drawing near to Roskilly before she roused herself enough to speak. "What are we going to do about Trefusis?" She kept her voice down low for fear of disturbing Yves. "He meant for Yves to die or get lost in those tunnels. That's obvious."

Nat looked up at her. "Intent is not an action he can easily be held answerable for."

"I know. That's what I'm afraid of."

"The best I can do is ask my grandfather to dismiss him."

"You ought to do that as soon as we're returned. Trefusis will no doubt be hoping by now that Yves has gone for good."

Nat nodded. "I'm looking forward to seeing the look on his face when he sees us back with him."

Caroline shifted in the saddle to ease her aching back. "And I shall make sure I keep Hetty and Yves as safe as possible until he goes."

"Which will be today, if I have my way."

The track led them down to the corner of the Roskilly gardens and round to the stableyard. Young Pascoe came running, his eyes shocked at the sight that met his eyes. "What's been goin' on, Sir?" His eyes ran over Caroline's bedraggled state as she relinquished her precious load to Nat with relief.

She slid down from the cob's broad back, glad to have her feet on solid ground that wasn't down a deep, dark hole.

"Master Yves got lost in the old adit in Penmar Cove," Nat said. "Take Casworan's horse for me and see it well fed. We had to make our way up to Jenny's workings and come up by the ladder shaft. We couldn't have walked back from there." He had Yves almost over his left shoulder.

"I had an adventure, Tom," Yves muttered. "I went exploring."

"Looks like you did, that, young master," Tom said, taking the cob's reins. "A right brave'un you are." He led the horse into the stable block and Nat carried Yves into the house, Caroline right behind him.

Mrs. Treloar met them in the hall. She had Doctor Rescorla with her, but whether he was on his way in or out was debatable.

"What's this?" she said, her eyes going from Nat and Yves to Caroline and back, lingering rather too long on the parlous state of Caroline's gown. "Where on *Earth* have you been to get like this?"

"Yves has been down Wheal Jenny," Nat said. "Or rather, up it, as he began at the old adit in Penmar Cove. He fell into a flooded shaft from which we rescued him. Doctor Rescorla, can you examine him if I carry him upstairs?"

Doctor Rescorla, a bluff, prematurely balding gentleman in his thirties, nodded his agreement. "Of course, of course. He looks as though he's had a bit of a shock to the system."

"I had an adventure," Yves corrected him in sleepy indignation. "I'm an explorer."

"Nearly a dead one, by the sound of it," the doctor said as he followed Nat up the stairs toward the nursery. Caroline made to follow, but Mrs. Treloar put a restraining hand on her arm. "What has happened to your gown, Miss Fairfield? And how did you get so dirty?"

Fury washed over Caroline. "I need to be with Yves. If you'll excuse me, I'll have to tell you all of that later." She yanked her arm free and ran up the stairs after Nat and the doctor, leaving her employer standing irate in the hall. She was past caring about offending her.

Nat laid Yves down on his bed in the nursery and the little boy stirred, his eyes opening. He yawned as the doctor bent over him. "These clothes are still damp. Get him out of them immediately and send a maid for hot bricks to warm him. And some hot broth to warm him from the inside, too."

Bridget had emerged from her room, her face a picture of shock when she saw the state they were all in. Although whether that was to do with their appearance or the fact that Yves was not dead, Caroline couldn't be sure. It very much depended on how much Bridget knew. Probably not a lot more than her own role in this. However, it gave Caroline great pleasure to send her running to carry out the doctor's orders. To which she added, "And fetch Patience up here." She'd have to go to her room to change in a while and didn't intend to leave Yves unattended and at Bridget's mercy. Patience would have to sit with him.

Once Yves was in his nightgown, the doctor put his ear to his chest and listened to his heart for a minute, then laid his hand on his forehead. "No temperature as yet. You might be lucky, and he may not get a chill from this. I recommend sleep, which is a great healer. And no excitement for several days at least." He looked back at Yves. "Bed rest for you, my boy. Bed rest." With that, the doctor departed.

"I don't want to stay in bed," Yves complained, sleepily. "But if I have to, can I have Dash with me?"

Caroline nodded. "Of course you can. Nat will go and fetch him for you." She glanced at Nat. "Can you do that now, do you think?"

With a sigh, Nat departed.

Bridget arrived accompanied by Patience, whom she'd made carry the hot bricks. These Caroline arranged around Yves in bed, sitting him up propped with pillows. "You may go, Bridget. Patience can sit with Yves while he eats his broth. It smells most appetizing." And she didn't want Bridget adding anything untoward to it. Not now Yves had just been rescued. How easy would it be for her to slip in an overdose and for it to look as though Yves had succumbed to shock from his near drowning.

With a surly look, Bridget departed, and Caroline turned to Patience. "I have to wash and find myself some clean clothes, so I want you to stay with Yves no matter what. He is not to be left alone, and above all, he is not to be left with Bridget. Don't leave him. I won't be long, and I'm trusting you to keep him safe for me. Mr. Treloar has to go and see his grandfather when he's brought Dash up, so he can't stay with him."

Patience regarded her out of nervous, wide eyes. "Yes, Miss."

Caroline caught her arm. "Do *not* leave him even if there's a fire. Do you understand? Even if Mrs. Treloar orders you to."

The girl's eyes went to Nat, who'd just returned with Dash, as if for corroboration of this strange order. He nodded. "Do as Miss Fairfield says. I won't be long, either."

Patience nodded. "Even if the house is on fire. I'll do that, surr."

Caroline got up from the chair she'd sat in. "I'll be in my room if you need me. I'll leave the door ajar, and this one. You can shout if you have to, and I'll come."

Patience nodded again. "I got a loud voice."

Caroline and Nat left the room together, and Nat continued on down the corridor leaving Caroline to go into her room. The pitcher and bowl of water from breakfast time still stood on her washstand, so she stripped off her ruined gown and petticoat, and stood in just her stays and drawers to wash herself as quickly as she could. That was better. Then she undid her hair and attempted to brush the accumulated dirt of the tunnels out of it.

Not so easy. She was just braiding it when Hetty arrived.

Her face was pale and streaked with tears.

Caroline's heart skipped a beat. Again. It was doing that a lot lately. "What is it?"

Hetty dissolved into tears. "Grandpapa has suffered another apoplexy."

Of course. That must have been why Doctor Rescorla was in the hall. He'd been to see Sir Hugh. "Oh, my goodness." She'd nearly emulated Nat then, and sworn. That would have surprised Hetty. "Is he all right?"

Hetty shook her head. "I don't think so. They won't let me in to see him. That awful Rodgers is looking after him. Mama and Mr. Trefusis went in to see him though. Mama said I was too young to go in a sick room." She frowned. "Mr. Trefusis was with him when it happened. He called the doctor."

A clawed hand seized Caroline's heart. Trefusis again. Was it pure coincidence he'd been with Sir Hugh when he'd had his apoplexy? Had he done something to the old man? He must have thought Yves already dead in the mines, never suspecting that she and Nat had gone in there to save him. That had to be why he had struck.

"I'm sorry, Hetty. Let me see if I can get you in to see him. But first, can you help me with my gown?"

Hetty glanced at the crumpled, filthy heap of the old gown on the floor, seeming to see it for the first time. "Whatever happened to that one?"

Caroline shook her head. "I'll tell you later. But I need you to stay with Patience and Yves. To keep him safe. He's had a terrible experience."

With Hetty's help, she struggled into a clean gown and exchanged her filthy boots and stockings for clean ones. That was better. She could face the world now. "Will you stay with Yves while I go to find out what's been happening?"

Hetty nodded. "I'll stay."

Caroline set off in the direction of Sir Hugh's room.

Chapter Thirty-Three

NAT STRODE DOWN the corridor to his grandfather's room, his muddy boots clacking on the wooden floorboards, and rapped smartly on the door.

After a few moments, it opened to reveal Rodgers, her square face creased in a scowl. "Yes?"

"I've come to see my grandfather."

"Much good it'll do you."

He glared back at the woman. "Get out of the way and let me in."

She stood back with surprising meekness for one normally so aggressive to visitors, and Nat entered the room. Immediately, the realization that the room had transformed from simple bedroom to sickroom bore down on him. An unhealthy, stuffy miasma pervaded the air, and his grandfather lay flat and still on the big bed, his slight body raising the covers only a fraction. Beside the bed, on an upholstered stool, sat his stepmother, her bony hands resting on the covers, with Aunt Agnes beside her in a high-backed chair.

Nat approached on hesitant feet. The left-hand side of Sir Hugh's face had fallen to one side, as though a heavy weight were dragging it down, and his skin had the sunken, waxy look of death, that Nat knew well. Only his stertorous breathing told Nat he still lived.

"What happened?"

His stepmother raised her head. "He had another of his turns first thing this morning when Jan went in to see him. Jan wanted to discuss some matters of business that needed your grandfather's approval." Her hands gripped the bedclothes so hard the knuckles whitened. "We sent for the doctor straightaway. He's been here all day, bleeding Sir Hugh, but to no avail. He was about to leave when you returned. Where have you been, I'd like to know, while the house has been in crisis? We looked everywhere for you after it happened, but it appears you were out gallivanting with the boy and his governess. Doing what, I cannot imagine, having seen the state you were all in. Still are." She ran her gaze over his filthy, coatless attire and her lip curled in a sneer.

Nat ignored most of what she'd said as being not worthy of a reply. "Can the doctor do anything for him?"

She shook her head. "He bled him copiously, but can do no more. He said it's just a matter of time, now."

"Going to meet his maker, he is," Aunt Agnes put in. "Be with Robert and Kenver, he will." She chortled. "And I'll be goin' there soon, meself. Mark my words."

Nat's stepmother shot her a malevolent glare, as though she saw the old woman as an unwelcome intruder in the sickroom.

Nat studied his grandfather's ravaged face. His stepmother had played no part in this, he felt sure. But what about Trefusis? Was it not rather more than a coincidence that the blackguard had been in here when the apoplexy had occurred? He'd set Yves on the path to explore the beach adit and counted him lost or drowned, which he would have been but for Caroline. No doubt it had been he who'd interfered with Nat's saddle then removed the evidence. And now Sir Hugh was handily at death's door. After a visit from Trefusis.

Nat felt grief, of course, but his grandfather had reached a far greater age than most, and he'd disliked being bedridden and at the mercy of Rodgers. No life for a man who'd always been so active. Common sense told him not to feel sorry for Sir Hugh. And besides, Nat had other far greater worries to attend to. The first of which was to get rid of Trefusis before he did any more harm.

"Where is Trefusis now, Mother?"

"Downstairs. Waiting in the parlor."

Nat turned on his heel and marched out of the room.

The patter of her light slippers told him she'd followed.

Without pausing, Nat descended the stairs and went into the parlor, shoving the door open so hard it banged against the wall. Trefusis was by the window, but he turned as Nat came in. He must have been able to tell by the expression on Nat's face that all was not well.

"Get out of here," Nat began with, not being one to beat about the bush. "You're dismissed. I want you gone."

The man's dark face darkened even further. "What the hell are you talking about?"

Nat crossed the room and stopped in front of him, almost nose to nose. "You heard. Pack your things and go. You are no longer employed here."

"Now, wait a minute," Trefusis said, his normally calm voice edged with tension and his gaze going over Nat's shoulder toward the still open door. "You can't do that."

Nat didn't bother to look behind him, but guessed his stepmother had come into the room. "Can't I? You watch me."

Trefusis's lip curled in a sneer. "You don't have the authority to dismiss me. I'm not your employee."

Nat's face must have matched his. "Don't I? You think so? We'll see about that. If you don't want me to kick you down the drive, then you'll leave right now. Or I'll call the Pascoes and have them throw you out. We'll all kick you down the drive."

"What do you think you're doing, Nathaniel?" His stepmother finally found her voice, an icily cold one. "Jan is needed here. We can't manage without him."

Nat didn't take his eyes off Trefusis. "No. He is not. How do you think my saddle came off my horse, *Mother*? Someone damaged the girth straps then went out and threw my saddle over the cliff or down an old mineshaft before I could find the evidence. Trefusis delayed Pascoe from retrieving it when I asked, so he could get there first."

"Rubbish," Trefusis snarled. "Your fall has addled your brain."

"That is a ridiculous accusation," Nat's stepmother said. "Why on earth would Jan do that? He has no reason to want you to have an accident."

"To want me dead, you mean."

"I don't want you dead," Trefusis snapped. "Perhaps you should look at the way Old Pascoe looks after the saddlery and lay the blame where it truly belongs. On the shoddy work of one of the staff. The man is a drinker."

Nat grit his teeth. "And you sent Yves out this morning to explore the adit in Penmar Cove, knowing full well how dangerous this would be and that Yves would do it on his own."

His stepmother blustered, not quite so confident now. "That isn't true. Yves wouldn't do that. He's far too sensible."

"He did, Mother, he did. Caroline—Miss Fairfield—and I have just returned from Wheal Jenny. Thanks to her prodigious detective skills your plans have failed. We followed Yves into the adit on the beach, but the tide was fast coming in, and the only way out was to make our way up through the workings. Yves is safe, thanks to Miss Fairfield. Hetty overheard your friend Trefusis telling Yves about where to get into the adit and recounted it all to Caroline. He knew a boy like Yves couldn't resist the adventure of it."

Trefusis's already darkened face now reddened in anger, turning a disturbing shade of puce. "How could I have known he'd do that? I don't have the power to see into the future. If the boy was stupid enough to go down there by himself, it has nothing to do with me."

Nat prodded Trefusis in the chest with a long finger. Hard. "And you were with my grandfather when he was taken ill. One of these things you might have been able to wriggle out of, but not all of them. And on top of that, there's Yves's medicine. Bridget has been trying to dose him with laudanum, as no doubt you both already know. Which one of you gave it to her? Which one of you persuaded her to dose him hoping that one night she'd give him too much and he wouldn't wake up?"

His stepmother had come round to stand shoulder to shoulder with Trefusis, her face ashy pale. "Why would Jan want to do that?" Her eyes glinted like sharp flints. Nat's heart did a leap of fear as he recognized the guilt in them. It was her. Caroline had been correct. Perhaps she had no knowledge of the rest, but she was behind the poisoning. Knowledge of her crime was written all over her face.

"Because he wants all of us gone," Nat said. "As do you. Yves and I stand between him and what he's come to see as *his* inheritance. What you've allowed him to come to see as his. Because he plans to marry Hetty and get his hands on this estate."

His stepmother's eyes widened in shock, all appearance of sangfroid flown. She hadn't known that one. "That's not true," she blustered. "Tell him it's not true, Jan. It's me you love, not her."

Trefusis must have realized his case was lost. "Why would I want a dried-up old hag like you, when I could have a fresh fruit ripe for the picking like Hetty? You stupid woman. I've had enough of pandering to you and your vanity."

Her hand jerked back and the sound of the slap ricocheted around the parlor. "How dare you presume to cast your filthy gaze on my daughter! Get out! I never want to see you again. Get out right now." Her coldly furious gaze looked daggers at the man she must have thought she loved. How swiftly love can turn to hatred. In the blink of an eye.

It seemed Nat wasn't going to have to kick Trefusis down the drive. His stepmother might beat him to it.

Trefusis threw them both a furious glare and, shoving between them, stormed out of the parlor. Silence reigned for a long half minute, before Nat swung round on his stepmother. "And you needn't think you're staying. I know it was you with the laudanum, you murdering, cold-hearted woman. You made my life a misery when I was a boy, then you made Hetty's life the same. I won't allow you to repeat history by doing it to Yves. And you can take that shrew of a nursery maid with you. I know she's in your pay. Go on. Get out."

Her mouth hung open, for once lost for words.

"And don't go anywhere near my sister before you leave." He marched out of the parlor and into the hall, buzzing with pent up anger. Maybe he should have punched Trefusis in the nose. Several times. That might have drained away some of this emotion and made him feel better.

Having dispatched a shocked Ennion to give Bridget her immediate marching orders, he paced up and down until his stepmother emerged from the parlor. Ignoring him, she stalked up the stairs, back ramrod straight. "And don't you touch any of the silver," Nat shouted, as a parting shot. Maybe he was behaving in a rash and petty manner, but compared with how he felt, this outburst was nothing.

She disappeared from view, and Nat strode up and down again, fists clenched by his sides, chest heaving. A thought fought its way to the surface of his jumbled mind. Caroline. He needed to tell her what he'd done. Some of the tension fizzled out of his body at the thought of her, but by no means all of it. He took the stairs two at a time in a run.

He met Caroline, much cleaner now than she had been and wearing a fresh gown, in the gallery and ground to a halt facing her. "Caroline. I was coming to look for you."

"And I for you."

She sounded breathless, her cheeks a becoming pink. She'd only had time to braid her hair but had not put it up on top of her head. It suited her. She had a hairpin in her hand which she quickly tucked into the bodice of her gown.

The world stood still around him, the sounds of the house

receding into nothingness.

He gazed into her eyes, lost in their depths, for an eon of time that might only have been seconds. His heartbeat pounded in not just his chest but throughout his body, and he felt himself harden with desire again. She was quite the most beautiful woman he'd ever seen, even with a smear of dirt high on her forehead that she'd missed.

For once he had to let impulse have its way.

Stepping forward, he caught her in his arms and her face turned up to meet his. Her compliant body molded against his and she must have been able to feel the extent of his arousal, but he wasn't embarrassed. This time, though, he ought to play the gentleman and seek her permission. Her face was so close to his he was breathing her in. "Do you mind if I kiss you again?" The words came out a little hoarse.

Her dark eyes flashed. "I should like it very much if you did, Nat."

He needed no further bidding but bent his head and pressed his lips to hers. They parted, his tongue slipped in and met hers and her hands came up to grip his shoulders. His head spun and he might have fallen had there been something handy like a bed to fall onto, preferably with Caroline still in his arms. But there wasn't, and he had to remain upright, his now throbbing arousal pressed against the softness of her stomach, something that only added to his ardor.

She kissed him back with enthusiasm, her hands rising from his shoulders to bury themselves in his hair, careless of the bump on the back of his head, pulling him ever closer. How small and delicate she felt in his arms despite her height, how fragile for someone who had just traversed an entire mine.

Eventually, they had to come up for air, breathless and gasping. But neither released their hold on the other. "Nat," Caroline whispered. "Oh, Nat…"

He couldn't resist the sound of his name on her lips. He kissed her again, drowning in the depths of her mouth and the willing body pressed against his own. Oh, how glorious it would be to whisk her into his bedroom right now and throw her onto the bed. To remove her clothes bit by bit, to kiss each newly exposed bit of skin, to finally part her legs and let his hungry manhood slide inside her where it belonged. He had a feeling that right now she might do nothing to resist him if he tried this. With great difficulty, he remembered he was a gentleman, and gentlemen didn't behave like that with any young lady, particularly not one of their employees.

He released her mouth and stepped back, disentangling himself from her arms. "I-I must apologize for my behavior, Caroline." His voice came out hoarse still, and squeaky as though he was back to being fourteen with it newly broken. If only he were carrying his coat, he could have put it in front of his trousers. She must be able to see all too clearly what he was thinking.

"You have no need to apologize," she said, her face serious. "For I enjoyed being kissed like that enormously."

His cock twitched at her reply, trying to influence him again. He had to get it under control. "I am glad to hear it."

She laughed, a gay, carefree sound in the glum silence of the house. "Oh, Nat, do not look so worried. I am a woman, not a goddess you fear defiling with your attentions." Her eyes twinkled. "Come, kiss me again, for I fear I shall faint for wanting you to."

This time his passions nearly got the better of him. This time he found he had her pressed up against the wall, his cock pushing against her stomach so hard he felt it might burst already and disgrace him. And she kissed him back with as much passion as he had himself. Her mouth hungry for his, her hands sliding up under his loosened shirt onto the naked skin of his back. Oh God, how much he wanted her to touch him all over.

A discreet cough disturbed them.

Oh my God. Hetty. She was standing at the far end of the gallery looking extremely interested in what he'd been doing. What they'd both been doing. A complete passion killer. No need for a coat to hide anything now. The shock had returned him to normal in a trice.

"Does this mean you're going to marry Caroline?" Hetty asked.

Nat looked from her to the woman still in his arms. "Yes," he said. "I think I am, if she will have me."

Chapter Thirty-Four

CAROLINE GAZED UP into Nat's deep blue eyes, conscious of his hand resting on her waist, the heat of it radiating across her skin. What had he just said? Had she heard him correctly?

Nat released his hold and dropped to one knee in front of her, if a little stiffly. "Caroline, Miss Fairfield, will you do me the honor of becoming my wife?"

At the far end of the gallery Hetty clasped her hands and jumped up and down with an excited squeal. "Ohmygoodness! Wait until I tell Mama."

Nat caught Caroline's hand. "Will you, Caroline?"

What to say? Of course, she would like nothing better than to be married to Nat, but did he mean it? Or was this proposal brought on by the strain of the last few days and given only on impulse or perhaps just because Hetty had surprised them in an immodest embrace and he felt duty bound to make the offer? Did he really feel as strongly about her as she felt about him? Or was it lust? She wasn't stupid. She'd felt his arousal pressed hard against her as he kissed her, and she had some idea about the way men were driven by their bodies. Did he only want to have his way with her? Would he tire of her as soon as he'd had what he wanted?

"I-I don't know," she whispered. "This is so sudden."

His hand gripped hers as though it would never let it go. "I think I've loved you for a while now, but just didn't know it," he said, keeping his voice down low, perhaps to avoid Hetty eavesdropping. At least she'd had the sense to stay at the far end of the gallery. "But today made me realize how much I admire you, how truly unique your qualities are, and that I can't live without you in my life."

This was better. Good reasons for a man to want to marry. She wet her lips. "Do you truly love me?"

His face clouded. "Do you doubt that I do?"

She bit her lip. "I-I just don't know. I don't know what love feels like, so how do I know if you love me or I love you? I feel something in my heart that makes it want to soar, but at the same time I feel a deep anxiety, as though something terrible is hanging over my head that I can't name."

He caught her other hand and kissed it, seemingly now oblivious to Hetty who still stood with her hands hopefully clasped, probably straining her ears to hear. "Unlike you, Caroline, I've loved deeply and lost that which I loved the most. And I thought I'd never love again until I met you. My heart was broken for many years, and I would have welcomed death during all that time. But fate was unkind to me, or perhaps kind in its own way. It brought me here, to you. And I know that I've found love again."

She gave a sharp indrawn breath. He'd had so many bad things happen to him. Her kind heart ached for him, but was that sufficient to prove she loved him? That she wanted his body, she had no doubt at all, and that she liked his companionship. But was that love or something else? "I-I'm all confused. Today has been so strange. Will you give me time to think about this? It's not a decision easily made in a moment." She managed a smile. "And do, please, get up off your knees."

Nat rose to his feet, still holding her hands. "If you don't say yes, I will go into a decline, I swear it." His eyes twinkled at her. "You are the woman for me, Caroline. Today has revealed to me the woman you truly are. A woman with the heart of a lioness."

"Oh, do marry him and become my sister!" Hetty cried, bouncing up and down on her toes. "It would be so perfect."

Caroline gently retrieved her hands as just his touch was proving distracting and might influence her decision. "I cannot choose to marry Nat just to suit you, Hetty."

At that moment, Mrs. Treloar emerged from the corridor to the east wing, carrying a valise. Hetty's eyes flew wide. "Mama, where are you going?"

Caroline looked at Nat, seeing a grim smile curve his mouth.

"She's leaving," he said. "She's decided to go and visit a relative in… Warwickshire."

Was he making her destination up? It seemed likely.

"Will you be away for long?" Hetty asked.

Mrs. Treloar paused at the top of the stairs. "I shall be away as long as suits me. You are to remain here with Nathaniel. Goodbye." And she swept down the stairs.

Caroline leaned in close to Nat. "How did you do that?" She kept her voice to a low whisper as this wasn't something Hetty should hear.

"Told her I knew what she'd done and she was to leave. I daresay she decided her best option was to flee before I called in the local magistrate." He paused. "I did the same with Trefusis and Bridget as well. They'll both be leaving today. I doubt very much if my stepmother will be leaving *with* Trefusis though—I managed to let slip his intentions for Hetty."

Good heavens. While she'd been washing and dressing and sorting Yves out, such a lot had been going on. "Are we safe now?"

He nodded. "I believe we are. And now, I think I might leave you to work out whether you wish to marry me or not and become a surrogate mother to Yves. I would very much like you to do that, if you can bring yourself to ignore my disfigurement."

She put a hand to her mouth. "Never think that it is your scar that makes me hesitate. Not for one moment would that be the case, for in fact, I don't even see it when I look at you. It's just that I hardly know you yet, and I am not a woman who does things in haste, for fear of regretting them later."

"Not unless it is plunging into an ancient mine in search of a lost child."

"Well, that had to be done. I had no choice."

He smiled. "I hope you will make the right choice now."

"And so do I."

HETTY AND NAT went to sit with their ailing grandfather, while Caroline repaired to the walled garden. He was not her grandfather, and if he had little time left, then they should be allowed to spend it with him in peace. Bridget had already left, and there was no sign of Trefusis anywhere, so she felt it safe to leave Yves with Patience again, once more with strict orders to stay with him.

With her head in a whirl after Nat's offer, she wandered the narrow gravel paths until she reached the rosebush her mother had favored and shared, all unknowing, with Nat's own long-dead mother. Some of the blooms were going over and in need of deadheading. She'd have to ask the gardener to attend to it tomorrow. Too late now, as he must have finished work and gone home for his supper. She chose one of the newer blooms and, having pinched out the thorns, settled it in the bosom of her dress, its heady fragrance wafting to her nostrils. Her handy spare hairpin held it in position.

What would Mama say to this, a proposal at her age? She'd be so pleased, as she'd probably given up on her only daughter ever marrying. What if she said yes to Nat, and he allowed Mama to come here to live with them? Would that not be perfect—just as she'd always wanted? And if she and Nat had children, Mama would be overjoyed to be so close to her grandchildren. Already, in her head, Caroline could see a brood of small children with Nat's deep-blue eyes running about here in the garden while she gathered roses. But being at last able to help her mother was no reason for matrimony.

Did she love him? Did she feel as Morvoren so obviously felt for Kit? Did she think of him every moment of the day? Well, yes, she did, now she came to think about it. How odd. Did she fear that if she said no, she'd never see him again? And the answer to that was yes as well. Did her heart leap whenever he walked into the room? Did it ache now she was away from him? Yes, and yes again. Did she have an inexplicable feeling of pure desire coursing through her body when she thought of him? Yes, again, only this might be put down to baser feelings of lust rather than purely love. However, from talking to Morvoren, who seemed well informed on matters of love, this, too, was a kind of love.

So perhaps she did love him. The fact that it had come upon her this suddenly had stunned her with shock. Of course, she'd read romance novels in which the hero and heroine fell in love at first sight, but she hadn't thought it possible in real life. Although, really, she hadn't done so quite on first sight when he'd seemed so aloof and bad-tempered and a possible suspect in an attempted murder. But, soon after, she'd begun to fall for his charms, well-hidden as they were.

She stopped in the far corner of the garden where a small wooden gazebo sheltered against the high stone walls, open on one side and with cushioned seats around the other three. Yes, she would tell him yes. She would marry the man she loved.

Trefusis stepped out of the shadows of the gazebo.

Caroline retreated a step, one hand to her throat.

Trefusis glowered at her, but there was more to his expression than anger. There was lust. Hot, vengeful lust. Not like the lust in Nat's eyes, born of love. No. This was born of anger and a need for revenge.

Caroline's heart leapt with fear. If she ran, he would catch her, hampered as she was by her long skirts, and there was no one in the garden to come to her aid. No one, even, in earshot. She swallowed. She had to brazen this out. "What are you doing in here?" She injected as much cold superiority into her tone as she could.

His lip curled. "You interfering nobody. Spying on me and plotting against me. Pretending you were meek and mild and all the while with your eye on the fortune for yourself. You've spoilt everything. Your lovely Nat's thrown me out, and it's all your fault."

Caroline could feel her heart hammering in her throat, but she wasn't going to let him see that. "On the contrary, you are the architect of your own demise." She was amazed at how calm she sounded, and it instilled more confidence in her.

"Your clever words will get you nowhere. You've deprived me of Hetty's ripe young body and the fortune that should be mine, and now you've got your claws into that upstart soldier boy, you think you've won. Well, you haven't. I'll be having the last laugh here." In one swift movement he lunged forwards and grabbed Caroline's wrist, swinging her body to crush up against his own, his other hand going to her breast and squeezing hard.

For a moment, Caroline had no idea what to do. His grip on her breast hurt. His thick-lipped, moist mouth moved toward hers, intent on stealing more than a kiss, that was for certain. His other hand had seized her posterior in a vicelike grip, pressing her body up hard against his evident arousal. Instinct told her she was on her own, and her actions now would either condemn her to his lusts or save her. She went limp in his arms, a sizeable weight for him to hold up, and he swore as she sagged away from him.

In that instant, when he was least expecting any fight from her, she slid the long hairpin from where it had been holding the now crushed rose to her bodice and stabbed at his face. She wasn't aiming for any particular part of it, but as he moved, so did his face, and the pin jabbed hard into his left eye, stabbing like a sword thrust.

He let out a blood-curdling scream and dropped Caroline to the gravel path, his hands clawing at his eye.

She didn't wait to see if she'd killed him, which she rather hoped she had. Instead, she scrambled to her feet and ran, her feet scrunching on the gravel, one shoe gone, aware that this was her only opportunity to escape. However, no sound of pursuit followed her. He must be in agony. She scrabbled for the gate latch, glancing over her shoulder, but he'd gone. Where, she didn't wait to see. Instead, she flung open the gate and bolted for the house.

A very surprised Ennion greeted her in the hall. She grabbed his hand. "Where is Mr. Nathaniel?"

"Upstairs, Miss. He went to change out of his dirty clothes."

Caroline raced up the stairs, careless of Ennion's disapproving expression, and along the gallery to Nat's bedroom door. She didn't wait to knock but threw it open and stepped inside.

Nat was standing by his washstand wearing only his breeches, his hair and face dripping with water as he turned to look at her.

"Yes," she burst out. "The answer is yes, I'll marry you. And I've just stabbed Trefusis in the eye."

"What?" Nat's eyes widened. "Not 'what' to your answer of yes, but 'what' to the fact that you've stabbed Trefusis."

Caroline ran across the room into his arms, careless of his near nakedness. If she were to marry him, she'd soon be seeing that every day. Something she relished perhaps more than was proper. He smelled a little of sweat but mostly of soap. "He was in the walled garden where I went to think. The man had the cheek to try to assault me. So I stabbed him. I think I've probably blinded him."

"He tried to assault you?" Nat struggled in her grasp. "I'll kill him."

She hung on tight. "No. You don't need to. I did it for myself. I'm not some milksop woman who needs a man to fight her battles. I think you'll find a hairpin jabbed in his eye will cause him far more problems than a beating from you would."

He stopped struggling. "You firebrand. I was right when I said you were a lioness."

She laughed. "Kiss me, then, if I'm to be your wife."

She offered up her lips, and Nat bent his head to hers. "We'd best make it soon," he said. "For I don't think I can wait long to have you in my bed."

She pressed up against his evident arousal. "I feel the same." She ran her hands down the skin of his back and felt his cock leap to attention against her stomach. "Do we have to wait?"

His arms held her tight against him. "I'm afraid we do, my little lioness."

Chapter Thirty-Five

S IR HUGH LINGERED on two more days, allowing his family to say their goodbyes. He never regained the power of speech, but his faded blue eyes still held their fierce intelligence. Caroline was able to report to him how Trefusis and Mrs. Treloar had been both outwitted and dismissed from Treloar. His grip on her hand as she told him that Nat and Yves were now safe reassured her that he'd understood. Without Mrs. Treloar to turn to, Rodgers became much more biddable and inclined to oblige, and after Sir Hugh's death, she was given a glowing reference and sent on her way.

After the funeral held in the small chapel at Kennegy Downs, the rector called the banns for three Sundays in succession and on the Saturday following the final calling, Nat and Caroline were finally married. Only immediate family attended, along with Caroline's mother who'd arrived a few days before, Ysella and Sam Beauchamp, and Miss Hawkins, who came out from Penzance especially to celebrate not just the wedding but the future security of the young Sir Yves Treloar, baronet, aged nine and a half.

"I don't want to be called *Sir* Yves," he complained, several times a day. "I just want to be plain Yves again. Nat can have the *Sir* bit of it. It would sit much better on a grown man than it does on me."

"It's yours by right," Caroline explained. "And one day you'll be a grown man yourself and glad to have the title. But at home, we'll just call you Yves still, have no fear. I can hardly tell a baronet off for getting his Latin verbs all wrong if I have to call him Sir."

"You won't need to tell me off," Yves retorted. "I shall be good and studious, for a start. And on top of that, you won't be my governess any longer." He wriggled on his seat. "But instead, I should very much like to call you Mama, if I might? I've never had a mother, and Aunt Ruth never offered for me to call her that." He paused. "Not that I wanted to, because she was so horrid to me. But I've always felt it unfair that Hetty had a mother and I didn't. I'd like *you* to be my mother, if you don't mind."

Sudden tears moistened Caroline's eyes and she had to wipe them away in a hurry and hope he hadn't seen them. She put her arms around the little boy and hugged him close. "And I've never had a little boy before, either, but I should be most honored if you were to call me Mama. In fact, it would be a dream come true for me, for I love you like my own already. How could I not?"

Yves hugged her back after that for a long time, and she suspected he, too, might have had wet eyes.

After the wedding came the wedding breakfast at Roskilly, which lasted from early afternoon until the middle of the evening, with even Yves allowed to stay up late to celebrate and drink a small glass of claret, which made him first, squiffy, and then, sleepy. When the meal was over, two young men with fiddles came in from one of the nearby farms to play for the dancing. The servants were invited to join in to create more workable formations for the sets, and because, as Yves announced as he partnered a delighted Patience, there were "only the nice ones left."

The last dance was by special request from Caroline—the waltz. And it was just for her and Nat. He took her in his arms just as he'd done on the night of the ball at Carlyon Court, and swept her around the dance floor, one hand on her waist, his touch hot on her skin through the thin gauze of her beautiful wedding gown. When the music finally ended, they were at the foot of the stairs.

He didn't release his hold on her. "Shall we go up?"

She ran her eyes over the assembled crowd, which the wedding party had swollen to with the addition of the now tipsy servants, and met her mother's joyful face. Tears were running down her cheeks, but tears of joy, not sadness. She was holding fast to Yves's hand, as he'd adopted her as his new grandmother and refused to be parted from her. Mrs. Fairfield, to Yves's delight, would be staying on after the wedding. "Goodnight, everyone."

A rousing cheer, mainly from the servants, greeted this farewell. And Ysella blew her a kiss. It would have been wonderful if Morvoren and Kit had been able to come, but they were expecting another baby to add to their growing family.

Yves suddenly wrested his hand from Mrs. Fairfield's and ran forward holding a single rose and thrust it into her hand. "For you, Mama."

She lifted it to her nose and inhaled the scent. Her mother had one pinned to the bodice of her gown, no doubt also presented to her by Yves.

Then she and Nat turned and climbed the stairs, leaving the party to slowly wind down behind them.

IN THE QUIET of their bedchamber, Nat closed the door behind them and shrugging out of his coat, threw it down on the chair in the corner. Caroline walked over to stand beside the bed, staring down at it, perhaps a little afraid of what was coming next.

He unbuttoned his waistcoat, and that joined his coat. His fingers, trembling a little in anticipation, went to his cravat.

Caroline turned around. Never had she looked more beautiful, standing with the single rose held to her bosom. Hetty's lady's maid had wrought wonders with her hair, but all he wanted now was to unpin it and let if fall in all its glory over her pale shoulders. He let his cravat drop to the floor and rolled his right shoulder a little. It still pained him from time to time, and he'd always have to be careful it didn't slip out again, but apart from that, and a few now barely visible bruises, he'd recovered well from their adventures.

Now to do what he'd wanted to do some time ago. Unwrap her slowly, appreciating every tiny exposure of her body, kissing every new inch he found. He stepped up to her and lifted his hands to her hair, pushing a stray curl out of her eyes. "I love you, Mrs. Treloar."

It was the work of a moment to loosen her hair, allowing luxuriant chestnut tresses to tumble over her shoulders. He lifted them to his face, breathing in the scent of the rosewater on them as her hands went to the buttons of his shirt. His breeches felt suddenly far too tight, barely able to contain his arousal. If she were to drop her hand to it…

"And I love you, Mr. Treloar," she whispered, a feather-light finger sliding over his ribs.

He bent and kissed her. Softly, at first, then with more passion, and she responded, her mouth opening beneath his, her tongue meeting his, and her hands slipping inside his shirt to the bare skin of his chest, then straying lower. God, how he wanted her. But he refused to hurry this moment. Neither of them would ever have it again—this first time, this discovery of each other's bodies, and he wanted it to be memorable.

Their lips parted. "Turn around," he whispered.

She meekly turned her back to him. Damn it. He'd intended to undo her gown and petticoat with steady fingers but he could hardly still the tremble. To hide it, he bent and, pushing aside her hair, softly kissed the back of her neck and down to her bare shoulders, her skin satin beneath his lips. He felt her shiver with excitement or pleasure… or both, and under his fingers the dress ties finally came undone. He slipped the gown off her shoulders and let it pool at her feet. The petticoat followed.

She was glorious.

Now her back was exposed, he let his lips trail over her skin as he started on the laces of her stays, his arousal throbbing uncomfortably in anticipation. Stay laces were harder than gown laces, he knew from experience. If he'd had a knife, he'd have sliced through them to get at her the quicker. At last, they were undone and the stays came away. Still with her back to him, she stood exposed in just her thin, gauzy slip and drawers.

He ran more kisses down her back, trailing them along her arms then back up to the nape of her neck, and gently turned her to face him. Her nipples, hard and erect, pressed against her slip. "Would you like to lie down on the bed?"

"I would."

He watched her as she lay on her back, eyes fixed on him. Time to take more of his own clothes off. He kicked off his shoes and stockings in untoward haste, pulled his shirt over his head and with his back to her, undid the fall of his breeches, letting them fall to his feet. That was better, but he didn't want to frighten her with the size of his cock. She'd be very unlikely ever to have seen one before. Not in this state, anyway. "Close your eyes."

"They're closed."

He climbed onto the bed beside her, for a moment leaning on his elbow and gazing down at her body, barely hidden by the thin slip and drawers. He mustn't hurt her. He must make this good for her as well as him. His first night with Julia had been fumbling in the dark, and that mustn't happen this time. He'd been a boy then, but now he was a man and he knew what women liked, what would bring a woman like Caroline to readiness.

Through her thin slip, he took a nipple in his mouth, caressing it with his tongue.

Her body arched and she gasped out loud.

His hand slid down her body, over her flat stomach and further down. It slid between her legs.

For a moment, she stiffened, and he let his tongue circle her nipple. She gave a little sigh, and relaxed. His gentle fingers continued their exploration, finding her already wet.

SHE BURIED HER hands in his hair, holding his head against her as his lips and tongue teased her nipple in a way she'd never known could happen. What had she been missing all her life? Well, for all her adult life. And his fingers, exploring deeper and deeper, massaging a part of her she'd never known existed. She never wanted him to stop. Her body arched and quivered and she clung onto him, aware of the length of his hot hardness resting against her thigh.

Should she touch it? Dare she? Her hand slipped over his cock, tentative and exploring as her fingers ran along the shaft, so thick and hard. She kept her eyes closed, made more confident by not being able to see. Half afraid that if she saw it, she'd be too frightened to continue.

His kisses began to descend from her breasts, tickling down her stomach, heading lower. She felt him pull her drawers off but didn't care. Her whole body ached for him, for his body, and above all for his cock. She wrapped her hand around it and felt it jerk beneath her touch like a creature with a mind of its own, astonished at the power she wielded in her touch.

And now his head was between her legs and his tongue… her body arched again, and she couldn't stifle the groan that throbbed out of her. His tongue… what was he doing? Nothing existed except the bed they were lying on, except each other, except their love.

His head came up just when she wanted to shout at him never to stop, and he moved to lean over her, one knee gently pushing her legs further apart. She didn't care. She spread them wide, ready to accept him, and felt the end of his cock nudging at her hot, wet pulsating center. She wrapped her arms around him and pulled him to her. "Yes," she whispered in his ear. "Yes. Now. Don't stop."

And he slid inside her, the sensation shivering through her like a long-awaited gift, a sudden stabbing pain and he was deep inside her and she was holding him tight as he thrust hard, his breathing fast, his body strong and powerful. Oh God, she wanted this. She wanted him to fill her, to pound into her, to... Her whole body pulsed with pleasure, waves of it shivering out from her center, down her legs and up to the top of her head, tightening her scalp. She couldn't help but cry out loud, his groaning in her ear.

His body relaxed on top of hers, heavy and languid, both of them gasping for breath.

"Oh, my goodness," she breathed. "That was... I don't know. Wonderful. Like some sort of magic." She paused as a delicious aftershock ran through her. "Can we do it again?"

He rolled off her, his body shaking with laughter. "You're meant to be satisfied after doing this once, not calling for an encore. You'll have to give me time to recover. Men are not like women. We can't perform to order in quick succession."

She rolled to face him. "How could anyone be satisfied with only once, when it's such exquisite joy? I never knew it could be this good. I had no idea."

He chuckled again. "Well, that might well be because I'm good at it..."

Her turn to chuckle. "And modest too. I don't think I shall ask you how you learned to be so good at this. I probably don't want to know. You were a soldier, after all."

"Well," Nat said. "There's other things we can do while my poor body recovers, you know. Come here, Mrs. Treloar, and kiss me."

A long time later they lay naked in one another's arms, slick with sweat and exhausted by their own passion. Caroline's head rested on Nat's chest, the curling hairs tickling her cheeks, and his arm protectively around her. She never wanted to have to move from this position again. Not ever. Her own arm lay across Nat's flat belly and she could feel the gentle rise and fall of his chest as he breathed. He must be almost asleep.

By the light of the candle guttering on the bedside table, she examined his face. So handsome, even his scar. Happiness settled on her like a warm blanket and she closed her eyes. This was how she'd always dreamed marriage would be.

THE END

About the Author

After a varied life that's included working with horses where Downton Abbey is filmed, riding racehorses, running her own riding school, owning a sheep farm and running a holiday business in France, Fil now lives on a widebeam canal boat on the Kennet and Avon Canal in Southern England.

She has a long-suffering husband, a rescue dog from Romania called Bella, a cat she found as a kitten abandoned in a gorse bush, five children and six grandchildren.

She once saw a ghost in a churchyard, and when she lived in Wales there was a panther living near her farm that ate some of her sheep. In England there are no indigenous big cats.

She has Asperger's Syndrome and her obsessions include horses and King Arthur. Her historical romantic fiction and children's fantasy adventures centre around Arthurian legends, and her pony stories about her other love. She speaks fluent French after living there for ten years, and in her spare time looks after her allotment, makes clothes and dolls for her granddaughters, embroiders and knits. In between visiting the settings for her books.

Social Media links:
Website – filreid.com
Facebook – facebook.com/Fil-Reid-Author-101905545548054
Twitter – @FJReidauthor

www.ingramcontent.com/pod-product-compliance
Lightning Source LLC
Chambersburg PA
CBHW060430310726
48977CB00001B/117